Traitor's Bride

No matter how many men I had met before or might meet in the future, there would always be Mark Wentworth . . .

"You see," he whispered as he captured my hand again, "I yearned for you. I dreamed of being with you. All my memories returned . . ." He pressed my hand to his lips. "Arabella, there's been a madness within me ever since. A need to possess you when you're willing. I knew I hurt you that first time but I also remember the moment when your hurt must have gone away because you became mine . . . *mine* . . ." He looked deeply into my eyes. "I see you remember too!"

He kissed me, held me to him and I remembered everything . . . everything . . . *the terror and the pain, the passion and the glory* . . .

TRAITOR'S BRIDE

JESSICA HOWARD

A JOVE BOOK

Requests for permission to make copies of any part of the work
should be mailed to: Permissions, Jove Publications, Inc., 200
Madison Avenue, New York, NY 10016

First Jove edition published December 1979

10 9 8 7 6 5 4 3 2 1

Printed in the United States of America

Jove books are published by Jove Publications, Inc., 200 Madison Avenue, New York, NY 10016

PART ONE

THE LADY

Chapter One

I should not have been standing in the dark, alone, uninvited, in a strange garden behind a strange house. I was fifteen, a budding woman, but because I came from a genteel family I didn't know much about the dangers a girl can face. At any rate, I intended no mischief. All I wanted was to peek into the windows of that big house and watch the masked ball, where couples in elaborate costumes whirled and bowed and drank and laughed and flirted—just as I would be doing in another year or two.

I had gone to stay overnight with Aunt Patience, my mother's unmarried sister. Aunty was usually the kindest person in the world, but sometimes she was a dragon—and she didn't approve of masked balls. She told me that when people wore masks you couldn't trust them. They did awful things they wouldn't dare do if they had to show their faces. And as for the costumes that some women wore at those balls! Women who came from respectable homes in our respectable city of Newport! She hoped that I, her only and beloved niece, would never think that just because my face was hidden I was entitled to bare most of the rest of me.

Meanwhile, down the street, that big house had glowed with lights and vibrated with music. And I *was* fifteen, and I wanted badly to be old enough to put on a mask and a costume with a slit skirt and a very low bodice. Telling Aunty I was going for a breath of air, I scurried around to where the fiddlers made such entrancing rhythms. Unseen, I whisked into the garden, stood amid the thick weigela bushes near the back fence, and swayed to the dance. I imagined myself masked and mysterious, dancing with an also disguised, magnificent young man. How he would beg to know my name! But I'd only smile and never tell, and I'd tap him coquettishly with my fan, and he'd sigh, and he'd call me his unknown charmer. . . .

7

A rear door opened and candlelight poured out. A man appeared, dragging someone after him—a woman in a skimpy Cleopatra costume. The costume seemed all the more revealing in contrast to the man's all-enveloping domino in red-and-white checks. He was obviously drunk, and as he hauled on the woman's arm he gestured toward the bank of weigela. He wanted her to go with him behind those thick bushes.

She struggled as he tried to rip away her skimpy, jeweled bodice. Finally she broke free and ran inside, her rouged mouth laughing beneath her velvet mask as she left the domino alone and sagging.

Not yet seeing me, the masked man took off the peaked, pomponned hat he wore above the clown-painted mask that covered his entire face. He mopped his sweating brow. I noticed he had only a fringe of graying hair—he must be at least fifty, I thought—and I saw a puckered scar that ran across his bald pate. He restored his hat, called angry curses back through the doorway. Then, turning to the garden area, he caught the moonglint of my white dress against the greenery. Instantly he stumbled toward me, trailing a reek of brandy that hung about him like a cloud.

Aunt Patience had warned me delicately about "rough men." I could have run away. But still, I wasn't Arabella Nobody. I was Arabella Downing, William Downing's daughter, and our family was one of the oldest in Newport. Who would threaten *me?* I rather pitied the besotted domino who lurched through the flower beds, and I thought to take him by the arm and lead him back to the ball.

He stopped squarely in front of me. His eyes glittered through the holes in his mask, and his fingers twitched as his hands made motions, outlining my form. I began to speak gently to him. But suddenly he grabbed at my bosom. At the same time he pushed me with all his weight and made me stumble backward, shocked. I never had met such crude insolence.

"Those women in there!" the domino snarled. "Driving a man mad with their half-naked breasts! Then they slip away with some damned callow young rooster. . . ." As he spoke he pawed and fondled, and pinched me in private places while I slapped at his hands and indignantly tried to get away. "Stay here with me!" he demanded. "Who are you? Somebody's serving wench? No; too well dressed.

8

You must be one of the young doxies from Big Beulah's house, trying to strike up business."

By then my poise had been replaced by shivering fear. But as I opened my mouth to scream, the masked man slapped a hand across my lips. I kicked his leg, broke free, and ran, pursued by foul curses. But I had run deeper into the bushes, and suddenly found myself trapped back there in a corner of the high fence. I turned, ready to kick and scratch and shriek—but I paused in fascinated terror. In two sudden motions, the domino had dropped his baggy trousers and his drawers, and he stood giggling drunkenly, facing me.

I had never seen a man more naked than the occasional laboring slave who was stripped to the waist. All I could have said surely about the male body is that men don't have breasts. But now I saw. Like a stallion!

The masked man giggled. "There it is, all ready for you. Come on, girl—quick—on your back—before anyone sees us."

A man was like a rutting stallion when it rears upon a mare. . . .

Coming out of my paralyzed stare, I tried to get past him. But he pulled me down, fell upon me, again closed my mouth. "Come, don't be silly," he muttered as he thrust his free hand beneath my skirt. All my kicking and scratching did not stop him from reaching up between my thighs while I writhed in outrage. "Silly girl, stop being coy," he panted. "I'll pay you two bits . . . four bits! You can meet me in my stable twice a week. I'll be your regular customer. Come on, come on!"

He *dared not* put his hand where it was! With the strength of frantic terror, I bit his palm. He howled, jerking away a hand that showed blood. I rolled past him, and leaped to my feet. Hampered as he was by his disordered trousers, he couldn't catch me. I ran like a deer through the garden and down the street.

When I stopped and brushed twigs and leaves off my dress, I was shaking as much from disbelief as from fright. I was Arabella Downing! Nobody did such things to *me!*

But someone had, and something worse had almost happened. It was true, then, that when you got past thirteen you had to beware of being alone with the wrong kind of man. But how was one to know? That domino had seemed so foolish and helpless. . . .

9

Shamed to my soul, I was tempted to tell Aunt Patience about the man who had exposed his nakedness to me and had felt my body in that dreadful way. But it was all over, and I had suffered no real harm, so I never told anyone of the awful thing that had nearly befallen me . . . let alone that, at fifteen, I was not quite sure what I had escaped.

I was nineteen and it was spring, 1805, when the masked man—unmasked, this time—came back into my life.

By then I was fully formed, and well formed if I may say so, and a responsible woman. My mother had died when I'd been sixteen, and ever since I had taken charge of our big old house. My father was having business troubles, and I had had to learn hard lessons in managing money. At the same time, Father was growing crippled with rheumatism and had been warned about his bad heart. So I spent much of my time at the Downing Ironworks, the business that my great-grandfather had begun, where I tried to be useful, at least with the paperwork.

For a long time I had had nightmares about that nasty scene in the bushes. But by now I had outgrown it. Unlike my Aunt Patience, I had no fear of marriage. I had sewn endlessly on a lovely, floating nightdress, all for the sake of having a magnificent husband lift it off me in the privacy of our chamber. I knew what would happen then, and I wanted it to happen—as long as I surrendered my virginity honorably and lovingly, in marriage.

We were having a delightful spring. Father and I decided to forget our business worries and go for a stroll in Washington Square. It was his favorite area, for he had served on General Washington's staff, and he never tired of telling me stories of the Revolution. Other strollers greeted us, sometimes with friendship, always with respect. I saw a man of pompous dignity come toward us, highly dignified in a wig even though wigs had gone out of style. His gaze fastened upon me. He pursed his lips, adjusted his cravat, and walked a bit faster.

I had never before met Mr. Aubrey Brinton, but I knew he was a man of solid fortune, Father's banker. I didn't like his air of self-importance. As he was bowing and telling me how beautiful I was, his wig slipped just enough to expose his fringe of gray hair and the end of the puckered scar that I suddenly knew ran all across his head. I caught my breath. I wanted to tell him what I thought of a man who would try to force a young girl's virtue. But he never recognized me as the near-child he had tried to rape in the bushes.

He said, all oil and glitter: "I'd heard you have a charming daughter, Major Downing, but I never knew how charming."

My father looked at me significantly. I knew my duty. "Thank you, Mr. Brinton, but I think it's just the spring air. We were going home for tea." So much was truth. The rest was a lie: "I'd be glad if you'd join us."

How that detestable widower ogled me as we had tea, and how he undressed me with his eyes! Worse yet, he began to drop in once or twice a week and stay after tea while Father—who no longer could manage a pen and rarely went to his office at the ironworks—dictated his letters and business papers.

Mr. Brinton always pretended jolly amazement at the fact that I wrote shorthand. I had had a tutor come down from Boston, and was proud of owning a skill generally used only by male clerks. The ancient art had been much improved, and I could capture words as quickly as Father could speak.

"Amazing!" Mr. Brinton would say, standing behind me to marvel at the little hooks and circles and dots my quill made. Was I to tell Father that Brinton placed himself so he could look down my neckline? No, I *must* be gracious and pleasant. The banker held Father's note for a large sum. The note was long overdue, and I dared not do anything that might annoy him into foreclosing it. Worse yet, I knew Aubrey Brinton wanted a wife, and I knew in growing dismay that he soon would "pop the question."

One afternoon while Father and I bent over a ledger, our constant visitor came down the path from the front gate.

Sighing, I received the usual compliments, rang for tea, took my usual place in the window seat. Father shuffled over painfully from the mahogany desk his grandfather had brought from England, and settled himself where the sun could warm him. Mr. Brinton sat on a Queen Anne sofa that was almost a hundred years old, but I don't think he knew what he was sitting on; he had eyes only for me, watching my every motion while I writhed inwardly beneath his gaze.

We spoke of the unexplored wonders of the Louisiana

Purchase territory, recently acquired from France; of Napoleon's rise in France and his threat to all Europe; of the price of rum and I know not of what else. It didn't matter anyway. What did matter was my increasing certainty that Aubrey Brinton wanted to marry me, and soon would speak to my father about it. What if I said no? Would he force the ironworks into bankruptcy?

I tried to smile as our Indian maid, Mary Crow, brought in the tea tray and set it on a delicate Sheraton stand, then curtseyed as I had taught her. But although sunshine poured through the window and warmed my back dread crawled up and down my spine like icy fingers. Accomplished as I was in the ladylike arts, I nevertheless clinked the teapot against a cup and spilled tea into the saucer.

The cup I handed Brinton was imported Chinese porcelain in the Famille Rose pattern. The service of which it was a part had been especially made for us in Hankow, and had been delivered two years after it had been ordered. My gracious mother had handed George Washington one of those cups, and he had remarked that his own Mount Vernon tea service had a similar pattern.

Mr. Brinton knew that much, and handled his cup with care. But nothing would ever change the noisy way he drank. Mr. Brinton's huge house was very new and garish, built in poor imitation of Thomas Jefferson's classical taste. It stood near the harbor and had little relief from summer heat. Our own house had been built in 1745. It stood on The Hill, which the earliest Newport settlers had chosen for its fine view and welcome breezes. The carpet in my father's study, where we sat, was a seventeenth-century Tabriz, made in Persia. Some of our chairs had been made in England by Mr. Chippendale's own hand. Our downstairs walls were paneled in rose cedar. Upstairs we used fine damask wall coverings, and much of the bedroom furniture was also covered in a silk damask that—I sometimes remarked to other ladies on The Hill—could no longer be purchased in our country.

As for Mr. Brinton, he had been brought up as an ostler in his father's stable, where a horse had once kicked him in the head—not hard enough, alas! True, he had since made a fortune; but on The Hill we called such money "new money." Among the Newport gentry, money, like furniture, was supposed to have a proper patina of age.

12

Stirring my tea, I murmured, "I trust your children are well, Mr. Brinton?"

Nodding, the wealthy banker gave me a small hard grin. Let the Downings show off their manners! He knew that even had I been able to find more of that silk damask, we couldn't afford to reupholster our worn pieces. He knew too—his smirk showed it—that we kept only three servants now, compared to the six we once had had, and thát Mary Crow had become less my personal maid and more the parlor maid and shopper. In short, we might have the breeding but Brinton had the gold.

He observed meaningly, "Yes, my children thrive. I've a nurse and a tutor for 'em, and if I ever marry again, my second wife need never be troubled with their care."

"How fortunate for your second wife," I replied. But I saw Brinton's puffy little eyes go round while his whisker-bordered lips parted. He stared at my bosom, and only then did I realize that the low afternoon sunlight streamed through my clothing. I was dressed in the Directoire fashion, all airy and gauzy, with a high ribbon-belt to accent the bust and a straight skirt that showed the outline of one's limbs. True, I wore enough beneath the thin *mousseline-de-soie* to hide any peekaboo under ordinary circumstances. But that revealing sunlight struck right through my dress, showing the outline of my bosom almost as though it were bare.

Mr. Brinton licked his lips. The shadow-show aroused his desire for me. I could tell, because he was too pot-bellied to sit with his legs crossed, and the fashion for men was tight pantaloons. The boorish banker forgot himself so far as to pull up his waistband to ease his discomfort, and I felt my face flaming as I imagined having such a man undress me and press his nakedness upon mine.

Painfully I recalled that I had turned down offers of marriage from two young men of good family, right there on The Hill. I knew they said around town that Arabella Downing was too choosy for her own good, and that when a girl reached nineteen—well, she should bear in mind she'd never grow any younger. But I had wanted a husband I loved passionately, and I had said no to those well-mannered young men.

Should I have said yes to one of them? It would have been a way to save the Downing family business . . . and probably extend my father's life, for the business was his

13

life. He worried badly about having Brinton's note hanging like an axe over his head.

I had turned away to hide my body's outline. Staring out into the front garden, I tried to handle the question: *When Brinton says he wants to marry me, what will be my answer?*

I didn't know, I didn't know!

Out there in the garden, our purple-red flowering quince had put forth its blossoms, but I hardly saw its beauty. I was blinking, and the man who opened the front gate seemed to swim in a mist. He had stridden some yards down the flagged path before I could really see him. I recognized him as a seagoing man, as any Newporter would. Noting the erect authority of his bearing, I was sure he was a ship's officer who had dressed well before coming ashore. He was about twenty-five, olive-skinned, lean-hipped, with a good span of shoulder. His pantaloons, with pearl buttons at the calves, clung to legs that were beautifully muscled. In one hand he swung a big leather portfolio.

We all heard the sharp rap he made with our brass knocker. Two minutes later, Mary Crow whisked into the study and closed the door behind her. Mary was a Narragansett and I was the only lady in town who employed a full-blooded Indian domestic.

Now Mary's dark-copper face, usually expressionless, showed real alarm. Breathlessly she addressed my father: "Mr. Downing—a captain come. He say see you."

Ship captains were no novelty as callers. We made and sold anchors, chains, mast fittings, and the like. I wondered at Mary's unease.

"Ask the captain to kindly wait," said my father. "But didn't he tell you his name?"

Mary began to speak, had to try again. Finally, "Yes, sir."

"Well?" Father prodded gently.

"Him say . . ." Mary stopped, gave me an imploring look I could not fathom. "Him say he Captain Mark Wentworth."

Mark Wentworth! I had been ten years old when I had last seen him, so of course I hadn't recognized him instantly. Now I saw how the name had filled my father with rage, while Brinton looked uneasy. No Wentworth would ever be welcome in our house.

"Show him out!" Father shouted.

"Yes, sir," said Mary.

"And never again mention that name in my presence!"

"Yes, sir."

She had not seen Mark before, but like everyone in Newport, she knew that the Wentworths had left Newport nine years ago in a cloud of jeers and insults. She turned quickly, her long black braids swinging beneath the starched white cap she wore.

That was how close Mark Wentworth came to being sent away. But with sudden urgency I wanted to have him in the room. Of course he was a Tory and his family had been Tories and I hated them all. But still, when you've last glimpsed a person when he was sixteen, it's natural to want to see the kind of man he's grown into.

"Wait!" I called, stopping Mary. My father glared. But I remembered the crush I had had on sixteen-year-old Mark, who had hardly known I existed. Oh, he'd been so strong and gloomy and black-browed . . . and magnificent!

"Father," I protested, "this is *Mark* Wentworth, after all. The son, not the father."

Not old Job Wentworth, once my own father's dear friend, now his mortal enemy.

Back in '75, even before the new nation had been born, Father had made the long, bitter march with the New England forces that had futilely, in winter, attacked Quebec. Later he had nearly starved at Valley Forge. At the Battle of Monmouth he had taken a bullet through the leg. His love for the United States was in his very blood. When he spoke at Fourth of July celebrations, he always said he was still willing to die for our united, indivisible, independent nation.

And now I wanted him to receive the son of a rich Newport Tory who had deserted the United States! No wonder he was outraged!

Still surprised to find myself arguing with Father, and astonished at my need to see a man who, as a youth, had ignored me, I protested to Father that at least he should hear what Mark had to say.

"He's a Tory and the son of a Tory! I'll never—"

"But Father, he knows he's not welcome here. The very fact that he's come to our house shows it can't be on any trifling matter."

"Arabella, I—will—be—damned if I let any spawn of Job Wentworth's set foot on my property!"

Softly but insistently I repeated that this was not Job, long detested, but only Mark, the son, who could not be held responsible for his father's misdeeds. At heart Father was a reasonable man, and at length, after some exchange of pleadings and refusals and a great show of indignation, he grumpily agreed that it could not hurt if he merely spoke to Mark.

He told Brinton that young Wentworth would get short shrift, "and that only for the sake of my stubborn daughter." With a touch of wry humor, Father added, "Heaven protect an old man from a managing female!" To the astonished but nearly expressionless Mary, he said, "Pray bring Captain Wentworth in."

My heart raced as I straightened my dress and patted my bright blond hair. When I last had beheld Mark it had been at a dramatic and violent confrontation, and even though I'd been only a small girl at the time, that scene flashed vividly through my memory.

It was back in '96. I was standing on Long Wharf, down at the harbor, holding tightly to my parents' hands. A British ship was waiting. A family dressed in their finest—father, mother, and sixteen-year-old son—walked down the wharf with deliberate slowness. We Downings and other reputable citizens watched in silent scorn, but various 'longshore loafers howled and jeered at the departing Tories. A hail of eggs and vegetables pelted the Wentworths, who looked straight ahead, pale, never hurrying.

Two young toughs ran out and smeared tar on the younger Wentworth's back. And now, although it was nine years later, I could see Mark whirl, his dark face made even darker with rage. His fists flew with amazing speed. I saw one loafer fall flat. The other staggered away, moaning, blood spurting through his fingers from his smashed nose. Mark glared around. Child though I had been, I had seen he had no fear. And when he resumed walking with his parents, it was no retreat. The sailors on the English ship cheered wildly. As for Mark's parents, they looked as though they had expected nothing less from their son.

Job Wentworth had already spent some time in the Bahama Islands, taking up one of the plantations that the

Crown had granted to self-exiled Loyalists, as they called themselves. He had returned briefly to Newport to sell his house and fetch his wife, his son, his slaves, and his household goods. Few of the patriots who watched them go wished ever to see them again.

Few, I say. Not all.

I knew now, as I had not known when I'd been ten, that four or five of the men who had come to Long Wharf had been *well* acquainted with Mark's mother.

My memory brought her back—that beautiful, ageless woman who sauntered the length of the wharf with swaying hips, a mocking smile, a bold glance sent slowly around at the men who watched, as though she were counting those with whom she had made scandal while her husband had been away.

Her name was Prudence. There had never been a woman more poorly named.

Now her son, grown to be twenty-five, strode into my father's study. Holding the beaver hat that Mary Crow had forgotten to take from him, he cast his bold, dark, vital glance around the room. He saw me but he didn't know me, which was not surprising, for I had changed far more than he. I felt a queer little thrill as I noticed he still looked dour, challenging, ready for a fight.

He bowed to my father. "Mr. Downing, my respects, sir," he said, and I noticed his resonant voice—of good use to a captain at sea—and how the sunbeams played in his black, wiry hair. His accent told he had been born to Newport gentry, but something softer had become blended with it—some cadence known in the islands to the south.

"Captain Wentworth," growled my father, and no more.

There was a pause in which neither offered his hand.

"I trust I find you well, sir," said the younger man, who did not smile.

"You find me ill and old, and without the strength to throw you out," said my father gruffly.

He introduced Mr. Brinton with little grace. The banker chose to be condescending. "Well, well, young Wentworth, you've grown into a tall 'un! And you're a captain now?"

"Aye," said Mark, who seemed not to have relished being patronized.

"Captain of what ship, eh?" said Brinton as though asking what toy the youngster was playing with.

"*Royal Arms,* tops'l schooner."

17

My father snapped, *"Royal Arms,* is it? So you're all still monarchists, down there in the Bahamas?"

Mark replied without embarrassment, "Indeed we are, sir." He added in the same cool manner, "You may be sure the new generation still remains loyal to our King."

I was as much a patriot as my father, and I thought Mark's statement hateful. Still I found myself noting the attractive glow that the tropical sun had lent his olive skin. Come now—I told myself—you only had a silly childish crush on the fellow. Yet he still stirred me, and my becoming annoyed at myself made no difference.

Father was rubbing his painful hands together and scowling. He demanded, "If you prefer the rule of King George, what are you doing here in the United States?"

"Trading."

There was nothing my father could say to that. Newport welcomed anyone who wanted to load or unload a cargo. This included smugglers, who were winked at. Also, despite the slave trade's having been outlawed in Rhode Island, slave ships still outfitted in the port, and nobody really knew—or cared—if they landed a cargo while they came and went.

Father found a way to cover his annoyance. He indicated me, in the window seat, and said, "My daughter, Arabella."

Mark was startled. When he bowed to me, his forehead wrinkled because he kept looking up at me from beneath his dark lashes. He still didn't smile—it seemed to me his face wasn't made for smiling—but something like pleasure touched his features. "Miss Arabella . . . it *is* Miss Arabella! You were just a little girl when I left Newport, years ago." He straightened from his bow, and a look of admiration came and went across his face, all in an instant.

I glanced away.

My father was saying meaningly: "Now then, sir, I'm a busy man."

"And I have business with you, sir," Mark Wentworth said, turning away from me—reluctantly, I thought.

"Well," Father grunted, "take a chair." Then, as though trapped into the motions of hospitality: "Arabella, perhaps Captain Wentworth will have tea. Or if he prefers rum—" Father waved stiffly at a bottle of very fine rum that Brinton had brought.

18

"Rum by all means," said Mark, seating himself and placing the big leather portfolio beside him.

He poured himself a good three fingers, smelled the rum, tasted it with a thoughtful face while the banker watched him indignantly.

"Medford," said Mark. "We get a deal of it in the islands."

Aubrey Brinton stuck his thumbs into the armholes of his embroidered waistcoat—a gesture more fitted to a shopkeeper than a financier—and announced, "Medford is the best rum in the world when it's well aged. Now, *that* rum was twelve years in the cask."

Mark tasted it again. "It's better than most Medford. But the best rum is the fifteen-year-old Jamaica, although I do have some regard for the Batavian, the kind they call arak."

Mr. Brinton didn't care to have his rum belittled. Huffily he demanded, "You get Batavian arak in the Bahamas? Batavia is half a world away."

"It comes by way of Africa," said Mark Wentworth.

"By way of slavers, you mean," said Brinton with indignation, although I knew his bank financed several slave ships.

"By way of slavers," Mark agreed, not in the least abashed.

I detested slavery, and once hearing that the Wentworths had a hundred slaves on their Bahamas plantation, I had announced, "It simply shows their character!" At least slaves in the North were generally carpenters or other sorts of artisans, and did not labor under the lash, out in the fields.

At the same time, a good deal of New England's wealth came from the southern slave trade. Down in the Bahamas and the West Indies, slaves tended great fields of sweet cane that was made into sugar and molasses. Much of that molasses was shipped to New England, where distilleries smoked night and day to change it into rum. Barrels of the raw "clairin" went into the holds of vessels that took it to Africa to be traded for human flesh. The slaves were then brought back across the Atlantic—dying like flies on the way—to grow more sugar cane in the islands or tend cotton in our own South.

Mark might have been thinking just that as he raised

19

his glass and said, his voice edged with sarcasm: "Miss Arabella—gentlemen—your health."

My father growled, "I half expected you to toast King George."

"Not in your home, Major Downing," said Mark, at least showing some sensibility. I felt my eyes widen as he tossed down half the rum without a blink, doubly insulting Mr. Brinton, for this was sipping rum. "And now, sir," he went on with the air of one who has done with trifles, "I have a letter for you. It's from my father."

Communication after all those years! But my own parent shook his head. "I see no reason why I should accept a letter from such a source."

Nevertheless, Mark drew a sealed sheet of notepaper from his inner pocket. "Sir, my father is ill. He won't live many more years. Moreover, his sight is failing. You'll see how badly he writes."

My father made no move to take the letter.

Mark went on almost gently: "We get occasional news from Newport, and my father bade me say he is sorry to hear of your own problems of health."

"He is *sorry?*" Father cried.

"Yes, sir. And he realizes your rheumatism must arise from the hardships you suffered during the late rebellion, and he says he respects any brave soldier."

"Humph!" But my father had been touched nevertheless. He sat looking at the rug, struggling with old bitterness. At length he asked, as though hardly believing: "You say Job is going blind?"

"That he is, and was losing his sight rapidly when I left San Isidro." San Isidro was the island in the Bahamas where Job Wentworth had his plantation. "For all I know, he may be blind by now."

Father cleared his throat, rasped, "Well, well, go on. I haven't all day to listen to you."

I didn't want to exchange an understanding glance with Mark, as though we both understood an old man's pride. Nevertheless, that is what happened.

Mark went on in his direct way: "Major Downing, you and my father were once great friends. He feels his end is near, and he would have me say—and he wishes he could tell you himself—that in the common bond of age he wishes to be your friend again. As you know, he is alone. . . ." I saw Mark's expression of complete unhap-

20

piness. Everyone knew that his mother had not been a year in the Bahamas before she had taken a lover. Then she and the man had disappeared. Mark finished: "Major Downing, my father asks that bygones be bygones, and he hopes you will agree."

Again Mark held out the letter. After a moment of hesitation, Father took it. He turned over the folded sheet, inspected its seal, and said in surprise: "Why, Job sealed it with that same big old signet ring of his!" In a heavy silence, the sheet turned over and over in the stiff hands. "Job's sight is failing?" Father still seemed not to have accepted the fact. "Why, he had the eyes of a hawk. Did you know, sir . . . did you know that when we were young, your father and I would go hunting like Indians, with bow and arrow?"

"He has spoken of it many times."

Father seemed to peer away into a forest. "Why . . . why . . . Job could see deer that were invisible to me. I've even seen him hit a running rabbit with an arrow."

Mark nodded gravely. "Down in the islands, I'd throw up a coconut and he'd shoot an arrow into it, in midair."

"And now he's going blind?" Father shook his head, betraying how he had been affected. The letter trembled in his fingers.

I knew he wanted to open that letter. Going to his desk, I found the old knife, honed thin, he had worn in his belt when he marched on Quebec. I lifted the wax seal for him, returned to the window seat. Meanwhile, I wished Mark had not gazed at me approvingly, as though I were on *his* side! All I had wanted was to ease a task for my father.

While Father squinted at the letter, Mark rose. He came toward me, meeting my startled eyes with his own dark glance.

"You're about nineteen now, Miss Arabella?" Mark's voice had gone softer than I'd thought was possible. And I hadn't realized how big he was—not till he came close.

"Yes," I said, lifting my chin.

"I remember your mother. We heard she'd died, a few years ago."

"Yes."

A pause. I might have imagined it, but as Mark looked down at me I thought I saw the faintest twinkle in his eye. He said in the New England way: "Happens you favor your father."

I nodded, thinking that Mark certainly favored his dark, dark-eyed mother. I had never seen a more perfect example of female beauty transmuted into male ruggedness. How hard it must have been for the growing boy to have had such an eye-catching, shapely, wicked, openly unfaithful mother! In her younger days, Prudence had had dozens of suitors. Some said she had married the successful merchant, Job Wentworth, only because she was already carrying his child.

"Apparently you live here with your father, so I presume you're not married, Miss Arabella?"

An impertinent question! For reply, I merely lifted my left hand to show Mark it was ringless.

"I'm not married either," he said, "although my father keeps hinting." I resented his saying it, as though implying it mattered to me. Moreover, I had had enough of chatting with a Tory's son who obviously continued in his father's ways.

But Mark leaned down as though to keep our words from other ears, and my heart beat faster. He was murmuring, "Do you know, Arabella . . . years ago . . . my father always said the Downing girl was a dear little sprat."

"Did he indeed?" I replied with some hauteur.

A twist of Mark's mouth told me he had caught my tone. But he only remarked, "In those days, I found ten-year-old girls not at all interesting."

How well I had known it!

"But what a difference the years can make!" Again those dark, clear eyes caught mine as he murmured, "I'll tell my father that the dear little sprat has grown into a remarkably beautiful woman."

"Tell your father what you wish," I replied, but wished my voice had been steadier. His litheness . . . the power in his shoulders . . . the forcefulness of his chin . . . all these were having a disturbing effect on me.

Now my own parent had finished reading Job Wentworth's letter. He sighed and again looked far away. "Yes, Job tells me he's going blind. Why . . . he used to identify ships far out in the Sound, when the rest of us needed telescopes. Well, as to being his friend again . . . I'll think on it. I'll think on it. How long will you be in port, sir?"

Mark again seemed reluctant to turn away from me. "Ten days or two weeks, depending on how many crates of candles I can stow, and lumber and beef and cheese, and other needfuls."

"Well then, come and see me in a week's time. I'll have an answer for your father."

"Yes, sir, I will. And now," said Mark briskly, "to the matter of business. We need a new set of iron rollers to crush cane at our sugar mill. We'd like Downing Ironworks to make the rollers and the machinery that goes with them." Father reared back as though he had seen a snake, but Mark went on, quite in command: "I'll be returning to Newport in three months. Can you have it all ready for me by then?"

Before Father could object, Mark's quick hands had flipped a batch of papers from his portfolio. They were mechanical drawings—patterns of objects to be made in iron and steel—the very lifeblood of the ironworks.

I saw Father try to resist, but he could not help glancing at one. "Hmmm. Those gears will be turned by a waterwheel, I suppose?"

Mark Wentworth shook his head. "No, sir, we have no streams in the Bahamas. We depend on windmills."

"So," said Father thoughtfully. He reached for his pipe. With true courtesy, Mark brought him the lamp from his desk and lifted the glass chimney to expose the flame. While Father inspected to make sure the fine Virginia— also a gift from Mr. Brinton—was lit all around, I held my breath. His pride might make him say no. But we desperately needed large jobs on which we could turn a good profit.

"Well, business is business," said Father, to my relief. "But as to whether I'll be Job's friend again—that's quite another matter."

"Understood," said Mark.

"A good many castings and forgings indicated here," said Father, poking his pipe at the drawings. "Expensive, and I'll accept no personal bills of exchange from Tories. Bills must be drawn on a good bank."

Mark gave Father a hard look, but kept his voice level. "I have a sufficient draft drawn on Mr. Hamilton's bank in New York City."

Mr. Brinton, seeing a chance to reprove the younger man, said, "You mean the *late* Mr. Hamilton, sir."

"I am aware, sir," said Mark, "that Mr. Aaron Burr had a duel with Mr. Alexander Hamilton last year, and because of it Mr. Hamilton is dead. Nevertheless, it was he who founded the bank, so I say it's Mr. Hamilton's bank in which my father has money deposited."

"Aaron Burr!" said my father with no pleasure. "There's another man who was once my friend and comrade-in-arms, but whose name I don't wish to hear. He came to be Jefferson's Vice President by trickery—by trickery, I tell you! And now he's been disgraced, as he deserves, and they say he's conniving with Tories in some scheme in the Southwest, to break off part of the Louisiana Purchase and form a new nation. That scoundrel!"

"What's more," Aubrey Brinton put in, "why are Tories dealing with Hamilton's bank? He was Burr's archenemy."

Mark Wentworth snapped, "It would go ill with my father's affairs and mine if we allowed politics to sway our need for sound banking. Well, Major Downing? Will my draft be good enough?"

"Good enough."

Mark reached for his hat. "You'll undertake to build the rollers? I can count on loading them aboard in three months?"

"Yes. Before you sail, I'll have the particulars of billing ready."

"I thank you, sir."

"I thank you for your custom, sir."

Mark replaced the drawings in the portfolio and stood it against the desk. He said, "My schooner is at Long Wharf, should you wish to find me."

As he rose, that dark, unsmiling face seemed to reflect a darkened soul, as though he were weighed upon by secret worries. He made his departing bows in order of seniority. His final bow, to me, was deeper than the others, and again he kept his gaze on me, so his brow wrinkled as he looked upward through his lashes.

His face was toward me, his back to the others. His lips formed two words very softly, almost silently. "You're beautiful." Something that was almost a smile hovered around his sensitive mouth.

I did not want to flush, but there was no way to prevent the tide of heat from rising to my throat and face. I tried to make myself angry at Mark's presumption, but I couldn't, and all the while my heart pounded and my

24

breath came quickly. As I watched his broad back and the challenging swing of his walk, I realized that although there is a great distance of years between a girl of ten and a youth of sixteen . . . when the girl becomes a woman of nineteen and the youth becomes a man of five-and-twenty, the distance vanishes to nothing.

Chapter Two

I set out next afternoon in our gig, with Mary Crow driving. Later she would go alone to Newport's historic Brick Market for a supply of food, then take the gig home. As for me, I had business to attend to at the Long Wharf—although not with Mark Wentworth. Then I planned to pay a surprise visit to darling old Aunt Patience, as I had done on and off during the past four years.

A wet east wind fanned our faces, promising rain. I drew up the hood of my woolen cloak. I had not slept well. I had had that old, unwelcome dream again. I had been lost in a jungle of weigela, and wherever I ran I met a giggling figure in a red-and-white domino who fondled my breasts and groped between my thighs with greedy fingers. Then, in my dream, the domino had changed into Mark Wentworth. The bushes became a bedchamber, and Mark told me "You're beautiful," as I stood in my bridal nightdress, trembling, waiting. Wakening in confusion, I had cried, "No!" into the darkness. Didn't he know I hated him for a Tory?

We stopped the gig at the ironworks, where Cason, the foreman, was having men load three hundredweight of fetters into a dray. Make no mistake; it was Downing Ironworks that had manufactured those scores of handcuffs and leg irons for use in the slave trade. I turned my face away from the grim, clanking objects, reminding myself that business is where you find it.

When the loading was done, one of the men, Peter Brown, drove the dray to Long Wharf while Mary and I followed sedately. In theory, Peter alone could have gotten the fetters aboard a waiting slaver, the *Bridgewater*, and collected payment. But Peter could not read, and Father suspected that the slaver's master, Captain Chance, would give him some piece of paper and be off to Africa before we discovered his draft was no good. No one else

27

could be spared, so I had persuaded Father that, unusual as it might be, *I* would board the vessel and collect in gold and silver, just this once.

Thus it went with me. Sometimes I was the elegant lady, and sometimes I was deep in some business that other Newport ladies—and how they could sniff—thought hardly genteel. But I still felt I could go anywhere in Newport and be quite secure. When Mary and I passed the White Horse Tavern, even the idlers waiting to beg drinks lifted their caps to William Downing's daughter.

Driving out onto the wharf, we passed the *Royal Arms* where she was secured to the stringpiece, loading. I noticed that Mark had moored her with her stern facing shoreward, displaying her name in gold letters across her counter for people on nearby streets to read. A Tory defying us patriots, and I liked him even less.

I noticed a couple of women strolling on the wharf who were—well, less than ladies. No doubt they were Big Beulah's girls. One of them was keeping company with a burly loafer named Thatch whom we sometimes hired to help with heavy jobs at the ironworks—if he wasn't in jail. Thatch sat on an upended hogshead, and the moon-faced girl sat on his lap and giggled mechanically as he pushed his hand into her bodice. Seeing me, Thatch touched his ragged cap as though to lift it to William Downing's daughter. But he merely jammed it down over his eyes and laughed, showing jagged stumps of teeth, then spat tobacco juice. I ignored him.

Resignedly, I pulled my hood closer as thin rain began to fall. Dusk was approaching, and I hoped I'd get to Aunt Patience's house before it was really dark. I found a boatman to row me out to the *Bridgewater,* where I asked the mate on duty to send one of his own small boats to pick up the fetters. He complained that the simple task would take a long time, since almost the entire crew had gone ashore.

Eventually the job was done and I confronted Captain Chance in his cabin below the quarterdeck. Sure enough, he made difficulties about paying in good metal. But I faced him down, and in the end he paid me out of a considerable chest of coin—for they were all rich, those slavers. Not trusting him, I made a quick mental calculation of the value of the Spanish, French, and Dutch pieces, then demanded and received three more florins.

Captain Chance was something of a dandy. His saturnine rake's face was partially framed by elaborately coiffed, pomaded black whiskers, beneath which a great bunch of silver-tinted lace spouted out from the vicinity of his Adam's apple. He complimented me on my sharpness with figures, and went on to say he had been in ten different ports during the past year but nowhere had he seen so comely a woman as I. I thought him clever-minded rather than really competent, and there was no mistaking the eye he had for the ladies. I was sure that were it not for the status of my family he would have made advances.

He said lazily that he'd call Mr. Haversham, the first mate, who was on watch, and have me rowed ashore with my bag of money. I thanked him coolly, meanwhile wrinkling my nose at the unmistakable odor of a slave ship. This one was empty, but it seemed that no amount of vinegar or burning sulfur could get rid of the stench of packed bodies.

Now I found to my surprise that there was a white woman aboard. Chance had nodded to someone beyond me, and when I turned I saw she had come to his door.

I inclined my head and she did the same for me, politely and as though she had breeding. I thought her some five years older than I, although quite smooth-faced, and I noticed she was of my own height and figure. Her eyes, like mine, were a darkish blue, and her blond hair was nearly the same light shade as my own. She too saw our resemblance to each other, and we exchanged a smile.

"Ah, here's Anne," said Chance in his lazy way. "Miss Arabella Downing, may I present Miss Anne Burney, who is a—ah—a warrant officer of the *Bridgewater*."

Now I noticed that Anne Burney's Directoire dress was quite in style, not unlike my own, and its light lawn was cut low but not daringly so. Strangely, she had added several large, gaudy scarves—around her throat, across her hair, one tied to each wrist, one knotted beneath her bosom. But her clothing interested me less than her status. A warrant officer? I made no sign of not believing Chance, but I was most suspicious.

Miss Burney acknowledged the introduction in a cultured, English-accented voice that went with her peaches-and-cream complexion. "How do you do, Miss Downing. It's so pleasant to have you aboard." To Chance, she said with a touch of eagerness: "If Miss Downing is going ashore later, I can go with her."

Chance lost his easy manner. "No you don't! You stay right here."

This was odd and unsettling. I pretended not to notice.

Seeming to dismiss Chance and his reaction, Anne Burney said to me very pleasantly, "Miss Downing, do stay a bit. I so seldom have a chance to chat with another woman. Won't you have a bit of late tiffin with me?"

I hesitated. Few captains carried women who were not either their wives or paying passengers. If they did carry a woman for any other purpose . . . well ,it was for one purpose only.

However genteel Anne Burney seemed, I thought I should not seek her company. Still, the cold rain was coming down hard on the deck above our heads. Peter would already have departed with the dray, and Mary had taken the gig to the market. I'd have to walk a good way and get chilled and wet. But if I waited, the rain might stop. So why not take an English tiffin with this pleasant stranger, who, after all, might be a perfectly respectable person.

"Why yes, I'd enjoy some refreshment, thank you," I said.

"Treat Miss Downing well, Anne," said Chance, yawning negligently.

Taking up my cape and my heavy little moneybag, I found myself being ushered into the cabin next door. It was dark. A strange, squawking voice startled me: "Ahoy, matey, blast your eyes! Ahoy, matey, blast your eyes!" When my hostess lit her lamp, I saw the speaker was a bright green and yellow parrot on a perch. It was part of the clutter in that strange, crowded little room. On both sides were shelves full of jars labeled *Senna* and *Colocynth* and *Dandelion* and such, and bunches of dried herbs hung from the overhead. I saw a spirit lamp and various chemist's vessels. There was an array of liquors in a rack, and, above it, four grinning skulls, one a baby's. Skulls of slaves? I wondered, shuddering. In one corner hung a little bag covered with odd beaded designs and decorated with a bunch of flamboyant cock feathers and little bones. I thought it a fetish bag, or *ouanga,* such as I had seen slaves wear. The oddest object of all was a kind of crown made of brass that hung on a nail. It looked positively barbaric, and I thought it might once have belonged to some African chieftain, along with the goggle-eyed little black-wood statues that stood here and there, frankly displaying private parts that had been made three times their proportional size.

"I'm ship's chemist," said Anne Burney, as though feeling some explanation was necessary.

"Really?"

"Oh, yes. It runs in my family. They were alchemists, hundreds of years ago."

I must say this information left me astonished. But I smiled and sat on the berth while Anne sat in a chair, draped with odds and ends of brocade, that had been wedged into a corner. How odd she was! And there was something so very peculiar about her eyes . . . the white showed all around the pupil, so that each eye seemed like the bull's-eye in a target. Add the scarves that floated about her, and the strange furnishings of her cabin, and you had a woman who was peculiar indeed. She seemed all the more strange when she pulled down a tiny table that had been folded up against a stanchion and said, as though we sat in some Devon parlor with phlox nodding outside, "So sweet of you to drop in, my dear."

Tiffin as I knew it was an in-between munch, generally of tiny sandwiches, cookies and the like, along with tea or cocoa, or buttermilk in hot weather. But my strange hostess served a mellow peach liqueur and plain, hard ship's biscuit. We spoke of the styles, as two ladies may, and I noticed that Anne had a way with cut and pattern, and apparently had access to excellent materials. She said she whiled away the time on long sea passages by making her own clothes. But did I have a current style book? I did, and promised to send it down with my maid.

Changing the topic in the oddest manner, Anne Burney told me of the dreadful heat in the Gulf of Guinea, on the African coast, and how they had taken on a load of Mandingoes and Fulas and Ashantis. To her, slaves were merely merchandise. Still, she fascinated me with an account of how Chance had given a ball for the few whites in the slave-gathering area, turning his ship into an outdoor ballroom festooned with paper lanterns; and how an Arab trader had come to watch, with all his four wives huddled behind him. Also she mentioned that she had sold two stylish dresses to the Portuguese factor's wife, whose wardrobe was ten years old. But the woman had had to steal the money from her husband.

"I wonder what happened to her when he found out," Anne said offhandedly. "Oh, you've finished your liqueur? Do have another."

The liqueur was warming and pleasant. Anne assured me on her honor as an apothecary that it would fortify me against the wet, and really, it was the mildest kind of ladies' drink.

Again switching topics, Anne took the parrot on her finger, cooed at it, called it pretty-pretty. It was when she told me, all in the same breath, how she serviced the master and mates of the *Bridgewater*, that realization began to dawn in my shocked mind. Most earnestly, my hostess explained that Mr. Haversham, the first, had no staying power. One-two-three, and he'd let out a banshee howl and it was all over. Really it was annoying, because all he did was arouse her and leave her unsatisfied. But I knew that kind of man, didn't I? Weren't they terribly trying?

What was I, a virgin, to reply? "Well—" I said, then, "Well, you see . . ." Then, at last, I put everything together—the weird eyes, the eccentric plumage of scarves, the strangely furnished cabin, the disturbing mannerisms, the wildness of the woman. It came over me that Anne Burney was utterly mad. I must not stay! I must go— instantly! But I felt so languid, I couldn't rise. What was wrong with me? Anne was mad . . . Anne had uttered dreadful insults to my virtue . . . and yet my backbone had gone so weak, I hardly could hold up my head.

Dizzying me worse with another change of topic, Anne said with a fond smile, "I'm so glad we have the same kind of hair because I want all my ladies-in-waiting to be bright-blond, like me."

"I beg your pardon? W-what ladies-in-waiting?" Confused and growing faint, I was not sure I had heard aright.

"But Miss Downing, you know I'm a reincarnation of Anne Bonney, the famous pirate."

"Oh . . . you are?"

"Yes. Isn't it wonderful? My name is nearly the same, and Anne Bonney was a bright blonde too. Years ago it came to me . . . I am Anne Bonney, containing her soul reborn on earth! Oh, she was a wonderful pirate! Brave and bloodthirsty as any man!"

Dimly I realized I had heard of Anne Bonney. She had stolen and slaughtered in the Bahamas and along the islands and bays of the Carolina coast a hundred years before. She had been known for her cruelty and her ability to command. . . .

". . . and when I have my own ship I'll call it the *Caribbean Queen*," the madwoman was saying from somewhere. She sat close by me, but she seemed far off. "Because I'll be queen of the Caribbean and the Bahamas too! Oh, I'll be merciless!" Following that blood-chilling statement with a hospitable smile, she reached to fill my glass again. I was too befuddled to stop her.

Now she set the brass crown on her head, whispered insanely, "And when I have my own ship I'll capture the *Bridgewater*, and wait till you see the revenge I take on Hiram Chance!" She snatched a curved, small knife from her stocking. "I'll cut him!" she gloated. "I'll cut him!"

"Oh dear . . . but why?" I asked faintly. It was all I had strength for.

Anne Burney hissed, "He keeps me prisoner. You see, I was wanted for murder in Savannah. Got away to the docks. He took me aboard. Now he says if I try to get away from him he'll bring me back there and have me hanged. And sometimes he whips me and locks me up—down there with the slaves!" She smoothed the clip-winged parrot and cooed, "Pretty, pretty!" In that atmosphere of madness, it did not seem strange to hear the clacking voice respond, "Ahoy, matey, blast your eyes!"

"Dear Miss Downing," said Anne Burney, still cooing, "you're a charming woman and you have breeding. I'm going to make you my chief lady-in-waiting and you're going to know all the secrets of my court."

I could smell the herbs and hear the whoop of wind and the swash of rain. Beyond that, nothing seemed real anymore.

"Come now, Miss Downing! If you want to be my chief lady-in-waiting you must give me a court courtsey and say Your Majesty."

Humor her, I thought dazedly. Get to your feet—she's given you a good excuse—and back up to the door. Slide it open and run!

When I rose from the berth, the cabin swam around

33

me. Nevertheless I curtseyed deeply, saying, "I shall be forever grateful for the honor you have done me, Your Majesty. I promise upon my faith to serve you always."

I saw eager delight upon Anne's face. But her features wavered. The cabin tilted. No, I had fallen and was looking up at an angle. Then I had half-risen, helped by the madwoman, and I heard her speak as though from a great distance: "There, there, Lady Arabella, you're going to be a trifle paralyzed, but it goes away. There was a bit of water hemlock in what you were drinking, and just enough opium, and other things I know, and you didn't notice that I drank from a different bottle, poor dear. Lie down, now. You won't be able to move or talk, but it passes, it passes."

I was lying helpless on the berth, able to hear and see, but not to speak or move. As Anne Burney spoke in the friendliest fashion, I was gradually engulfed in a black mist of helplessness and terror.

"I'll borrow your cloak, dear. And the money. And I must take along my lamp so I can signal for a boatman. No one's on deck, and I'll get to shore, you'll see. Thank you, Lady Arabella. You have helped your sovereign win her freedom, and you shall be rewarded when we meet again." Mad, mad.

My sight went dim, returned, went very dim, while my heart thudded and faltered, thudded and faltered. Vaguely I saw Anne Burney wrap herself in my cloak, draw the hood closely around her face. I saw her start to put the parrot into its cage. Then she muttered, "Keelhaul the creature. Why take it along? It'll only squawk at the wrong moment." Just as dimly, and with hardly presence enough to feel horror, I saw her hold up the bird and glare at it. "Ahoy, matey—" was cut off as she wrung its neck. Feathers drifted as she tossed the little corpse behind the herb jars.

The black fog closed around me and I must have gone unconscious because my fright and bewilderment disappeared. Everything disappeared.

When I opened my eyes, the cabin was dark save for a small streak of light that came through a crack in the bulkhead. My limp body seemed without life, all one great numbness, but only in my mind did I suffer. How long had I lain unconscious? I had no way to tell. Had the

Bridgewater gone to sea? For a while I was sure it had, and I'd never see Newport again. Terror seethed in my reeling mind . . . I was to take Anne Burney's place, *servicing* those four men! At last I realized there was no swaying motion, and the ship must still be anchored in Newport Harbor.

With my consciousness coming and going, I realized that the streak of light came from Captain Chance's cabin, next door. Vaguely I remembered that Anne Burney had told me she would take revenge on Hiram Chance . . . she'd cut him. Was Chance dead, then? Had Anne run amok with her knife, killed him and others too?

No, all she wanted was to get ashore . . . and even as the thought came to me, I knew Chance was still alive because I heard his drawling voice behind the bulkhead. He was saying, "Take a chair, my dear fellow." Came a murmur, then nothing, as the cold darkness returned. When I was again awake, I heard Chance still speaking: ". . . two months on the Middle Passage. Put sixty-eight of 'em over the side, but the rest fetched a good price in Savannah." He laughed. "Ah, I had some neat wenches! Traveled 'em in the rope locker. Kept 'em clean. They sold well to the young bloods who come to slave auctions to get—cooks, hey?" He guffawed and I heard him slap his thigh.

Blackness came over me. When again I had my senses, but still lay helpless, barely able to move a finger or a toe, I made out some talk of rum. "Try this jacmel," Chance was saying, "It's from Sàn Domingo, and there's something in the soil. . . ."

A different voice, male, vaguely familiar, said, "It's a good brandy rum. But not what you trade with, I fancy."

Chance let out a roar of laughter. "What we trade with would scrape the lining from your throat! So now, Wentworth, we were saying. . . ."

Wentworth! That vaguely familiar voice had been Mark's! He had come aboard the *Bridgewater* and sat within a few feet of me, in the next cabin!

The men talked, and I heard snatches of what they said, but as I lay there between waking and sleeping I made out very few of their words. Then one name reached my fuzzy mind and stayed there. *Aaron Burr.* Of course one noticed the name of a man who had been Vice President. But it was more important to me that my father had known Burr—then a young lieutenant—during that terrible time in the snow before the heights of Quebec. And I knew that, before my father had come to detest Burr as a plotter against the United States, the future Vice President had visited us in Newport.

I tried to concentrate as Mark and Chance talked of Burr. I gathered they were associated with him and with someone named Wilkinson in a secret venture. Wasn't Wilkinson a general in the army? Drugged as I was, I couldn't remember.

The men in the next cabin paused to toast each other's health. Then they spoke of a missing cannon. Someone had hidden a cannon and wouldn't say where. Mark Wentworth mentioned his father, but I didn't get the connection, if any. Cannon . . . Burr . . . Wilkinson . . . the words all vanished as I remembered that my own father knew I had planned to make a surprise visit to Aunt Patience. And so, because Aunty had not been expecting me, no one would miss me. Everyone would think I was elsewhere, safe!

Now I heard Mark Wentworth say, we-ell, he'd take just one more glass of that good jacmel rum, but he really ought to return to his ship while he could still walk.

Chance laughed and said, "If you'll be my guest for another half-hour, you'll find it worthwhile. You know I've a woman aboard—eh?"

"You mean your blonde Mad Anne? I've seen her on occasion, looking ashore and wishing she could swim."

Chance laughed again. "Ah yes, she'd love to get away from me! Meanwhile, my officers and I enjoy bouncing her. But I tell you, Wentworth, when she has a mad spell she can be a real tiger bitch. Queen of the Caribbean! You should hear her chained below, howling! Oh, she's a good enough chemist to physic the slaves, and she knows that if she ever tries to poison anyone aboard, I'll roast her over a slow fire. But my dear friend Wentworth, she's still a woman and she has everything a woman should have—if you know what I mean—so why don't you take a go at her, eh?"

Mark said, "Well—"

"Go on! After all your weeks at sea, remembering those juicy black wenches you had to leave behind! Go on, give her a good roll. Y'know, after I make one more trip to

Africa I'll be coming to the Bahamas, so why don't you make her want to see you again?"

"Well," said Mark, "it *was* a lonely voyage." They laughed together.

My mind had cleared a little, enough to let me be indignant at the male way with women. With them it was all lust. But at least, when Mark and Chance came to Mad Anne's cabin, they'd find me and rescue me.

The sliding door opened. They fumbled their way in. "Now, where is that loony?" Chance muttered. "Her lamp's out . . . no, it's gone. Odd. So's the parrot. Well, I see there's a bit of light coming from my cabin, so you can see to unbutton yourself, eh, Wentworth?" He chortled and said, "There she is, dead drunk in her berth. Anne, you lazy bitch, wake up. I've brought you a lusty fellow. Oh well," he added while cold fear crept in to push aside my hope, "she always wakes up, and don't worry, she'll heave you out o' bed yet! Come back to my cabin when you're done with her and have another rum to see you off."

"Delighted."

When Chance left, sliding the cabin door closed behind him, I was alone with Mark Wentworth, who knew me, knew my father, knew the Downings' standing in our community. And yet I saw him take off his brass-buttoned jacket and pull his shirt over his head!

With terrible effort I stirred in the berth and uttered a wavering moan. It was all I could do to show my terror. But it brought no message to the man who cheerfully prepared to take me, for I could not form words.

How amiable he was! "Ah, you're waking up, Anne? Good. We'll sport it together. I'm partial to blond women —did you know?" For the second time in my life I saw a naked man, however dimly. I closed my eyes, but opened them in the vain hope he'd notice my dumb stare of shock as he went at my skirt and petticoat, and his hard hands ran up my leg. "Too addled to undress yourself? But I hear you may be the lost daughter of some good English family, so I won't treat you like a shoreside doxy and merely toss your skirt above your head. Come now, help me slide you out of your dress, Annie-girl. You *are* drunk! But here it goes. And now this comes off. And this. And this. And the little silken cups," he said with interest as he bared my breasts and I could do nothing to defend myself, nor even voice my shame. "Ah," said the Tory, "here's a fine proud bosom. I wish we had more light. . . ."

For the first time a man kissed my breasts. It was horror to me, but he obviously enjoyed himself as he trailed his lips along the pearly skin and pressed his mouth deeply into the yielding softness. I *must* fight him off! But even when an incredible effort lifted my hands against—it seemed—leaden weights, they only slid down Mark's arms and fell away, while once again blackness flickered. Helpless, I knew only my own frantic thought: How dared the man knead my breasts and make toys of my nipples! But when I was able to summon another low moan, he only chuckled. "Why, Anne, your body is a treasure! I've a mind to steal you and keep you for myself."

When he ran his prickly cheek along my belly and felt me all over, sparing nothing, and flicked me with his tongue and gave me little pinches inside my thighs . . . how could I tell him that no man dared take such liberties with a decent woman? I tried to make myself believe this awful thing wasn't really happening; Anne's drugs were giving me delusions. But only for an instant could I fool myself. When Mark Wentworth—who knew me—whom I never again could look in the face—when that lust-driven man lay down beside me and I felt the touch of his hard male organ, I wanted to die of despair. Surely, by now, he was only pretending to believe I was Anne Burney! Surely he realized what virginity and purity meant to my father's daughter!

Nevertheless he dallied with me, remarking on the smoothness of my skin, patting my buttocks, making me feel unutterably vile. After a time my body glowed, my nerves tingled . . . but of course it was only the natural reaction of skin that receives so much caressing.

"What a treat it is to find such a lovely form!" Mark's own body had grown hot against me, and he breathed quickly as he rose, came down upon me and pulled my legs around him. I resisted with every shred of my will but I could make only the smallest motions and he interpreted them in his own way: "Well now, Annie-girl, I'm glad to see you're conscious enough to return a little passion."

For the first time, a man's hairy chest pressed upon my bosom. He was finding me . . . I felt his thrusting strength. He paused. Silent screams raced through my mind in streaks of wild fire. I heard the rapist's conquering growl

38

of pleasure, then his exclamation of surprise. All the while, the drug was slowly wearing off, and shreds of unintelligible sound proved to be my own voice begging him to let me go. But he could not have understood a word. I'm sure it would not have stopped him. He pressed again. Pain tore a shriek from my throat. Mark gasped in amazement but kept pressing . . . pressing . . . I fell away into blackness. . . . I came to, and the pain had receded. I was panting. My panting was in rhythm with Mark's, for he was carrying me along in great surges—as though, while I had been briefly lost in merciful *nothing*, my body had found an existence independent of my mind. With an awful effort I forced myself to lie still, and my arms—which had been gripping the man while he possessed me—fell away to either side of the berth. But I felt strangely different. . . .

All he did was to clutch me low and force my loins up against his and again into his surging. I was too weak to withstand the force of that conquering rhythm. It carried my body away. It made molten stuff of my body and came up into my mind and burned away my fear, so that I surged into a different world of strange, fierce, exquisite yearning. . . . The yearning became laced with agony, but it was all an agony of fiery need.

For a time I floated as though on clouds of ecstasy—blissfully knowing that the man I gripped with all my limbs was writhing in his own rapture as he poured his essence into my body.

I said his name.

"But Anne . . ." he said wonderingly.

He lay still, his hand upon my cheek. At last he pushed himself up on his elbows, demanded, "Anne, what kind of woman are you? It doesn't seem possible, but I'd have sworn you were . . ."

He withdrew from my body and reached downward to touch me. He held up his hand and I could see the dark stain as he whispered, "Blood . . ."

All my terror rushed back in a cold wind of loathing. " 'M . . . nah . . . Anne. Nah . . . Anne," I sobbed with numb lips, then cried out as pain returned between my thighs.

"What?" Mark asked dazedly.

"Nah . . . Anne . . . but you . . . raped me. . . ."

"Not Anne? But who . . ." He looked around wildly

39

at the dim rows of jars. He bent and smelled my lips "Are you drunk or drugged?" He stared closely. I heard the hiss of breath through his teeth.

He rolled off the berth and stood beside me. "Stand up!"

When he saw I could not, he lifted me, held me sagging but upright with one arm thrust beneath my armpit and around in front, crushing my breasts. He grabbed my hair and made me slant my face to the tiny shaft of light that came through the crack in the bulkhead.

Out of an instant of dreadful silence came: "Oh . . . my . . . God!" And in rasping disbelief, while his hand tightened painfully in my hair: "No wonder you were a virgin! You're Arabella Downing!"

He dropped me back upon the berth, strode to the cabin door, slammed it open and roared, "Chance! God damn you, Chance, come in here. Bring a light."

When the lantern shone upon me, I was clutching a blanket across my body, shaking, sobbing, telling Mark to go away, I hated him.

Chance said, "Why, it's . . ." He couldn't finish, and his rake's face looked completely stunned as he stared around the cabin. "Anne's not here! It's—"

"Well, you bastard?" Mark grated. "You've tricked me into ruining Arabella Downing. I'm going to beat you till you're—"

"I didn't know! I swear it!" I heard Chance's teeth chatter. "That bitch Anne drugged her! Took her cloak. Yes, I saw a woman in a cloak being rowed away, all huddled in her hood against the rain. Wondered why Miss Downing hadn't waited for my mate to escort her ashore!" He kicked the draped chair—Mad Anne's throne—in frustration. "That dirty bitch Anne—she's gotten away from me!"

He was going off into bewildered ranting when Mark stopped him. "Listen, you fool! Are we the only ones who know what happened—the mistake that was made?"

"I reckon so . . . sure! Most everyone's ashore and whoever's aboard is staying out of the rain. No night watch posted yet. We get kinda loose on watches when we're—"

"But Arabella screamed. Someone surely heard her."

"Heard her myself. Thought it was Anne. Anne always screams when we swive her. Her way of enjoying it."

Mark's voice was hard. "Listen to me, Chance. If you

40

ever tell anyone that Miss Downing was—was swived here tonight, I'll kill you. Do you understand?"

"Aye," said Chance sourly.

"Now you'll help me take Arabella ashore without her being recognized. And back to her home . . . Gad! Her father will have men out looking for her by now!"

Barely able to make myself understood, I mumbled, "Get me to my aunt's house on Spring Street. I was going to surprise her with a visit. My father knows I'll stay with her tonight." It wasn't that I wanted to shield the man who had raped me—but I thought of what the news could do to my father. Strange that I could think at all.

Mark hauled me to my feet, thrust my clothing into my arms. Still naked, he ripped the bloodstained sheet off the berth, rolled it up, told Chance to burn it in the galley fire.

"Get dressed," Mark told me. To Chance: "Doesn't Anne have a comb somewhere?" While Chance found it, he demanded of himself: "But how will she explain the loss of her cloak? Yes! It blew into the water! Do you hear me, Arabella? Your cloak blew into the water."

"The money," I moaned.

"Anne took that too? Of course she would. Chance, you'll replace the exact sum this minute."

"Damned unfair," Chance grumbled. "But—all right. And I think I've another leather moneybag, somewhere."

Mark took me by the chin, lifted my face to make sure I understood. "Arabella, we'll leave the lantern for you. And here's . . ." Silently he handed me a roll of bandage cloth from the surgical supplies. "Knock at Chance's door when you're ready." He turned, hesitated, looked back over his shoulder. "You do realize I thought you were Mad Anne? If I'd known who you were, I'd never have . . ." He scowled, trying to find something more to say, but never found it. Perhaps he had come too near apologizing, which would have been a retreat. At any rate, he turned away brusquely and left me alone.

Moving like an automaton, dry-eyed, still lanced with pain, I washed myself with cold water I found in a pitcher. When at last I had managed to pull on my clothing, I leaned weakly on the chair. Lingering terror still shook me, and my throat suffered spasms of dry sobs.

Even so, the question of "ruin" and reputation occurred to me. But as long as no one but Chance and Mark knew

41

of my disgrace, I'd never tell anyone else. Would *they* tell? I hoped desperately they wouldn't.

Now I remembered that Mark Wentworth would soon return to the Bahamas. I wished his ship would sink before he ever got there. I wanted him dead, dead, *dead!*

Chapter Three

Three days later, my father was glad to see that my color had returned after my "indisposition"—although he didn't know how hard it was for me to force a smile.

Meanwhile Father had been preoccupied with Job Wentworth's letter. When at last he made up his mind as to how he would reply, he could hardly wait till I sharpened a quill. He dictated his answer and I took it in shorthand and transcribed it, never knowing what a profound effect that letter was to have upon my life.

To Job Wentworth, Esquire, at Wentworth Hall on the island of San Isidro, in the Bahama Islands:

I pray God has spared your sight, that you may read for yourself in my own words, although in my daughter's hand, that I am pleased at your offer of renewed friendship and do most heartily extend my own, letting bygones be bygones. . . .

Well, I thought, it *is* better for Father to be rid of that long-standing grudge. And it doesn't obligate me to have anything to do with the Wentworths, father or son.

I think I hated Mark all the more because I had no one in whom I dared confide, and so must keep my secret festering in my own heart. But also, after he had finished with my body on that dreadful night, he had not finished with insulting me. This is what had happened after he had taken me ashore from the *Bridgewater;* enough, you will see, to make me want to tear him apart.

Stunned, I had walked beside him the length of Long Wharf, huddled miserably in a man's borrowed cloak, in that cold rain. The best I could hope was that we'd meet no one. But here and there in little open sheds, or beneath tarpaulins, men idled with bottles or dice or cards. Or women. One of those men was the monstrous Thatch. He noticed me, and I saw the peering puzzlement on his battered features. Thoughtfully he spat tobacco juice and I saw him whisper to the blowzy, moon-faced whore with whom he was sharing something out of a pan. He still had not seen my face, but I wished he hadn't seen me at all, for I knew the man was evil.

All this time, Mark and I said not a word to each other. When he touched my elbow to help me across a muddy place, I pulled away. We stopped at last near the arched rose trellis that marked Aunt Patience's house, and I was dully relieved to see she still had a light in her window.

"Well, Arabella," Mark began awkwardly, removing his sodden beaver as though he merely had escorted a lady home and it was time to say goodnight.

Although I was ready to collapse and weep, I found strength enough to flare, "I never gave you leave to call me Arabella."

Fathomless eyes in a wet face regarded me through raindrops that flashed and were gone in the faint light. "At least, *Miss Downing*, I no longer call you Anne."

My hand flashed out and I slapped him hard enough to make him jerk his head sidewise. He swung his own hand hard—but stopped it in midair, controlling himself with a visible effort.

In a tight voice he asked: "Miss Downing, aren't you aware I believed you were Mad Anne? You're both blond . . . it was dark . . ."

"I am aware that I was almost unconscious. I'm aware that you were willing to ravish a woman who could not defend herself."

"Lower your voice before your neighbors get ideas."

"Oh! You're concerned about my reputation!" In truth, nobody could have heard us above the roar of the rain and the wind. "A Tory comes back to Newport to attack its women, then tells them how to behave!"

Mark said in unsmiling jest: "Only one woman, so far."

"So it's an occasion for jokes, is it?" In utter fury I kicked at his shin and made contact. But my backhanded slap, that should have drawn blood from his mouth, was

44

stopped by his own hard-knuckled fist, and I was hurt more than he.

He said with exaggerated patience, "I've told you I regret it was you and not Anne Burney."

Was it pity I heard? All the more infuriated, I demanded, "And what is any woman to you? A body for your pleasure. Go away, Mark Wentworth," I half-screamed, my nails digging into my palms with my tension. "And don't worry about your order for cane rollers. I'll send them to you, and may you rot with them. Get out, get out!"

As I turned away, he remarked, "You were brought up to hate the Wentworths, weren't you?" Then he yanked me back by my cloak. "Miss Downing, I still have something to say to you."

I beat at his hand. "Let go of me!" He didn't, and I went on beating that rugged hand till I was exhausted and ready to sob with frustration.

"First of all," he said with maddening patience, "can you realize that when we Loyalists shook the dust of this raw nation from our feet, you lost a good proportion of your gentlemen?"

"So you say!"

"I am a gentleman's son and a gentleman. Be quiet! You've heard of the gentleman's code. The difference between a good woman and a bad woman is fundamental to the gentleman's code. So I know the difference between a slaver's whore and a virgin lady. I know I have harmed you, but also I know it was through no wish of my own. Nevertheless I have done you harm and I wish to offer amends."

I laughed, near hysteria. "You know you can't undo what you've done to me."

"I do indeed know it. Nevertheless, as a gentleman, I offer you the only amend I can make. I offer you marriage. It can be marriage in name only if you wish."

Startled out of speech, I thought: What? Spend the rest of my life with this man who acted as though he were doing me the greatest favor in the world? Yes, he *pitied* me from his superior height, and if there was anything I would not accept, it was pity!

My words came like stones dropping one after another.

45

"I wouldn't marry you, Mark Wentworth, if I were eight months pregnant."

He growled at my retreating back: "You'd save nothing of your reputation if you waited that long."

Thunder crashed and lightning flickered. Alas, he was not stricken dead. I knocked at Aunt Patience's door and took refuge with that sharp-minded, sensible woman. I was cold and wet and exhausted, so she didn't question my need for a bath and bed.

Now my father had agreed to be Mark's father's friend once more. Very well!—so long as *I* never had anything further to do with the Wentworths, father or son!

Father became increasingly ill. During the next week, I dealt with the customers who wanted iron gates, boot-scrapers, etageres and so forth, and tried to keep the books up to date. Arthur Cason, besides running the shop, helped me run the office. I don't know what I would have done without that good man.

The shop had just finished a number of iron frames and racks for a new rum distillery up near Fall River. Peter was sent with his dray to carry the heavy sections to be loaded on a brig, down at Long Wharf. There was a freightage problem to be discussed with the brig's captain, and since my father was quite ill I once again stretched a point and went down there to take care of it.

Walking this time—for the weather had turned pleasant —I passed the *Royal Arms,* still at her berth, and noticed how trim and taut she was kept; all a-tanto, as sailors say. Mark Wentworth was at the binnacle, conferring with Mr. Mapes, the compass adjuster. He looked around suddenly as though I had called him—which of course was the last thing I'd have done! It was the mysterious force that tells you when someone is staring at your back— only I hadn't realized I was staring, and I looked away in confusion.

Thatch was on the wharf, leaning on a pile of lumber, picking his teeth. He and other idlers were watching the iron frames sway up in the brig's tackles, and I too watched, waiting till I could see the captain. I smelled something offensive. It was Thatch, who had come up beside me.

"Howdy, missy"—in a foul whisper. "Want to speak with ye."

Strangely frightened, I said without turning my head: "Go away."

"Now, missy," the lout whined with false humility, "I'm not beggin'. It's just that I wanted to tell ye—'twas Mad Anne who came ashore in your cape, t'other night, and 'twas *you* came ashore later with the Tory captain, weren't it?"

Stabbed with panic, I looked at Thatch as though he were a worm I could step on. I said nothing, dared not speak.

The broken mouth grinned and said, "What went on 'board the *Bridgewater* that night . . . makes me think you're no better than Sukey, my doxy, over there." He meant the moon-faced trull, who watched us eagerly.

"You're blocking my way. Please let me pass," I said; but fear crawled in my bosom.

"I'll tell ye what I know, missy."

"Why should I be interested in anything you know?"

"'Cause I know Cap'n Wentworth plowed you that night, missy."

I must lift my chin. I must keep my poise. I must admit nothing. "I don't know what you're talking about," I whispered. *How had he found out?* Through Chance? Not likely; Chance would have much to lose and nothing to gain. *Who had told him?*

Far from getting out of my way, Thatch only leaned closer, almost overpowering me with an odor of rum and unwashed skin. "Why, missy, *I'm* not talkin'. 'Twas a certain honest seaman o' the *Bridgewater*'s crew talkin', as had stayed aboard when the rest went off whorin'. As had gone quiet-like to the lazarette"—the private storage area beneath the officers' quarters—"and was helpin' hisself to a mite o' strong waters. Now, this worthy man comes to me later and he says, 'I was right beneath the captain's cabin and Mad Anne's, and that Tory, Wentworth, was there, and seems Miss Arabella Downing had come aboard too, and I heard every word, and let me tell you what was goin' on,' the honest seaman says, 'for there could be money in it for you and me.' "

Horrified, I said, "Yes, I was aboard the *Bridgewater* collecting money owed my father."

"Ye didn't collect from Cap'n Wentworth too?" Thatch

looked over at Sukey and winked. "I mean, considerin' . . . but never you mind, missy. I told this honest sailor off the *Bridgewater,* I told him: 'We'll not say a word to hurt Miss Downing's good name.' "

Blank with despair, I waited.

"And he says to me, this worthy tar, 'You know Miss Downing and I don't, so you handle it, and all I want is half.' "

I gasped, "Half of what?"

"I heered that your dear departed mother, God rest her soul, left you some joolry?"

"No!" I gasped at the clouds. Not those few beautiful mementoes I was saving to wear when I was a married woman!

But Thatch said that of course I would bring him a trifle or two, rather than have it known around town that the Tory captain had plowed me.

"No! I can't!"

"You mean you won't? I think you will, out o' fear for the health o' your poor sick father. I heered talk from one servant to another—ye never know what goes on backstairs —I heered all about 'em jools and 'specially a purty brooch. Rubies in it? You go home and tell your father that Cap'n Osgood is too busy to talk today, so you're comin' down to the wharf tomorrow. *You bring that brooch.* And don't think I'm fool enough to try and sell it around here. I've a friend who'll handle it for me in a certain big"—he chuckled—"wicked city."

Next afternoon, on the wharf, he came at me with his hat in his hand, fawning and bowing and scraping and begging for a penny, for he'd had hard luck, and everyone knew he was an honest workingman. What I dropped into his dirty paw was a gold-and-ruby brooch that had come to my mother from her mother, and my heart went dead when I let it go.

I whispered savagely, "Don't make the mistake of asking me anything else!"

"Me, ask? Never fear, missy, never fear. I'm satisfied. Thankee, thankee!"

But of course he blackmailed me again, right at the ironworks, where Cason had given him work unloading casting clay. I had to give him the ruby eardrops that went with the brooch. Oh yes, he must have known maids and footmen who had made him familiar with the jewelry of Newport! He said he now had a good batch to sell, and he'd not bother me anymore.

That night I locked the door of my room, with its damask-covered walls and its queenly four-poster. I opened my jewelry box, tried not to weep over my mother's treasures. For a moment I thought of getting help from Mark, who was still in Newport. After all, I could tell *him* what was going on! But no! My pride wouldn't let me. Well, suppose I told Thatch I had already sold some piece he demanded. And suppose he didn't believe me? If he told what he knew, I never could go on living in Newport. And my father . . . might not go on living at all.

"Oh God!" I whispered. "What am I to do?"

Then, when I was at the Brick Market, conferring with the butcher on what cuts I would take from a calf he was about to slaughter, Thatch looked out from behind a stall and motioned me to follow him. Helplessly, I did.

He told me that he and his friend, the unnamed eavesdropper, were leaving town. All he wanted from me—ever again—was my mother's lovely pendant, a gold chain from which hung a lustrous black pearl. I was to bring it to him at dusk, on a street near a certain livery stable.

"Dress warm, missy," he said as though he really were concerned. "More rain's comin'."

I told Father I was going to visit a friend and would have an escort home, so he was not to worry if I returned after dark. When I put the Ceylon pearl into my reticule, I wept. In the new hooded cloak I had had made in a feminine cut, I walked muffled in the rain and the gathering darkness, my head down, my eyes smarting.

The stable was in a lonely area near the waterfront. I was within a couple of squares of it when a horse clattered up beside me, its flanks steaming in the rain.

"Good evening," said Mark Wentworth.

He was responsible for all this! "Go to hell," I said. I had never used such language before.

"No, I think I'll only go as far as the stable." Then: "But I'm surprised to see you in this neighborhood at this hour."

"My business is not your business."

He made the horse clop-clop beside me as I stamped on down the deserted street. He said, "I offered to marry you as an amend of the wrong I did you—even though it was not my fault. The offer still stands."

"How kind of you, sir. *No!*"

"Well then," he muttered, gathering his reins. "'Ware the mud off the horse's hoofs." He trotted the animal toward the livery stable. Silently I screamed at him that because of his lust I was being robbed of my jewels, and I'd live forever at a ruffian's mercy.

I saw Mark walk away from the stable. When he saw me he lifted his hat and kept on walking. I supposed they rode a good deal on the Bahamas plantations and he missed the exercise. As though it meant anything to me!

Thatch materialized out of an alley. He wore a wet canvas poncho. When he had the Ceylon pearl in his cap, he said he'd now be off to the wicked city with his friend, and good-bye missy, and he hoped I didn't think he was too bad a fellow. To which I said nothing as I turned on my heel in a mist of misery and walked off as quickly as I could.

Very soon, a wagon covered with a canvas hood came along from behind me. It was a large, heavy conveyance drawn by two big percherons. I paid it no attention till its driver, very wet on the outside seat, said, "Bad night, ain't it, missy?"

Thatch. I glared at him, caught my breath when he dangled my mother's pendant from an outstretched hand. As I automatically quickened my pace to keep up, he said, seeming not too unpleasant: "Now, missy, we've enough to keep us, and we've Sukey with us to earn a bit, so here's your pearl back, for you're a proper lady and has helped me, and I wish no harm to you."

He was actually holding out the Ceylon pearl to me. He had stopped the wagon and was stretching down to put the precious object into my hand.

I took the pendant, clutched it to my bosom, stared up at Thatch, trying to find words. Sukey and another man ran out from an alley behind me, and as Thatch leaped from the wagon's seat, Sukey gripped my arms while the other man whipped a sack down over my head. Thatch grabbed my legs. The two men slung my struggling form into the wagon like a sack of meal.

They gagged me with burlap, wrapped me in rope, and let me lie on the wagon's floor, bruised and gasping. I heard a man's growl: "Sukey, you take off that pearl afore I swat you." Sukey's whine: "Oh, lemme wear it!" The man: "You put it in the box with them other jools, and mighty quick." Sukey: "But I won't hurt it if I wear it, and it's so purty!" The sound of a hard slap, and Sukey sobbing, "Oh, all right!"

When the wagon began to lurch, hurting my bruised ribs, I knew even in my terror that we were out on a rough country road. Where were they taking me? Why? I couldn't get enough air through the gag and I felt consciousness leaving me, knew I could choke to to death, could do nothing to help myself. Then, blackness. I awakened to find the sack gone from my head, the strange man bending over me, and Sukey splashing water into my face.

"Name's Blagdon, miss," the man told me. "Jake Blagdon, as has jumped ship off the *Bridgewater*. Happened to hear your conversation, t'other night. Very bad thing that Tory Wentworth did to you." As he spoke, he slipped a wire noose around my neck. "Mustn't talk! You try screaming and we draw the wire tight, and it's thin, sharp wire. Can cut right *through*." He turned to Sukey. "You hold the end of the wire and if she makes a sound, pull."

"Where are you—" I began unwisely. Sukey yanked the wire and made my eyes sting with tears of pain.

"Where are we goin', you want to know?" Blagdon had a deceptively mild manner. "To the end of Aquidneck"— the large island on which Newport stands—"and over on the ferry and around to East Branch, where we know a man who buys pretty young ladies. He'll give you a nice voyage down to Rio. Down there it's all dark women, but they like their whores with fair hair and skin, like you, miss, for you're very pretty if you'll pardon my saying so."

"I'm purtier'n her!" cried Sukey.

"If I look at your bum, mebbe, not your face," Blagdon said .

The wagon jounced on and horror flowed in my mind like molten metal. I was to be sold into prostitution in Rio de Janeiro. Oh, merciful God!

But William Downing's daughter was learning that she was only one more woman in a world full of lustful men.

Three or four times we passed wagons going the other way on that country road. Greetings were exchanged, and the most ordinary comments: "Bad night, neighbor." "Wet spring brings dry summer." Thatch, out on the driver's seat, could have been a farmer anxious to get home.

They untied one of my hands, sat me up, and gave me bread and cheese and a swig of rum. They stopped the wagon and we went into the wet roadside bushes, I on my wire leash, accompanied by Sukey, to whom Thatch gave a cocked pistol. They bound me again and the wagon rolled on. Sukey watched me with an almost unblinking stare in which there was no mercy, no sympathy of woman for woman.

Only one thought possessed me. I must escape. Bound as I was, I still could draw up my knees and kick with both feet. . . .

But the very effort would tighten the noose around my neck.

Futile plans went on like a drumroll in my head. Till the wagon stopped, and Thatch looked back through a flap in the cover into the dimly lit interior, where a lantern had been kept burning.

"Water's in sight," he said. "Rain's over and the moon's breakin' through. Carrick said he'd take us across anytime we arrived, didn't he?"

"Anytime," said Blagdon. "I gave him a dollar to keep the ferry out, and he said he'd wait."

Thatch climbed back into the wagon and inspected me, grinning, poking my breasts. "There's a track in the woods so we'll pull off the road a while. I want to take a better look at what we have here."

"Now that you mention it, I'd like to take a better look at 'er meself."

My shuddering did not prevent Thatch from pulling down my bodice and flipping his finger against the nipple of an exposed breast. "You two strip 'er while I get the wagon out of sight."

I shrieked, then—for the instant I had before Sukey yanked the wire so hard she drew blood from my tender neck.

"What do you need *her* for? Sukey whined. "You've got *me*."

They took off my clothing carefully and bound me, naked, onto a corn-shuck mattress, leaving only my legs free. In my desperation I kicked out one bare foot and caught Bragdon perilously close to the fork of his canvas trousers. But the punch I took in the calf came so near to breaking my leg that I kicked no more.

They shone the lantern upon me, moving its dim light up and down my bare form.

"Now, there's a figger!" Thatch said. "When we take her to that fella in East Branch we'll strip her and make her walk up and down and roll her hips. That'll put the price up."

"I got somethin' else comin' up," said Blagdon, leering.

"She needs more meat on her," Sukey said, kicking me.

"Shut up,!" Thatch shouted. "Go on outside! Keep watch! Get out—go look at the moon!"

She departed, grumbling. And then Thatch said, breathing hard: "You hold her legs, Jake, while I plow her, and then I'll hold her for you. And if that damned Tory hadn't gotten ahead of a good American—by thunder, I'd bang her cherry till they heard it pop in Boston."

He was stripping. When he stood naked, bent by the wagon's low arch, I saw a creature more ape than man— furred, fanged, its great paws eager to grip me as its male lance rose. It stalked toward me, that organ of frightful size.

"Wanted you all the time . . . and now I've got you. Me, born in a gutter . . . gonna plow the finest lady in Newport. . . ."

When my wild screams filled the space around us, Blagdon not only jerked the wire, torturing me, but also brought his fist down onto my forehead, almost breaking my neck. Now Thatch was over me. Blagdon held my feet but I was able to squeeze my knees together, while in my throat I pleaded wordlessly, "No . . . no!"

I was taught, then, that if a woman will not part her knees, a raping man need only drive the edge of his hand repeatedly, with force, down between them. When they give a little he can chop at the inside of her thighs, where it's very tender, and at last her battered legs fall helplessly apart. I was taught, too, that if a woman tries to deny entrance by constricting the muscles of her groin, she can be subjected to a simple torture. It is done with one finger at the other opening of the body, and the vileness of it, I think, as much as the pain, made me give way.

Nothing was too dreadful. Bragdon went for lard to

53

make me ready. Then the great ape Thatch plunged into my womb, heaved up and pounded me, heaved and pounded, till I didn't expect to live through it and didn't care if I died. His climax was a frightful spasm, during which he smashed both fists into the mattress on either side of my face while Blagdon said admiringly, "There you go!"

He lay at his ease upon me, crushing me so that even my faint moans could not escape. At length he pulled away, but stayed on his hands and knees and gloated, pawed me, pinched my nipples, poked at the flesh of my most intimate parts.

"Come on, it's my turn," Blagdon complained. "You've got me horny as a ramgoat."

"You wait," growled Thatch. "I've had my eye on this piece for a long time and I ain't quittin' till I'm good and finished." His limp phallus, with its ugly blue veins, was becoming engorged again.

Again he raped me, taking joy in letting his weight smash down. It meant nothing, at first, when, pounded nearly into unconsciousness, I heard the two percherons whinny. It was their way of greeting another horse that I dimly heard arrive with a heavy thud of galloping hoofs. Sukey screamed a warning from the wagon seat. But Thatch had been caught in his moment of ecstasy and could not stop. In that moment the wagon leaned as someone must have swung from his saddle onto the wooden seat, and Sukey shrieked wildly as she fell backward into the wagon through the flap in the canvas.

Whoever had come riding leaped after her into the covered space. All I saw was a dark form. Bragdon snatched a pistol from his pocket just as the intruder, also pointing a pistol, shouted, "Put up your hands!" The weapons made a single roar and two flashes of orange fire. Bragdon slumped, fell across the lantern, extinguished it in a tinkle of glass. A wan, silver smudge of moonlight showing through the wagon's cover accented the sudden blackness within.

At the instant Thatch withdrew from me, snarling, the intruder shouted, "Arabella, stay where you are!" For an instant the darkness held only the sound of hard breathing. Faint glimmers showed here and there, but did not seem to belong to men. Sukey whimpered. I heard Mark Wentworth's horse come trotting back to join the two hitched to the wagon. And the instant stretched. And death waited. And a screech owl in the forest called with its unearthly wavering cry. Till Thatch leaped up and swung an arm through the wagon's cover, ripping it widely and letting moonlight flood in.

When I saw he had a gun I screamed, "Mark, look out!" But he was diving to the wagon's floor and was not hit as the pistol flashed and barked. He was instantly up, but not two feet from the floor, propelling himself horizontally at the other man's gross mass of flesh. His impact pushed Thatch backward through the canvas, but the naked man grabbed Mark's coat and they both tumbled outside into the mud.

Bent over, sobbing, I dragged myself to the torn canvas. Nude and brutalized as I was, I would have flung myself over to help Mark if I had not seen what was already happening—if I had not heard the awful crunch a pistol butt makes as it hits a head and the bone gives way. Mark rose, leaving the dead man-beast staring at the moon.

I realized then that Thatch also had a knife, and I saw blood seeping through Mark's right sleeve from his wounded forearm. Ignoring the injury, he vaulted back into the wagon, found the cowering Sukey, slapped her out of her daze, made her find a tinderbox. She managed to light the lantern's wick and it guttered and smoked.

Absurdly he demanded as he bent over me: "Arabella, are you hurt?"

Hurt? I was able to force a nearly hysterical laugh through a choked-up throat. Then all I could do was to sit hugging my knees against me, squeezing them together, shaking my head as though to deny Mark had seen what he had seen.

The horse walked toward Newport through late, moonlit hours. I sat sidewise behind Mark on the animal's crupper, and had to hold him around the waist so I could stay on.

Mark was no talkative man, but he made all sorts of remarks. It was long afterward that I realized he had tried to make me think of something besides my shock and pain and shame. He talked of the mysterious tower on The Hill

55

that some said had been built by Vikings. He talked about Bahamas shells. Also he told me that when he had been a boy he'd been fascinated by the tides, and would come to watch them scour in and out of a salt creek back in the woods, near where Thatch had stopped his wagon. So he knew that before the sun rose, the two bodies he had put into the creek would be carried by the tidal current down into the sea. He said somberly that he hoped no fisherman snagged a hook into either of them.

Before we left, he had warned the terrified Sukey that since she had been an accomplice to kidnapping and rape, she could hang. He had told her to drive the covered wagon to the ferry, cross, and keep going till she was far away from anyone who knew her. He gave her money, and judging by her eagerness she would do as he had said. But as she had driven away, she had turned that broad face, full of low cunning, and had given me an odd look, as though she knew something I didn't know. I'd certainly been in no condition to think.

"Arabella," Mark went on over his shoulder as I clung behind him, "on two occasions I've seen Thatch approach you on Long Wharf—and you and Thatch simply don't belong together. Well, after we'd met earlier this evening, and I'd returned my horse to the stable, I noticed that wagon. The ostler said Thatch was leaving town, and good riddance, wasn't it?"

"Good riddance," I repeated dully. The man was dead, his friend was dead, but the terror of it all had not yet reached me.

"Well, I got a feeling of—something's up. I hired a fresh horse and rode fast, going the way you'd go if you'd been walking home. Didn't see you. Rode to your aunt's house. No lights. Where were you? *Thatch.* By the time I'd returned to the livery and borrowed a pistol, he had left, heading eastward with his wagon. So I went eastward, and I met someone who'd passed a covered wagon driven by a big, rough sort of man. At the ferry I found it ready to run after dark. Made me all the more suspicious. I turned back and found the track a heavy wagon had made when it turned off the road. After that—you know what happened."

"Yes . . ."

"At least those two will never rape another woman."

Knowing how ungracious I was, told him venomously: "No, that's a gentleman's privilege, isn't it?"

He twisted around to face me, his dark eyes glinting rage. "Damnation, Arabella, I've not asked for thanks. But I'll not be demeaned for getting you out of that scrape."

"If not for you I'd never have gotten into it."

"What?" he demanded in a voice that startled birds into chirping in the trees.

In low, strained bitterness I told him about Blagdon who had heard so much aboard the *Bridgewater*. "Then he went to Thatch and Thatch blackmailed me. And made me meet him where he could kidnap me, then sell me. Now do you understand? It was all your fault, and you killed two men for doing no more than you did."

He shouted back wrathfully, "If you refuse to believe I thought you were Anne Burney—very well, that's your stupidity, not mine."

"Listen to me, Mark Wentworth. I never expect to meet a man over sixteen who has not had a woman. But despite that, Newport is full of decent men, and all the more since we drove out the Tories."

"Hell and damnation, what an ungrateful brat you are!"

For the rest of the ride he kept his back turned toward me. And I was sorry for it, and less angry at him and more angry at myself. The man had been concerned for me, and although he had not been able to save me from a frightful experience, he certainly had saved me from a lifetime— probably a short lifetime—of forced prostitution. But I'd had not a word of gratitude for him. Well, I'd watch my chance.

During that long trip into Newport we met a few other late travelers. One was a stud-man who said he was riding to a farm to pick up a stallion he had left there to service mares. When I recognized him as a Newporter, I ducked far back into my hood; but I knew I might have been too late. Anyway, aching and exhausted as I was, I wanted only to get home.

No one else was in sight when Mark stopped his horse within sight of my home, near the mysterious old tower. Dismounting, he lifted me down, held his bloodied arm, and grimaced.

"Good-bye, Miss Arabella Downing of the Newport

Downings. Does the salutation suit you? I sail tomorrow at sunrise."

I should have been glad to hear it. Yet somehow—taken all aback—I didn't want him to go so soon.

"Listen to me," he said. "At the risk of my own life I saved you from an ugly fate. I once felt obliged to marry you, but now I have canceled my obligation."

I thought: The code of a Tory gentleman is a wild and wonderful thing. At least I didn't *say* the words.

Shaking with the reaction of it all, and ready to drop with fatigue, I searched for a way to tell Mark that although I detested him I was not forgetful of what he had done for me. But already he had mounted his horse.

From the saddle, in his torn coat, he growled at me: "I suggest you tell your father you were hit by a runaway horse and tossed behind a fence where you lay unconscious. At last you recovered and came home."

He pulled his horse around and directed it toward the livery stable. I, still with my peacemaking words unsaid, stumbled toward my door.

A moment later I turned and was about to call him back. My mother's jewels! That was why Sukey had driven away in such evil glee! She had gained far more than a few dollars and two horses and a wagon!

But although I opened my mouth to call, I remained silent, too proud to accept Mark's help again. Anyway, all the frightfulness of Thatch's rape *had* been Mark's fault, and if I hadn't admitted I was grateful for his bravery—well, *let one thing cancel out the other!* I thought with the wild reasoning of people who know underneath that they're wrong. Still, considering what I had been through, I think I could have been forgiven.

At least I didn't have to explain to my father. Aided by pills the doctor had left, he had fallen asleep and never knew how late I had returned. Cook and our other maid, Thelma, had gone to sleep. But faithful Mary Crow had remained dressed and on the alert, ready to go and look for me if I hadn't come home by dawn.

I begged her to heat water and pour me a bath, no matter how late the hour. But I had to have a second bath before I felt clean again. At last I calmed my quivering nerves so I could sleep.

I needed many hours of sleep. And yet I awakened

briefly, an hour after sunrise, and went to my window. "Good riddance," I muttered, but fell silent as I watched a tops'l schooner head out into Rhode Island Sound and set her course for the open sea.

Chapter Four

My bruises healed. But for a time I wanted no more of
men. Brutes, every one of them! I had to admit that Mark
Wentworth had had reason to believe that the woman in
the berth was Mad Anne. But still, she had been a *helpless*
woman, and so he was as bad as Thatch—taking a woman
who had been unable to resist!

In time my feminine instincts rose above my bitterness.
One morning I found myself standing nude before my
mirror—and let me say this is not something that Newport
ladies do; or if they do it, they don't admit it. At any
rate, a certain memory made me look upon my body as
though its curves could solve a mystery for me.

I studied the contour that begins at the throat and runs
down the slope of the shoulder—so different from a man's
shoulder!—to the outward swell of the breast, then inward
to the waist, outward to form the lyre-shape of the hip,
then sweeping down to the long, smooth, tapered leg line.

My hips were not broad, but they were broader than a
man's. I remembered my mother explaining, in great embarrassment, that a woman's hips are broadened so she can
accommodate an unborn baby. A baby? Perhaps someday
I would have a baby . . . if I ever met a man who was no
leering Brinton, no apelike Thatch, and certainly no Tory
traitor who wrapped up his condescension in a "gentleman's code."

A memory returned. A slow tide of pink arose in my
breasts and spread upward. Disturbed, and holding my
hands to my flaming cheeks—although I did not move
from the mirror—I helplessly recalled my first man—Mark,
of course—his hands upon my nudity . . . and then the
male impact of his lithe, hard body. But the memory did
not end there. I remembered pleasure, could not deny that
the pain of being deflowered had been combind with an
ecstasy that still seemed to hide within me and sometimes

shiver along my veins. *That* was the really bothersome matter. And now, down in my loins, I felt a tiny reminder of rapture ... a tremulous yearning.

Damn Mark Wentworth for all he had done to me! And yet my breasts told me, with a prickling sensation at their peaks, that they remembered Mark's kisses. Oh, all it had been was carnal intercourse, no different from the coupling of animals! And yet, said a soft thought, some called the action ... lovemaking. Perhaps it could be that, if a woman were really in love with the man ... and then she would desire it. But some said a good woman never desired a man. But ... no. Why should a woman not desire a man when her hips are shaped not only to accommodate an unborn baby but first of all to cradle a lover?

Turning away in confusion, I dressed hastily. I guessed I didn't want to become a spinster after all. For every woman there simply *had* to be a right man ... but how did you find him in a world that was so full of male beasts?

My days were somewhat brightened by the fact that Mr. Brinton had gone away on a business trip. Nobody knew how many businesses he had, and it was whispered that some were unsavory, but all that mattered to me was the relief of being free of his ogling. Soon enough, however, I became greatly concerned about Father. He grew increasingly ill and weak. Being obliged to stay home made him all the more pettish.

It was at this time that Father was visited by a stranger —a man whose face I came to know well. Thomas Hedrick was his name, and he always entered quickly, stayed briefly, left with little ceremony, never shared a meal with us or even took tea. Or rather, I suspected, Father never asked me to pour tea in his study because he had highly confidential business with the man. Hedrick was lean, with sunken cheeks. His long black hair drooped limply on either side of his face, and he paid little attention to his clothing. But he was highly alert. He kept turning his beak of a nose this way and that like an inquisitive bird, and his eyes were like a bird's too, small and sharp and bright.

I was walking from the ironworks office early one evening when I saw Mr. Hedrick enter our house. I myself entered very quietly, just behind him but unobserved. The times were full of reports and rumors about Aaron Burr and his comings and goings around the mouth of the Mississippi—that new, very important part of the nation. Father had recently taken out some documents that had to do with Burr, and it seemed to me that Mr. Hedrick had gone off with some of those papers. This may not have been sufficient excuse for listening at my father's door; but that is what I did.

"Major Downing," the visitor was saying in a low, cautious voice that was full of concern, "the courier from Washington has told me that Burr is going south again. What's more, he spoke with Wilkinson in Kentucky." Instantly I recalled Wilkinson's name, last heard when I had lain drugged and helpless—and still a virgin—on Mad Anne's berth. I knew by now that James Wilkinson was Commanding General of the United States Army, and I'd heard rumors that he had been taking bribes from the Spanish in the Southwest. Some said the Spanish were bribing U.S. officials up and down the Mississippi in an attempt to stop our expansion westward.

With my ear against the door, I heard the two men talk about the possibility of troops under Wilkinson's command turning against their own nation. That was where Burr might come in. He might bribe the troops with promises of rich acreage in some private empire he wanted to carve out, down there. All this had been rumored in our local newspaper, the Newport *Mercury*, which had called the plan Burr's Folly. But Mr. Hedrick took it seriously. He said a word I had not heard before: Burriana.

My father repeated, "Burriana, is it? Damn the fellow, he has vanity enough to name a nation after himself. He's a rascal, but clever and brave and damnably persuasive. Back in '75 we had to get a message from Quebec to our General Montgomery, who had captured Montreal. Burr carried that message through one hundred fifty miles of enemy territory. Later he distinguished himself for bravery under fire. Watch out for him, Mr. Hedrick. I hate Burr as a traitor but I know that what he wants, he's likely to obtain."

"Thank you, Major Downing," Hedrick said briskly. "I'll take the rest of the papers to Washington, then. Meanwhile, since you know so many influential New Englanders . . ."

"Count on me," said Father. "I'll send you reports."

I slipped away. It seemed to me that Hedrick must be

an agent for President Jefferson, who was known to be worried about the security of the Louisiana Purchase lands. As for Father's knowing influential New Englanders and sending reports . . . it must have something to do with a group called the Essex Junto. They were men of money and influence who lived in Essex County, Massachusetts. They said that the prosperity of New England—a manufacturing and trading area, with heavy shipping interests —could not be reconciled with the interests of the agricultural South and the pioneer West. They thought that New England might have to break away from the Union . . . and it was also said they had been conniving with Aaron Burr.

I wished Father had not involved himself in those matters. And yet even I wished to have a hand in keeping the Union together, for I was as staunchly patriotic as he.

In the days after Hedrick left for Washington, my father had a good many callers. They included our congressman and other men of affairs. Only once did Father ask me to come in and serve tea, and I noticed that the men looked tired and depressed.

They were all saying their good-byes when I saw Father slumping in his chair. His face was gray. I got him to bed and sent Mary Crow running for our doctor.

It was Father's heart. The doctor shook his head. Four or five times that night we thought Father had passed away, but each time he rallied. Once he touched my tearful cheek and said, "There now! Mustn't." Near dawn he whispered, "Tell Job . . . friends again." The sky was graying in the east when he said his last words: "My sword." I took down his old sword from its hooks above the fireplace and laid it beside him, Thus, I like to think, he went to join General Washington, who had died a few years before.

They said on The Hill that a woman in mourning had no business doing what I did. But I had to act quickly, and nobody knew my fierce resolve to keep Downing Ironworks no matter what else had to go. Thus, with a lump in my throat, and with the feeling that ancestral ghosts would haunt me forever, I sold the house that had known so many Downing generations. Along with our fine furniture it brought more than I had hoped for; enough to pay off the banker and leave me a little cash.

I gave a month's salary to Cook and Thelma, sent them off with the best of "characters." Mary Crow stayed with me. It was her own choice. That darling Mary! Once, when I'd been traveling up to Providence with my father, we'd been stormbound at a mean little inn where I'd noticed a skinny Narragansett girl slaving at endless tasks. Worse yet, the half-grown girl had to satisfy the innkeeper and various male guests who felt casual need of flesh. Using my own money that I had had from my mother, I bought Mary's indenture. Then, after I'd fattened her a bit and had melted the terror from her eyes, I set her free. But she had remained with me, devoted. She came with me now to live with Aunt Patience, where she had to sleep in a tiny attic. At least Aunty benefited by having a maid in the house. I settled down in my own closetlike room and determined to make the best of matters.

But while I'd still been living in the old house and preparing to give it up, I had a fateful visit from Aubrey Brinton.

He had found me engaged in packing the Canton porcelain, which I had sold along with all the rest. It was a heartbreaking task. Old memories had brought me near tears, and I didn't want company—especially not Brinton's.

But he was paying a condolence call, and he said the proper words about Father and my bereavement, and I acknowledged them. Then the banker, taking a seat and smoothing his waistcoat, said he knew this was not a good time in which to speak to me of a certain personal matter. But nevertheless, since I was making great changes in my life, my duty to myself, and my status in Newport as my father's daughter, made it important for me to consider what he was about to tell me. He would speak from his heart, he said, for it was the only honest thing to do.

I wondered what he knew about honesty and I thought "heart" was only a euphemism for another part of his body. I did not sit, but leaned against the packing crate, rubbed my dusty hands together, and said, "Yes, Mr. Brinton?"

He said that of course he would respect my year of mourning. But, once I was out of my black—well, I must understand, he must make clear, it was his duty toward me to set forth without equivocation, that although there were other ladies in Newport, he surely would not remarry until *we* had spoken seriously together. As to the money owing on my father's note: "I mention it only to assure you it can wait." Pausing to let that sink in, Mr. Brinton inspected my bosom. I folded my arms, high. Making nothing of the gesture, he went on, sly and full of heavy meaning: "And right now, could I not help you keep—or buy back—some of the household treasures I've heard you are selling? You might wish you had them later . . . in your own home."

"Thank you, Mr. Brinton, but I have decided to sell everything and use the money to pay off your note."

That startled him. "But my dear, it's not necessary. I'll give you a year's extension—"

"No, thank you. And by the way, Mr. Brinton, I'll be living with my aunt, and I regret I won't be able to receive you there."

Brinton's surprise faded into a hard look—a banker's look. But he tried to turn it pleasant. "Silly girl," he said with an exaggerated smile, "don't you know you're going to live only a little while in that tiny house? In a year your home will be mine—the biggest house in Newport, and I shall be your adoring husband."

"Will you? It takes two to make a marriage."

"Oh, of course, of course!" He waved a hand to show he understood. "But you do see why I had to speak to you now of—of my intention to propose? Meanwhile, let me help you keep your favorite bits of furniture and the like, for I assure you my house is big enough to hold it all."

"No."

"W-what?"

"No. I'll devote myself to taking care of the ironworks instead of your big house."

His lips went thin. "I'll run the ironworks for you."

"No. Thank you for your interest in my well-being. I'll pay the note in a week or two. And shall *not* expect a proposal from you when I am out of mourning—or ever."

Now, as his face went hard beneath its puffiness, I knew the real Brinton would come through. Ruthlessness grated in his voice as he said, "You'll regret this."

"Perhaps. But, as you said, there are other eligible ladies."

"I want you." The words were said in a hiss, with frightening force and meaning.

"I've known that quite a while, Mr. Brinton. And now, if you'll excuse me—" I picked up a cup.

"You'll regret this, Arabella, and I'll have the ironworks anyway, whether or not you become my wife."

"How, when I'm going to pay the note?"

"How? Do you think Newport people will deal with a *fallen* woman?" I stared, unable to hide my fright as he snarled, "Share my bed, Arabella, and as my wife you'll lord it over other women. And," he paused, "no one will ever know you were not a virgin bride." To my shocked face, he whispered, "Defy me, and everyone will know. I'll make it impossible for you to walk the streets of Newport. The ironworks will fail—and I'll buy them for a song. So, Arabella? Shall I have the ironworks alone or both you and the ironworks? Which way will it be?"

My desperate words, "I don't know what you're talking about . . ." only made him laugh.

He leaned so close, I felt his breath upon my face. "You've been seen talking to a rough fellow named Thatch. He left town with a sailor who jumped ship and they drove east along the ferry road. Later that same night—long after midnight, my *respectable* Miss Downing—you were seen riding double with that damned Tory, Mark Wentworth. You both were returning toward Newport on the ferry road." As my mind screamed, *The stud-man!,* Brinton went on, "Yes, I know the stud-man. He finds it to his advantage to bring me bits of news."

"I'll go where I wish—when I wish!" I cried.

"Not if you want to maintain the appearance of virtue. Out there with Thatch and a ruffianly sailor and one of Big Beulah's prostitutes that Thatch stole . . . oh yes, I know! Joined by Wentworth. It must have been quite an orgy. I hope you enjoyed yourself. And don't forget, I saw how Wentworth looked at you, that day in your father's study. I saw it on both your faces—shameful, open lust!"

"You're not confusing your own feelings with Captain Wentworth's?" But the haughty question faltered. That Brinton's view of events was wrong in many ways would not help me if he chose to spread what he thought he knew.

"Well?" he was saying. "Do you still say you're not a fallen woman?"

I aimed a shot in the dark. "You're annoyed because Thatch has affected your profit. I've heard you have money invested in Big Beulah's . . . enterprise."

His glaring eyes told me I had been right. "I'll not dignify

67

that remark with an answer," he snarled. "But you are to remember this, Arabella, and I give you twenty-four hours to think on it. If you marry me, you'll live like a queen. But if you refuse me I'll see that nothing is left for you—neither your reputation nor your livelihood. Will you marry me one year from today?"

"No."

He rose, brushed his hat on his sleeve, adjusted his wig. "You have twenty-four hours in which to change your mind. Good day."

When Mary Crow came with some question about packing the linens, she found me standing motionless. Suddenly I broke. I held her. I told her everything. At least it made me feel a little better, for it's hard to keep all your pain locked up inside. And at least I had her few words to comfort me: "House go, Mary stay. Mary takes care. Always."

On the last day of June I moved from the house where I and my father and his father and his grandfather had been born, and went to live with Aunt Patience. She greatly approved of my paying Father's debt to Brinton. Mary, who took the money to the banker and had him receipt the note, reported he looked furious but said nothing. Nor, up till then, had he attempted to do me any harm —but I knew better than to think him forgiving.

On the third of July I was at work in the ironworks office when Mark Wentworth came in.

I was not surprised. The ship watch had reported a fast topsail schooner heading toward Newport. I had had time in which to decide I would receive Mark with dignity, have him pay for his cane rollers, and send him out of my life.

Why, then, when he entered the office with his muscular swing, did my calm desert me and that unwanted flush rise in a tide of heat beneath my fair skin!

He was as ever—dark and dour, touched with sun, and in the latest fashion, his hair cropped close in back and brushed forward above his forehead, his high collar coming up to his ears. Again, when he bowed, he watched me through those dark, long lashes.

"You're in mourning, Arabella?"

"Father died." It was not bereavement that made my voice unsteady.

"Your father died? I say . . . I'm terribly sorry . . . why, I remember him sitting right in that chair. . . ."

"Yes," I said, a bit too briskly. "I'm having your rollers loaded right now. Have you a draft for the balance?"

With a wry look, he handed over another draft on Hamilton's bank. "I'd hoped you'd be more pleasant after my not having seen you for all these months."

"Pleasant? Why?"

He grimaced. "Well, at least you're a beautiful sight after a long voyage." That submerged trace of a grin hovered on his sensitive lips. "And so you're running the ironworks?"

"I am."

But only that day, I'd heard that an old friend of Father's had ordered a big iron fence and an elaborate, scrolled gate from an ironworks over in Bristol. Was Aubrey Brinton letting whispers get around? *Arabella Downing is a fallen woman. . . .*

Mark asked, "May I wish you good fortune with the business?"

"I can't stop you."

"May I remark upon the fortitude it shows, especially in a woman?"

"You've already said it," I replied.

Yet I could not look away from his dark, searching eyes.

Producing a letter, he said, "Arabella, my father has written again to your father. He had to dictate to me word by word—he grew very impatient—I wished I could have taken it all down the way you do, in shorthand." He paused. "You see, my father's gone blind."

"Oh, Mark, I'm sorry!" Truly I had not wished Job that much misfortune. But immediately I regretted my show of sympathy to his son; I sat back in my chair and went on: "Well . . . nothing for you to do but take the letter back and tell your father that my father is dead."

Mark clearly had something else on his mind. "Will you read the letter? It concerns you too."

"Concerns *me*? How?" Mark waited. I took the letter, found my father's thin old knife I used as a letter opener, and lifted the seal.

Mark's handwriting was as bold and firm as I'd have expected it to be. Job Wentworth's words made me blink as I read his joy at once again having William's treasured friendship. He alluded fondly to those long-ago hunts with bow and arrow. He described the long, narrow island of

San Isidro, told something of his plantation, but intimated it had been hard to find enough good soil. He spoke of the beauty of the tropical waters, which, alas, he could no longer see.

Then he asked his old friend to come to San Isidro with his daughter Arabella, whom he understood had grown into a lovely young lady. Yes, both of us must come down with Mark in the schooner and pay a long visit—stay through the winter at the very least. Miss Arabella must not worry about being entertained, for there would be fishing and sailing, and trips to Nassau, and balls and routs, and many young people to meet, all of good family. As for William and himself, they'd have no end of good talk. It would take some time to prepare for such a trip, but Mark could wait even a month till we were ready. And what a welcome Job would give us when we arrived!

When I looked up from the letter, the clangor of the shop was vibrating through the office. Even so, Mark and I seemed all alone. I looked quickly away from his disturbing gaze.

"I hope you'll thank your father for me, but of course it's out of the question."

"Ah, but your foreman, Cason, is known as a capable man. He could run the business for you."

"No, thank you. I see no reason to visit."

"Why, just to see our part of the world!"

"Hardly reason enough. No."

"Well," Mark said. He hunched forward in his seat. "I expected you to refuse. But there's another reason I'd like you to consider. You could be a great help. Did you know my father is writing a history of the Bahamas?"

"No."

"He is, and he's become an authority on the subject."

"What has that got to do with—"

"You see, he wrote till his sight began to fail. Now, being blind, he needs someone who can take his words in shorthand. Such people are rare. You'd confer a great favor if you'd come down and help him finish that history. You'd work only a little while every day, a few days a week. Once you transcribed your shorthand notes—couldn't take very long—you could do as you wished, and of course you'd be our honored guest, I promise you."

The guest of Tories? Somehow I could think it angrily but couldn't say it, only: "Really, Mark, my place is here."

70

"Nassau's an interesting little city. Did you know that the latest London and Paris style books often arrive there before they reach Newport?"

"I'll not be thinking of style for some time."

"Perhaps not," he admitted, scanning my black dress of sober cut. "But even so—"

"Do thank your father for me."

"Well," said the man who had ruined my life, sighing and rising, "I'll go and inspect the rollers."

Mark retreating?

But when he stopped at the door and turned, he let me know the subject was not closed. "I'll drop in this evening at your aunt's," he said as though commanding from his quarter deck. "I remember her, and I've brought her a roll of silk that I traded for in Lyons some time ago. And there's another roll for you, a deep green that goes well with golden hair. I'll have them sent up from the schooner, and when I drop by we can continue this discussion."

Before I could protest, he bowed and was gone, leaving me furious. But . . . oh well, let him come to Aunty's! He'd soon find out how snappily she could get rid of any caller she didn't like.

A Narrangansett girl worked at the White Horse Tavern, on Marlborough Street, and she had become Mary's friend. Mary went to see her that evening, and it turned out that Mark Wentworth also was at the tavern.

One would have thought that the unspoken Newport motto—anyone is welcome if he comes to trade—would have prevented trouble. But this was the evening before the Fourth of July. Also, it appeared that Mark had spoken scornfully of the quality of the local rum.

At any rate—as I put together the scene from Mary's few words—a large man confronted Mark and spoke about Prudence, his mother. Did Mark realize how many men in Newport remembered his mother *very* well? Leering, he asked if Mark had heard from his dear mother lately.

Captain Wentworth had looked the speaker in the eye and had said very slowly and distinctly, in a voice that carried all over the inn: "I thank you for your concern about my mother, sir, and I offer my own concern about your own dear father. *Have you ever found out who he was?*"

Mary said there was silence in the big public room, and

you could smell death. The other man told Mark to name his weapon.

Mark said, "I prefer the pistol, but that would be murder. I shoot as well as Aaron Burr." He flipped rum into the other man's face and said, "My weapon is fists—here and now."

They tangled instantly. As Mary described the scuffle, her dark features positively glowed. Oh, Captain Wentworth was a fighter! I remembered the skirmish in the wagon and how Mark had killed two men who had wanted to kill him. Despite myself, I feared to have Mary tell me how the fight in the tavern had come out . . . and went limp with relief when she described that it had ended with the other man unconscious on the floor.

Mark, with blood dripping from his face onto his fine ruffled shirt, had turned slowly to face his audience. He had wanted to know if there was anyone present who had any further remarks to make about his mother.

Nobody did.

And then, said Mary Crow—I had never heard her talk so much—then Captain Wentworth staggered to the bar and dropped gold upon it. He bought a drink for every man in the room.

I thought: Fighting, drinking, and fornication; that's all they live for. Men!

And shook my head at a man's eye for color when I found my roll of silk—waiting at Aunty's house—was closer to peacock blue than green. Nevertheless it would go well with a fair skin and blond hair, and it was gorgeously exotic; from India, I think.

Aunt Patience inspected it, fingered her own roll of expensive French silk. "Bygones are to be bygones? Humph!" she said. "We'll see about it when your Captain Wentworth arrives."

Eight o'clock came, then half-past eight. We say in Newport that we stay up late—perhaps because the city is the center of a spermaceti candle industry, and whale-oil wax makes such a bright flame. But by nine o'clock, when it was almost dark, Aunt Patience was yawning, and I— again despite myself—wondered if Mark had been badly hurt in that fight.

Then, as Aunty's big clock finished chiming the hour, we heard the first rowdy catcall outside.

"Yoo-hoo, Arabella! Comin' out to the haystack?"

72

As Aunt Patience and I stared at each other, aghast, another male voice sang out, wavering: "Is the honorable Miss Downing in there? Is she lonesome? Does she need a bedmate?"

Objects hit the house with a squashing sound. Green tomatoes.

The hoodlums rattled tins and banged sticks together to make sure the neighbors heard. Despairingly I heard the next falsetto cry: "Yoo-hoo, Arabella! Couldn't the iron-works make you a chastity belt? Too bad, too bad!"

"Try me, Arabella! Five times a night and twice again in the mornin'!" All this and more, and a great deal of noise, and howls of drunken laughter.

Peering through the curtains, I dimly made out a rowdy, ragged group of loafers whom anyone could have hired for a bottle apiece. It was clear who had paid them. Aubrey Brinton! He had thought and schemed and decided to use this means to shame me openly.

I pulled back Mary Crow, who was ready to go out and fight those men. Then, facing Aunty's frightened stare, I could do nothing but tell her the truth about myself. Tell her I had been had by Mark Wentworth and by the brute Thatch, and that it was none of my own fault but that was the fact of it, and Brinton had drawn certain conclusions, and had tried to make me marry him. Now he was carry-ing out his threat to disgrace me.

Aunt Patience took me by the shoulders and squeezed till she hurt. She shook me and said, "Wait, girl! If it wasn't your fault . . . when I get hold of Aubrey Brin-ton . . ."

We heard a horse gallop up and we heard Mary cry, "Captain Wentworth!" The jeers and insults changed to shouts of alarm.

Running to the window, we saw Mark wheeling his horse right and left and slashing with his riding crop. He reared the horse and made it present its dangerous hoofs at the faces of ruffians who stumbled backward. As the men turned and ran, Mark spurred the horse among them and struck blows with his crop that brought blood from shaggy heads. Roaring, he kept at them till they scattered.

Galloping back, he leaped from his lathered horse and flung its reins over the hitching post. Meanwhile, Aunty and I clung together as we heard doors closing all around. Brinton had planned well. Whatever rumors had run through town before—rumors enough to make my father's friend take his business elsewhere—would be out in the open now, and nothing could undo the damage that had been done.

Mark flung open the door and was with us, one eye half closed, his face bruised, his voice slurred because he had a torn lip. "God damn them!" he shouted.

I was unable to speak. Aunt Patience walked up to Mark. She was a tiny person, but now she seemed six feet tall. She was generally a quiet person—but not when she had a certain fire in her eye.

She had it now. "You caused this to happen to my niece," she said in a deadly whisper. Now," Aunt Patience said, "Arabella will have to leave Newport. Brinton will take the ironworks as soon as it fails—and it will fail because of you."

"The ironworks . . . fail?" Mark asked dazedly.

"Because this is Newport, and in Newport the whores may crowd the wharves, but if a lady is even suspected of sin, that lady is *finished*."

My aunt's bony hand lashed out. Mark's face was already bruised from that fight in the tavern, and the slap must have hurt. His lip began to bleed again. But he only stared at me aghast.

"The ironworks? Lost?" He couldn't believe it. "And . . . sin?"

"How did Brinton find out my niece is *fallen?*" Aunty's voice was terrible even though she had not raised it. She told Mark about the stud-man and all the rest.

Mark ran his hand dazedly through his hair. "But I only went out on the ferry road to—"

"I know," I told him mercilessly. "You didn't come after me to rape me *that* time."

He shouted, "I killed two men for your sake!"

"No, you killed them to preserve your own life."

Before he could reply, Aunt Patience, her voice gone shaky and weary, said, "Sir, your rolls of silk are there on the table. Take them as you leave. Good night."

Mark Wentworth gave us a black-browed scowl. He tried to button his coat over his increasingly bloodstained shirt, and stared at it in a puzzled way when he found buttons were missing.

He stood tall and was the captain again. He told my

aunt: "Miss Bentley, I've something to say. What happened in Mad Anne's cabin should not have happened. Worse yet, I, who made the mistake, go scot-free, while you, Arabella, have suffered. And will suffer more. But *it was a mistake.* I had reason to think you were another woman. Because the consequences to you have been so bad, I can't expect you to treat it as a trifling matter."

"As a man does!" I cried.

"Be that as it may . . . Blast it, Arabella," he roared, and he kicked a stool clattering across the room. "What in the name of hell am I to do?"

I knew this was the nearest to an apology I'd ever get from Mark Wentworth. Not that an apology could help me or save the ironworks.

"At least keep the silk," Mark was saying. "For my father's sake. It was he who sent it. He remembers Arabella as a darling little girl, and he remembers you with great respect, Miss Bentley."

"I'd like to have you secured to the old whipping post," was my aunt's reply, "and have you sent back to your father with your back lashed to ribbons."

Mark hunched his shoulders. I saw by his angry grimace that the fight in the tavern had cost him a tooth.

Briskly Aunt Patience opened the door. "Take your silk and go, Captain Wentworth."

Mark stayed where he was and looked her in the eye. "If you don't want that silk, give it to charity in the name of Job Wentworth, late of Newport, driven out for the sin of being loyal to his king."

Aunt Patience glared. Mark had put her into a bad position. It would be a sin on her part if she did not give the silk to charity, nor could she refuse to say in whose name it would be given.

"Clever," she said.

"You don't think I'd return the silk to my father, a blind old man? He'll suffer enough when he hears his old friend has died."

"What is this person?" Aunt Patience asked of me. "A Tory who wants us to believe he has a heart?"

She stood in the open doorway. Mark stood firm in the center of the room. I stood to one side, shaking with reaction. Dark Indian eyes watched from a corner.

Aunt Patience's face softened. She looked off into mem-

75

ories. "Still, this was a manly lad even when he was twelve years old," she murmured. "Oh, when they're boys they can be sweet, but once they get hair on their chests they're monsters, all of them."

There wasn't a sound in the house, and only the sound of the wind outside as my aunt slowly closed the door. "Once you carried a parcel for me," she said oddly.

"Yes'm," said Mark. "I remember."

"You were decent enough—as a boy."

"I was brought up to believe that a man is strong so he can protect women, Miss Bentley."

"Too bad you didn't remember that when your ruined my niece!"

"Had I known . . ." Mark didn't finish.

"But of course you had to act the rutting ram!"

When Mark replied, "Yes'm, after a three-week voyage, I certainly did," he left my aunt startled.

She motioned me to a chair and I thankfully fell into it. She seated herself in her own rocker, with its needlepoint cushion hung on the back. "Sit," she told Mark.

"Now then," Aunt Patience said, "my father—your grandfather on your mother's side, Arabella—was a judge, and I've heard him say that when a crime is committed, there often is more than one villain. I see two other villains besides yourself, young man—Captain Chance and Anne Burney. They both got away. You didn't."

"I got away to the Bahamas and *came back*," Mark said, discomforting my aunt.

"In any event, Arabella," Aunty went on, "I am not implying that this . . . rutting boar should ever be forgiven. But it was dark in that cabin and he did have reason to believe you were someone else."

"What good does that do me now!" I cried.

"No good at all. Except that . . ." She paused, said to Mary Crow, "Dear, we'll all have tea with a teaspoon of my raspberry cordial in it."

Mark did not ask for rum.

"Captain Wentworth," my aunt said, "I hope even *you* can realize that an invitation to my niece to visit your plantation, under the circumstances, is nothing but an insult."

"I realize, ma'am, that the invitation was offered by my father in all good faith and friendship."

76

"That's true enough, I suppose."

"You may indeed suppose so."

My aunt glared at him. When she turned to me, she looked anxious and worried. "The fact is, Arabella, you should go away. Let things blow over. I'll do what I can to ruin Brinton's reputation—and I won't have to work hard, from what I hear. After all, you're a Downing. People would rather be on your side than his, but they'll need time to see it. Now, my dear, Cason really could run the ironworks, and don't worry, I'll keep an eye on him."

I said loudly: "I can go away, yes, but I'm certainly not going to the Bahamas!"

"Let's think, dear. You could visit your father's brother in Providence, but that's not far enough. I don't know where else you could go . . . I mean, where you'd be welcomed by friends or relations, have a decent place to stay. . . ."

"Never mind all that, Aunty! I'll go to New York or Boston and find work as a companion or a governess—or something!"

Mark cut in: "There's that matter of my father's history. And you know shorthand. . . ."

He had to stop and explain the matter of the Bahamas history, and how much Job yearned to have someone to whom he could dictate efficiently, now that he was blind.

My aunt rocked and thought. I sat silent, ready to say again I would *never* go to the Bahamas. But when Aunty at last spoke, she spoke to Mark. "Young man! Can I suppose you're away from your father's plantation a good deal of the time, in your schooner?"

"Yes. Fact is, I'm away most of the time."

"Now, suppose my niece decided to go after all. —Be quiet, Arabella! —Do you have a decent female of mature years, down there, to act as her chaperone?"

Mark gave us that near-smile. "We do indeed, Miss Bentley. My father's unmarried cousin, Miss Lavinia Dermott, from Charleston. She lives with us and keeps the house."

"Humph!" said Aunty. "Aren't we old maids useful, though! Now, I'd expect my niece to have the very best of quarters."

"That she will."

"Never!" I cried.

"Now, dear," my aunt said seriously, "Mary Crow could

go with you. And Arabella, your father did make his peace with Job Wentworth. And you really can perform a valuable service for Job. Besides, it would be good for you to have a little work to do, instead of being nothing but a guest who spends all day primping and eating."

When I said nothing, hardly trusting myself to speak, Aunt Patience said to Mark: "Go and wait outside, young man. Oh, you resent my giving you orders? Kindly remember this is my house, not your ship."

"Mary, dear?" said my sweet, fierce aunt when Mark had taken himself, scowling, outside. Mary Crow understood perfectly, and vanished.

Aunty and I went to each other then, and held each other close. I was terribly hurt yet full of love. "Child, you're the only one I have in the world," Aunty whispered. "God knows I'd hate to see you go away. But you must. Oh child, child, whatever anyone says about you—if they dare speak in my hearing!—*I* know you weren't at fault. They say time heals all wounds. I can't promise it will, but while you're away, I'll just—just—see what I can do. At least Mark Wentworth isn't the worst of 'em. He could be a real gentleman if he tried, I think. And you won't have to see much of him. . . ."

"But Aunty, I can't go and live among Tories!"

"Not many of the real old Tory generation are left. And anyway, all things considered, Job Wentworth is bound to treat you well. And you know, child, helping a blind man write a history is a Christian thing to do."

"That's hardly reason enough, Aunty!"

"I agree," she said with a twinkle. Then, very seriously, "But there's another reason. I'm not going to tell it to you. Think."

For two or three minutes I went on embracing my aunt's bony shoulders, one moment wondering what reason she could have in mind, the next moment telling myself it was utterly ridiculous for me to go to the island of San Isidro . . . no, I *wouldn't!*

Then something stirred deep in my mind. And then I knew, and said, "Yes, I'll go."

"You agree that your dear father—?"

"Yes. He'd have wanted me to go and help Job if I could. But I'm glad he never knew why I'm really leaving Newport."

Aunt Patience gave me another hug. She straightened her lace cap, called Mary to bring Captain Wentworth back in, then serve the tea.

As she poured, my aunt said briskly, "Now, Captain Wentworth, Arabella can't board your ship in Newport. She'll leave by coach for Providence and stay with her uncle. When you sail from Newport you'll go north to Providence and pick her up."

"Agreed," said Mark, who seemed—for him—almost happy.

"But of course, young man, especially since *you'll* be aboard, Arabella must be chaperoned for the entire voyage. Go and find some respectable couple who wants to go to the Bahamas, perhaps on the way to the West Indies or New Orleans."

This left Mark and me looking askance at each other.

"I have it!" said my aunt. "The Grahams. Do you know his shop? It's the chandlery near the harbor. He's come into some property in Antigua and has been talking of going to see it."

"I'll go and speak to Graham tomorrow," said Mark with evident relief.

"Of course my niece is to have a cabin of her own."

"I don't have that many cabins."

"Then Mary Crow will sleep in the same cabin. And," Aunt Patience added significantly, "just as well. Also, it's to be a cabin next to the Grahams' and it's to have a lock on its door."

"Agreed."

Aunt Patience sighed, leaned back wearily in her rocker. "May God forgive me if I have sent my niece into danger. Well, Captain Wentworth, don't get the impression that I enjoy having you in my house. But you may have an extra teaspoon of cordial in your tea."

After Mark had left, Aunty and I sat a long time talking. It was then I had a thought that put us into excited whispers. Down in San Isidro, among traitors, I might acquire valuable information about Aaron Burr's dangerous plots, to say nothing of knowledge of how the Tories might be working with him. Whatever I could find out I would tell Aunt Patience in a letter, and she was quite willing to take that letter straight to Washington, D.C., if she must.

79

It was a far-fetched idea, of course. But still it let me believe that my trip might help the United States. And so I prepared to go off to a distant island with a man who had raped me and was a hated Tory beside.

PART TWO

THE TEMPTRESS

Chapter Five

Even in summer, the northern seas were cold and gray. But as we ran our southing down, grayness gave way to all shades of indigo and cobalt; and the sky, a softer blue, bore little cottonwool clouds that marched peacefully into the west. Sometimes, great schools of flying fish rose out of the water with a hiss of their "wings" as they escaped some hungry creature below. Or we'd find ourselves surrounded by dolphins that curved in and out of waves, seeming to grin as they left long blue tracks behind them.

Often, at night, I watched mysterious flickers and lightnings in the water, said to be made by creatures too small to see. Or I measured with my fingers how the Pole Star slipped lower every night and the southern constellations rose higher in the sky. Many days I spent in the bows, leaning against the bowsprit while I knitted or sewed or read my father's old books that I'd brought along. Or I'd merely lounge on a coil of rope and enjoy the warm wind while I remembered all that had happened to me, and tried to make lingering pain and shame and terror leave my soul.

One day, some contrary wind brought a blue jay that settled in the schooner's rigging. It didn't seem well tailored, as jays generally are, but sat rumpled and dejected-looking, its head hanging, never bothering to preen its ruffled feathers. A land bird in the rigging is good luck, so one of the sailors climbed up and tried to get the jay to eat bread crumbs. The bird seemed too weak to avoid the man, but it wouldn't touch food.

Watching with interest, I suggested, "Perhaps it wants water."

They brought it a drink. Sure enough, the bird dipped its bill into the pannikin again and again. In time it preened itself, seemed happier, gave us its unmusical call—"Jay! Jay!"—and flew off westward toward the invisible shore.

I returned to the schooner's bow, leaned over the bulwark, watched how the waves frothed up on the windward side like fluffy white hands that reached for me but never touched me.

A man spoke behind my back. "How did you know it wanted water?"

I made no hurry about turning to face Mark. So far, he had kept himself very busy with ship's business. He had Mordecai, the aging slave who was both cook and steward, bring his meals to his cabin, leaving one of the mates to be pleasant to us passengers, who ate in the officers' mess.

Certainly I had not missed our captain's company. I hoped my cool expression told him as much when at last I did turn and say, "I merely thought it likely."

Mark Wentworth wore canvas trousers ragged at the cuffs, a striped jersey, and a peaked cap with a thin line of gold braid that was his only sign of rank. He had forsaken his sea boots and now went barefooted like the rest of the crew. But everyone knew who was the captain. I had not yet heard him give an order twice.

He spoke now in a nearly friendly tone. "A land bird flies to sea and the salt air dries it out. It's the kind of thing a woman would think of . . . the care of small animals, like the care of babies."

"Really? I had assumed your knowledge of women was limited to more earthy matters . . . Captain."

"Touché! Well, Arabella, I've been noticing you. Very silent. Very remote. But you're still patient with Mrs. Graham and her seasickness, and you endure Mr. Graham's endless games of cribbage. You're kind to that strange Indian maid of yours, and you never blame Mor'cai— so I hear—for not being a better cook. You also spend a great deal of time sewing, which is why I have come to disturb your reverie. You are sewing unsuitable dresses."

"Unsuitable?" Resentfully, I demanded, "Am I not to mourn my father's death?"

"Mourning is very soon put aside by Bahamians in summer. Everyone wears light colors. They reflect the sun. But black absorbs the sun and makes you hotter."

"I'll see," I returned, not willing to take his advice.

"You'll see better when you start to fry. But I'll make sure you have a chance to go to Nassau for whatever clothing you need. It's an interesting little city. I'll take you around."

"I'd rather go around by myself, thank you."

He folded his lip in displeasure. I felt a surge of triumph at having put that aggressive man in his place.

Still, with contact made between us, it became easier to live aboard the *Royal Arms*—and a ship is a very small world. Mark now came more often to the big, scarred table beneath a skylight where we had our meals, and his presence caused those meals to improve. We carried a ton of ice secured from an ice house near Newport, where it nested in sawdust all summer. Few captains would have bothered—but that ice helped us have fresh butter and eggs for half the voyage, and fresh meat rather than the salted stuff that is generally all you can get at sea.

By now I knew the officers and most of the crew. They all were respectful. But they were not really friendly. I wondered why, till I came to understand that every man of them was as much a devoted Tory as Mark Wentworth himself. No wonder I found them stopping conversations when I came near, then taking care to point out a whale or a cormorant, and muttering to each other again when I went away. The entire vessel was suffused with an air of secrets. Everyone knew my patriotic feelings, and nobody was going to let me overhear a word about devious schemes.

Nor did Mark ever mention Burr's politics or any other kind of politics at the dining table. Instead, he told us about the Bahamas. How the entire area, nearly seven hundred miles of scattered islands, had once been a great nest of pirates, for it was full of shallows and countless inlets and mangrove swamps where wrongdoers could hide. Pirates had been practically charmed into the area, long ago, for the route of the Spanish treasure galleons had gone through the Bahamas. Right past San Isidro, in fact.

"Wasn't there a female pirate named Anne Bonney, down there?" I asked with a bland face.

"Why, yes, she . . . uh . . . came later. Plied Carolina waters too." Mark cleared his throat and went on hastily, telling us Newporters that the hundreds of islands had known Spanish masters and French masters, but at last had come firmly into England's hands, and were governed from Nassau by a governor appointed through the Crown. He explained that the islands were low, a hill of a hundred feet being an unusual summit. Plantations had been started on various islands back in the seventeenth century, but had

85

failed because of poor choice of location. He told us of islands that were given over to the gathering of salt, which was done by evaporating seawater in shallow ponds. Many islands were still uninhabited, or bore only tiny settlements where freed or runaway slaves eked out a bare existence from garden plots and the sea.

"But we have very few runaway slaves," Mark said.

"A likely story!" I scoffed.

"The fact is, my dear Miss Downing, that if a slave escapes from one of our islands, unless he has a seagoing boat he's likely to drown."

I hardly believed it at the time, but I was to find out later how lost and lonely those islands were, and how widely separated from each other by tricky, reef-strewn sea.

So day followed day, and night by night we slipped southward beneath the incredible stars. I hoped to overhear secrets that could be harmful to the United States; but the voyage was two-thirds finished and I had heard nothing.

One night I finally heard a very few words that told me a great deal.

To begin with, at the previous noon I saw Mark and his first mate, Mr. Lynd, go to the quarterdeck with their sextants. "Shooting the sun" at noon was a regular routine. But this time the other two mates also came up with their sextants. After they had measured the angle of the sun above the horizon, they all adjourned to the navigation desk, below, for a session with mathematical tables. I heard Mr. Lynd say with satisfaction that we had reached thirty-north. He meant latitude thirty-north, one of those imaginary lines that help find a ship's position at sea.

A roar of orders sent the watch scurrying to man the braces. The quartermaster spun the wheel, and the vessel came around with her mainsail flapping thunderously. The yards on the foremast were trimmed, the foresail and staysails arranged for the new course, and the *Royal Arms* leaned gracefully to starboard as she ran close-hauled into a northeast wind.

Mark said, "Take her east for one watch, Mr. Lynd, then westward for a watch, then east again. He'll be looking for us on thirty-north, about two hundred miles east of St. Augustine."

It sounded as though Mark was to meet another ship. Men were posted aloft to watch all around the horizon.

Near sunset we heard the cry from a masthead: "Sail ho! Dead ahead!"

In a hot, fitful wind the two ships approached each other, till at last even we on deck could see a tower of canvas that glowed pink in the sunset, gradually went dark as the sun dipped out of sight. The Spanish three-master, *Nuestra Señora de los Dolores,* hove-to a short distance from the *Royal Arms.* A small rowing boat came dancing over the water. I stood on the main deck against the quarterdeck's forward bulkhead, a vertical eight-foot wall, and never realized how hard I was to see in my black dress, with a black veil drawn over my bright hair. When I did realize my near-invisibility, I kept quiet and still.

Because the night was so warm, Mark had had a small table and two chairs brought to the rail. He sat there with the flamboyantly dressed Spanish captain, whose great cocked hat fairly dripped gold braid. Mark spoke in a lame Spanish. His visitor—stopping now and then to dip the mouth end of his cigar into his rum—held forth in a torrent of words, out of which *El Coronel Burr* caught my startled attention.

I knew hardly any Spanish, so I caught nothing of what was said about *El Coronel Burr,* and *El Coronel,* and *Burr* again. In his next long burst of speech—with Mark futilely trying to slow him down—the Spanish captain said another name I knew: *Pickering.*

Coronel surely meant colonel. Burr, who at Quebec had been a young lieutenant, had become a colonel later. He was, indeed, often called the Colonel—*El Coronel.*

Before leaving on the *Royal Arms,* I had learned all I could about the Louisiana-Burriana situation. It was hard to separate fact from rumor. But certainly Spain maintained armed forces to the east of Louisiana, in her Florida territory, and also to the west, in Texas. Now, pressing myself against the dark bulkhead in my dark clothing, in the overcast night, I realized that Burr must be dealing with Spain. Yes, it could be to Spain's advantage to have a friendly new nation set up right at the mouth of the Mississippi, strangling the United States' western trade.

Add to this the name Pickering. Timothy Pickering was a United States Senator from Massachusetts, and he was also a leader of that rebellious group called the Essex Junto. Oh! I thought, why can't Burr and Pickering and the rest simply be locked up? But part of the trouble lay in our dedication to freedom. No one agreed as to where freedom of speech ended and treason began.

In my distress I moved, and my face caught a vagrant gleam of light. Both men realized I had heard everything they had said. The Spaniard, however, had no reason to think I might not be a Tory. He made a great bow, sweeping that cocked hat in the most elegant, old-time fashion. He came and kissed my hand, and with motions of his cigar and many Spanish words and a few in English appeared to say he was overjoyed, carried away, swept off his feet because of my highly decorative presence. He was something of a mountebank, that great-mustachioed man, and because of the menace he represented, he was all the more annoying. Before he left in a renewed cloud of compliments, he gave Mark a number of large sheets of heavy paper tied in a long roll. Mark gave him a letter . . . a letter from Burr? As soon as the Spaniard's men began rowing their captain back to his ship, Mark wheeled and glared at me.

"How much did you hear?" he demanded.

"Everything—"

"God damn it, you have no right to—"

"—and nothing. I don't know Spanish."

"In any event, I'll thank you not to eavesdrop."

"I stood in plain sight, sir, on the open deck. Can you deny it?"

It was not a small thing to frustrate Mark Wentworth so badly that he could do nothing but turn on his heel and walk away.

The *Royal Arms* swooped south from thirty-north toward twenty-seven, where we'd find the Bahama Islands. But the wind died and the sun came up in a vague blob behind thick clouds, watching us roll on an oily sea. A puff of wind ruffled the water, sang in our rigging with a low, ominous note, died away. The next puff had strength enough to lean the ship, and at Mark's roar men scurried aloft to strip the masts, leaving only a few small stormsails. Within half an hour, the ship labored in a frightful gale. We passengers were sternly told to stay below, where we huddled together. Even the stormsails tore out from their boltropes, and the schooner staggered as waves rushed across her deck.

I spent most of my time with poor Mrs. Graham, who was sure she would either drown or die of seasickness, and didn't seem to care which way she went. Her husband sat by, wringing his hands. The storm ended in another heaving calm, and at last Lucy Graham made peace with the ship's motion. But she yearned for chamomile tea. If only she could have a cup of good, hot, fragrant, New England chamomile tea to soothe her stomach!

The ship's cook had never heard of it. But Mary Crow whispered that she and Aunt Patience had packed a selection of chamomile, comfrey, and other home medicines into one of my chests—for who knew what I might need, down in those lost islands?

We needed Anne Burney and her pharmacopeia, I thought wryly. Accompanied by Mary, who carried a lantern, I went down a ladder into a storage space beneath the schooner's cabins—an area reminiscent of the *Bridgewater*'s lazarette, where a man now dead had heard so much that had besmirched me. In a small compartment we found a heap of old sails, along with the luggage not needed in the cabins. Fortunately my chests were on top of the pile, and we uncovered the row of spice jars, all neatly labeled in Aunty's writing.

It was hot enough on deck to cook eggs—almost—but below decks was still cool after three days of heavy rain. I sent Mary up with the chamomile and stayed in the compartment both for the sake of its coolness and for the chance to be alone. I had to sort out what I knew and what I had guessed about Burr and Wilkinson and Pickering—and Mark Wentworth.

When I rested on the heap of sails, I realized how tired I was after all those days and nights of little sleep and constant bracing against the ship's motion. As the schooner rocked to and fro in the swells, I was simply and comfortingly rocked to sleep. . . .

Gradually I came awake. The ship was rolling harder, creaking in all its timbers, and the little compartment was full of noise. Gradually I became aware of the unshaven man who crouched, watching me in the lantern light, barefooted, wearing canvas trousers ragged at the bottoms and a salt-stained gold-trimmed cap pushed back on his springy dark hair.

When he saw my eyes were open, Mark growled, "Damn

it, girl, never set down a lantern when you're below decks. It could get knocked over and start a fire. Hang it where it can swing." He had already done just that, and we were swept by rhythmic changes of light and shadow.

I sat up, pulled my dress down around my ankles, lifted my chin. "I had no intention of starting a fire."

"I presumed as much. But what are you doing down here? I saw you go—you and your Indian."

He had seen me even though he had been frantically busy with repairs needed after the storm. He had noticed me even though his eyes were sunk into his head with weariness, for his only sleep in three days and nights had been catnaps on the rainswept quarterdeck, where he would lie on the bare planks with a tarpaulin wrapped around him.

I told him about the chamomile tea.

"So that's it!" The fleeting flicker of his near-grin made him seem quite pleasant and reasonable. "You may tell Mrs. Graham she'll feel better now. Once she gets to Nassau she'll be able to proceed to Antigua with little discomfort."

"I'll reassure her, thank you."

I was rising, ready to leave, when Mark whispered, "Wait."

Hesitating, I stared at him, able to think only of what we had been to each other. His male presence seemed to fill the small space. We were alone. Beware! said my mind. But my heart didn't say it; my heart knew only that I was glad to see Mark uninjured after his long ordeal. My heart said: Stay with him, chat with him. Fiercely I told myself I wouldn't stay with him unless he promised not to touch me. Yet that would be most difficult to ask. . . .

Still, we had a continuing quarrel. I'd concentrate on that. "Mark, I know the Spanish captain didn't come aboard to smoke a cigar. I'm sure it's all part of a plot against the United States."

Mark glowered. "Shall I be flattered at your interest in my affairs?"

"But you Tories left the U.S.A. of your own free will. Why do you plot against us? We offer you no harm."

Mark shouted, "We left of our own free will, you say? We were spat upon . . . had our homes burned in many cases . . . our cattle scattered . . . our property stolen. Even some of us who approved the Boston Tea Party . . . the

Sons of Liberty tarred and feathered them and rode them on a rail. Do you know what happens to a man who is ridden on a rail?" he demanded.

I knew. They tied a man's hands behind his back and sat him straddling a thin rail. Carried him around, jouncing him up and down with the rail gouging into him while they laughed at his agony.

"Well, Arabella?"

"Well . . . some patriots were ruffians too. But when England landed thousands of troops, bled us with more and more taxes—"

"England bled *you*—America—with your unlimited land and resources? And still you wouldn't do your share of protecting your own frontier. A frontier now expanding, but it could have remained a prosperous part of the great and growing British Empire. . . ."

"We had outgrown the Old World! We were ready to be free and independent!"

"No. You gave yourselves into the hands of Sam Adams, Tom Jefferson, and the like—the New England merchants and the Virginia planters who saw how to grab power. Thirteen colonies united under English law became thirteen jealous states quarreling with each other."

"You know we'll resolve our quarrels. The United States has everything it needs to make it a great, powerful nation."

"Yes!" Mark Wentworth shouted. "That's why now is the time to strike—now or never!"

His words left us glaring. At last I sat back on the sails and smoothed my hair. Mark scowled at the lantern, adjusted its wick. But he didn't go away . . . and somehow I hadn't wanted him to go. I had missed him during the days of bad weather.

Now he sat against a bulkhead and scratched his dark bristle. I thought I saw in his face what I felt in my heart —that we both were relieved to have our quarrel over, at least for the time being.

"Well," he said, "I ought to shave and take an hour in the sack before mess."

"You must be terribly tired."

He yawned and nodded, sat silent, and I was silent. At last Mark said, "Have you heard any talk of steamboats?"

Glad enough to be off on a neutral topic, I replied, "The *Mercury* said there is one working in and out of

Philadelphia, that a Mr. Fitch constructed. But nobody in Newport has ever seen one and I hardly know whether to believe there is such a device."

"There is. It's a cranky, unreliable thing, and the people who ride on it get full of smoke and cinders. Still, it makes eight knots."

"Will there ever be a steamboat out in the ocean, do you think?"

"It's possible. But I see more of a future for them as towboats, helping large sailing craft in and out of narrow places. They could pull a vessel right against the wind."

"I see. The way no sailing craft can go by itself."

"Do you see how that can help you?"

"Help *me?*"

"Certainly. If we're going to have steamboats, then Downing Ironworks might look into the manufacture of steam-tight cylinders and the like."

"Oh . . . thank you." I should have thought of it!

I watched Mark's head sink upon his chest, thought his eyes had closed, but saw their dark glint through those long dark lashes. He was watching me. I shifted on the sails, became very much aware that we were a man and a woman alone together.

"Arabella."

"Yes?" Unsteadily.

"Even though it turned out sad, it was wonderful that our fathers became friends again."

I nodded.

"And when you consider that they'd hated each other for twenty years or more . . . and that you and I have been snapping at each other for a mere quarter of a year . . . seems to me we could sample being friends too."

"I'm not so sure about that."

"Too much politics in the picture? Well then, how about a truce?" He waited. "Or even a mere cease-fire?"

To that much I could say yes, and I said it, the one word oddly trembling. Mark smiled. Something in the rare warmth of his smile communicated itself to me. I glowed all over and found myself smiling too.

"Well," he said, "I don't know how women seal a bargain, but men shake hands." He held out his hand.

I gave him my hand knowing that he would hold it warmly and firmly.

Leaning very close, he whispered, "Arabella, you stayed below all the time during the storm, didn't you?"

"Yes."

"You have witnesses?"

"Why, yes!"

"Can you believe that during the worst of the storm you visited me on the quarterdeck?"

"But—"

"I lay down a few times. And each time . . . just for a moment . . . I didn't seem to be resting my head on wet wood. I seemed to be resting on your bosom."

I gasped and pulled my hand away.

Mark murmured, "If our acquaintanceship were proceeding in the usual fashion, I'd expect you to slap me. But matters have gone beyond that."

"They have indeed," I replied, and even laughed a little—however wryly—at the fact that a slap would come much too late. Also, as I look back, I see I had come to realize that no matter how many men I had met before or might meet in the future, Mark Wentworth would always be a very special man in my life. It was he who had changed me from girl into woman. Certainly the physical fact would never be made "right" by marriage, for the man was still a Tory. But I knew it would always be hard to sort out my feelings where Mark was concerned.

"You see," he whispered as he captured my hand again, "I remembered that proud and lovely bosom. There I was with my ship in great danger . . . thirty lives in my hands . . . but my thoughts went to you. I yearned for you. Even when I slept in the rain, ten minutes at a time, I dreamed of being with you in Mad Anne's cabin. All my memories returned. Even how I had said to myself, back then: Here is a female form that affects me so deeply, I can't stop caressing it. . . . Can it be possible that this woman has been had by many other men? And: How can this dainty loveliness belong to such a one as Mad Anne? Of course it wasn't so!" He pressed my hand to his lips. "Arabella, there's been a madness within me ever since. A need to possess you when you're willing and all-alive, not drugged! I knew I hurt you that first time, but I also remember the moment when your hurt must have gone away because you became mine . . . *mine* . . . ah!" He looked deeply into my eyes. "I see you remember too!"

He kissed me, held me to him, and with mind and body

93

I did remember . . . everything . . . the terror and the pain . . . and then, shutting it out, the surging discovery of passion, the abandon and the glory. It overwhelmed me, made me return Mark's kiss, open my lips to his while a tug of vital need shivered in my loins and a thirsting need possessed all my body. Yet I still tried to force one word against the conquering force of my desire: "No!" And a person who no longer existed—a virgin Newport lady— did try to slap the man who caressed her, but only felt her hand draw tenderly along his face as she gave in.

"Dearest . . . my dearest," Mark whispered while his hands searched out fastenings that opened and let cool air bring even more excitement to my burning skin. The last of reason left me in moans of want as my clothing fell away. He flung his after it. When his unshaven cheek found my breasts I said, "There . . . there!" and pressed him into the softness. His contented sigh echoed my own.

A suspended moment ended with his head turning, his lips seeking and finding and drawing from me a cry of delight. Then, as he had months ago, he kissed me where he wished and every part of my body wanted his kisses. I lay back with my arms locked around him, pulling him downward. Did he penetrate me? No, it was I who drew him in, could not get enough of his strength within my body. And once again we discovered the rhythm, the writhing joy, the surges and small cries and eager gasps that climaxed in rapture as wild and boundless as the sea.

He actually fell asleep upon me, that mighty man who nevertheless had a limit of endurance. But he wakened instantly when there was running on the deck above our heads and excited cries that must have echoed a shout from the masthead: "Land ho on the starboard quarter!"

"It's the islands," Mark said while he fondled my breasts and let their yearning crests know his lips again. "I must go topside. It'll be a gala dinner tonight. You'll dress the part?"

Sighing with reluctance as he rose from my body, I teased him: "I'll change my dress if you'll shave."

"I'll shave and I'll even put on my shoes."

"So formal!" I laughed and pulled him toward me. But he could take no more time for dalliance.

Getting into his trousers, he said with mock ceremony: "Pray present the captain's compliments to Mrs. Graham and inform her that whatever the menu may be—and I hope Mor'cai has found the good, aged steak I told him to put aside—she may have gruel if she wishes."

"Mark Wentworth, there is kindness in you somewhere."

"A kiss for that." A long one . . .

We heard a hatch open and a male voice call, "Cap'n, you below?"

"Don't come down, I'm coming up," Mark shouted to his bos'n. He whispered to me: "Climb the ladder in five minutes. I'll have everyone on deck and the cabin passageway clear. Nobody will see you." He squeezed my bottom and left me tingling, a bit dazed, thoughtful, happy.

Once I was in my cabin, my bliss was followed by a bad half-hour with my conscience. Of course, every precept of my upbringing told me I should not have yielded. And yet, I told myself, my yielding might have shown me a way to handle Mark. If arguing wouldn't do it, tenderness might. Not that I really expected to turn him into a patriot, and not that I didn't know I'd face friction on San Isidro, and perhaps real trouble. But . . . well, I'd see.

The guilt passed. I knew I looked my best when I came to the gala dinner with my black clothing temporarily put aside. It made me quite blissful to have Mark attend me, slide my chair beneath me, say, "There's nothing like sea air to make a beautiful woman more beautiful."

He looked so impressive in his dress uniform that I wished he'd always wear it. It was I who proposed a toast to our gallant captain who had brought us safely to port.

Mark had to leave the table to confer with the mate as we approached Lucaya, the first of the Bahamas. Mrs. Graham took the occasion to whisper to me: "Isn't he handsome?"

Knowing how I flushed, I whispered back: "He certainly is!"

Chapter Six

Next morning I gazed with wonder at islands that rested in great curves upon the dazzling sea. The land was low, but had hills enough to make contours of dusty green that seemed almost like great waves rising out of the water, and I saw winding beaches and white-limestone, green-curtained cliffs. A couple of miles eastward, a row of little cays seemed to have gone swimming. Farther out, long reefs broke the ocean swells and turned them into lines of spouting spray that caught the low sun and transmuted it into little rainbows.

As the sun rose higher, it seemed to paint the most glorious colors in the water—great splotches of purple, pearl, every shade of blue and green, dark mysterious brown, and cheerful yellow. That water took its hue from the nearness of the bottom and what grew on the bottom —sponges, or flats of eelgrass, or fantastic coral gardens, or sparkling sand, or white marl where you could actually see the shadows of great fish and turtles as large as a dining table, although you might not see the creatures themselves. I realized why the Bahamas had taken their name from the Spanish word *bajamar*, meaning low water.

The sailors, however, told me they saw little beauty in the reefs and shallows. Those dangerous waters discouraged the captains of European ships. They felt safer if they picked up cargoes of cotton at mainland ports such as Savannah or New Orleans. This added one more difficulty to the planters' lives. Already some Tory families had given up the struggle to survive and had gone to live in Europe. A very few had returned to the United States.

San Isidro turned out to be higher than the other islands we passed, and it had areas of very rugged land. But the wind had turned fluky again, and it was three days before we reached our goal, miles down its long, winding coast.

Twice we had to drop an anchor into one of those gorgeous sea bottoms and wait for the tide to change a contrary current that might have put us on the rocks. I didn't mind the delay. I basked in delicious peace and a wonderful harmony with Mark. We never touched each other. We said little. But our eyes kept making a warm, expectant contact. We knew we had better not try to hide away, for it had been the merest luck that we hadn't been discovered in the sail locker, and I hardly could go to the captain's cabin and remain behind a locked door. But the thought was in our glance; it was in Mark's delightful hint-of-a-grin; it was even in my turning away from him—but only to let the wind cool my cheeks so that my flush would not betray me.

Once we went ashore I'd be the only patriot in a world of Tories. Now everything was peace and beauty and I wanted it to go on and on. How could I ever have thought I hated Mark! Really, it was too bad that I never could allow myself to love him.

We caught a breeze. The schooner, following a "tongue" of deep water, rounded a jutting area of rocks and bluffs. Everyone cheered as a wharf came in sight. We saw a house shaded by huge mahoganies and silk-cotton trees. We saw fields stretching away from the shore, and the sailors pointed out yam and guinea corn and pineapple, and the inevitable sugarcane planted near a windmill that looked very Dutch with its turning sails. In the cotton fields we saw slaves bringing in the small summer crop. They dragged tubular sacks that trailed after them like great gray serpents that grew fatter as they were fed with the bolls.

The boom of a small cannon and a puff of smoke announced that the *Royal Arms* had come home. Slaves waved from the fields. As we closed with the land I saw that Wentworth Hall was built of wood, and resembled the rambling, white-painted house the Wentworths had inhabited in Newport. The extra verandas and jalousies must have been added to make life more pleasant in the hot sun. The slope leading up to the house was dotted with exotic plants I later learned to recognize as bougainvillea in purple and salmon pink, gaudy oleander, and huge bushes of red hibiscus. Those bushes seemed to shimmer oddly, but I found out that the shimmering was caused by tiny, jewel-like hummingbirds.

As I watched the strange new scene, two black men appeared at the top of the slope, carrying a gilded sedan chair. Years ago, that chair had been one of the sights of Newport and a symbol of Wentworth pride and standing. Surely only Job Wentworth could be riding in it. He was attended on one side by a neatly liveried black man, no doubt a house slave. On the other side walked—or billowed—a lady of imposingly large figure, followed by a black maid who held a parasol above her mistress's head. Surely that lady was Lavinia Dermott, Job's cousin, now presiding as hostess of Wentworth Hall.

When the bearers put down the sedan chair on the wharf, the black man helped a blind white man descend from it. Handsomely attired and carefully groomed as he was, Job still seemed terribly aged and bent. He cocked his head, judged the nearness of the schooner by the creaking and gurgling sounds she made. With quick impatience he called orders to take her lines and belay them to this bollard and that, unerringly remembered.

As we moored, Mark vaulted the bulwark and went to embrace his father, then the large lady, who fondly pinched his cheek. I, following more sedately, faced Job's blank eyes and questioning smile. He expressed surprise at the height of the hand he took, and told me, in a familiar phrase, what a dear little sprat I had once been. When I said I had come to take his dictation and help him finish his history of the Bahamas, he was overjoyed. Wonderful! My house was his.

But his unseeing gaze went beyond me. When he dropped my hand, his own still remained raised and pitifully questing, wanting another old hand to find it. It was then that I told him as gently as I could that my father had died.

"William . . . dead?" Tears came to those blind eyes. Job's attendant put a lace-edged kerchief into his hand, and Job hid his face while Miss Dermott fluttered her fingers and uttered a cry of dismay.

But my host rallied quickly. He sought my hand again, patted it, found a shaky smile amid his wrinkles. "No-no, I must not depress our guest," he said hoarsely. "My dear Arabella, you bring me as much of William as is left upon this earth, and I cannot tell you how grateful I am that you have come." Turning to his servant: "Tibbal, I want you to tell everyone that Miss Downing is to be our most honored guest. Nothing is too good for her. She is to be treated as though she were my own daughter."

Tibbal, silent and grave, made me a respectful bow. His name was Theobald, but I was to find out that Job had taken up the Carolina style of calling slaves by abbreviated nicknames.

At last formally introduced to Lavinia Dermott, I found I must call her Cousin Lavinia, that she had been perishing for lack of female company, that she was charmed with my sweetness, that she'd make sure I'd have a wonderful, wonderful visit at Wentworth Hall. This lady of a certain age had touched her white hair delicately with blue and wore kohl on her eyelids. Puffing beside me as we ascended the slope, she complained of various ailments, as old maids do—except such as Aunt Patience who rarely give in. Still, she seemed kindly. She gave away her age by speaking of Charles Town, not Charleston as it had been known for some years. I thought her a former Charleston belle who would never forget those happy days.

Now Cousin Lavinia—fluttering—told me she had chosen a bright little black girl as my personal maid. I thanked her but said I preferred my own Mary.

Startled, Lavinia gazed from Mary's white cap, unrelentingly starched, to her own maid's Southern bandanna. "But your girl is an Indian slave, isn't she?"

"No indeed, Cousin Lavinia. She's free."

"But anyway," said Lavinia with a wail in her voice, "I've heard that many Yankees keep slaves."

"True. But not the Downings. And the custom is rarely followed anymore." Not wishing to seem sharp, I added, "Anyway, I don't need much maiding and Mary knows just how much I like."

Lavinia was distressed. At length she carried off the scene by saying, rather grandly; "But of course, Arabella-love, we all want you to be pleased."

Later, Lavinia must have remarked to some gossip-hungry planter's wife that I wouldn't accept a black maid. Then—one supposes—as the story went down the thin line of plantations and over to the other islands, it grew stronger. No one would be impolite to the Wentworths' guest, and everyone knew there had been other Yankee visitors among the Tory families. But it was I who became known as "Wentworth's Yankee," and I always thought the label implied suspicion, if not dislike.

When I entered Wentworth Hall, I noticed how similar this house was, in its furniture and decoration, to the house I had sold. We too had had a curio cabinet filled with milk-glazed *blanc de chine* and crowned with a great scallop shell molded in plaster. Like the Downings, the Wentworths favored mahogany highboys with carved finials projecting down from the bottom and up from the top, and lovely little candle stands in cherry, the favorite wood of Newport craftsmen.

Tories, yes . . . but also the Wentworths were people of quality, just as the Downings were. I had to admit that the two families had much in common that no question of politics could becloud.

There was no way to prevent slaves from carrying my luggage upstairs. Commanded imperiously by Mary Crow's pointing finger, they arranged my belongings *there* and *there*.

It was a lovely room, graced with hibiscus blossoms floating in crystal bowls, and no lady could have wanted a prettier little vanity table, with three mirrors on hinges so you could see both sides of your face. Tibbal, who seemed to be the major domo as well as Job's attendant, came with his quiet tread to make sure the jalousies were arranged just so, to keep the sun out and let the sea breeze in. The upstairs maid came, in her apron and turban, partly to stare unbelievingly at Mary and partly to assure me I wouldn't find a speck of dust—which was almost true.

Then Mark looked in and inquired if I was well settled. And even the trace of his smile was gone. I'd known it! To keep real peace between us we had to be away from Tory-land. Nevertheless, as he was leaving, he paused and glanced back over his heavy shoulder. He seemed only to want to look at me again . . . wistfully, I thought.

Then came Cousin Lavinia, fluttering in and out like a fat hen worried over her chick. When at last I was alone with Mary, I stood at a window gazing at the far-reaching palette of the shallow sea, remembering the arrangement I had made with Aunt Patience.

Mary, briskly unbuttoning me down my back, said, "Tonight wash hair. Salt out."

"Yes." Fresh water was not used for such a purpose when one was at sea.

"Now change. Lunch."

I only nodded. Lunch with the Tory Wentworths! How impossible it would have seemed a month ago!

Over in a corner stood a graceful writing stand. I lacked nothing.

"Mary," I said, feeling the tightness in my voice, "please make sure I have plenty of candles. I'll want to write to my aunt tonight so Captain Wentworth can take the letter to Nassau when he brings Mr. and Mrs. Graham there."

"Yes'm."

It would be perfectly natural for me to write to my aunt Patience Bentley, telling her I had arrived safely. But the letter—routinely sealed with the stick of wax I saw on the *escritoire*—would also contain my first secret report. The Wentworths never would know how carefully I would describe that meeting at sea . . . the Spanish captain and the name of his ship . . . the exchange of papers . . . Pickering . . . *El Coronel Burr* . . . all the evidence that Burr had acquired an important ally in his plot against the United States.

Job could hardly wait to take me into his sedan chair with him—it was a squeeze—and have us carried around the plantation. The chair's cordovan-leather lining was cracked and mildewed, but he told me proudly it was the only sedan chair within a thousand miles. At least he ordered two more slaves put at the chair's poles to carry the extra weight.

I soon realized how crops flourished in pockets of good topsoil but were stunted elsewhere. Job had had fair luck in his location, but even so, it was amazing that a Newport merchant had found such success as a planter. Beside the crops I had seen from the water, he had orange and lime trees and a great planting of sisal, a kind of hemp from which rope is made. He even had a bad-smelling but important "crawl" where sponges were laid in the sun till the animal matter rotted out of them and they could be dried and shipped to England.

Job had had to give up the active management of his estate. But it was still *his,* created by his own clever plans, and his dedication was still felt on every field. At the same time this Yankee-born man continued as the leader of the Loyalists. I saw horsemen gallop in for quick, secret conferences with him, and suspected that almost every boat or ship carried some message that his unfailing memory stored away.

As I grew to know the neighbors—none very friendly, and none very near—I found that although Job was admired, he had done *something* that was resented. Or rather, he seemed to have left something undone, and it had become a source of worry up and down the islands.

Once I asked Renzo, the black plantation foreman, what Mister Job had neglected to do. Renzo and I were old friends, for in Newport he had been the Wentworths' gardener. To me, he had been the smiling slave who, when I passed the Wentworth house, would say, "A purty little flower for a purty little lady," and hand me a peony or whatever was in season.

So I thought he would tell me what it was that Job should have done that he did not do. But sturdy old Renzo only scratched his woolly head and said, "Don' know, Miss Arabella." He wasn't a good liar. I was sure he knew, but was keeping the secret.

I was surprised when I learned that Renzo had been manumitted—but for business reasons. Job thought it not good for a foreman to be a slave. Renzo could have left the plantation, yet he stayed. "Young mans go wanderin', but old mans don' muches that," he said, meaning he didn't much like the idea. Once I saw a runaway return, take his lashes, and get back to work. It was better than starving in the bush or braving the hungry sea.

My sightseeing expedition with Job often took us to the rocky peninsula I had seen from the water. Job liked the wind and the near-coolness out there. He had us carried to a windbreak of coral blocks that had been set up along with stone seats and a stone table. It all made a kind of picnic grove, shaded with trees, near the bluff at the end of the point. The "tongue" of navigable water came right to the base of the cliff, very deep and very blue, and waves washing below the cliff made strange boomings in the hollowed-out limestone.

Until his eyes had failed, Job had written his history on that stone table. He told me: "Soon I'll be dictating to you out here, Arabella. But first we're going to give you a grand reception and a ball. I want all the island families to know my dearest friend's daughter."

By now I had come to see how true it was that one should not wear black when the sun is almost overhead. I had light-colored dresses with me and on very hot days I did modify my mourning. I decided I'd let the reception and ball signal my putting it aside. But the coming reception made my mind hum with a deeper thought. Amateur spy that I was, I had to give myself every possible chance to gather information. And I wasn't likely to find out much from the local women. It was the men who *knew*. In that case, I should get myself noticed by men. Approached by men. *Be bold, Arabella!*

Despite England's long war with France, Bahamas fashions had become mildly Frenchified. Lavinia assured me that a marvelous little French dressmaker in Nassau would make sure I was modishly attired. Mark was going back to Nassau in a few days, and he'd take us along.

"Good!" said I, and made plans I hoped I'd be able to carry out.

On the schooner, we covered the three hundred miles to Nassau amid summer thunderstorms. Since this was a "family" cruise, Lavinia and I invaded the sacred quarterdeck and made seats for ourselves on the edge of the skylight. We sewed and chatted. I learned about social life in Charleston and a deal about life on the great plantation where Lavinia had been born. Given a roaring market for your cotton and indigo and rice, your house became so big that you hardly knew how many rooms you had, to say nothing of the number of black faces down in the quarters. For the men, it was all fox hunting, dueling, drinking, gambling; a flamboyant parade. For women of that class life went gently and smoothly, with hardly the need to lift a finger save in ladylike pursuits.

I had heard that Southern plantation owners had duties as well as pleasures, nor were they free from crop failures, and sometimes they went broke. So I took whatever Lavinia said with a grain of salt. The real point was that no matter how much money you had, the Southern style of life was unimaginable in stony New England. I realized all the more that the North and the South were very different places.

I've mentioned that the big table of the officers' mess stood just below the skylight. One afternoon, while Lavinia chatted on and on, and the table was empty, someone sat down to it and opened a roll of papers that had been tied with twine. I knew the man's wiry black hair.

Lavinia was telling me how her fiancé had died, long ago. Touching her kerchief to her fluttering eyelids, she related how he had fallen from his hunter and had been carried home with a broken neck. But still, she said, if poor Winthrop had had to go, she was consoled in knowing it had been a gentleman's way to die.

I don't know what I said to that. Standing as though to stretch my limbs, I was able to look down more clearly through the skylight's slanted glass. Mark was studying big maps that showed the entire southern part of the United States and part of Texas. I recognized the Mississippi Delta with its many winding passages, and I noticed how close West Florida—in Spanish hands—came to the city of New Orleans.

With brass dividers Mark was laying out distances just inland of the swampy coast and then jotting figures in the margin of the map; mileages, I supposed.

His interest was not in the sea. It was in the land. I tried to remember the exact areas of southern Louisiana that he measured. Was he laying out the supposed boundary of Burriana? Was he involved in measuring an area to be taken up by future Loyalist plantations?

As I watched, Mark shifted his dividers eastward, brought them to the chart's distance scale, made a note, opened them wider and brought them back to West Florida again. Was he laying out a route for an invading Spanish army that would come from Florida and help the Loyalists carve away a piece of the United States?

I stopped peering lest he see me, reminded myself that Mark was still one of the enemy—no matter what else he might be. At any rate my next letter to Aunt Patience would warn Mr. Jefferson that West Florida had become a sword pointing at Louisiana and the key city of New Orleans.

Nassau Harbour, protected by a cay just offshore, was dotted with the stubby, single-masted vessels that plied the islands. Farther out lay several large ships, with whom the *Royal Arms* joined company as her anchor went down. Still farther out, a tall-masted armed cutter showed a busy scene of gun drill as her sailors rolled her guns to her ports so that they seemed to watch over the harbor and the shipping. Ashore, whitewashed houses glared in the sun, while older houses were barely visible beneath a profusion of bougainvillea, vivid red poinciana, and brilliantly hued parrots that seemed like flying flowers. Nassau was a busy place, a crossroads of far-flung trade, and after sleepy San Isidro it looked very exciting.

Lavinia had us rowed ashore by one of Mark's polite, secretive sailors. She puffed me up the hill to be presented to Governor Cameron, who was polite enough but not very warm toward Wentworth's Yankee. Then, on Bay Street, we promenaded past a surprising number of well-stocked shops. When the city had been a pirates' nest, rich West Indian planters would come to deal openly with the cutthroats who supplied them with stolen silks and satins, fancy foods and wines. The pirates were gone—or almost so—but Nassau remained a shopping center. Well-dressed ladies and elegant gentlemen were to be seen everywhere. Every lady was accompanied by a slave girl who held a silk parasol above her mistress's head. Just so was I followed by Mary Crow with a parasol and Lavinia by her black Nessa—Vanessa—who was in a panic because she was afraid of Indians.

As Lavinia said comfortably, you always met people you knew in Nassau. But a good many of the nods and how-de-dos were directed right past me. Very well. I was at least able to take note of a cross section of Bahamas styles. Every woman I'd seen was dressed well but cautiously. In that case, if I wanted attention from men, I must not be cautious. True, one suited one's dress to the occasion. But an occasion was coming up when I could throw caution to the winds.

"There's the dressmaker's, Madame Marcellot's," Lavinia said, nodding toward a flower-covered cottage. "She's quite wonderful. Except that, being from Paris, she's apt to be a little—well, Parisian as to designing one's décolletage. And of course, Arabella-love, you'll be ordering your ball gown. But I'll explain to her. . . ."

Perfect. From the moment I had heard I'd have a French dressmaker outfit me, I had been carrying a subdued excitement. Napoleon was in power, and his tastes as to décolletage were very well known. I was about to spend heavily from my small store of ready cash, and I would

106

not spend to please the Loyalist ladies' ideas of decorum;
I'd spend to attract the Loyalist men. Yes, I must talk to
men, listen to *men*, draw confidences from *men*.

Instantly, when Lavinia introduced Madame Marcellot
to me, I knew I'd come to an understanding with the
slight, gray-haired woman who gestured with needle-worn
fingers. Especially when she assayed me, murmured, "Mamselle brings me a lovely figure," and sighed and rolled her
eyes, looking from me to Lavinia significantly, then from
Lavinia back to me.

I winked. The small French face returned a quick look
of joy.

Madame Marcellot had all the latest fashion books and
endless rolls of cloth, for she preferred to be her own
draper. Lavinia and I hunted through silks, damasks,
mousselines, and linens, all fresh from Europe, English
blockade or no. Beside a ball gown I wanted several dresses.
They might not be reckless but they would not be cautious
either.

As I laid a bolt of cloth aside for further inspection, I
nudged the dressmaker and whispered, "Get rid of her!"

"Mamselle Dermott," murmured the Frenchwoman,
"Madame Beauregard of Acklin Island was here this morning. She saw the *Royal Arms* come in, and she hoped she
might find you. I was to tell you she'd be at the boot-
maker's. Anton's, you know? He has had a shipment of
Austrian kid. . . ."

"Austrian kid!" cried Lavinia. "I must have a pair of
slippers in Austrian kid! And—Ernestine Beauregard! I
haven't seen her for ages! But—" She looked at me doubt-
fully.

"Don't let me keep you from your friend, Cousin
Lavinia," I said. "You can certainly trust Madame Marcellot with the fitting."

"Yes . . ." said Lavinia, worrying. "But . . . the styl-
ing . . .

The Frenchwoman nodded, moved a finger across the
base of her throat.

"Oh!" said Lavinia in relief. "You do understand."

"Certainement"

"Then I'll go along," said Lavinia to me. "And I'll come
back for you soon and make sure that—"

"Oh no, do have a good visit with your friend and I'll

find you later." Anything but have Lavinia return at the wrong moment!

"That's kind of you, Arabella-love. Look for me, then, over at Anton's. Anyone can tell you where to find his shop. Or if we go elsewhere, I'll leave word with Anton as to where we'll be."

Lavinia wagged a finger at Madame Marcellot, who again drew a finger across the base of her throat and made gestures of assurance. Lavinia sailed away like a waddling ship of the line, but the little dressmaker still kept rubbing the base of her throat.

"It is an eetch," she told me solemnly.

"Of course. It has nothing to do with a neckline."

"Surely Mamselle Dermott did not think—?"

"Why no, she never said a word about the neckline."

"Then we do not deceive—eh?" The dressmaker winked.

I winked back in the greatest delight. When I turned to look meaningly at Mary Crow, she surprised me by also winking. I stripped to my underclothes, and Madame Marcellot sang cheerful French roundelays as she got to work with cloth, measuring tape, and pins. My ball gown definitely would not rise to the base of my throat. Not by several inches. In fact, Madame would have to invoke French magic to keep it from slipping away from my bosom's pink crests.

I had a bit of trouble in finding Lavinia, later. It turned out that Ernestine Beauregard had indeed asked about her, but it had been during the previous week, when we had not been in town. A slip of memory on the dressmaker's part, no doubt!

We had ourselves rowed back to the schooner, where we could dine and spend the night out on the moderately cool water. There we found Mark superintending the loading of a small bargeload of fancy foods that would be consumed at the reception. He also had bought an amazing number of cases of wine, some of them oddly speckled with little white barnacles. They had lain underwater and had been salvaged from a wreck. Lavinia explained that many delicacies consumed in the Bahamas were hauled out of broken ships that lay beneath the shallow seas.

"You must be pleased with your new wardrobe," she told me. "You look like the cat that ate the cream."

I hardly could wait to have my new dresses delivered. Especially that ball gown!

On the voyage home we had a fortunate slant of wind. At night it was exciting to go rolling and foaming through the black water till we rounded the southern end of San Isidro. The wind picked up, and we swooped like a great white ghost past the island's hundred-mile stretch of bluff and beach. Hardly anything was visible—only the faint loom of the low land, and an occasional light from some dwelling. Once I saw a cluster of lights that looked like the anchor lights of several ships lying together. That must be a harbor, I told a sailor. "No, miss," he replied, "them's more likely wreckers' lights to make a strange cap'n think the harbor's there when it's really ten miles away." And so another vessel might be "assisted" in going onto a reef where wreckers would pick her clean. In addition, there was not a single lighthouse in all the Bahamas, and I marveled at Mark's skill and confidence as he drove the *Royal Arms,* wind whistling in her cordage, through the moonless night.

I went to my favorite spot in the bow and watched froth leap from the schooner's cutwater, born startlingly white out of the dark sea. When the wind disordered my coiffure, I put all my pins and ribbons into my pocket and let my hair fly. It came forward and seemed to hold me, all alone, in a small, airy, reeling world.

"Well, how do you like our islands?" Mark Wentworth said behind me.

Again I did not turn immediately to speak to him. Where Mark was concerned, my feelings were still unresolved. Moreover, during the three weeks I had been in the Bahamas I hardly had seen him. When he hadn't been off with the *Royal Arms* he'd been occupied with installing the new grinding rollers in the windmill, and during our trip from San Isidro to Nassau he'd gone back to his old habit of not coming to meals.

When the trembling warmth in my body made me turn, I quivered with the realization that the bellying foot of a foresail hid us from view of the watch.

Mark was waiting for my answer. I managed at last: "I like the islands well enough, but I do miss Newport."

He surprised me by saying, "So do I. And I miss winter. In January or February the Bahamas sometimes get a whiff of cold weather, perhaps down to forty degrees for a couple of hours, and I want it to be zero so I can go ice skating. Or just walking on the crunchy snow."

"And then comes spring—"

"When everything wakes up—"

"When you see the first crocus poke out of the snow . . ."

And we stood very close and he had leaned down toward me.

What's happening to me? I asked myself. But I knew, oh, how well and warmly I knew the tugging and the yearning that now came very quickly because they had so recently been aroused and fulfilled. As I waited for Mark's kiss my entire being wanted kisses and more than kisses. I was lost . . . I was his. My taut nipples told me, and that tug across the loins, and my rapid heartbeat. Where would we hide? He must know. My eyes closed. My lips parted.

But Mark didn't kiss me. My eyes opened, saw his face was no longer close to mine and that the faint loom of his body seemed awkward and uncomfortable.

He said, "Well, about winter . . . at least we can agree on that."

What was I to say? I still trembled, I still needed, but a coldness in my bosom told me something had gone wrong.

"I nearly kissed you," he said. "But—"

Why didn't you? I cried within my mind.

"—but it wouldn't have been fair."

His words seemed utterly ridiculous. "Really?" I said, a woman scorned, my voice sharp with hauteur.

"Damn it," he whispered, "I want you. But I've been thinking about our—our relationship—and about our being on opposite sides of a vital cause. . . ."

"I see. But you don't think well when you're in a sail locker, is that it?"

"Look, Arabella, that—that was when we were caught between worlds. Look . . . what I mean is . . . the issue is joined. I saw you spying on me through the skylight."

I cried with the wrath of guilt: "I was merely standing there! Happened to look downward—"

"No, Arabella. The slanted glass makes reflections onto the glass-fronted case on the bulkhead. That's how I know you didn't just happen to look downward. I saw your interest in my maps."

"Oh, You're *so* sharp-eyed, *such* a fine renegade, *such* a *capable* traitor!"

He sighed. "We *are* very much on opposite sides of the fence, aren't we? I don't want to be rough with you, Arabella, and I do want to dance with you at the ball. But you've been spying." He bent again, but only to look straight into my eyes as he said, "You had better drop any further idea of spying."

"If happening to glance down a skylight can be called—"

"It's more than that. I know it's inevitable that you'll find out a few things you shouldn't know and put two and two together, as you did up there at thirty-north. But whatever you find out, it won't do Thomas Jefferson any good. Because you'll never be able to get the news to him."

Unwisely, I blurted, "You can't stop me!"

"Can't I? Remember that any letter you write must leave San Isidro by some boat or ship. And there's no one—*no one*—who'll accept a letter from you without turning it over to me, or to one of the men who works with me, for our inspection."

"Just what does that mean, sir!"

"It means your very revealing letter to your aunt never reached her. But I know everything it said."

Aghast, I cried, "You opened my letter!"

"Yes. And will open every letter you write unless you hand it to me unsealed, so you may as well do so. Still, there's no need to let your aunt worry about you. Write to her that you're well. Write about the scenery, the birds and the flowers, the broad Carolina accents you hear. I'll let that kind of letter go through . . . gladly."

Ready to bite and scratch and kick, I hissed at him: "And if I choose to leave San Isidro?"

"Don't choose," said Mark Wentworth rather too softly. "Because, like it or not, you're going to have a long stay with us. You'll soon be busy helping my father with his history, and, as your wise aunt said, it's better to have work to do than loll around as an idler." He paused, and the black night added to the impact of those challenging dark eyes. "I repeat, you are not to go off San Isidro. You are not to attempt to send messages regarding our affairs, here, or Colonel Burr's. It won't work, and it will cause much unpleasantness for you—even confinement if that is necessary."

111

Though shivering silently, I stood proud, showing him I was still defiant. Eight bells—midnight—sounded from the quarterdeck. Mark gave me a salute and a bow. "Good night, Arabella, and pray excuse me. I've ship's business." He strode away.

Frantic with helplessness, I hammered on the bulwark till my fists hurt. Not only would my letters be read, but also my every movement would be watched.

No matter what I might find out, no matter how important it might be to the future of the United States, I was locked onto San Isidro by the will of plotting Tories and the beautiful, dangerous sea.

Chapter Seven

I was astonished at the effort that went into preparing my presentation to Loyalist society. First there would be an afternoon of feasting and gossip—and matchmaking among the local families, I was sure. Then we'd have a grand ball, along with whist and euchre and an array of other games to play if anyone didn't care to dance. On the following day we'd have horseracing on the beach and more feasting in my honor. But I realized how much these people needed an occasional grand get-together to lighten their spirits and catch up with friends who lived far away.

Certainly I was willing to mingle and dance and chat. But also I would make the festivities serve my main purpose, which was to gather information. Let Mark keep me prisoner and read my mail! All I needed was one willing male confederate. The reception should give me a chance to find such a man.

Meanwhile my New England conscience would not allow me to be idle. I bustled about the house and grounds and even went into the kitchen, which a Southern lady would not do. Outdoors, I chatted with my friend Renzo, whose white woolly head bobbed here and there as he managed the outdoor preparations.

I also met Gumry—Montgomery—a younger man who would be foreman someday. Stripped to the waist, he was a beautiful mass of sweat-gleaming muscle, and I smiled when I saw how Mary Crow followed his motions with big eyes. Gumry was, I suppose, three-quarters black, but a tint of copper along his broad cheekbones told of the Arawaks who had lived in the Bahamas long ago. Proud and aloof, Gumry managed work gangs with a fierce competence. He got a huge pavilion set up on the lawn, and made sure its canvas was stretched tight as a drum.

Field slaves dug trenches where pigs, whole sheep, and

sides of beef could be turned on spits over glowing coals. At the proper time, Tibbal led out the house slaves— who contemptuously turned their backs on the field slaves —and they arranged long tables in the pavilion's shade. These they covered with the finest napery while Lavinia prowled and peered to make sure that the edge of each cloth hung exactly straight. Next came solid old silver. Glancing at a tureen, I recognized the work of a Newport silversmith who once had made my mother a sugar-and-creamer. I felt a lump in my throat.

Some guests arrived on horseback. Some pushed through in various light vehicles on the almost nonexistent roads. Others sailed up in tubby sloops. Moored at the wharf, the sloops and Mark's schooner would offer sleeping quarters for a number of men. Lavinia and I found ways to squeeze out sleeping quarters in Wentworth Hall for the older ladies, and sent the spryer ones down to the Trumbulls, our nearest neighbors, who opened their own home for the occasion.

The aroma of roasting meat filled the air, contending with the scent of soap and lotions as ladies bathed and dressed. None of us looked toward the wharf, where the men splashed naked in the sea. Already I had grown used to taking a tub in the open air, on a terrace surrounded by vine-grown trellises. That day, for the first time, I allowed Mary to bathe me, and I remained unconcerned as she passed a sponge along my belly and breasts. It was strange to be, all at the same time, aware of my body and yet more matter-of-fact about it. Glancing at Mary, I almost remarked on what a difference it had made in me to have had experience with men. She would understand. Nevertheless I kept my silence. Regarding men, I did not want even to hint at an action I might have to take. How could I best induce a man to carry a secret letter? Knowing, I glanced down uneasily at the ripe pinkness of my curves.

When Mary produced my filmy petticoat from between two wet towels, she came as near to being gleeful as ever I had seen her. I'll not pretend that a damp petticoat is comfortable to wear, but it does cling and show the shape of one's legs. A clever web of black ribbon contained my golden hair and made it look all the brighter. Riding on the back of my head, utterly useless and marvelously pretty, soared a Paris afternoon bonnet with a foot and a half of curved brim going almost straight up, framing my features. It would come off later for the ball.

But before the bonnet, the gown went on. And Mary, viewing me, said a great deal. She said, "Oh-h-h-h!" The gown was brocade on net, in apricot with black and gold touches. You could see right through it, as Lavinia had known; but my chaperone had not suspected how much I'd leave off underneath. The high belt was a tasseled cord that swung almost to my gold-colored slippers and matched a similar cord on my bonnet. As for the décolletage . . . at last the twenty-year-old woman was wearing the style that the fifteen-year-old girl had dreamed of. I can only say it did justice to my high well rounded form.

"Good," said Mary Crow, her eyes shining.

In Newport the gown would have been considered too elegant for an afternoon rout. But Lavinia had told me that the Loyalist ladies would bring along only one gown for both afternoon and evening, rather than fuss in the summer heat. More likely it was a matter of economy. Be that as it might, with the aid of Madame Marcellot I was ready to defy Bahamas convention with an exposure that would bring every man's gaze my way. A final adjustment by Mary to my remarkable bonnet, and I went downstairs with a shawl of gossamer silk draped across my back and nestling in the crook of each elbow, to flutter as I walked.

Lavinia, in an elaborate lace fichu and a velvet train, waited with Job at the foot of the stairs. Job, knowing my step, looked up and smiled, but of course could not see me. When Lavinia looked up I thought she would have an attack of the vapors then and there. After a paralyzed instant, she turned to Job and fussed over his cravat. Slowly, then, as though trying *not* to look, the elderly spinster turned once more. Her jaw dropped. Her smile seemed pasted on.

Where was Mark? Playing the gracious host in the pavilion, I supposed—a task for which he was remarkably ill-suited. Well, he too would see me soon enough. With my arm in Job's I strolled across the lawn in the first coolness of approaching dusk. A slave held aside the canvas flap that allowed entrance to the pavilion. We entered; the flap closed behind us. I gazed around casually. Mine was not the richest gown I saw. But had Napoleon I, Emperor of France, been there, he would have had eyes only for me.

Meanwhile a hum of voices had died away. Suddenly

the women all turned back to one another and began talking, presenting stiff backs to the shameless Yankee puff. As for the men . . . some of the younger ones had forgotten to stop staring. From the older ones, in the presence of their wives, I had cocked eyebrows, little grins of appreciation.

"Oh dear," Lavinia whispered faintly. "I was going to suggest you put on a fichu, Arabella-love. But that gown simply won't take a fichu. And it's your only ball gown. But . . . oh, dear me!"

I hardly heard her, for my gaze had clashed with Mark's. He was at the other side of the pavilion, a glass in his hand, chatting with a red-haired young woman. She had a delightful figure well contoured in saffron yellow, satin-striped silk gauze; but once she saw me, she knew that compared to exposure, contour was not enough. It was odd to be looked at and instantly hated.

Mark had come far from his role as a barefooted captain. He wore a cerise brocade coat, and rather than tight pantaloons he had chosen gray silk evening breeches. White ribbons held up the white stockings that encased his muscular calves. I saw how the cascade of ruffles down his chest moved with the long, admiring breath he drew.

Now Lavinia said we must stand where great masses of flowers had been banked against a wall. I was sure that every man, young and old, noticed my swaying walk.

Lavinia's agitated fingers and beseeching eye brought Mark to join us. The long round of introductions began. The men bowed their evident pleasure. The women stabbed me with their gaze. And I, holding out a hand in an ineffably chic long black fingerless dance mitt made of Paris net: "Charmed, sir . . . ma'am . . . miss . . . delighted I'm sure. Oh yes, the voyage down was most interesting. San Isidro is most interesting. Yes, I do look forward to helping Mr. Wentworth with his history. It will be a great contribution to scholarship. My gown? Oh . . ." As though surprised at the compliment. "Thank you, sir. So kind of you to say so." And a small, inviting smile.

Trying not to overdo it, aware that a woman of the world should be subtle in her ways, I still tried to pick out the most vulnerable of the men, smiled warmly at those who evidently wished they could take me away to a dark room. While the ladies edged their words with poison and the gentlemen told me how much they hoped

116

to dance with me, I realized the devastating potential I had attained. I was a prisoner, yes. But my captors were not people who wore dresses. And they were being treated to the company of a woman who was new and unusual in their closed society, and who dared them to be all man.

I must never let on how the proper lady, deep beneath, shuddered at the sultry temptress!

There was one man I didn't meet immediately. He stayed at the buffet, busily feeding, but he certainly took notice of me. He was sandy-haired and bony, full of sun and health, with the mark of the sea upon him. Once, when his Scotch-blue eyes caught mine, the most delightful grin lit up his freckled face. But he never came to take my hand, which made me all the more anxious to meet him later.

Just as I thought we had finished with introductions, another man entered the pavilion. He recognized Job and Lavinia and Mark with a blink of heavy-lidded eyes, glanced about as though world-weary. This was an elegantly slender man, richly but soberly dressed, in clothes of an old-fashioned cut, and he had an air of wealth and position—and boredom. Coming toward us, he found me out, and for a moment the ennui left his half-closed eyes.

I was to learn that this aristocrat was Bartley Holdridge, a widower of about thirty-five who kept an elegant house on an island called Eleuthera, to the southwest. He had come a full two hundred miles from his plantation, but in comfort, in a bargelike craft propelled by both sail and oars. I learned that as his yellow-painted boat approached Wentworth Hall he had remained seated on a little balcony aft, reading Catullus, and had never looked up till the barge was secured.

Now he neared us. His face was all shadows and hollows, and his eyes were sunken into dark nests. Like Hiram Chance, captain of the *Bridgewater*, this man had a dissipated, rakish face. But Chance, rake or no, looked strong, while Bartley Holdridge seemed at the point of exhaustion.

"Miss Downing, I welcome you to the islands," he said as though he owned the Bahamas. His voice was deep and strangely hollow and his hand was cold.

Trying to ignore a very uneasy feeling, I said I had heard Eleuthera was a lovely island.

"It is indeed. But it would be made all the more lovely

117

by your presence if you would honor me with a visit one day." Holdridge glanced at Lavinia, Job, and Mark and added, perhaps a bit reluctantly: "Of course I mean a visit from all of you. You know I have a big, empty house."

Job said, "Thank you, Holdridge, but you know my health has not been good. I don't travel if I can help it."

Mark said very drily, "When it's cooler, perhaps, if I can find the time."

Lavinia, going quite flustered, said, "I'm sure it would be a wonderful visit for my Arabella, but she's going to be very busy with Job's history, you know." She fussed nervously with the artificial flowers she wore in her hair that had begun to droop over her face.

Holdridge paid little attention to what had been said. "Do you like gardens, Miss Downing?" he asked, still holding my fingers in his.

"Yes, I like gardens. I had one back home." Why did this man make me so uncomfortable as he watched me with his tragic eyes? Obviously he was attracted to me, yet I felt repelled by . . . something.

"I am an esthete," said Holdridge, "and I remember, although it's been some years since a woman shared my home that a woman picking flowers is a lovely sight. I'd like to see you gathering a bouquet in my garden."

This was all rather peculiar. But the man himself was like no one else I had ever met. The cold hand. The voice from a tomb. The handsome but ravaged face. I was relieved when, with a kind of superior smile at the necessity of good manners—I thought—he let go of my hand, bowed, said in the old-fashioned manner, "Your servant, Miss Downing," and moved on.

I had been aware that a small slave had accompanied Holdridge, staying close as a shadow behind him. Now we all saw a very short, overfed black boy who was dwarfed all the more by a huge turban pinned with a ruby. He was dressed like a Turk in an embroidered vest, a velvet shirt, baggy velvet breeches, and soft shoes with their toes turned up. He had a strange stare, almost as though he were blind. But he was not. That stare was his permanent expression. The stunted black boy scurried short-leggedly after his master.

I informed Job: "Mr. Holdridge keeps a little blackamoor in fancy dress. I thought that custom had ended."

118

Job seemed annoyed. He snapped, "Holdridge is odd in more ways than one. I've no wish to visit him."

Said Lavinia, all a-flutter: "Nor I! He's wicked!" For emphasis she rolled her eyes and held a hand to her bosom. Then, as though anxious to drop the subject: "Now, Cousin Job, you come with me and I'll see that you have some refreshment."

"Stop treating me like a child," Job grumbled. But there was affection between Job and Lavinia, and he allowed her to lead him away.

Puzzled, I watched people whisper behind Holdridge's back. Contemptuously at ease, he seemed aware of it and uncaring.

Since I'd been left alone with Mark, I asked him: "Is Holdridge really wicked? How?"

Mark didn't like the question. "Well . . . he has a certain habit that . . . that is more common in the East than in the West."

"Does he smoke hashish?"

"Perhaps that too. Let me say only that Bartley Holdridge is the richest man in the Bahamas and is very generous in supporting our cause. Otherwise we'd cut him." Mark took my arm, and not wishing to show open antagonism, I walked with him toward one of the long tables that groaned with food and drink. "So, Arabella, you've become the *femme fatale*. I own I'm astonished."

"Because I'm no longer the innocent you met in her father's study?"

Mark gave me a long look. "You never were the innocent," he said.

"Not since I was sixteen. But I was pure, Captain Wentworth. Chaste. Untouched. Or however you want to say it, since you certainly take my meaning. Then you—"

"Quite so," he agreed, greatly annoying me by offering no excuse—not even the perfectly good one, that he really had thought I was Mad Anne, which I had long since accepted. "But really, Arabella, your—ah—new status still left you with a deal of modesty. What's come over you now? And you've been giving all the men a sultry survey. Which they return in kind, although they don't look you in the *face*."

"Do you object, sir? By what right?"

"I, object? You have nothing left to show that *I* haven't seen."

I knew he had tried to "get my goat," and he had. I stamped my foot. "That is the most ungentlemanly, caddish remark that I ever—"

"My point was merely that I don't object to other men's looking as long as they see less than I have."

"Thank you, Captain Wentworth, for at least revealing your truly hateful side. Since I have nothing left to show you, I don't know why you look at me at all."

"True enough. But a woman's glory half-revealed will always make a man yearn to see the rest . . . as you ladies found out long ago."

I merely nodded.

Mark almost smiled. "Once I was in an English tavern —a rather low place. They had a barmaid who was as well endowed as you and wore the same kind of bodice. The men flipped farthings at her to see if they could—"

"Never mind!"

"But you're after . . . what *are* you after?"

"That's my affair, sir!"

"I suppose you'd like me to go away so you can talk to other men?"

"You're most acute, sir!"

"Still, it's my duty to see that you sample our green turtle soup. It's a great treat of the islands, and we ought to have some before any drunkard dips his sleeve into it. Ah, Macgillivray!" he said then, nodding cordially to the freckled Scot who was busy with boar's meat at the far end of the table.

Macgillivray gave me a bow but still did not approach to be introduced. I was charmed by his grin, as open as a boy's.

Mark signaled a slave to fill silver cups from the steaming tureen. The thick, sherry-laced soup was fragrant and delicious. Sprinkling it with grated, hard-boiled turtle egg made it even better. Mark watched me thoughtfully. Trying to ignore him, I gazed around with a cool invitation, hoping another man would approach. And yet my heart reminded me that it was Mark and no other man who stood beside me. Try as I might to treat him with disdain, to remember he was my enemy, to resent that bitter scene in the dark aboard the *Royal Arms,* my treacherous body betrayed me.

Now he growled, "Well, here comes someone to make

conversation with you. I suppose every man is entitled to a closer view of the Yankee Hills."

I knew the type of young man who approached me, for I'd seen such youths at Newport balls. If any woman stood out from the others, they would screw up their courage and go and talk to her—but they'd still be shaky and pink-faced with their own daring. This seventeen-year-old left his parents glaring after him as he headed toward a blatant . . . whatever word they used for me. I knew how conspicuous he felt, and I tried to help him with a smile as he came straight where his instincts led him.

Mark did casual honors. "Miss Downing, you've surely met Mr. Brian Roscoe? Of course. Well, I've my captain's . . . er, my duties as a host, so do excuse me, and Mr. Roscoe will see to it that you sample the best of our island fare. Mr. Roscoe, where Miss Downing is concerned we must put our best foot forward."

"C-c-certainly," said young Roscoe, who looked as though he would have given a million pounds to get rid of his nervous stutter.

He commanded the slave to serve me crayfish in aspic, minced blue crab in its own shell, and everything else in sight. He told me, stuttering and shaky, that he was one of the new Loyalist generation, Bahamas-born. That his father had owned five thousand acres in the Carolina lowlands and had been very rich; but here crops were short and cash was low. That he lived for the cause and hoped soon to play his part. Suddenly feeling he might have offended me, he added that I might not be one who'd share his devotion, but he hoped we could be friends.

I still thought that my ideal confederate would be an older man who might send letters to a factor or agent in the United States and would enclose a sealed letter to be forwarded to Aunt Patience. Of course I'd ease his conscience by assuring him that my letter concerned only private financial matters, and he'd believe me if he wished. Brian Roscoe was no man of affairs. But his eyes were glassy with admiration, and if the older men thought they had better not be too obvious about squiring me, this young chap might do.

I said softly, "I'd like to be your friend."

"You w-would?" He was flooded with joy. "B-because you're so l-lovely and I hope you don't th-think I've been too bold . . ."

Fussing with my shawl as though embarrassed, I whispered, "A man should be bold." Bold enough to slip my sealed letter into some local trader's hands, with instructions to relay it to some northward-bound captain.

Smiling to Brian Roscoe, I wondered if he had ever had a woman. And was quite ready to initiate this young man if it served my own cause.

"W-won't you have some p-pralines, Miss Downing? They're from New Orleans, and awfully good. More syllabub? More—"

"Oh, I mustn't! Or I won't fit my gown."

"It's a gorgeous gown." But he didn't dare look below my chin. "And your bonnet is so—so—modish."

Pretending doubt, I looked around. "But it doesn't seem quite the style for Bahamas ladies."

"You'll set the style, Miss Downing!"

Exactly what I had wanted him to say. "Thank you," I breathed.

We chatted, then, about the problems of running plantations and about my shorthand ability, which, I found out, some Bahamas people thought must be a skill of the devil, for they could not understand how simply it worked. Soon enough, however, I was fanning my face with my shawl and saying, "Oh dear, this pavilion does hold heat. And there are so many insects."

"The lights attract the insects, Miss Downing," Brian informed me brightly.

"Yes, it happens that way in Newport too."

"Does it really?" My young man's view of the world had limited scope. Flushed, he glanced around. His stout blond mother, her kohl smeared with sweat, watched as though ready to run to his rescue. Almost visibly reinforcing his courage, Brian asked me desperately, "Y-you wish to go outside, Miss Downing?"

"Would it be too unconventional, do you think?"

That left him only one possible answer: "Of course not." I rested my fingers lightly on his arm and we walked toward the exit through thick silence. For an instant, our path was blocked by that cheerful, freckled, sun-smitten man to whom I had not been introduced. Brian frowned uncertainly. Macgillivray gave me his wonderful grin and a wink, and stepped aside.

Outdoors we found a little breeze, not quite enough to sail my bonnet away, and a full moon that seemed poised above the eastern horizon with a hilly cay silhouetted against its orange disk like a black-paper cutout. Since events were moving rather too rapidly, I paused within easy sight of the pavilion, not far from the strip of woods that hid the slave quarters.

Brian drew ohs and ahs of admiration from me as he spoke of hunting alligators in East Florida. The hides were valued in Europe. And fearsome beasts they were. Enormous jaws! Slither out of a swamp and take off a man's leg!

When I asked timidly if the hunters hadn't worried about Florida's being Spanish territory, Brian said nobody gave a thought to *that*. The country was vast and mostly empty. He said proudly that he had done some smart trading with the Miami Indians, and promised to present me with a string of rare shells he had acquired.

Brian listened, impressed, to my discussion of Newport galas I had attended. Oh, dozens! Doing justice to the role I had assumed, I made Newport sound rather like an annex of Paris and I made every gathering sound as risqué as that masked ball. Poor young man—he listened raptly. But I took care to turn the conversation back toward where I wanted it to go. Since Brian had mentioned being his father's heir, and would eventually run a plantation, I asked him if the growing conditions wouldn't be very different in Burriana—for that was where the new Roscoe plantation would be, wouldn't it?

He hesitated. "I . . . I shouldn't t-talk about Burriana."

Blinking up at him in the moonlight, I asked, "Why not? Oh!" I drew away. "You've been taken in by that nonsense about my possibly being a Yankee snooper!"

"Of course not! Why, that's just g-gossip spread by jealous women!"

I, leading him on: "But what have they to be jealous about?"

"Your beauty," he blurted.

"Oh, Mr. Roscoe! But really, what does a woman know of all these shufflings of territory? Why, just as you say, all the land along the Gulf of Mexico is a great big swampy mess, and if you Loyalists are brave enough to settle yourselves in Louisiana, I say you deserve the chance. There's land enough, heaven knows. Why, the Purchase lands stretch so far north and so far west, they'll be hundreds of years in getting settled." I made sure to add: "I mean, that's what my father told me."

"Well," said Brian cautiously, "there *is* a certain amount of good, tillable land not far inland along the Gulf Coast." I knew very well there were millions of good acres. "And the swamp along the shore has its own uses."

Now I remembered Mark's dividers touching the map in places where I knew the land was half water. Innocently: "Do tell me, Mr. Roscoe, how is a swamp good for *anything*?"

"Well . . ." He'd become uneasy.

Again I drew back. "If you think I'm snooping . . . !"

"Oh, no!"

"Then what *is* a swamp good for, outside of giving pirates a place to hide?"

Faced by the necessity of either answering or enduring my displeasure, Brian suffered. Suddenly and wildly he plunged. "Those swamps are going to hide our invasion force. Oh . . . this is confidential, please, Miss Downing! But we'll have Cajuns waiting to guide us—Acadians, you know—originally from French Canada—and help us get our horses and cannons through on trails they know. And the Spanish are getting a secret invasion fleet ready for us, and will furnish a thousand men, who'll wear our uniform. And we're recruiting in the West Indies, promising payment in gold. And . . . oh, Miss Downing, when I think that I'm going to be one of the force that marches into Louisiana before Washington knows what's happening, I'm so excited that I—"

He caught himself, turned away in chagrin, kicked at the ground.

I touched his arm. "Dear Mr. Roscoe, is something wrong?"

"I shouldn't have told you! I'm sworn to keep it all secret!"

"But Brian, really, I give you my word I'll never say anything to anyone." My hand crept along his arm. "I never before met a man who was devoted to a great cause and willing to die for it if need be. How can I tell you how much I admire you?"

"You—admire me?"

"Of course a woman admires a brave, dedicated man. And, Brian, how can I help but know about the militia and the cavalry that drill all the time? Those drums and

124

bugles sounding in the woods, and the practice volleys!"
Job Wentworth had assured me that the islanders were
raising a defense force only to guard against a possible
French invasion of the islands.

Brian still watched his foot kick at the earth. "But we
planters' sons—we'll be the officers, of course—we formed
a sworn brotherhood in arms, took an oath that we'd
never . . ."

"But Brian, you've not broken your oath. You've only
shared your oath with me and made me so terribly pleased
and proud! Because I've really come to admire the Loyalists, and I see that back home I was told a lot of lies about
your people. And I would never, never do anything to
spoil our friendship."

"Our friendship?" He said it again, wonderingly. "Our
friendship? Arabella—may I call you Arabella—you're so
very lovely . . ."

"Not lovely," I murmured, "but honest, I hope, and
worthy of a brave man's regard . . ."

My hand rested on his shoulder as I gazed worshipfully
upward into the turmoil that showed on his face. He
couldn't believe what his senses told him. He, a callow
youth, had turned a woman of the world all dewy and
desiring.

I should have stopped there, insisted we return to the
pavilion, whispered we'd speak again, later. But instead I
breathed, "Life is short, and if you're going away to war
I want you to know that I . . . that I truly admire you.. . . ."

I should have known what could happen, once that
mother's boy had been tempted toward the world of passion. His hoarse whisper, "I love you!" frightened me; but
already he had grasped my bare arms where sleeves clung
like tiny balloons to my shoulders. For the first time he
really looked at all of me, and went over the edge. With
a choked cry of abandon he forced me against him with
one hand while the other sought my breasts.

He was pulling me toward the woods! We'd return to
the pavilion much too late and no doubt disheveled—and
Brian was beyond caring! I realized that even though I
was no virgin and my eyes had been opened to the nature
of men, I was also no accomplished seductress. I might
own my share of women's wiles, but I was trying to act
a subtle, wicked part for which I was woefully unsuited.
True, my motives were a patriot's, and if I wanted infor-

mation I had to get it at every opportunity and with every means at my disposal. But in not playing my lure more coyly I had made a bad mistake. What could I do now? I dared not scream. Already my dress was on the point of tearing, and my frantic objections had no effect on the wild eyed young man who had gone almost mad.

Chapter Eight

I heard a rustle and a cough—the kind of cough that tells
people they are not alone. Twisting out of Brian's arms, I
left him glaring at two dim figures who came out of the
woods. The moon revealed they were Bartley Holdridge
and his blackamoor. Holdridge made a polite pretense of
having seen nothing. He looked more dissipated and exhausted than ever, and the little boy still stared beneath
his jeweled turban and panted as though he'd run a long
way.

"Good evening," said Holdridge in that buried voice.
Suave, aristocratic, strange, he was repellently fascinating
—and almost unreal.

As I returned a greeting and Brian muttered something
with bad grace, Holdridge turned to the blackamoor and
snapped his fingers. The boy responded by holding out a
gold snuff box to Brian. He didn't know what to do. Be
bold and take a pinch? Then sneeze and be ridiculous in
my presence? I understood very well and so, I was sure,
did the waiting Holdridge.

Brian refused the snuff. Politely, Holdridge also took
none. At a wave of his hand, the blackamoor closed the
box and tucked it back into his sash.

"Your pardon, Mr. Roscoe," Holdridge now said. "But
I have come a two-day journey to do honor to Miss Downing. Unfortunately I must begin my trip home to Eleuthera
at dawn tomorrow. I had hoped to have a few words with
Miss Downing and may have no other chance. There will
be dancing later. The lady will surely favor you with her
company then. As for me, I do not dance . . . and so," he
finished in his exaggeratedly courtly manner "may I hope
for your indulgence?"

In short, he wanted Brian to go away. Nor could Brian
stand up to the older, far more polished man—especially
when I said not a word to encourage him. It was better

127

for him not to have tried to go further in intimacy—better to have him think he might have succeeded.

"Well, sir?" I demanded of Holdridge when Brian had returned to the pavilion, no doubt to be swept up by his indignant mother. "A few words are yours if you want them, but it's time I returned to my hosts."

He said, "Beautiful as you are, your bonnet has been slightly disarranged by the young man's ardor." He added sardonically, "If I may say so."

"And it offends your esthetic sense?" I didn't touch my bonnet.

"I enjoy talking to a woman of spirit."

"It takes two to make a conversation," I told the strange, cold man.

"So it does. You act as though you've heard some unkind words about me."

"I have."

"What did you hear?"

"That you are wicked."

"Wicked? How?"

"Nobody said how."

"They hardly believe it possible," he murmured. "They're all so unsophisticated. They need time in Europe to refresh themselves on what civilization is all about. But as for conversation. You and I could have wonderful talks together. It's unfortunate that you're merely visiting the islands. I suppose you have some shivering bluenose waiting for you back in Newport, to bear his brats and mend his woolen stockings?"

"I find you insulting, sir!"

"I find you ever more interesting and challenging. And since time is short I'd like you to know me better. The Holdridges are a good old Cambridgeshire family. My own branch was in South Carolina for five generations, having enjoyed the favor of Charles II. The word Carolina is after the Latin for Charles, did you know?"

"You need not educate me, Mr. Holdridge."

His sunken face became almost animated. "I like that retort. You and I might quarrel, but if we knew each other better we'd get along." Watching me, Holdridge adjusted the diamond in his cravat. His jeweled fingers glittered in the moonlight. "As for my estate here in the Bahamas, it's located on the finest soil, and will continue producing richly for generations. You'd like it, I know. And you'd like my house. It's the original seventeenth-century house that my forebears built of English brick, and I transported every brick and re-erected it exactly as it had been. There is no mistletoe in the Bahamas, but I still call my estate by its old name, Mistletoe. None of us is entirely free of sentiment."

"You seem to wish you were."

"Ah! We *could* get along! I was about to say that my house is far too large for a single man, and I spend too much time alone in my library. Nor have I an heir."

"All that is of no importance to me."

"You *do* attract me. You're so different from our Bahamas young women. They're brought up to be a namby-pamby lot. You're very vital. Let alone being very lovely, very shapely, and very brave to wear a gown that flies in the face of local custom. I trust you'll bring it with you when you visit Mistletoe."

"If my hosts decide to visit you, I daresay I'll go with them."

"I'd like to see you at my table in that gown . . . touched by candlelight. Would you oblige me by wearing your hair down? It's beautiful hair, and should be better displayed."

He made me want to pull my scarf across my bosom, but I refrained from showing the man that he disturbed me.

"Come visit with as many others as you wish," he was saying, watching me closely with those heavy-lidded eyes. "I've a long dining table. They may sit along the sides. You'll sit at the end of the table opposite me, where I can feast my eyes on you. You might even find you'd like that as your permanent seat for dining . . . at the foot of my table."

As it is a man's wife who presides at the foot of his table, It seemed I had had a proposal of marriage on five minutes' notice. Significantly I lifted my skirt an inch as though ready to walk away.

But the exhausted-looking man murmured, "Tell me, have you visited other plantation houses besides Wentworth Hall?"

"Not yet."

"When you do, watch closely. See how the planters try to hide their creeping poverty. Take note of draperies and rugs that show wear, and porcelain that has become chipped but is never replaced. See how the house slaves shuffle about indifferently. Slaves take their style from their masters, and they know when their masters have little left to feed their pride. You may see spermaceti candles burning. Be assured it's only when company comes. Many a big Bahamas house is generally lighted with burning rags soaked in pig's fat."

I said acidly, "But of course it's going to be all milk and honey in Burriana, the promised land."

"In time it will. But not for those who go as pioneers. I assume that with your display of female endowments you are husband-hunting? Beware. Almost any local swain would expect to take you to Burriana with him. There, you'd live in a miserable log cabin with panthers and Indians howling outside. But I am wealthy, and I have no thought of deserting my comfortable home. Although I do go often to Europe. My wife could look forward to seasons in Paris, Rome, Madrid."

"That could be interesting," I said, then realized I had not sounded sufficiently sarcastic. Because it really might. But certainly I would never marry a man who reminded me partly of an overbred, cynical courtier and partly of what the slaves called a jumbie—a person who had died but still walked sepulchrally among the living. I snapped, "So you'll let your neighbors fight and die for Burriana while you stay comfortably here?"

He replied, "Of course." The way he said it made me shiver. Then: "Miss Downing, about that intriguing gown you wear. I confess a weakness for the skill and imagination that can be displayed in women's clothing. I like to see a woman dressed as a work of art—like a painting so composed that it gives a single, perfect effect. But you have a fault in your costume. I'll tell you how to turn that fault into a virtue."

So indignant that I was tongue-tied, I watched Holdridge lift the turban off his blackamoor's head and unpin the great ruby that held its folds together. He dropped the cloth back on the boy's wool, and the stunted slave stood motionless with yards of rich cloth falling around him.

"Marvelous as your gown, is, Miss Downing, and so well displayed upon a marvelous figure, you still need a more emphatic focus at the center of attention. A jewel would give you that focus if you wore it . . . here."

He held the ruby to the center of my bodice, where it would accentuate my breasts.

I slapped away his fingers, told him angrily, "I'll thank you to keep your hands to yourself, sir."

"Yes. At any rate, I can hardly give you this ruby and expect you to appear out of the dark wearing a prominent jewel you didn't wear before. I was only sampling the joy I could have in draping and decorating you." He dropped the ruby into his pocket. "By the way, do I understand you've not yet begun to take dictation from Job Wentworth? We're all looking forward to reading that history of the Bahamas."

"Mr. Wentworth will begin next week." I lifted my skirt very definitely.

Holdridge bowed. "Miss Downing, do visit me at Mistletoe. I promise you elegant quarters, elegant food, elegant wines, elegant living."

I replied as I turned away: "Mr. Holdridge, *do* have a pleasant trip home."

When I re-entered the huge, striped pavilion, I saw Brian Roscoe talking to a girl who was precisely the type I'd imagined his mother would want for him—blank and milky and well covered. He gave me a despairing glance. I smiled noncommittally at his glaring parents and went to pass a few words with Job, who at least knew me only by my usual words and manner.

For a while I remained shaken, and badly worried over whether I had seemed ridiculous. But, to my great relief, I found the situation could be saved. A planter—not a planter's son!—drifted to me with a fatherly smile to ask if I had ever visited the Carolinas. Another, of equal dignity, thereupon thought it time to stand equally close. I tried to let them do the talking. In fact it was interesting to hear again of the old life on the Southern plantations, where—they said—a man could spend his time in horse talk and playing billiards or piquet, and laughing slaves brought pitchers of toddy through gardens full of Cherokee roses.

When I did speak, I made sure to say that we Northern people simply didn't know *anything* about the delightful South and its people. I tried to show that my Yankee-ness might not go deep. This instinct worked, at least with men old enough to be Brian's father. They competed to drive insects away from me. They brought two slaves to keep me cool with huge palm-leaf fans. With half-humorous gallantry they paid their respects to youth and beauty, as older men in Newport—and everywhere—always will. A girl is supposed to believe she is safe with an older man because he may *look* but he won't *touch*. At the age of fifteen, trapped against a fence behind weigela bushes, I had learned better. But of course it was the older men who kept up a business correspondence with various parts of the United States; so I tried to assess each of my graying friends as a possible letter carrier, while younger men, looking annoyed, remembered their Southern manners and did not push ahead of the old.

When everyone was full of food and drink and neighborliness, and Mark and the red-headed girl seemed to chat themselves out, we all strolled to the big house for the ball. When we ladies went to freshen up, the red-headed girl treated me to a cold appraisal that I returned in kind, for we didn't like each other. I could feel it. Since I had met everybody I must have met her . . . yes, she was the Trumbull daughter, Rosemary, and nature had given her a striking combination of red hair and green eyes, to say nothing of an excellent figure that her pure-white virginal gown with many-cuffed sleeves *à la mameluck,* however modest as to neckline, displayed very nicely.

Back in the ballroom, the musicians struck up a stately pavanne, as much a procession as a dance. It let us honor Job by parading past him, just as had been done long ago in the courts of Europe, when courtiers and their ladies paraded past a king. The blind man, in an armchair, was much gratified.

Later came a quadrille, and then dignity gave way to merriment as everyone sampled a fresh tureen of syllabub. It's a Carolina specialty brought from England, consisting of wine frothed up with whipped cream and sugar; it's bad for the figure but it's delicious. I drew much attention from an elderly gentleman who kept telling me what a rascal he was, but never explained what he meant. Then I chatted with four young men at once, but resisted all suggestions to stroll outside; oh no, the insects out there were dreadful!

The next dance was a type of minuet in which ladies are handed along from partner to partner and a few words may be exchanged as one twirls and bobs about. Poor Brian and I were ill-matched partners. Otherwise, I found it most enjoyable, and good for my self-confidence, to smile

132

slightly and say little to a changing array of interested male faces.

Inevitably I became Mark's partner. For a moment we danced in a searching silence, for the plane on which we met was always in question—friends or foes, fighters or lovers? At length I innocently asked him why there had been so much shooting in the woods. Soldiers?

He returned, "You don't hear soldiers. You hear hunters. The woods are full of chickcharnies."

So he was back to his unsmiling banter! I said, "I don't believe in chickcharnies." They are Bahamian goblins.

"They are real," Mark said. "But nobody knows what they look like. We fire when they squeak from the bushes, but we haven't hit one yet."

"But so much shooting?"

"So many chickcharnies."

"If you don't want to explain the shooting, very well. But I am not a child, Captain Wentworth."

"No child could fill that dress the way you fill it, my dear."

"I am about to pass you on to Miss Trumbull. Don't waste all your compliments on me. Save some for her." I twirled beneath his uplifted arm and bobbed away, trailing my scarf airily. But I wondered at the place of Rosemary Trumbull in his life.

I danced with others in a Schottishe, a breathless galop, an Allemande. Then came that new dance, the waltz, in which partners nearly embrace each other. It caused concern among the older people, but the younger ones were all for it.

The Bahamians did not follow the custom of having men write their names on ladies' cards to claim dances. Three men came at me at once, eager to engage me in that daring modern dance in which you did *not* change partners. But Mark Wentworth stepped ahead of them. "May I have the pleasure, Miss Downing?" His arm caught me around the waist.

I marveled at the strength of the arm that swept me out upon the floor, and marveled too at how so big a man could be so light on his feet. Unwilling to be pleasant, I said, "The Newport dancing masters say a distance of six inches must be kept between waltzers."

"In Boston it's a foot. But since I don't think there's a dancing master in the entire Bahamas . . ." He pulled me closer. "Will you not gaze at me adoringly? Well then, I can admire your hair. It's especially lovely tonight."

"I thought you were partial to red hair."

"It's pretty, and it indicates a sprightly temperament."

Rosemary Trumbull was waltzing with a lanky young islander who also seemed to like red hair. But she kept darting glances our way. I had noticed that all the men treated her with deference. Were the Trumbulls, then, of noble English blood? Or . . . but I couldn't imagine what the reason might be, nor why Rosemary carried herself with a certain aloofness, as though she were set apart.

"So red hair indicates a sprightly temperament?" I asked as we waltzed. "Is there a language of hair color? What about dark-haired women? You must have met many in France."

"I did."

"And you found out—?"

"That dark hair indicates a passionate and willing nature."

I grew angry at the remark, then angry at myself for being angry. French charmers, black-haired wenches . . . what did I care?

Then I went breathless. Mark had come so close that his starched shirt ruffles tickled my bare skin. Besides a flush, my traitorous body provided another reaction that certainly showed through my clinging bodice, and I could only hope it would go away before anyone saw.

Mark was out to annoy me. "But as for golden-haired women, folklore tells us they are always virtuous."

The beast! "I'll slap you before all these people!"

"You'd earn the gratitude of the ladies. They'd have something to talk about for a month."

I glared, recovered my poise. Green eyes watched us, and I wasn't going to let Rosemary Trumbull think there was friction between Mark and me. I saw nothing sprightly about her. I guessed her to be possessive and determined —and didn't think it had anything to do with the color of her hair.

"By the way," Mark said as we whirled amid the other whirling couples, "I was going between the pavilion and the house, earlier this evening, and saw you out in the moonlight with Brian Roscoe. He looked ready to have himself baked and served up to you with an apple in his mouth."

"Indeed!"

"Later he returned to the pavilion alone, looking disorganized. A few minutes later, you came in, straightening your bonnet. What happened?"

"You surely aren't interested in my doings with other men?"

"That's a leading question, Miss Downing. But I'm curious about this new Arabella, the *femme fatale*. Considering that you come from Newport, Rhode Island, you do quite well. But you need practice. I've seen women in Paris who'd make you look like a blushing schoolgirl."

"Then kindly leave for Paris tomorrow and stay there."

"Happens I'll be off to Charleston soon. Will that do?"

"Anyplace will do as long as you never come back."

Mark circled with me, one-two-three, one-two-three, but now there was really a foot of air between us. And there was challenge. And there was wariness. And, despite sharp words, there was the heat of desire and longing. All the mixed-up anger-and-passion had returned to me. Mark's sudden deep breath told he felt it too.

A mask of hardness came over his face. His voice whipped as he said, "You're still spying."

"I don't know what you mean."

"You do know what I mean. Your gown. Your suddenly assumed man-gathering ways. Very well! Write to your aunt. Tell her the younger Wentworth is an impossible boor. I promise I'll pass that on to her. But I warn you for the second time, Arabella, that if you want your aunt to receive your letters, say nothing of Loyalist plans. I don't know if you tempted Brian Roscoe into telling you secrets. I'm sure you tried. But whatever you may dazzle some youngster into revealing . . . or whatever you may tease any other man into whispering into your shell-like ear . . . remember, it never will reach the United States."

We whirled and dipped, our eyes locked in challenge. My heart beat rapidly in frustration and despair.

"I see through you, Arabella. I suggest you modify your bodice and abandon your plan." The music ended. Mark bowed me to a seat, asked me to excuse him, and returned to Green Eyes.

135

Chapter Nine

Faint grayness showed on the eastern horizon before the ball ended. I went wearily to bed, but lay sleepless. Checkmated! Worst of all, I could not banish the memories that had caught up with me in the closing moments of that fateful waltz. Damn Mark! He didn't own me! But I had come to know how much of me *was* owned by that man.

The great star Venus was rising just ahead of the sun. It seemed to mock me as it peered into my window. I turned my back on it and at last fell asleep.

Mary wakened me in time for a very late breakfast-for-fifty that I felt obliged to attend. Rosemary Trumbull was there, observing me. Mark was not. After two hours of sleep he had gone off with a party of dedicated hunters to shoot the little island deer. Hearing this, I came wide awake. With Mark out of the way, I still might be able to do something for my country.

I persuaded Mary to put away the silly parasol. At ease and becomingly outdoorsy in a wide-brimmed straw hat and a sufficiently high-necked, pale yellow, red-striped dress —chosen because its light muslin would cling on that breezy day—I chatted with a group of guests as we all walked to a nearby strip of beach. I attempted no *femme fatale* maneuvers. In fact, with a scarf tied under my chin and around my hat, bending its sides upward, I felt more dashing than sultry. I was single, I was approachable, everyone knew I came of good family, and I was, so to speak, the new girl in town. Add an arangement of my hair that allowed a few long strands to escape and whisk about . . . it should be sufficient.

Also I knew I'd be the center of attention because the young men were going to race their horses on the beach and I, as guest of honor, was to be the judge. I called the winners as fairly as I could, standing close to the finish

137

line, laughing and dodging as clods of hard sand flew off the horses' hoofs.

Declaring Brian Roscoe the winner of the last race, I received his faint, guilty smile. But I'd been startled at the way that race had been run. Controlling their mounts with their left hands while they galloped like fiends, those reckless horsemen leaned far out and cut with sticks—that could have been sabers—at invisible foes in an imaginary battle. "Take that, you Fed!" they shouted, meaning a Federal soldier. And: "Put your head under your arm and take it to Thomas Jefferson!" We ladies didn't have to pretend to shudder. You could almost see the blood!

The races done, we turned to the buffet that Tibbal had set up beneath an awning. It was then that I noticed the sunny, sun-browned man named Macgillivray. He stood alone, nourishing himself, at the end of a long table, and a certain look passed between us. I don't know how to describe it save just that way; it's a certain look that a woman gives a man and a man gives a woman.

I waited, chatted, flirted a bit with men who fed me buttered turtle and gumbo. But the seagoing, solitary man was the one I wanted. Idly I strolled along the edge of the water, stopping here and there to pick up a bit of coral or a pretty cowry shell. When I was off from the others—

"Donal Macgillivray at your service, ma'am," said a pleasantly burred voice. "I present meself since no one had me name on his tongue last night."

I smiled to the pure Scottish face. "I'm pleased to know you at last. But I've wondered why we haven't met."

Ruefulness deepened the tiny wrinkles around eyes that were a lighter blue than mine; Scotch blue, of course. "Why, Miss Downing, I'm not gentry, ye ken. Squire Wentworth said to come and fill my craw wi' goodies, but it was not for me to meet the Yankee lady o' quality."

"Really, Mr. Macgillivray, that was a shame." I meant it. "You're a seaman?" I hazarded.

"That I am, and pickled in salt."

"But more than a foretopman, I think?"

"We're careless about captain's papers i' the islands, ma'am, but I do own and run the *Grappler*. She's a salvage schooner, and if you care to squint, you can just see her out yonder, near the spoutin' reef. We're searchin' beneath an old wreck to see what heavy metal may have dropped through her timbers into the sand. A salvor is a scavenger, y'see."

"A scavenger?"

"A-weel, the wrecker, now, the wrecker skims a new wreck and runs, and never gives the Crown its lawful share. The salvor works openly on an old wreck, more likely, and finds what's left over. Sometimes it's good."

"Treasure?"

"I'm waitin' to find it. If I get rich, I'll be a gentleman. Ye look at me fashed?" He meant puzzled. "Ye make money, ye build a big house, and the gentry welcome ye to their company."

I could see that "gentry" was a sore point with Macgillivray. I was about to ask him if he was well acquainted with the Wentworths when he continued, as he ambled along with me: "Right now I'm on contract with Squire Wentworth. He buys all of a"—the sandy man hesitated—"all of a particular kind of metal I bring up. But never mind!" He waved away salvage with a blunt-fingered hand. "I'm talkin' at last to the lady who brings men around her like bees to honey. And bein' close to you, and breathin' of your sweetness, I tell meself, They can keep the Macgillivray off in a corner, but he turns out the luckiest mon of all."

"Now really! I'm nothing but a Yankee, and tolerated only because I'm the Wentworths' guest."

"*Nothing* but a Yankee? I'm most pleased to have you exactly that. What Scot would be on England's side? Let alone that I came to live in York State ten years ago, straight from the heather, and that makes me summat of a Yank too, eh? Aweel, I've learnt to tolerate the English. But"—he frowned—"not since the day of Bonnie Prince Charlie in '45—nay, not since the day of Robert Bruce lang ago—has a Macgillivray of Dunmaglass not wished to murder the English king." He leaned close, winked. "Aye, but these aren't real English here anyhow, these Loyalists. They're American but won't say it. For what's the blether between patriot and Loyalist but the blether between two kinds of Americans, by now?"

"I see." In a sense, he was right.

"Still, ma'am, I was born across the sea. So I take no side in the family bickering. I stick to my trade and may be no gentleman, but does any other man try me, he'll find the Macgillivray is a man for a' that."

139

"Why, Mr. Macgillivray, I run an ironworks when I'm at home. I've never thought it lowers anyone to be in trade."

"An ironworks, now! You're a most uncommon and charmin' lady."

"And you're a most charming and unusual man." Even though a bit childish, I thought. But this hearty Scot ran a seaworthy schooner. . . .

"Charmin', say ye?" He chuckled hugely. "I'll tell ye what my wife Fiona used to say o' me. 'You're a bold and lovin' man, Macgillivray,' she said, 'and a laughing man do you but hold your temper, and you're a—' He caught himself. "Now, there was somethin' else Fiona told me, and she had reason to know, that I'll not say to a lady I've but recent met; but it's no disgrace to a man to be what Fiona called me." He winked joyously. He meant passionate, I was sure.

"You've lost your wife?"

"Aye. But a man's a man still, and a blue-eyed woman is always a proper woman for a Scot to admire."

I was pleased to be able to say, "My ancestors came from Cumberland, right on the border."

"Right across from Scotland! I knew it! Ah, and there's a Scot or two in your line, I can see!" He beamed upon me. Then, looking toward the outdoor buffet; "Now, I'm fresh off the *Grappler,* where we live mostly on salt pork and fish, and the smell o' Wentworth's vittles is makin' my mouth water. Come with me to that wee buffet that gives the gentry strength to watch horses running."

Another local wild boar had been baked and sliced—I wished it hadn't had a New England apple in its mouth! All in all, the "wee" buffet could have fed a small army. Macgillivray did justice to everything. As for me, I allowed curiosity to overcome delicacy and had a fine rum drink that was three-quarters fruit juices, topped with mint. It had been invented in Jamaica and was called a planter's punch. Eager men were ready to push ahead of Macgillivray and wait on me, but I pointedly stayed with him despite certain glares and mutters to which he returned his cheerful—and defiant—grin.

While we sipped, I asked in as idle a tone as I could manage: "Isn't it bothersome to be always anchored over the reefs? Don't you go off on trips sometimes?"

"Oh aye, I've fetched across twice to Europe wi' loads o' cotton when the price was right."

I hoped I was hiding my excitement. The *Grappler* might be small but she was fully seaworthy, and Newport, Rhode Island, was certainly within her range!

At last I murmured that, since I was the guest of honor, I really should be affable to the other guests. Macgillivray said he agreed it would be manners, and all he wanted was that I should be twice as affable to him, for he'd taken a great "warm" to me. At any rate, Job Wentworth sent for him, so we parted. I didn't lack for male company. But always, with a glance here and a smile there, I let Macgillivray know we'd talk again.

Luck was with me in another way. As I passed by old Job and the Scot, on another man's arm, Job, not aware of me, raised his voice.

"Yes, yes," he said testily. "I know you can't guarantee there'll be cannon and cannonballs down in the sand. But England can't supply all we need and we must have them, man, especially the six-pounders."

He meant cannon that fired a six-pound iron ball; light guns that could be mounted on wheels and bring death secretly through a Louisiana swamp. I walked on, pretending to have heard nothing. But cannon would certainly be mentioned in my letter along with the Cajun guides, the cavalry charge, and all the rest.

We entered a time of yawning. Guests drifted off to the house or the moored boats to take naps. Freed at last from a group of ladies who had determined it would be Christian to be cordial to me, I wandered to a shady spot out of sight. I tossed crumbs to tiny, orange-colored lizards and waited, knowing I'd not be long alone.

A rustle in the bushes. A burred and hearty voice: "I watched ye, lass, and thought you'd not be displeasured if I followed."

"I'm far more pleasured than displeasured," I said, smiling up into Donal Macgillivray's open face. That bold and loving man, that laughing man, that man who kept a temper somewhere—I knew very well how deeply he was attracted by me. He knew very well I was leading him on.

And now every word I said—every smile, every hint or half-promise—would be vital in persuading Macgillivray to carry my letter. And I certainly didn't have money enough to pay him for voyaging three thousand miles. All I had to give was myself. It amounted to selling myself, and I grew frightened and ashamed. Or would Donal carry my letter without payment, merely because it was so important? I didn't know . . . but I did know that his eyes blazed with an emotion that had come very near the surface. Little could hide on that face.

I was ready to blurt out my need for a courier, but stopped. I must be patient and very, very careful, for I couldn't tell which way Donal's sympathies lay in the Burriana matter. So I asked him about lizards and land crabs and the amazing, hungry creatures that lived on the reef. He was willing enough and he knew a great deal; but somehow, with every word, he signaled the "warm" he had taken.

Idly I said I had met a most charming Miss Trumbull. Did Donal know her?

"The Trumbull lass? Aye, though it's not a near knowing, for I'm not o' the gentry, you'll remember."

"I guess Mark Wentworth has known her all her life."

A shrewd glance told me I had betrayed my interest in Mark. "Aye, he's watched her grow up into marryin' age."

"Marriage must be on the girls' minds a good deal around here, because I can see there are more young women than young men."

"So there be, and worryin' the more that a batch o' young hot heads will get themselves killed in Louisiana. But Miss Trumbull has little worry."

"Because she's so attractive?"

" 'Tis more of a muckle than that. Her father and Job Wentworth would mightily like to see the two married, and they'll announce they're bespoke one o' these days, or so goes my guess."

Something hurt in my bosom as I said, "They'd make a good-looking couple."

"Good-lookin', aye, but position and rank is what that hoity-toity lass is after."

"What do you mean?"

Donal rubbed his cheek thoughtfully, watching me. " 'Tis too early to talk. There's many a slip 'twixt the cup and the lip, and many a league 'twixt San Isidro and New Orleans, nor do I fancy that yon Mr. Jefferson is sleeping."

He had not answered my question. But I told myself sternly that I was *not* more than casually interested in Mark's marriage plans. Remembering that he had once

142

offered to marry me, I realized how abhorrent it must have been for him to face giving up his darling—and no doubt virtuous—Rosemary because he had unwisely raped someone else. But he'd had his gentleman's code, that also worked insolently backward, and he'd canceled the offer soon enough! How forced and insincere his proposal to me had been! How humiliating it had been to be offered marriage under such conditions! Well, I'd never let him touch me again. Of that I was sure.

"You're frowning," Donal said, peering, his face close to mine.

"Oh . . . it's only the heat. Well . . . I was thinking, now that I've been presented to society I might have more time to myself. I want to see more of the countryside and the seashore."

"Do ye? Then let me show you the sights, for I know them well. Now, a bit down the shore is a rare fine spot for a picnic. It's called the Pirate's House."

"Sound's interesting."

"Then we'll go and look . . . eh? Ye ken . . . the pirate's not been at home for a hundred years?"

He was telling me we'd be alone. I had to gulp before I asked, as I thought I should, "Would it be proper?"

"Would anyone have to know?" he returned, breathing hard.

"Of course I'd take my maid along." I knew I had better not fly in the face of convention too openly.

His face fell. "Your maid it is, then." He winked. "I'll bring wine and get her drunk," he said with a boy's glee.

We understood each other, and my flush—that old, helpless flush—told my doubt and shame. He interpreted it differently and bent to kiss me, but I drew away, taking little notice. I told him that Mr. Wentworth wanted to start dictating his history the next day, and I thought I should work a week with old Job before taking a day off. This was quite true and rather handy, since it would make Donal wait for me and whet his desire.

He sighed, " 'Twill be the longest week I ever lived. But a week from today at an hour before noon—can it be so, Miss Arabella?"

I nodded. He cheered up. "I'll come in my wee work sloop to meet you." He described a nearby place on the shore where Mary and I could embark. That we would not be seen went unsaid; but it was well understood.

"Au revoir till then," I said, giving him my hand. I thought him likable, but I felt no real attraction. Nevertheless, for the sake of the United States, as I walked away I turned and confirmed our assignation with a smile.

The hunting party returned with deer. The guests began to leave, and I was properly at hand with Job, Lavinia, and Mark to say good-bye and thank them for coming to my reception. Meanwhile, hard-muscled Gumry was managing a crew that took down the pavilion and rolled it up. I noticed how my Mary stayed nearby, admiring him, speaking to him when she could. It was the first time I had seen her take more than passing notice of a man, and I was glad to see she had overcome the soul scars that her bitter early experience with men must have left within her.

Lavinia, taking me aside, fluttered and evaded and in the middle of it all had a headachy misery. But at last she came to her point and I promised I would not order any more shocking gowns. I had grown fond of silly old Lavinia, and also it had occurred to me that the less tension I caused at Wentworth Hall, the more I'd be able to walk about at my will and connive against the Tory traitors.

Mark had *not* checkmated me, and fate, which had supplied Donal Macgillivray, was playing into my hands.

Once again, next morning, I squeezed into the sedan chair with old Job and four men carried us to the rocky point. This time a box of reference books and notes was strapped to the top of the chair. Also I took along my traveler's writing kit and a bundle of quills, and, as always, the quiet, well-dressed Tibbal walked attentively alongside.

When Job felt the bearers slipping on an abrupt slope, he told me: "It's all loose shells, here. They show where the sea level once was higher. The Arawaks made their arrowheads out of sharp bits of oyster shell." He added reminiscently, "I used fine steel arrowheads your father once made for me."

After some time of climbing and sliding along the tumble of ridges, we found the windbreak of coral rocks. As Tibbal made his master comfortable in the shade of sea grape, I noticed that the recent moonlight had brought some of the guests out there. I saw a hairpin, an empty bottle. On the surface, the Bahamas Loyalists were even more respectable than the Newport patriot gentry. But in Newport we had our masked balls, while here they had their picnics.

"Are you ready, Arabella?"

"Quite ready, sir."

Job gazed—or seemed to gaze—out across the sea, and listened a moment to the thunder of waves that rolled through unseen caverns. He said, "I'd gotten halfway through the history when my sight left me. Those were written words and these will be dictated. There'll be a difference, so I'll make a fresh start."

I thought it odd, for Job hardly seemed in condition to take on the extra labor. But I dipped my quill, and my little pothooks and slants and dots flowed across the notebook as he began:

"Like all the rest of North America and South America, the Bahama Islands remained unknown to Europeans until the fateful year 1492. It was then, on the 12th of October by the old calendar, that Christopher Columbus made his famous landfall on San Salvador. But the great navigator thought the Bahamas were islands off the coast of Japan. When he sailed on and found a much larger island, Cuba, he thought he had reached Japan at last. Of course, he really had found islands of the New World. Within a few years, Spanish settlements had been established on Cuba and the adjacent island of Hispaniola. But for some years the Bahamas remained almost unexplored."

Pausing, Job asked, "Am I going too quickly?"

"No, sir," I replied. "I have every word."

"Do you have it exactly as I said it?"

"Yes, indeed."

He snapped suspiciously, "Read it back to me."

When I read it all back without any trouble, his face cleared. "Very good! And I daresay you're the only person who can read those notes, within hundreds of miles?"

I did not then understand the significance of the question. I thought Job was only glorying in being exclusive, as he did with his sedan chair.

"No doubt you'd go a long way to find anyone who can read or write shorthand beside myself," I told him, and he seemed oddly satisfied.

Now we settled down to work. It was pleasant out there, high above the sea's palette of shifting colors, the *Grappler* just visible, far out, and a fishing boat or two nearby. A

145

covey of red-legged thrushes hovered about in their inquisitive way, taking shelter in the dangerous-looking plant called Spanish bayonet.

I filled my notebook with the story of how the early settlers soon killed off the Indians of Hispaniola and Cuba, who could not stand the dreadful labor in the silver mines. It was then that the Bahamas were really explored, but only for the sake of bringing in shiploads of gentle Arawaks. Poor Indians! They believed that the souls of their ancestors had gone to live in a paradise to the south, and expected to have a joyful reunion with their ghosts. Instead, they too died in the mines. The labor problem was solved by the importation of black slaves from Africa. Thus the American slave trade began.

I grew puzzled at Job's strange procedure. He dictated two chapters a day. The first went at a fast pace. The second went slowly. Job often paused, tapping the fingers of his left hand into his right hand in the oddest way. Was it an aid to thought? Perhaps. But, in that case, why did he tap his hand only when he dictated his second chapter, never when he dictated the first?

I would read back the day's dictation. He never made changes in the first chapter. In fact, he'd seem impatient for me to get through with it. But he took every second chapter and twisted the words this way and that. Tapping his hand, muttering inaudibly to himself, he would take what *I* thought a perfectly good sentence and change it into something awkward, even ungrammatical. This was very strange, for Job was a graduate of Harvard College.

Each evening, back in my room, I transcribed my shorthand notes into plain English, being careful to have each word exactly right. I was at this work, one evening, when Job arrived on Tibbal's arm. He asked me how I was progressing.

"I've very nearly finished transcribing, sir."

"Excellent. You'll read it all once more to me, tonight, and I'll send it off."

"Are you sending it to a publisher in London?"

The blind man made a nervous start. "Don't you know I send my history to Colonel Burr in New Orleans?"

Colonel Burr in New Orleans! "I didn't know, sir."

"Mark should have told you." But I thought it more likely that Job had preferred to say nothing of the matter till now. "Well, my friend Burr is the learned descendant

146

of a learned family. His grandfather was the well-known cleric, Jonathan Edwards, and his father was president of New Jersey College, in Princeton. I'm greatly obliged to Burr for the corrections and notes he'll provide. He's a fine man. They try to make a traitor out of him, but he's perfectly well entitled to go into the West and buy up land."

"I see." But I saw nothing but treachery.

While I read the first section of the history aloud, Mark sat in Job's study with us and glowered at me from a shadowed corner. Time and again—always at an even-numbered chapter, the second chapter of a day's work—either Job or Mark would ask me to read very slowly. While I read, Job tapped his hand. Mark tapped his knee. At last both were satisfied. Tibbal came with waterproof oilskin wrappings and sealing wax, and carefully packed the pages. Mark addressed the parcel to Colonel Aaron Burr at the Hotel Phillipe in New Orleans.

Mark took the parcel to a trading vessel that lay at the wharf—its crew Loyalist to a man, I was sure. Tibbal escorted Job upstairs to bed. Settling myself in the library, I read Walter Scott's *The Lay of the Last Minstrel*, which lately arrived from London. I was lost in the long-ago when something began to nag at the back of my mind.

Why had Job so often tapped his hand when dictating a second chapter? And Mark, tapping his knee . . . it must have been for the same unknown reason.

The answer lurked in my mind but I could not find it. I went to bed. But I wakened, found myself again looking out at stars that rode above the first faint grayness in the east. All that tapping . . . tapping . . .

As though counting?

But what could a blind man have been counting while he dictated thousands of words?

Why . . . just that! *Words!*

Now I remembered a code that merchants use in communicating confidential information about prices and supplies. Agreeing in advance with an agent, they'd send an innocent-seeming letter; but the agent would know he had to get a message contained in, say, every fifth word.

I must try it. Daylight found me writing: "Perhaps I ought to buy a few ribbons and more cloth for summer dresses. Cotton dresses, I think." The merest woman chat-

147

ter? But an agent who checked off every fifth word would be told: "Buy . . . more . . . cotton."

Of course, it could be every third word or every tenth word, for example. Or the sequence could be: third—sixth—ninth—twelfth—or any other, regular or irregular. I was sure that Job Wentworth and Aaron Burr had arranged some elaborate, tricky sequence of words that would be almost impossible for anyone else to untangle. Also, they could have arranged to change the sequence with every packet of papers, to further confuse meddlers and spies.

No wonder Job had spent so much effort in turning good sentences into bad ones. Grammar didn't matter. What mattered was to get the key words exactly in the right places. Then, if any snooper got hold of the history on its way to New Orleans, all he'd be able to make of it was a history of the Bahamas. But for Aaron Burr the "history" was a steady stream of secret, valuable information—concerning how many cannon were ready, I supposed, and how the militia's training went, and what news might have come from Havana or Madrid. And, as the plans for the attack on Louisiana progressed, Burr's "corrections" to the history could carry code messages back to Job—to be read to him by Mark or another trusted person.

It occurred to me that the entire area of the Gulf Coast and even the Bahamas might harbor many spies. Some might be Thomas Jefferson's. But they didn't know me and I didn't know them. I must work alone. Well, I would, and damn Mark Wentworth if he thought he could scare me or stop me!

Moreover, I still had my shorthand notes. Working cautiously, I could make my own secret transcription of the entire two-faced history. Certainly they used codes and ciphers in the State Department in Washington. They'd have men who could break Job's code. The old problem remained; how was I to get a letter to Washington? But I was going to meet Donal Macgillivray the next day, and a tingling in my bosom and a shivering in my thighs gave me reason to believe he would help me. If I persuaded him.

I reached into the drawer where I kept my notebooks. They were gone.

I searched everywhere. But my notebooks had been taken away and I bitterly suspected they'd been burned.

Damn Mark Wentworth for being as smart as I! I tried

not to stamp my feet as I went down to breakfast; I was that angry. When Mark suggested I try the mushroom omelette I knew why he was being so polite, and I think he understood when I glared the rage that filled my heart.

"I'm not hungry," I said.

That day I wrote two letters.

One told Aunt Patience about my wonderful reception and ball, and my "darling" gown. I also spent a page in comparing the local thrushes with our own Northern chickadees, who would eat out of your hand and sit on your shoulder. Could I be more innocent?

The other letter, which Mark would never see, was also addressed to Aunt Patience. It covered all I knew about the Burr-Loyalist plot . . . the conniving with the Spanish . . . the cannon. The cavalry. The Cajuns waiting as guides. The foot soldiers being recruited, to be paid, apparently, from some secret fund. All this must be brought to Thomas Hedrick if he could be found. Or, better yet, to James Madison, who was Secretary of State. Or, best of all, hand my letter to Mr. Jefferson himself. I thought: If anyone could make her way into the White House, Aunt Patience could!

In this letter I also said I hoped an agent could be posted to intercept parcels of manuscript that came to Aaron Burr at the Hotel Phillippe in New Orleans. It would be most useful if the agent copied every second chapter of that manuscript, exactly, word by word. I told why.

There! Let Mark threaten me! Let him keep me prisoner on San Isidro! That one letter might insure that Burriana never would exist.

I folded the letter tight and small, sewed it into the hem of a light linen jacket I intended to wear when I visited the Pirate's House with a man who wanted me . . . and who certainly would listen when I told what I wanted of him.

Chapter Ten

Plum rose grew here and there in poor soil near the shore, reminding me of the lower-growing shore rose of New England. In Rhode Island we called the fruit rose hips, not rose plums. But I told Lavinia I was sure it would make the same kind of preserves.

So we went off to pick rose plums, Mary and I, where they grew thickly a quarter-mile down the shore. Soon enough, a small sloop came slipping along, and Donal Macgillivray waved happily from his seat at the tiller.

As he took us aboard, he gave me a quizzical lift of those sandy briar patches that were his brows. "It's reemarkable to have a proper lady aboard this wee work sloop o' mine. Can it be that the lady has found a fondness for a rough seaman?"

I only smiled beneath my straw bonnet, and pulled my blue linen jacket around me to ward off the sun. Seated on a mat near the bow, I kept Mary between Donal and myself.

In time he produced a barnacle-spotted bottle of Madeira. He urged Mary to drink plenty of it, and winked at me. But I only asked him to anchor where the clear water revealed a coral garden. He had a bucket with a glass bottom, and when you pushed the glass just beneath the surface, it took away the ripples and gave you a window into a fantastic world. I saw great branching arms and domes of red and white and yellow coral, and little fish swarming all over, dressed in the most fantastic hues. Schools of silver fry turned all together, flashing tiny lightnings through sunlight that penetrated down and down, so that we seemed suspended in air over a grotesque landscape rather than floating in water.

"It wouldn't do for you to be away too long," said Donal anxiously.

I nodded, glad that Mary and I at least had a small

basket of beach plums to show. Donal brought up the anchor. Again we watched the shore slide gently backward. In some places you couldn't tell what was shore and what was sea because the land was edged with mangroves. I wouldn't have believed that trees can grow in salt water, but there was the dense, low forest standing in brine on stilted roots.

Donal pointed out the ruins of stone huts where the rich pirate had kept his slaves. Nearby we saw the remnants of an orange grove, planted more recently. As Donal gybed the sloop around and headed her into a small bay, we saw the ruin of a great house. Its wooden roof had long since fallen in, and large trees reared from inside above the jagged walls of coral rock on which orchids made spots like flame amid the creeping greenery. I noticed the vestiges of a road that ran back from the sea, and imagined free-booters in jackboots swaggering about the grounds, long ago.

Macgillivray hauled up the sloop's centerboard, anchored her almost on the beach. I rode his broad back ashore. Mary lifted her skirt and waded. I think she noticed how Donal moved his hands beneath my thighs.

In that deserted place he showed us pits, lined with blackened stone, where great feasts of lobster, turtle, oysters, and fish had been cooked in wet seaweed. Very like a New England clambake, save that the local *langouste* wasn't real lobster and didn't have those big, meat-packed claws.

Donal showed us other holes that treasure-seekers had dug. Chuckling, he said everyone thought that where a pirate had lived, there had to be buried treasure. Then we had the lunch that the *Grappler's* rough-and-ready cook had packed, and fresh raw oysters that Donal plucked from exposed mangrove roots. All this with barely restrained impatience, as though the real feast were yet to come. And I had been unsteady ever since I had felt his hands upon my upper legs, and the strength of his back, and his muscles rolling against my bosom, and the clean scent of his sun-bleached hair.

We were silent where we sat on a bit of old coral-block wall. Donal looked significantly at Mary Crow—who had taken one drink only—and again at me. His unspoken words blazed in his eyes.

I took a deep breath, gathered my courage. "Mary dear,"

152

I said, "it would be so nice to have one of those oranges we saw. Will you get me one?"

She looked along the shore. The orange grove was far out of sight. "Yes'm," she said.

"And Mary, you may . . . you may stay there awhile . . . eat some oranges . . . I know you'll enjoy them . . . and . . . and take an hour for yourself. Or an hour and a half. You can gauge the time by the sun."

Macgillivray put in: "There's a wee shallow pool in the rocks where you can have a dip. Go right along the beach and you'll find it."

"Yes, do," I said. "A dip will refresh you."

I knew Mary was always ready to please me. But never before had I asked her to leave me alone with a man.

"Watch sun," said my faithful Mary, rising, her face as devoid of expression as a bronze mask. There was something over-vigorous in her walk as she proceeded down the beach, her black braids bouncing. When she moved out of sight, the woods and the ruined house seemed full of enormous loneliness, while the glistening water lay empty as far as the eye could see.

Quickly I told Donal: "I want to speak to you about a very great favor you might be able to do me. I could only ask such a favor of a—a real friend."

"I hope I'm that, lass, for there's no woman since Fiona died that made me feel warmer i' the heart."

"But it's a secret."

"It's safe as the grave wi' me."

I slipped out of my linen jacket, gave it to him. "Feel here, in the hem."

"Here? Papers, by the crinkle of 'em."

"It's a letter. You see, they've been reading my mail. . . ."

"Well, y'know, lass, they've big plans they don't want spoiled, and I've heard they're suspicious o' Wentworth's Yankee."

"I know, Donal, and they've reason." I hesitated, bit my lip, hoped Donal would not betray me. "I've heard of matters that should be known in Washington, and I want to send that information for my country's sake."

"Ah! I told Wentworth I take no side i' the quarrel."

"Well . . . I'd hoped . . . you'd side with me."

"I've a powerful yearnin' to do that, but . . ."

153

"I mean, you have a seagoing vessel. And so you could—"

"Ah, I can see my ship might be of use to you. But let Loyalist fight patriot. I'm out o' the argle-bargle."

My heart sank. But still I'd hardly yet tried real persuasion. I waited while Donal went to get another bottle of Madeira that he'd been keeping cool in wet straw, in the shade. He pulled the cork and poured fragrant wine into a cracked mug. We listened to the gurgle of wavelets upon the beach and watched how the color of the sand changed, growing dark when wet but turning coral-pink again when the wave retreated.

At last Donal took my hand and murmured, "These are light little fingers to do spy's work. But when a woman spies among men, graceful hands and a pretty face are no disadvantage. Nor a creamy bosom. Nor a canny head, and that you have too, for you know the U.S. will be carved up if Burr has his way."

"And we'd soon be prey to European powers. Why, we might find ourselves English colonies again!"

"And that would be an advantage to King George, who's no friend o' mine," Macgillivray said mostly to himself. "Aye, Scotland was its own nation once, till the sassenachs forced the Act o' Union. And I'm thinkin', lass . . . a man can care not a whit to take other people's sides, but his own side a canny mon will take, and I'm thinkin' . . . there's more use for shipping by a nation wi' two coastlines, Gulf and Atlantic, than wi' Atlantic only. And so I'll finish my work for Wentworth but privately to you I say I've decided I'm for the U.S.A."

I raised my other hand to his shoulder. "Then will you take a letter to Newport, privately? I've an old aunt there who'll bring it to Washington. Please, Donal? I've no one else I can trust."

Donal Macgillivray turned away and seemed to search for his schooner among the spouting reefs. The curve of the San Isidro shoreline had put it out of sight. He cleared his throat, rubbed his hand along his cheek. "Lass, I'm busy here."

"But it's so important to get the information to Washington!"

He regarded me with a sorrowful face. "Do you know the cost o' taking a ship and crew fifteen hundred miles? And this without a cargo?"

"My aunt will find you a cargo in Newport! Or just go to the Downing Ironworks and tell the foreman—his name is Cason—I said he should—"

"I'm to go one way, then, wi' an empty hold? Oh, lass, lass!"

Without asking him to look away, I pulled down my bodice and found, where I had hidden them between my breasts, two jade earrings in fine gold settings and an emerald ring. Silently I held them out, warm, upon my palm.

He gently closed my hand upon nearly the last of my mother's jewels. "No, lass, I could na' take them." He mopped his face and looked down, around, anywhere.

"Please, Donal. If you do this for me . . . for the United States . . . why, I'll . . ." But the words had no way of coming gracefully. How *does* a gently reared Newport woman simply offer herself to a man?

Donal Macgillivray gazed down the beach. Took the initiative. "I'm thinkin' of yon Indian girl. By now she's cool in the water. I've a mind meself to go in for a bob and a splash. Turn your back, lass, whilst I skin meself and go in up to my brisket." He indicated mid-chest. "I'll stand wi' my back to you. You're surely as warm as meself, so hang your clothes on yon sea grape and come in too?"

Go naked into the water with him? It wouldn't be merely to get wet. I'd known of a certain swimming hole in the woods back of Newport. I'd never gone there. It was for bad girls. I'd heard that "it" could be extra fun when you did it in the water.

Undress, then? Wade in and join this passionate man who'd know exactly why I had joined him? It would be purely a matter of *body*. It would be payment given for— assuming he carried my letter—value received.

"Yon Mary Crow will not come sneakin' to watch," Donal chuckled. "Don't be worrit."

He thought that was all that worried me. And yet, why should he not think so?

I tried to think of all that was at stake, and at last I nodded. Again he wanted to kiss me, but I turned my back and said, "Tell me when you're in the water."

A pulse thudded hard in my throat as I waited. In a very short time I heard, "I'm in, and I'm facin' seaward. A seaman will never look at a beautiful body when he can look at the bonnie water."

155

He chuckled. I almost wept.

But I undressed. Naked and shaking—although certainly not with cold—I folded my arms across my breasts. If you're raped you can't help it. If you're seduced . . . well, at least you didn't plan it. But to *sell your body* in the most cold-blooded way! . . I stopped thinking, walked into the sea, waded toward the broad back, thatched with sandy hair, that Donal kept turned toward me.

Slowly the warm and silken water rose past my knees and rippled up my thighs, bubbled around my slender waist, lapped upon my breasts with an insinuating show-and-hide, show-and-hide motion. As I came up next to Donal, instinct made me bend my knees to make sure no skin showed below my shoulders. But I still wanted to keep my hair out of the water, so I couldn't go in too deeply. When Donal turned his massive chest toward me, he watched with delight as wavelets rose to my collarbones, then passed on, leaving depressions in the water that exposed a good deal. No way to help it. Nor any way to help the tugging, warm reaction that told me my body could feel the near presence of a naked male.

"I should have looked sooner," Donal chuckled. "Now I've a mind to go for the water glass."

Despite the ripples, I knew he saw more of my form than a wavering mystery. The crystal-clear water showed me his aroused manhood when I looked—then looked away.

He bore a tattoo on his chest—the letters *D* and *F* in a heart, intertwined.

"Aye, Donal and Fiona. But after the smallpox took her . . . a-weel, a man is meant to have women."

That stirred my guilt, and cried, "You males! You'll not say a woman is made to have men. Girls are brought up to not believe it, and then one day they—they have to change all their ideas!"

"Is it so?" he asked, winking, then roared with laughter. "Now I mind me, back i' the heather, when a baby is born on the wrong side o' the bed, they say, 'It's the Old Adam.' He's the one who makes all the trouble, y'see. But I never heard tell of Old Eve."

A larger wave rose and put me on tiptoe as it wet my chin. Before I could duck down, it passed and I felt air upon my nipples. Donal saw, and moved toward me. I

156

backed away, ready to plead I had made a mistake, such was my panic.

But he could move faster than I, and his hard hands came down thrillingly upon my bare shoulders. "Lass," he whispered. "Lass." I gave in, did not evade the warm yearning of his kiss as he pressed me to him. "Arabella, darlin' woman, you've asked me to go a long voyage for you. And you'll pay me wi' yoursel'. Good. And we'll put it in the bargain that you're to be mine many a time, aye, again and again. Now, were you an ordinary woman I might not think it enough. But to have a lady o' the gentry! I, the Macgillivray, rough-born, rough-reared, not fit to meet you, put in my low place, and now risen to yours in a most special way! This I count a laugh in all the gentry's faces. Let alone the great warm I have for ye . . . aye, the great heat. So I'll do it."

Speaking against the thick muscle that ran across the top of his chest, I asked, "You'll carry the letter?" I could hardly speak.

"I will. And worry not, lass, for I can always find me a cargo o' molasses and sponges somewhere i' the islands. But you knew I could, I'm thinkin'. I'll make profit. But the real prize is you."

My knees had gone weak, down in the gliding, glittering water. *My letter would reach Aunt Patience.* But why had I not been swept by grateful gladness? Why—outside of a few preliminary quivers—was my body not ready to be held up buoyantly against Donal with my legs around his waist in those bouncing little swells? No, I was not eager —not even when Donal lifted me by my elbows to bring my bosom out of the water and savaged my breasts with an eager mouth.

Even as he drew me up against him and his penis sought my womanhood, I winced and doubted. In the end I knew I must give myself . . . and give myself again and again, and be Donal's woman, I supposed, for as long as I stayed in the Bahamas or as long as he wanted me. But still I sought some reason for delay.

"Donal, is there no place ashore? You've told me about the sting rays and other creatures in the water. . . ."

"Why, lass, the bottom is clean and clear. But what'er I can do to make ye happy . . ." He swung me up into his arms. "And yonder I know there's a heap o' seaweed left over from old picnics, that's all dry i' the sun."

All the way in, he searched my body with avid eyes. In a few moments he placed me upon the warm seaweed, behind a clump of casuarina, and kneeled over me, truly an attractive male, sturdy and virile and greatly ready to enter me, as much of a man as any woman ever saw in her most secret dreams. So why not be grateful that my new lover was strong and lithe and hardly thirty, rather than some big-bellied, married planter who was three times my age?

If I sobbed inside, Donal didn't know it as I smiled to him and wound my arms around his neck, drawing him down upon my body.

He was finding me . . . in seconds I would have been his. But in that moment we heard the sound of voices and the clop-clop of horses approaching through the woods.

Donal snarled an oath and leaped to his feet. We were not only naked, but had not a shred of clothing anywhere near. Peering through the feathery casuarinas that were far too thin to shield me, I saw three people on horseback just as they stopped their mounts a short way down the road. A man and two women. The man had been riding ahead —and it was Mark Wentworth, and the shock and rage of his expression told he had seen Donal and me.

He wheeled his mount, waved the women back. In that voice that belonged on a quarterdeck: "Go home! Something bad is happening here!"

"But Mark, what is it?" one woman called from her side-saddle. While riding in the shady woods she had slipped her hat down on its ribbon so it rested between her shoulders. A pert, heart-shaped face. A thrusting figure. Red hair. Mark had not been around that morning, when Mary and I had gone to "pick beach plums." Now I knew he had gone to visit Rosemary Trumbull.

Mark roared, "Nothing! I mean—it's not for you. I'll take care of it. Go home, please, and pardon my abruptness, but—go! I'll ride around later and explain."

The other woman was Rosemary's black maid with a picnic basket tied behind her saddle.

As the two who had not seen me—or so I hoped—went away, Mark spurred his horse into the area that had been a garden and leaped from his saddle, his face a thundercloud. Naked, Donal walked out to confront him. His rage thickened his brogue. "I'll welcome ye anither time in anither place, Captain Wentworth, and wi' pistol or sword

158

if ye wish. Now go awa'. The lady I am with . . . her name is none o' your concern."

Mark stood with hunched shoulders. "None of my concern, say you? When you steal away with a lady who is my guest, and then you——" He gestured at me where I cowered in the seaweed, my face averted, the rest of me all gleaming bare skin.

Donal growled, "She is under my protection. Go awa'!"

"She is under *my* protection!" Mark roared out of I know not what interpretation of the gentleman's code.

What happened to me then? I was doubly and triply shamed, and I had lost all chance of having Donal carry my letter. Beside myself with frustration, I leaped through the casuarinas and stood like a witch, my hair falling around me. My shrill voice screamed hysterical words—words that were loosed to the hot air before sense returned. "Under your protection, am I? Was I under your protection that night you had me aboard the *Bridgewater?* Or when you took me when I was—was—exhausted and helpless on your own ship?"

As I caught my breath and clamped my lips, Donal Macgillivray glared at me in utter shock. He passed his hand across his face, stared at Mark, stared at me, shouted, "Then it's true as I've heard—for they whisper all over San Isidro about ye—that ye came here not to aid Job Wentworth write a history but to share his son's bed!"

"No!" I gasped.

"Did he force ye to sail wi' him on the *Royal Arms?* Tell me that!"

"No, but you see—"

"Nay, nor forced you to share his cabin, I'll be bound, not, when you'd been his sweet jo-abed lang ago in Newport! So they said, but I would na' believe ye'd be so wanton as to roll from one man to anither—a lady!"

"No! He—Mark—means nothing to me!"

"Nothing! Bah!" Mad with jealousy, Donal swung toward Mark. "Admit it! She's not a lady who's at your house to aid your father but a dressed-up wench who's there for your pleasure, aye, every night!"

How childish it was for Donal to think he really had some claim on me! But the tension that grew between the men was nothing childish.

Mark grated, "I owe you no excuses. My relations with Miss Downing are none of your concern."

The naked man walked slowly toward the other, fists clenched. "Ah, ye do yourself well, Wentworth. I take it ye want us to clear out and let ye roll i' the seaweed wi' yon red-haired lass? And by tonight ye'll be ready for anither go wi' the very willin' Arabella?"

"Donal, no!" I cried brokenly.

He only flared at me: "So ye told me ye hated the Tories whilst ye were a-bed wi' the worst of 'em. And would be bouncin' wi' him again all the while I sailed three thousand miles for ye. Nay, I'll carry no letter now!"

Mark demanded, "What letter? Then, deeply and harshly, "Never mind. I know." To Donal: "Damn you, Macgillivray. I was bringing another lady here, yes, decently, with her maid, before I knew what a whorehouse you've turned this place into."

"By hell, I'm as good as you are!" Donal roared, his face red and wild. "And I'm done wi' bein' respectful o' the gentry and being put i' my place by the gentry and not good enough to meet a lady who's no lady at a'. I'm *better* than you are, and I'll show ye wi' my fists!

"You challenge me?" Mark's hands clenched, ready. His face was dark with anger but also it bore a strange joy.

I heard words that might have been a curse in Gaelic as the Scot leaped and the two men tangled. They broke apart, instantly came at each other again, cursing and swinging. With the strength of rage Donal flung Mark staggering into the bushes. The Scot rushed, head down, roaring like a bull to finish Mark off. He was met by a blow that knocked him backward, blood on his face. But when Mark aimed a terrible blow at his jaw, he caught the fist on his arm and punched below, with all his weight, into Mark's belly. For a moment Mark was left pale and gasping. He managed to grapple with the other man. They swayed in a contest of strength. As they broke apart, Donal, disadvantaged by his bare feet, stepped on a thorn. He was off balance at the critical instant when Mark swung a blow. Struck with frightful force, Donal reeled backward, arms dangling. He stumbled against the wall of the old house and managed to catch at some projection and stay on his feet.

Mark ran forward to finish the job. His toe caught under a root on that rough ground and he went flat in the instant that Donal recovered. The murderous rage that snarled from his battered face was dreadful to see. A bold man, a man with a temper . . .

In a scatter of ancient mortar, that projection on the wall came away in his hand. It was a rusty iron bracket that might once have held a hanging plant, and it was two feet long and heavy. Mark was rising. He was only half-way up when Donal leaped with his iron club, again sounding the wild cry that echoed of ancient feuds along the border. I saw Mark could not stop the pounds of iron that would crush his skull.

I screamed and leaped forward in terror, and Donal ran into me. The impact knocked me sprawling, but it held him back for the moment it took Mark to spring to his feet with a chunk of coral rock in his hand.

The two men paused in the reek of their sweat and the sound of their gasping.

Donal looked down at my nude body. The madness left his face. "Ach, no more," he muttered. As he flung away the piece of iron he seemed older and very weary. "It's the last time we'll see each other naked. Or any other way. If I needed proof that you're Wentworth's bedmate—and I good for naught but to be cozened—I had it when ye saved his life. A-weel . . ." He closed his eyes briefly, tried to shake the dizziness out of his head. "A-weel, I know I'll remember ye, but I doubt ye'll remember me. As for the letter sewn in your jacket, I'm thankfu' it ne'er came aboard my ship and I ne'er spent weeks sailin' at the whim o' my lady. My lady!" He tried to laugh. "I've learnt a deal about ladies today." To Mark he said dully, "So, Wentworth, I'll hae it oot wi' ye anither time, for I'm too sick i' my heart to fight longer. Tell your father I'm leavin' wi' my ship. Today. And I'll salvage no more cannon for him."

"I'll tell him," Mark said tightly.

"As for the one missin' cannon, aye, that important cannon that can na' shoot, that's so badly needed, that your father hid . . . I hope it's never found. For you're mad, you Loyalists—the lot o' ye!"

Donal Macgillivray turned his muscular buttocks toward us and walked to where he had left his clothing. He picked them up and waded out toward the sloop, not caring that his shirt dragged in the water.

Rising shakily, dirty and scratched, I tried to find some semblance of dignity as I walked toward the place where I had left my clothing. Mark, hunched and pale, watched me as I dressed. It took a long time, I was shaking so.

I was about to put on the last garment, the blue linen jacket, when Mark snapped, "I'll have that."

He came and snatched it from my despairing hand. I knew what he wanted, and had to watch him rip the seam and find the letter. He read every word of that letter which told everything, even the fact that I knew Job was using a secret code hidden in his history. My letter would certainly not reach anyone in the United States. And without doubt I had lost my chance to send another, ever.

I was to remember the look Mark gave me. The narrowed lips, pressed almost white. The raging eyes. Slowly his lips parted to show his clenched teeth. I saw more than rage upon that bloodied face. Something primitive seemed to pour like acid upon me, conveyed by that terrible expression that meant more than anger—an expression for which I could find no name.

But still I could defy him. I shouted, "Donal was right! You Tories are mad! And not only mad. You're pathetic! Playing soldier! Waiting for a disgraced plotter to settle you on stolen land! Hoping Wilkinson won't save his neck by turning against you. But you know how quickly the United States can rally another army right along the Mississippi, where every settler is brought up with a gun in his hand."

Mark and I had had many a quarrel on the subject. Now, for the first time, I had presented him with a hard fact when his emotions lay bare. The frightfulness of his face seemed to waver. I had struck home.

"Yes," I shouted more loudly, "the states do quarrel with each other, but you know how a common enemy draws them together. Why, we were all ready to go to war with France a few years ago!"

Mark asked in a deadly voice: "Is that our topic? I'll spare you a moment before I get to the real business at hand. Yes, John Adams acted as brave as a crowing cockerel back then. But your nation was divided and you know it. He was glad enough not to have to go to war. Of course you'd ignored the treaty made with France, who pulled your chestnuts out of the fire with her fleet at the Battle of Yorktown. You were supposed to help Louis keep his West Indian islands if England attacked them. You never did. But what else can be expected from a nation that keeps its rabble and exiles its men of honor?"

"Of which I take it you consider yourself an example?"

Mark laughed in my face, laughed in the scalding, mirthless way he'd learned as a growing youth who'd been publicly shamed by his mother. He tore my letter into small bits, let them blow away in the wind.

"Why did you get dressed?" he demanded.

"I prefer to be clothed." My voice was haughty, but my heart despaired as I watched the bits of my precious letter scatter all over, some in the bushes, some in the sea.

"Undress."

"What?" I cried.

"Need I translate plain English? Take off your clothing."

"Certainly not!"

With a leap and a grab he had his hand in my neckline, his knuckles bruising my softness, his fist ready to tear.

"Well? Do you undress or do I rip?"

Shaking with rage and terror, I got out of my dress, my shoes, my stockings, my chemise, everything. Yet I still tried to defy Mark by taking time to fold my garments and place them carefully on a flat rock.

When I had done, he scattered them with a kick. He untied his stock and dropped it on the grass. He slid out of his coat and dropped it.

I lifted my chin.

"So if you can't have Miss Trumbull today, Miss Downing will do?"

Speaking hoarsely through his shirt as he drew it over his head: "That Miss Trumbull is a virgin and will remain so till she is married has nothing to do with you. *You,* who were ready to betray our secrets . . . you treacherous bitch!" he shouted.

But it was not the letter that had made Mark so wild. Now I realized the depth of the male jealousy that had contorted his face.

I heard: "So you wiggled your tail and he came after you, drooling I daresay! Your errand boy! Well, I won you in a fight and I'm going to have you. Swive you till you're blue!"

He was naked. He was in the manly way. "You'll not touch me against my will!" I cried, futilely trying to cover breasts and lap.

"Do you see that grassy place against the wall? Go there and lie down."

"I won't! Oh . . . you're nothing but a rutting stag who has chased off another! I am *not* a mere female animal!"

What Mark told me had the ring of bitter truth. "There is very little difference. Go and lie down, I said."

"No!"

I turned and ran, had not gone three steps when he had me by my flying hair. Stumbling and screaming, I had to follow him lest he tear out my hair by the roots as he dragged me toward the sea, out into the water, where he flung me down waist-deep, instantly hauled me up again.

"Now you won't smell of *his* sweat!"

Near the broken wall of the Pirate's House he shoved me down upon the grass. I leaped up, screaming for Mary; but she was more than a quarter-mile away, and the waves had grown and made a constant swishing that drowned my voice. Mark tackled me and I fell hard. He rolled me onto my back, keeping my arms locked painfully behind me as he grabbed me at the mons.

"I'll swive you till you forget his touch. I'll swive you till . . ."

I struggled, but strength left me, breath left me, hope left me. Yet in all that time, somehow I was not really *afraid*. Indignant, yes, for I was not willing to be used merely to slacken a man's temper, but I felt nothing of the unbearable horror I once had felt when I had been raped by Thatch.

And then, when I'd had to give up and Mark lay within my legs in a heavy-breathing pause, and his chest flattened my breasts and he pressed manhood and womanhood together, and there was heat and sweat and the musk of sex, and a pounding of blood in my ears and a warm quaver in my loins, and his lips were bruising my closed mouth, trying to force it open . . . he still had not filled my body. Nor was it from lack of readiness, for I felt all the length and power that was pressed along my tissues.

"I'm a fool," he whispered as though to himself, and released my arms.

Instantly I pounded at him. "Let me up!"

He did not seem to feel the beating I gave his hard shoulders. "Strange that I should remember the time I took you against your will, and it stops me now. But by God, woman, you deserve not merely to be ravished but also to be chained in our lockup and fed on bread and water."

"You wouldn't dare."

"Spy that you are, you are damnably right. But I don't

know what in Hades makes me so forbearing, except that you're still our guest."

I knew that wasn't the reason. No, the real reason was something I had so often felt when that man was near me —it was the strange combination of liking and mistrust that had grown between us. I could not hate him yet he was still my enemy. Lying naked and helpless beneath him, I knew that truth again. And if I didn't really want him to take away his fourteen stone of weight . . . well, that was all part of the mystery.

He said against my brow: "I am beholden to you for saving my life. It seems that you care whether I live or die."

"No, I simply can't condone murder."

"I see," he said, accenting the doubt in his voice as he rose on his elbows and looked at me. "There was once an occasion near Newport, out on the ferry road, when I showed regard for your safety. There is no mutual regard, then?" I didn't answer. "Why do you look away?"

"The sun is in my eyes."

"But it's shady here."

"Kindly allow me to look wherever I wish."

"Damn it, Arabella . . ." But he didn't finish whatever he'd been about to say. He rolled off my body and lay beside me. "You know," he muttered, "I was damnably jealous."

Neither of us moved or spoke for a while. I told myself I should rise and dress, but all I did was watch a cloud of tiny yellow butterflies. Gradually I realized that Mark's anger at my spying had not been as strong as his rage at seeing me naked with another man. He had been jealous enough to kill.

After another moment, Mark said to the butterflies rather than to me: "I face the Devil's own situation. I chased Rosemary home. Now what am I going to tell her?"

"Do you think I care?"

"I wondered. Well, I'll say that some blancs had taken over the Pirate's House and were carousing in their immoral way."

I almost told him sarcastically, "You're never at a loss." But I remembered it would not be the first time he had invented a story for my sake.

Arabella Downing continued of her own free will to

165

lie naked next to a naked man. It was outrageous, but it was happening.

"Well," said Mark after another long silence. "Since I'm not going to put you in our lockup—which is wrecked, anyway, as you may have noticed—I suggest we forget the entire incident."

"Very well."

"I did treat you roughly."

"You certainly did."

"Don't try to send any more secret letters," he said in a tone that was full of warning. "Damn it, Arabella, I'm quite capable of losing my temper, and if I ever hit you, you'd not recover soon."

"You said a man's strength is for protecting women."

"Depends on what the woman's up to," he snorted.

Enough of this, I thought, and began to rise. But I lay back when a heavy arm dropped across my bottom ribs.

Mark turned to face me. "Stay a while. I wish I could see you naked more often. You're so beautiful right down to your toes."

I fought a sudden softening of resolve, said, "Let me get up."

He only bent his elbow to allow his hand to hold my right breast, where he must have felt an instant punctuation in his palm, for he uttered a deep, rich, rare chuckle.

"Does it occur to you, Captain Wentworth, that you have no right to paw me?"

"It's true we're not married—"

"Nor ever will be!"

"—but I do get so few chances."

"I'll not banter with you. Go on, hold me down. Trust a man! You only *said* you wouldn't force me."

"You know I'm not doing anything but . . . ah, by the way, where is Mary Crow?"

"Picking oranges."

"Over in the old grove, where you sent her, I'm sure." Mark removed his hand from my breast and sat up. "Do you know why God gave men two hands?"

I knew the answer and knew what was going to happen. But, just as it had gone in the sail locker, once I hadn't followed my first impulse to go away, a more primitive truth than any the mind can hold took charge of my body. Else why did my uncovered breast feel so neglected, and why did both pouting breasts welcome the two hands

166

that found them and fondled them and smoothed them and caressed them?

Mark and I knew we lived in two worlds—one of conflict, the other of rapture. Our ever-waiting need, that made its own rules and ran its own courses, carried us into that tender, thrilling world where we were mates. Not married, but mates. That, I saw now, was the immutable truth that told itself in my overwhelming yearning.

Did I really push at him, as though to make him go away? It was only old habit, and the push was light and tender. All Mark had to do was to find his smile while his cupped hands created twin centers of throbbing passion. My fingers found his face, and then his face rested between my breasts and his kisses filled the valley. His mouth discovered my parted, yearning lips, came down again along my body, making it ripple in anticipation and joy. He sought where my legs met and I sought him. Deliciously we teased and aroused each other, holding off, going at each other again until the yearning to be joined became unbearable. I guided his entrance. An explosion of pleasure came instantly as he filled me, stretched me, completed me. More rapture waited as our bodies rippled together, and together we found glory and held it, moaning and sighing with it, till at last we lay breathless, savoring the slow, sweet diminution of the afterglow.

Mark was still breathless when he whispered, "I had reason to be jealous."

"Nothing happened. But if you had arrived a moment later—!"

"Then I saved you for myself? But what did he mean to you?"

"A courier to be paid."

"That was all?"

"That was all."

"I like what you say." Mark kissed me. "And now, dearest woman, you can't say we're not lovers."

I feared the word, with all it meant—to me—of lifetime commitment. Did it really mean only sex to men?

"Mark, I . . ."

But we heard the sound of someone approaching along the shore. Mary, who could walk like a silent shadow, knew it was best to step on shells and make them rattle.

I called to her to stay where she was. As I dressed and Mark dressed beside me, the thought, we're acting as

167

though we're married, came and was banished. At any rate, Mark was again concerned about appearances. He said he knew Mary and I would have a long walk back to Wentworth Hall, but if he gave us his horse, how could we explain our having it? I said I understood, and that we'd use the occasion to pick more beach plums.

When Mary saw Mark riding away, she stared after him, stared at me, stared at a small sail that was heading toward the spouting reef, across the whitecapped water. She said nothing save to remark on the condition of my hair. She took out her pocket comb and handed me an orange.

I was late for dinner. So was Mark, whose face had been bruised when he had collided with a low branch while riding, he said, adding, although I knew he had many bruises on his body: "It's nothing."

"And how are all the Trumbulls?" asked Lavinia, beaming.

"Yes, how are they, all those fine people?" asked Job. "And especially, how is that charming girl Rosemary?"

"Charming as ever, and she sends her best regards."

Mark and I sat opposite each other at the table. I didn't care about the Trumbull girl . . . but why did I feel dismayed when Mark looked everywhere except at me?

PART THREE

THE CASTAWAY

Chapter Eleven

"Thank you," I said coldly to Mark Wentworth when he handed me a letter from Aunt Patience. She had written at intervals during the fall and winter, but this was the first letter that Mark had carried directly from Newport on the *Royal Arms*.

I said nothing to Mark about not having seen him for the three months of his voyage. Nor would I have admitted to the strange emotions that had swept me—fear and eagerness, annoyance and quivering warmth—when I first spied the topsail schooner threading her way in among the reefs. Now, still keeping the coldness in my voice, I glanced at the seal on my aunt's letter and said, "It doesn't *seem* to have been opened."

Mark snapped, "We don't care what your aunt tells you. It's what you might tell her that counts." After an instant of glaring he added in a softer voice: "She also sent you this." A small, squarish package. "It's a hyacinth bulb she put in dry moss. She said if you water it, it will bloom."

I felt a catch in my throat. It was spring again, and there'd be hyacinths coming up in every Newport garden. I almost asked Mark if he had been up to my old house and if he had seen the flowering quince. But I reminded myself I had determined to keep my distance from this man and choked off the words.

I merely asked, "Has Aunt Patience stopped slapping your face?"

The dark, dour features regarded me bitterly. "Yes." Mark turned away.

Later he rode off toward the Trumbulls', dressed in his best, with a package under his arm. A present for Rosemary, no doubt. I remembered that during Mark's absence I had grown to know Rosemary better—although no more

171

favorably. Indeed, we had had a scene, and I wondered if she would tell Mark about it.

It had happened at Brian Roscoe's wedding. Mark was still away on his trip when Brian had married Ethel Lamont, that milky little girl. The Roscoes couldn't help but invite me to the wedding, and I couldn't say no, so I had found myself, along with Job and Lavinia, at the Lamont house, northward on San Isidro.

The Bahamas Corps of Horse had made the wedding their occasion for coming into the open. Brian and his brothers-in-honor sported English-looking red tunics with gold-and-red waistbands, broad white sword belts, a dangling sabretache, and red-striped gray trousers worn most sportingly outside their boots. When the bride and groom turned away from the makeshift altar in the Lamonts' parlor, a sharp command brought the officers to attention in two rows. Sabres flashed out, clashed overhead in the traditional arch beneath which Brian passed with his blushing bride.

Brian took pains not to make eye contact with me. Ethel tried to crush me with a glance. Brian's father gave me a cordial smile. His mother, happily sobbing, gave me a look that said, "He's out of your clutches now!" I fluttered my kerchief, as all the ladies did, and hoped Ethel would not soon be made a widow.

After the wedding came one of those rare and precious times for visiting, and it was then that Rosemary Trumbull sought me out. Whatever we had had to say to each other up to then had been trifling and polite. It may be that we knew we had better keep out of each other's hair. But Rosemary had been watching me in a flushed, angry way, and now, finding me in the primping room, she took pains to stay till we two could be alone.

Her charming little face was knotted with hatred and her tip-tilted eyes flashed danger as she said, "It's time we had a talk, Arabella."

"Yes?"

She swept my dress with a sharp glance, was perhaps cheated of a chance to criticize when she took in the V-necked, long-sleeved redingote with a shawl collar that the wise Madame Marcellot had provided for certain occasions. Rosemary was no shy little Ethel. With a toss of that red hair, she said, "At least you're covered. You've such

172

a liking for nakedness! It certainly was more than satisfied when I saw you at the Pirate's House!"

Hauteur was the best mask for my discomfort. "Ah! You peeked!"

"I certainly did slip back through the woods to see what Mark was trying to protect me from—as though I were a child! And I saw—"

"Donal Macgillivray, I'm sure. Isn't he a rugged sight?"

"Oh?" She made a gesture of disgust. "When I realized a naked man was there too, I didn't look."

"How'd you know he was naked?"

"Don't try to evade the issue! I saw you for what you are!"

"And ran away from all the wickedness before you could be corrupted?"

"I went away, my dear Miss Downing, thankful that Mark Wentworth is gentleman enough to try to protect a *good* woman's virginal modesty."

"Yes," I said drily. "He has his gentleman's code. But it's too bad you didn't stay for the real sight—after Macgillivray sailed off."

"What do you mean?" Rosemary demanded.

I said nothing, and she cried, "Well, if Mark really brought you down from—from Yankee-land for the purpose of—of—because men are *that* way, he's gentleman enough to hide it. And anyway, all you mean to him is a way of relief. Remember that!"

"I must write it down so I won't forget it."

I almost did have Rosemary's hand in my hair. But she contented herself by raging, "He's going to marry *me*."

"Lucky girl," I said, my voice somehow not as sarcastic as I had wanted it to be. "It's official, then?"

She hesitated. "It's *understood*. And no matter what—what you are to him—and Macgillivray—and I suppose a dozen other men around here—while you shamelessly try to find out our secrets—remember, you have no claim on Mark. None whatsoever!"

"None whatsoever. So you and Mark will be braving the Louisiana wilderness hand in hand? You hope? Well, I suppose you could do worse." Why had an ache appeared in my heart? I added: "Still, the Wentworths have status."

"Yes!" said Rosemary. Her face glowed. She looked beyond me. "And the Trumbulls and the Wentworths

173

united . . . everyone says it's a perfect match . . . two distinguished families."

"Oh? Are the Trumbulls distinguished?"

"Really!" Rosemary's anger returned. "Back in South Carolina the Trumbulls were judges and legislators and my uncle was a senator in Washington. Let me tell you, Miss Downing, there is a great deal you can't appreciate about Carolina families."

"I should remember I do come of Newport riffraff after all."

But as I spoke, face to face again with dreams of Burriana, I thought of Aaron Burr and realized he was not a young man. When—or if—he became president of the new nation, it would be time to look for a younger man who, after Burr had served one or two terms, could take his place. Mark was the son of the Loyalists' present leader; Mark was active in their secret affairs; Mark, when his father died, would certainly be looked upon as a man of authority, ready to carry the torch. Already there might be an understanding that Mark Wentworth was to be the second President of Burriana. Of course Rosemary wanted to marry him and become the First Lady, the foremost hostess, the most admired and respected woman in Burriana's capital of New Orleans.

"I see," I said with perhaps too much knowing in my voice.

"You see what?" demanded the red-headed girl.

"I see certain advantages in marrying Mark Wentworth." Turning, I walked out into the Lamonts' drawing room, where furniture had been arrayed to hide the frayed ends of draperies, and the house slaves lounged around as though waiting for the end of an elaborate charade.

Now Mark was off to see Rosemary. Thoughtfully I watched his broad back, atop the cantering horse, disappearing into the woods. The second President of Burriana?

Sighing, I sat down to re-read Aunt Patience's letter, which in one way had given me hope, but in another had only increased my loneliness and frustrataion.

Dearest Niece Arabella:

I am so relieved to hear you are well, although you haven't told me *enough*. I'm glad to know you are trying to get the black children to eat more greens.

174

I do believe there is a connection between the eating of greens and the prevention of rickets. Do tell Renzo I remember him as the Wentworths' slave-gardener, although how he learned his kindly ways in that household I never will understand.

Since you are far from the source of news on *political developments,* you may not know that our ex-Vice-President *Mr. Burr* showed up in Philadelphia last December. He also spent some time in Washington, where we hear he visited both the *English* and *Spanish* ambassadors. Rumors are flying thick and fast about his *doings in the Southwest,* but when people cry out for his arrest, that clever little lawyer challenges them to present grounds for their accusations of treason. Nobody has. Of course, his indictments for the murder, if it was that, of Alexander Hamilton are good only in New York and New Jersey, but he stays away from those states.

Yes, for some time the packets of manuscript that went to New Orleans had been addressed: "To be forwarded according to Colonel Burr's instructions."

Aunty certainly was hinting broadly that she wanted me to send her information worth taking to Washington, which I was not able to do. Those underlinings gave the hint. But she was smart enough not to ask, in writing, "What do you know?"

I read on:

Mark Wentworth has brought me a great jug of cane syrup made in his own vats. He had the effrontery to suggest I might prefer it on my johnnycake to Vermont maple syrup, made by free men. Still, he brought me word of your well-being, so I could not send him packing. I heard later he'd gone up to *Essex County,* Mass., where I daresay he will find bad company to keep.

It is not my way to retail backstairs gossip, especially that of a sordid nature, but I feel you are entitled to know all I know about that nasty person, Aubrey Brinton. It is being whispered that the fellow is having difficulty, these days, in arousing his natural powers, and requires the services of three low females

175

to attend him in his stable in ways which have not been described to me, nor would I listen if they were.

This failure of vigor may be due to a depression caused by his business troubles. When I told around that it must have been he who had hired those foulmouth ruffians to shout insults at you—and cause horror to the parents of young girls for blocks about —I found that a good many people have been simply waiting to believe evil of him. At the same time they are loath to believe ill of you. I have been assured over and over that even a fine woman of fine family can be tricked into unsavory situations. I've been told recently that it's Brinton and not you who should have left town. At any rate, Banker Brinton is finding himself and his bank avoided while the Downing Ironworks, Cason tells me, has more orders than it can handle.

So you see, darling niece, you can return home when you wish. It's true that when it comes to actual marriage, Newport men may shy away from you, but there are other cities where a man good enough for you can be found. I know you'll stay dutifully to help old Wentworth finish his Bahamas history, but I hope it won't be long. Do write and *tell me more.* Your letters are interesting but not as *significant* as I could wish.

> Your loving and lonely aunt,
> Patience Bentley

> Second of April, 1806

In time the hyacinth bulb pushed its stem up from the dampened moss. The spikelets came out all around. Delicate blue flowerets appeared, and filled my room with a heavenly scent of home in the spring. I admit I wept over that flower, wondering if I'd ever see Newport again. I was now being watched very carefully—far more carefully than when I had gone to "pick rose plums" with Mary Crow—and I writhed with helplessness while the birth of Burriana drew closer and closer.

One day the little cannon boomed for another incoming ship. Squinting out into the sun-dazzle, I thought I might

176

have seen her before. I had. In fact, I had been aboard that vessel, and was not likely ever to forget. She was the slave ship *Bridgewater,* from Africa by way of the West Indies and Nassau. Her hold was now empty of black bodies and their terror and their cries. Her captain had come to help the Tory cause by shuttling among the islands and back and forth from New Orleans.

Hiram Chance, bowing over my reluctantly offered hand, looked as healthfully rakish as ever. Some perfumed African unguent gleamed in his black hair and mustache and his very elegant, twin-pointed beard. Soon enough he was sitting with Mark over pipes and mugs, calling him "my dear fellow" and guffawing over slaving adventures with comely black women and the Portuguese factor's wife. I pointedly stayed away from such conversation. But one evening at dinner I found myself listening with interest to Captain Chance's knowing drawl.

First he had glanced at me with a wink and very slight shake of his head. As he proceeded, I realized thankfully he would not reveal what had happened to me aboard the *Bridgewater.* He went on to say, in a rum-touched yarning voice, that he once had met a woman named Anne Burney who was very intelligent, a competent chemist and apothecary and yet quite mad. This poor deluded soul had decided she was a reincarnation of Anne Bonney. Anne Bonney—Chance explained to Lavinia Dermott—had efficiently run a pirate ship, back in the days of Blackbeard and others of his ilk.

"A female pirate? Oh, no!" cried Lavinia, gasping like a fish out of water.

"It's quite true, cousin," said Job, who had listened with interest. "My great-grandfather once saw her. He said she was a striking blond woman who dressed like a man, and her cutthroats were proud to serve under her. It set them off from ordinary crews."

"Oh, heaven help us!" said Lavinia, fumbling for her pills.

"Well," Chance continued, "I hadn't seen Anne *Burney* for some time, nor heard of her, till I encountered a government cutter while coming up through the islands, not a hundred miles from here. The cutter's captain was warning shipping that a pirate vessel called *Queen of the Caribbean* has been rampaging in these waters, and her master is a woman named Anne Burney."

177

Amid the murmurs of surprise I sat silent, remembering Mad Anne, the cluttered cabin, the skulls, the herbs, the "tiffin" that at length had made me fall to the cabin's deck with pools of blackness whirling before my eyes. I glanced at Mark, caught his stare and his quick turnaway. I remembered the ribbon of light that had illumined my face as he'd held up my fainting form after he had raped me. I remembered the choked cry that had heralded, for me, one misery after another: "My God, it's Arabella Downing!"

And now the madwoman who had pretended to be me was actually a pirate preying on vessels in the Bahamas! It was hard to believe. "How is it possible?" I asked. "How could she get the money she'd need—the men—the ship?"

Chance replied, "She's very resourceful and utterly unscrupulous. Wanted for murder in Savannah, in fact, and —ah—not averse to using her charms—ah—carnally, to persuade men to take her side." Another glance from Mark, at that. "Also, she comes of some good family in England, though she never mentions their name, which can't be Burney. She seems to have been their black sheep. I believe they banished her to America and pay her regularly never to come back. She spends much time at sea and it may be that a banker has accumulated her money for her. At any rate, she seems to have proved to her own satisfaction that she really is a reincarnation of Anne Bonney, for there's no quarreling with the fact—she has a ship and she's a pirate. Well," he told us, reaching for his glass, "the *Bridgewater* is armed, and if I meet the *Queen of the Caribbean*, depend on it, I'll send her to the bottom."

I thought: He remembers that Mad Anne hates him. He won't feel safe till he gets rid of her.

"Oh, we'll none of us sleep till someone sinks that dreadful pirate ship!" said Lavinia faintly. "Remember the motto on the Bahamas coat of arms: *Expulsis Piratus, Restituta Commercia.*"

"Pirates expelled, commerce restored," said Job, nodding. "You are right, Cousin Lavinia. Pirates deserve no grave but a watery grave."

Off and on through the winter, the blind man had been ill. His history of the islands lagged, and sometimes he dictated to me when I knew he should have been in bed.

We sent off packets to Burr that contained no more than ten pages. And yet there were always two chapters, the second far more carefully done than the first. Always Job tapped his palm as he counted to make sure the key words were in the right place. Always Mark double-checked. Always I was the unwilling accomplice in sending secret messages that might destroy my country.

I had to admit that Bahamas history was fascinating. For example, a group of French Huguenots had settled on the island of Great Abaco in 1625 and then had vanished. Why? Whence? No one knew. Later, after the beheading of Charles I, Puritans who became unpopular in Bermuda came to Eleuthera and began growing crops. But they had not found the area of rich soil that now sustained the Holdridge plantation, and they returned to Bermuda when they could. Despite my writing thousands of words in shorthand, then in plain English, I never had a chance to make a copy of my notes. Tibbal had been ordered to watch me transcribe. He not only took away my transcription, but also tore the pages of shorthand out of my notebook and took them as well. He did this with grave courtesy and the utmost soft-voiced respect. But I knew how quickly I'd be dealt with if I tried to evade his watch.

Trying to make the best of things, I waited to hear one part of the history I had already heard in Newport and knew I'd enjoy hearing again. It was the story of how Commander Ezekiel Hopkins, with eight small United States vessels, captured Nassau in 1776, dismantled the forts, then sailed away with the governor as his captive.

But Job never reached that part.

In July, the fever season, the blind man had a touch of dengue. He recovered, but was left thin and shaky. When he sent for me. I found him reclining on a wicker chaise beneath an awning, facing the sea, with Tibbal fanning his sunken, yellow face.

"A chair for Miss Arabella," Job said faintly when he recognized my step. He asked about my own health, which had been good, and wanted to know if I had sampled one of the new strain of pineapple that had been grown from cuttings brought from Cuba. Hardly aware of my answer —I had—Job went on to say that Mark should soon be returning from a trip to Charleston. Sightlessly he quested the horizon as though watching for the *Royal Arms*, but I told him that only the *Bridgewater* was in sight where

179

she lay at the wharf. When he said, testily, "Yes-yes, I knew," I realized he had something on his mind he found difficult to mention.

At last Job whispered, "Don't tell Lavinia. She'll go to pieces. But I feel my death is not far away."

"But Mr. Wentworth, you're looking better today and I'm sure that within a few days—"

"No, don't protest, my sweet Arabella. I feel I've only a few days left to me. There is something I want you to do for me before I die. It's very important. Listen to me now." The old man tried to smile. "You've grown quite used to listening to me."

I listened, then, leaning close as Job's voice weakened, turning sometimes to gaze with astonishment into Tibbal's expressionless face and opaque dark eyes.

Job whispered, "There is a certain very large, very old cannon. It can't be shot. It holds something of great value." The cannon Mark had mentioned long ago in Chance's cabin on the *Bridgewater!* The cannon to which Donal Macgillivray had so bitterly alluded! "I wanted to keep it hidden," the wavering voice went on. "Hidden and safe for Aaron Burr. But inevitably others found out where I kept it. . . . I locked it up in that little building with barred windows that formerly was our jail. No doubt you've noticed it's wrecked? They blew it open with gunpowder, one night. Masked men. Fortunately Mark is a good shot and our plantation guards—Renzo trained them—they were faithful. We saved the cannon. . . ." Job had to pause. Tibbal gently wiped his face with a cloth moistened in cool water. "We saved the cannon, Arabella," Job repeated while I listened breathlessly, "but certain deaths had to be hushed up. I'd known the cannon had become a challenging prize for some of our piratical wreckers, but—but—there are also Loyalists who have grown tired of waiting for Burriana. Yes," the blind man cried harshly, *"they* would have stolen the cannon if they could! And so we had . . . deaths . . . in certain well-known families. But no one dared take revenge on me. And some came to ask my pardon. Had I known how desperate they had become? Yes, I knew."

I waited tensely. The cannon held something of great value. Of great value for Aaron Burr. Of great value for the Tory cause. What could it be but a store of gold or other treasure?

"And so," Job went on shakily, "I prepared another hiding place for the cannon. A place I alone knew. When I had it ready, I sent everyone off the plantation. I brought in a work gang of six slaves who had been loaned to me by a friend in Jamaica. They rolled and skidded that cannon to its new hiding place. They had no way to know its value. Quickly I sent those men back to Jamaica— rewarded, you may be sure. Nobody else in the Bahamas knows the plantation they came from. Arabella . . ."

"Yes?"

"Not even Mark knows where the cannon is now hidden. I am the only one who knows."

Mark didn't know? But of all the people in the world, surely Mark could have been trusted?

"Brandy," Job whispered. He barely moistened his lips, rallied, went on, seeming almost to time his words to the pounding of my heart. "You are bright, Arabella. Perhaps too bright. I think you know by now how my neighbors have worried about my dying before I told the secret. If I did, the cannon would be lost forever, and our cause would be lost. But I had to take the chance that I wouldn't die suddenly." He leaned forward, his blind gaze weirdly seeking mine. "The time has come when I must tell the secret. But only Aaron Burr must know it. Only Aaron Burr must find that cannon." I recoiled as Job Wentworth uttered a strange, cracked cry: "Only my *friend*, Colonel Aaron Burr!"

Something he did not say shook him and contorted his face. He fell back upon his pillow. "Burr is back in New Orleans," he whispered. "I have sent word to him that Captain Chance will soon bring him the very important secret he has been waiting for."

But how did I figure in all this? I thought I knew, and in growing excitement I tried not to move, not even to breathe.

"I trust my faithful Tibbal," Job went on when he could. "And I am about to free him. But he can neither read nor write. I would dictate the secret word by word to Lavinia, but she'd know I spoke in anticipation of dying, and after that I could trust neither her hand nor her judgment. I know how accurate your shorthand is, Arabella, and how carefully you transcribe it." Now I really held my breath. "And so, this afternoon, Tibbal will have the sedan chair ready and you will kindly be prepared with paper and quills and ink. We'll go out to the point. We must be all alone while I dictate certain clues that Burr must follow to find the cannon."

Then *I* would know the clues! "I understand," I said tensely.

"Arabella, you are my guest. And you are all that remains on earth of William Downing. I am going to protect you as well as I can." I did not understand what he meant, but I said nothing. "We'll leave at four, when we'll have shade. Wear sturdy shoes and an old dress. You'll ride out to the point with me, as usual, but later I'll ask you to do some climbing about."

Job lay back and Tibbal hovered over him. After a bit I stole away, trembling with hope and bewildered with puzzles.

Again Job and I sat in the swaying sedan chair as four slaves bore it out toward the point that thrust a rocky finger into the sea. Job leaned back against the cracked leather upholstery, his eyes closed in his parchmentlike face. He fumbled at his coat, smiled weakly when I opened it for him. I had noticed long before that he was partial to silver buttons with a rose design.

The slaves were carrying us up that hill littered with loose shells when Job whispered, almost sobbing: "She left me . . . Prudence left me . . . after all that I had forgiven. . . . I knew . . . she was one of those women who must have many men. . . ."

Embarrassed, I could only maintain my silence. I had never heard Job mention his unfaithful wife before.

"She . . . was everything to me. . . ." It hurt to see the tears on his face. "But she ran away with him. Ran away. Everyone thinks they were killed in Florida by hostile Indians. But they ran away . . . together . . . and disappeared. . . ." Job sighed, found his kerchief. "Do you know his name?"

Unwillingly I replied, "We heard in Newport that it was Sir Brendan Stratton."

"Stratton it was. Oh yes. Yes. Stratton. A statesman. Member of the Government. A famous man. He offered her money and position . . . I suppose. Was . . . powerful enough . . . to face out the scandal . . . or didn't care, because he was mad about her! Mad!"

"You mustn't excite yourself, Mr. Wentworth."

But he shook both fists and an unhealthy flush crept beneath his paleness. "Prudence knew we'd never get rich in the Bahamas and she had no faith in Burriana. Then Brendan Stratton came with secret messages from Whitehall . . . a ladies' man . . . not the first wife he'd seduced! He couldn't take his eyes off her. And she led him on . . . oh, she knew how! Maybe he thought he'd take her to Australia, where so many people live under assumed names. . . ."

"Please—" I began.

"We had many guests. Everyone wanted to meet the famous Sir Brendan Stratton. And even in the sight of guests, he'd . . . And I took him aside, out in the garden, and told him to desist or I'd kill him. He laughed in my face. I struck him. We might have had it out then and there, but there was a couple. . . ." Job paused and gasped. "There was a couple sitting on a garden bench and they came running to stop us . . . because they'd heard me threaten him. And others were aware we'd been quarreling. I'd had enough of shame. Later in the evening I challenged Stratton to a duel before a dozen people. He laughed again and said I was not of his rank so he could not duel me. I told him I'd kill him like a dog, then, if he didn't get off my property. That was the night he went away . . . and took Prudence with him." Job Wentworth uttered a long, tortured sigh. "They didn't go to Florida. I know where they went."

"But why did you never . . ." I stopped myself, glad that Job had taken no notice of my unfinished question, only sat shrunken and weak, his head lolling in rhythm with the sedan chair. Whatever reason he had had for not pursuing the runaway couple could mercifully remain in his own heart.

We had almost reached the wall of coral blocks when the old man whispered, "It's only that . . . now that I'm about to die . . . it would be easier . . . if she returned to me . . . for just a little while . . . and held my hand . . . and helped me . . . go." He reached shakily into his inside pocket, drew out something that his fingers partly covered. It was about the size of a playing card, and it gleamed. "I still carry it, but what's the use," Job murmured, and let the object drop back into his pocket. But he never said what "it" was. When the chair stopped and the bearers set it down, he said, "Well, here we are!" With a ghastly, forced cheerfulness: "Tibbal! Send the men back. Make sure they know they're not to return till you summon them."

As we had done so often before, we settled ourselves in the shade of the seagrape, Job in one stone chair, I in another, my notebook ready on the stone table. I opened the sealed inkpot, dipped my quill, and waited.

Job turned blindly this way and that. "Tibbal! Look behind the wall! Behind the rocks! Make sure nobody's hiding and listening!"

It was hardly possible, but Tibbal looked nevertheless. Meanwhile I noticed a small vessel being rowed past the point, out in the shimmering water, a quarter-mile offshore. It was yellow. A tiny-seeming man sat on a balcony aft, reading, while the oars rhythmically dipped and rose, carrying him along. It was Bartley Holdridge, unconcerned about the world. He certainly could not hear us.

"I must tell you, Arabella," old Job said, "that Burr and I have been communicating in a secret code. It's been hidden among the words of the history."

"Really, sir?" I hoped I sounded genuinely surprised.

"But I can't encode the directions I'm going to dictate now. I don't have the head for it. I can only hope I still remember. I was a week in memorizing the clues, years ago. You'll never be able to remember them all, and what's more, they're no good unless they're memorized exactly in order."

And how could I possibly make an extra copy of my notes with Tibbal silently, steadily watching me?

The blind man said in a fierce whisper, "That cannon is hidden not four hundred yards from where we sit. It's down in a cave. There's a great system of interconnected caves, hollowed out by the sea. Perhaps a few fishermen and"—he hesitated strangely—"others . . . have found some of them. But I know all those caves." His blind stare was as fierce as his voice. *"All."*

"Yes, sir."

"You could search a year and never find that cannon unless you had the clues. So! Let's begin."

He tried to compose himself, but once again I saw his face twist oddly as he began: "To Colonel Aaron Burr, who has waited long for these directions, and who, in following them carefully, will surely find the cannon, whilst I, who by then will be dead, will care not a whit how wounding the discovery may be to his pride."

Burr's pride? I kept my silence, but it was evident that Job Wentworth and Aaron Burr were not the friends they seemed to be.

I dipped my quill again, and Job dictated: "Go first to the wall of coral blocks where it has been my wont to dictate my history of the Bahamas. It is on the highest point of the rocky area north of Wentworth Hall. Once at the wall, walk from its eastward end thirty paces to a clump of poisonwood. Push it aside and you'll find a mound of shells. Dig into the shells and you'll find a block of coral with an arrow chiseled on it. Go the way the arrow points. Go straight, no matter how rough the country. You will come to a vertical wall of rock ten feet high. You can climb it by working your toes into cracks. At its top, stand in a line with the poisonwood bush and the northwest corner of Wentworth Hall, visible in the distance. Turn directly around and go in a straight line till you find the skull of a cow spiked into a stone. Go in the direction the left eye socket points."

Old-time pirates had been known to give that sort of clue for finding buried treasure. They had had the same reason for complexity—to make it almost impossible for the treasure to be accidentally found. Surely it had been a younger, more active Job who had worked hard and alone on a complex system of indicators that traced a crooked path amid the natural tumble of the region.

As I quickly jotted my dots and lines and loops under Tibbal's unwavering eyes, Job went on, his voice growing weaker. But his trained memory delivered clue after clue. Toward the end of his dictation he seemed frighteningly feeble. But he had given me some twenty additional marks, all requiring great care to find. Aaron Burr would eventually be led into a steep-walled gully. Three more clues would lead him to a line of flat stones that Job had laid out. He was to lift the ninth stone. "Beneath that stone you will find the underground road to the cannon," said Job Wentworth, hardly conscious. Then all I heard was the wind in the seagrape leaves and waves booming in the mysterious hollows they had worn in the rock.

"Transcribe it all, now, Arabella," Job said, recovering. While my quill made plain English words out of my shorthand, he brooded, his hands working nervously upon each

185

other, his gray head sunk upon his chest. I did my best to remember what I was writing. But, just as my host had said, it was hopeless. There were too many directions, they were too complex, it would be too easy to get them out of order, and Tibbal's gaze never wavered from my hand.

At last I said, "I'm finished, sir."

"Good. You may hold the transcription for the time being. But give your shorthand notes to Tibbal. Tibbal, you have them? Burn them."

Tibbal showered sparks from a flint into his tinderbox, blew till he had fire. I watched my shorthand notes become pale flags of flame, then ashes blowing away.

"Now," said Job, "I must consider that one or more of my signposts may have been covered by a landslide or washed away in a hurricane. Tibbal, Miss Arabella will now read the clues to you, one by one, and you will make sure that each clue still exists as I have described it. You already have memorized the last three clues. Are you sure you know them?"

"Yes, Marstah."

"Then you'll know what to do when you find the gully. And make sure Miss Arabella does not enter the gully."

"Yes, Marstah."

I was not to see Tibbal uncover an underground road—no doubt the entrance to a cave.

"Go ahead, then," said Job. "But be sure to use a stick when you move the branches of the poisonwood." He told me: "It's a good deal worse than New England poison ivy."

I found a stick on the ground—and also I saw something that at first I thought was a small dark stone. But it was not a stone. It was far more interesting.

"Here's a stick for pushing aside the poisonwood, Tibbal," I said, bending to pick up the stick for him.

"Thank you, Miss Arabella ma'am."

He had not noticed that when I had picked up the stick, I also had picked up the interesting object. It was a flattened lead bullet, relic of a hunt out there, I supposed. Lead will leave a mark on paper. That bullet was going to be very valuable to me. I read the first directions aloud and followed Tibbal thirty paces to the poisonwood shrub. While he poked gingerly with the stick, I stood behind him. At the right moment, while he concentrated on uncovering the buried block of coral, I whipped out the sheets of

186

blank paper I had taken along in my pocket, hoping I'd have a chance to make secret notes with the quill. The lead needed no ink. I had the first clue scribbled in shorthand, and the paper back in my pocket, before Tibbal could see the arrow carved in the rock.

He carefully reburied it. I read the second clue aloud. We made our way, with difficulty, to the cliff. I couldn't possibly climb it. Walking around an easier way gave me time in which to write secretly with the bullet: "Stand in line with the poisonwood bush and the northwest corner of Wentworth Hall, visible in the distance." And the rest. When I met Tibbal I complained that my throat was dry and my dress torn. I didn't tell him that my heart was exulting.

We went on and on from clue to clue, missing some, searching, at last finding. Some were high, some low. Twice, when we were on high spots, I caught a flash of light from the sea. Holdridge's barge was merely drifting out there among two or three other boats and he was fishing. I couldn't imagine what had caused the flash.

I felt parched and broiled by the time we reached a large arrow made of stones fitted roughly together, the whole thing almost buried under sand. The arrow's head pointed invitingly; but the seeker was not to go that way. Instead, he must first face that way, then go directly to his right. When Tibbal and I walked the required number of paces, we found the vine-shrouded entrance to a gully. It looked like a dozen others in the area, but somewhere, in it, I knew, the seeker would find an entrance to a cave.

I was not to enter. In fact, I stood innocently on the arrow while Tibbal entered the gully. I heard the rattle of stones and after some time I heard a strange, rumbling, groaning sound. Tibbal came out blowing on a skinned hand. He grumbled something about having had to move a lot of stones because there'd been a small landslide.

Meanwhile I had had plenty of time in which to copy the final clues. Now I had my own complete, secret set in my pocket. With idle curiosity—at least I hoped it sounded that way—I asked Tibbal if he had found the underground road to the cannon.

He shook his head evasively. "Too dark down there, ma'am. Don't know."

We made our way back to Job Wentworth. He'd been sleeping, I think, then had heard us returning and come wide awake—but you could see the effort it cost him. Tibbal assured him that every clue had been checked. Instantly he held out his hand and said, "Arabella, I'll have the transcription."

At his direction, Tibbal folded the papers and put them into an oilskin pouch. It was carefully sealed, and later would go on the *Bridgewater* to New Orleans, where Aaron Burr waited.

Using a razor, Tibbal carefully cut the stitching of the cracked old leather that lined the sedan chair. He tucked the package deep into the horsehair padding and resewed the seam. It did not show amid the many cracks and stains.

"You see, Arabella," Job told me faintly, "I'm going to send Burr a present—my sedan chair. He knows the chair is coming and he knows where to look for the hidden papers. Even if someone has suspected I've been sending him coded messages, they'll watch for parts of my history. They'll pay no attention to an old sedan chair."

"It was cleverly planned."

"And it will work. And Burr will find the cannon, and —" Job looked away. He touched his pocket, where that shiny object rested. Suddenly he turned back to me. "*You* couldn't find it, could you, without the written directions?"

"Not a chance," I said truthfully.

He chuckled a bit. "Exactly as I planned. But you see, Arabella, I really have protected you."

"I don't understand. Protected me against what?"

"Well . . . whenever I've been ill I've had many visitors. All afraid I might die and leave the secret untold, of course. People I trust and people I don't trust. But you see, Arabella, we never made any public announcement of my illnesses. I don't know how the news always got around. I'm afraid one of my slaves has been suborned. So it's also possible that word may have gotten around that at last I was going to dictate the secret of the cannon. To *you,* they'd surely surmise. Still, nobody can torture the secret out of you because you can't remember all the clues."

Aghast, I cried, "Mr. Wentworth! You're saying someone might torture me?"

"I tried to protect you," Old Job repeated. "But, as I told you, there are those who want the cannon not for the sake of the cause but for the sake of the wealth it will put into their hands."

188

"But . . . such people . . . couldn't they torture the secret out of *you?*"

"They know they couldn't torture me two minutes without killing me. As for Tibbal, he's going to New Orleans to make sure Burr gets the sedan chair. Then he's continuing into the West as a free man. Nor could he remember all the clues and all in order, either. But you—"

"You've put me into terrible danger!"

I would have sworn the blind eyes glared a new emotion at me. It was not fatherly affection for William Downing's daughter. Job rasped with his old asperity: "I shouldn't have to remind you that spying is a dangerous business."

I said nothing. There was nothing to say.

"By the way, when we return to the house you may expect to be searched to the skin by one of our trusted maids—not your Indian. Tibbal couldn't have watched you every minute while you went around with him, and I don't know what you may have been up to."

This man was clever!

"As you wish," I said.

I had to get rid of the papers in my pocket. At the same time I had to make sure I could find them again. I still hoped I could have that cannon found, not by Burr, not by pirates or disillusioned Loyalists, but by an armed force of the United States. I had *not* reckoned on the possibility of torture.

While Tibbal was standing on a high rock, his back toward us, and signaling the bearers to return, I quietly picked up the wine bottle that picnickers or lovers had left behind. I rolled my notes into a small cylinder and slipped them into the bottle. I plugged the bottle with a bit of wood, tucked it down into a crack in the wall, dribbled dirt upon it to hide its glassy shine.

Job had drawn upon his last reserves of strength. When Tibbal and one of the bearers carried him into the sedan chair, his skin had gone a dreadful, dull color and he barely was able to mumble, "Home . . . get to bed." We stretched him out in the chair as well as we could, and I walked beside it, with its door open to give him air.

We were near home when I saw the sick man try to sit up. He fumbled at his inside pocket, then was quiet. As we arrived at Wentworth Hall, Lavinia tottered out, vexed because her cousin had been away from his bed so long. When the bearers set down the chair, Job rolled out of it

and lay limp upon the ground. I bent quickly over the old **man**, and if ever I have seen the face of death, it was Job Wentworth's face as I saw it then.

Lavinia burst into hysterical screaming. I, reaching futilely for the dead man's pulse, saw that next to his open hand lay an oval object the size of a playing card. It was a miniature of a woman of thirty, dark-haired, olive-skinned, long-lashed, bare-shouldered in a ball gown of years ago. Her son Mark's features, made lovely and delicate, looked from that sultry face. Her right hand, resting upon her lower throat, displayed a large opal ring.

Job had still carried his wife's portrait, still had seen her in his mind's eye.

How beautiful she had been!

Or . . . still was?

Where was she now, I wondered as the faithful slaves bore her husband's corpse away.

Chapter Twelve

Job's passing left me saddened, but Lavinia was devastated. Her deepest emotions had been focused on her blind cousin. Now she was left rootless. She went to pieces, wept till I feared for her sanity, and wondered at the same time if she and Job might have had more than a cousinly relationship with each other. I could not comfort her. Old Renzo, himself in tears, shook his head worriedly as he watched Lavinia walk the house like a ghost, touching everything that had been Job's, crying out that he couldn't be dead—it was impossible.

"I don' muches the mel'choly," he told me when I gave him a black band to wear on his sleeve. "The mel'choly tooken a-hold, it sometime never let go."

In Newport there had been a woman who dragged herself about in perpetual black and spent most of her time at her husband's grave even though he was ten years dead. That was the melancholy.

Tibbal was mourning, I knew; but he was not with us. Hiram Chance had insisted that the sedan chair must go immediately to Aaron Burr, and Tibbal had gone off on the *Bridgewater* not two hours after his master had died.

One shock followed another. On the day of the funeral, the armed cutter we had seen in Nassau came to our wharf. An officer in blue coat and white breeches approached the house with every appearance of haste. It was I who spoke to him, for with Mark away and Lavinia incapable of speaking to anybody, I had become the highest-ranking white person at Wentworth Hall.

I hardly could digest the officer's news. It was only later that I realized its full import. He was spreading an alarm. We must urgently beware the pirate brig, bristling with guns, captained by that blond woman. Anne Burney had met the *Bridgewater* off Lanthorn Point, on the route to New Orleans, and had sunk her.

"Sunk her!"

"The *Bridgewater* was seen to burn to her waterline and go down in deep water."

"Was anyone rescued?" I asked breathlessly.

"No, ma'am, there was no known survivor among all the souls aboard. You'll spread the word up and down the island, ma'am? I must keep going. My guns are shotted, and if I find the *Queen of the Caribbean,* I'll sink her."

The cutter was heavily armed. Still, I thought, shuddering, Hiram Chance had been confident he could send Anne Burney to Davy Jones' locker. Now he himself lay on the ocean's floor with all his crew.

Directly after the funeral, Renzo made sure that a guard was posted day and night at the end of the wharf, watching the water. He also had his trusted men keep their muskets handy even when they worked in the fields. How strange it was to know that slaves could be armed and yet not turn against their masters! It would not have been possible on the mainland.

Lavinia somehow had stayed on her feet for the funeral, but afterward she took to her bed, and caring for her and trying to keep the household running hardly left me time to think. Luckily the chief maid, Ora—Isadora—was able to supervise the housekeeping, and the kitchen, tyrannized by the monstrous female cook, ran according to its own laws. Everyone watched for the *Royal Arms* to return. Mistah Mark would stay home now, said the slaves hopefully.

Meanwhile we received comfort from a strange source. An elegant dark-clad man entered the house with a little dark-clad figure toddling after him like a shadow. A glance through a window showed me the yellow rowing-sailing barge, the *Argo,* secured at the wharf.

I greeted Holdridge with little warmth. But I had to admit he had shown delicacy in clothing not only himself but also his blackamoor in funereal garb. His sunken face was full of sorrow. He said it was too bad he had missed the funeral, but it was a long trip and funerals had to be hurried in the tropics. Too bad, too bad, he sighed, and it was hard to recall him as the supersophisticated esthete. He seemed to be merely one more plantation owner who had come to express his sincere sorrow at Job's passing.

I brought him to Lavinia, where she lay helpless on a chaise with Nessa scurrying to bring her powders and potions. At first she shrank from him. But he took no notice, only spoke to her gravely, in his sepulchral voice, of God's will and of the end to which we all must come, and of Job's goodness as a man and as a leader. And he murmured that Job would have wanted Lavinia to be brave; but there, he knew how hard it is to stop the tears when a good man goes to his eternal rest. I listened, and I must admit that after a while even I felt comforted. We had no clergyman to help us, and I think Holdridge supplied something of what a clergyman might have given—appreciation of the dead, comfort for the living, and . . . call it a good graveside manner.

When at last I left the room, I told myself I still distrusted the fellow. But when I returned after an hour I found Lavinia sitting up, propped with pillows. She had refused all food and drink, but now, at Holdridge's gentle urging, she was taking a biscuit and a little wine. The man still might be wicked, but he certainly was comforting to the grief-stricken woman. Her tears had dried. She seemed both bewildered and faintly pleased at this different and most acceptable Holdridge. Again I had to give him credit for being one of those rarest of persons—a good listener. He sat silent, listening with attention and respect as Lavinia talked out every detail of her years with Job. I knew how hard it was to be so patient.

Later, Nessa told me that Miss Lavinia had invited Mr. Holdridge to stay over, and he had said he would— but only as long as he could do her some good. I had a room made ready. I sent Mary to find Gumry and have him make sure the men on the barge had food and a comfortable place to sleep. Obviously my Mary was a woman in love, and I knew she would enjoy doing the errand.

Holdridge wanted to go home the next day, but Lavinia again begged him to stay, and he did. They walked slowly up and down together, in the garden, and later everyone in the house paused and listened when he read the Bible to her in his grave, deep voice. She confided in me that she had terribly misjudged the man. And I, after three days in his correct, respectful company, wondered if I too had not misjudged him. Well, I told myself, it wasn't *I* who had accused him of wickedness, and then had let the wickedness remain unnamed. And as for his having so blandly let me know he'd like me "at the foot of his table"—meaning in his bed—well, he wasn't so different from other men.

When I went to the new grave with orchids and poinsettia, I found the slaves had been there before me with pathetic little bunches of acacia, spider lily, sea oats, or anything else they could gather. As I was distributing my own flowers over the raw, spaded soil, Holdridge and his shadow appeared.

"Job Wentworth led us in our fight for our cause, but never lived to see our victory," said Holdridge, standing with clasped hands and bowed head. "He will be remembered as one of the founding fathers of Burriana. Ah, well . . . *requiescat in pacem.*"

"May he rest in peace," I echoed, noting meanwhile that the headstone was only a slab of wood. There was no hard native rock, and the permanent headstone probably would be New England granite.

Holdridge mused, "No doubt we'll elect Mark to take his father's place as our leader. He has all the qualities of leadership. But right now, poor fellow, he'll come home to very bad news." Holdridge shook his head. His voice was as buried as ever and I still felt a strange uneasiness that made me dislike being near him. Yet the cold patrician did show signs of humanity.

He said as we turned away from the grave: "And there are other deaths to be regretted. That poor chap Chance and all his crew. It's been a long time since Bahamians joined in a pirate hunt, but we may have to again."

"Wasn't it dreadful?"

"Fate, fate," said Holdridge, shaking his head. "I understand that your man Tibbal also was lost with the *Bridgewater.*"

"Yes. He must have been."

"Odd that Job would send him to New Orleans."

This brought my sidewise glance, trying to ferret out a certain *meaning* in the words. "Tibbal had been freed," I said.

"So have others. But—New Orleans?"

"Perhaps Mr. Wentworth wanted him to carry some message to the business agent there. At any rate, Tibbal would let people know of Mr. Wentworth's death."

"Yes," said Holdridge. "I see. Although Captain Chance could just as easily . . . but then, I must not presume to have known Job's mind." We were silent, approaching the house, till he said, "So your work with the history of the Bahamas is over, Miss Arabella? I wonder if Burr will complete the book. I presume Chance was carrying the current part to Colonel Burr for his usual reading and correction."

I dared say only an untruth: "Yes." But as Holdridge bowed and left me, my mind whirled as I tried to think coherently of my own predicament. It was tremendously important to get word to Mr. Jefferson about that cannon, and tell him why I felt it must hold some great treasure, and let him know that if Aaron Burr found it, Louisiana would be invaded and there might be dreadful consequences to the United States. But at the same time, our president must be told that the indispensable list of clues was lying somewhere on the ocean's floor; and that I had made a shorthand copy, and that I was the only one who knew that copy existed, hidden in an empty wine bottle. Let him send armed men to rescue me, and I would be able to find the treasure and present it to the United States!

But I was still being watched. Even when I had gone to the little cemetery, a black man had unobtrusively followed. When the half-dozen neighbors who had been able to attend the funeral had stood at the grave with me, their glances had told me: *Even with Job gone, you'll never get anyone to help you. Even with Mark away on a trip, you'll never get a letter off the island unless it is first opened and read.*

Holdridge stayed another day and another, but only because Lavinia begged it of him. She was constantly in his company. Still there were times when she wept uncontrollably, and I admitted to Holdridge that I worried over her state of mind.

"As do I," he said, holding me with his world-weary, heavy-lidded gaze. Everything she sees reminds her of the departed. She should leave Wentworth Hall for a time."

"Yes, she should. I'll try to get her to visit a friend in Nassau."

"I have always had regard for Miss Lavinia. I know she's heard tales of my—ah—wickedness, which, believe me, amounts only to being more sophisticated than the general run of honest, sunburned Bahamas people. One who is different from his fellows is bound to be misunderstood. But I am pleased to see that in her time of trial she is accepting my friendship. If she had not, I would not make the suggestion I am about to make, that she should come to visit me. On my estate she will have utter peace and quiet. Eleuthera is a beautiful island, and my estate is green . . . very green. To be surrounded with greenery is known to be soothing for those whose minds are . . . vexed."

Suddenly cautious, I said, "I'll talk to her about it."

"Green," Holdridge repeated as though the word were a talisman. "I've so much more moisture than you have here . . . my forest and garden are so much more calming to the nerves . . . restful to the spirit. In Nassau, Miss Lavinia would be forever having to excuse herself from being sociable. On my estate nothing will be asked of her save to recover in quietness and peace. And since I've no other suitable female companion for her, and she speaks so warmly of you, won't you come with her? I don't think she'd consent to go alone, and you too would enjoy a change of scene, would you not?"

I went wary, then, with a kind of instinctive bristle, and said once more that I'd speak to Lavinia.

Holdridge took note of my attitude with a wry nod. "You have little reason to like me, Miss Arabella. Allow me to offer an apology I have owed you for many months. You know I am a widower, a lonely man, and doomed by . . . by accidents of personality to be lonelier still. When we first met, I felt an immediate attraction toward your youth and beauty. Still, the gesture I made with the ruby was—how shall I say it?—ill-advised. And if I made untoward remarks—well, it was a festive occasion and I had been sipping freely of the excellent liquors that poor Job set out. Had had a bit too much, I'm afraid . . ."

He had not seemed drunk at the time. In fact, it was hard to imagine the man risking his suavity by drinking too much. Still, he was apologizing, and what could I say? "Well, Mr. Holdridge, I admit you did upset me, but bygones are bygones."

"Then you'll forgive me? I've worried a good deal over having offended you. It's the last thing I'd want to do."

Like my father, I could forgive. I didn't have to *like* the man, and I didn't seem quite able to trust him. With all that, I need not be so put off by an odd manner and a strange, lost voice.

"I forgive you, sir."

He bowed deeply. "I am your humble servant. Miss Arabella, in any way you may see fit to command. Dare I hope you will become my guest, along with Miss Lavinia, for as long or short a time as you may please? I await your decision."

That night, Lavinia came down to dinner. Peaked and pale, clad in heavy black, she clung to Holdridge's arm and he handled her as though she were made of cut glass. Still, her eyes were no longer so red and she managed a wan smile. She would recover, I thought, no matter how many times Renzo shook his woolly head and didn't muches Miss Lavinia's mel'choly.

At the same time, she *would* benefit by a week or two away from home amid pleasant, green surroundings. And if she did go off to Holdridge's plantation, she really should be accompanied by another female besides her maid. My conscience hurt me. Should I deny such a benefit to a desolated woman? But something within me shuddered at the thought of being so long in Holdridge's presence. As New Englanders say, if a person "puts you off," you're put off and there is nothing you can do about it.

Mary Crow had briskly seen me to bed and had blown out my candle when a thought leaped from the dark.

"Of course!" I said aloud.

"Ma'am?"

"Oh . . . nothing. Good night, Mary dear."

But it was a great deal. Of course I must visit Holdridge's plantation! He had mentioned that his pocket of good soil was located only five miles from the settlement of Aragon Wells, from which he shipped his cotton and cane. Which meant that ocean-going ships put in at Aragon Wells. Which meant that once I was down there on Eleuthera island, away from the strict surveillance I had to endure at Wentworth Hall, I might be able to get away on a ship that would take me home.

But I must play this cautiously. Lavinia was well aware that I was under "house arrest."

Having coffee with her on the terrace, next morning, I found her talking of nothing but Holdridge, his fine family, the depth of his education, the extent of his travels. "Oh, I was so foolish to think ill of the man! It's just that he's a bit too well, overbred. But they always were an overbred family, and overbreeding makes the nicest people seem odd, just as it does with horses."

She was quite serious. I nodded agreement, took the opening, told her we had an invitation to visit the Holdridge plantation for her health's sake. I'd go along to keep her company, of course.

Delighted, she said it was so darling and generous of Mr. Holdridge and she'd love to go. But shouldn't she stay home to break the bad news to poor, dear Mark when he returned from Charleston?

My only chance lay in leaving while Mark was still away. "Now, Cousin Lavinia, your health is at stake. It's important for you to go now, really it is, and I simply must go with you."

"Oh yes, Arabella-love, yes, you're quite right. I'm sure we can trust Renzo to—"

"Of course. But, oh dear," I sighed, and pretended to recall only just then that I was not allowed to leave San Isidro Island.

"Fiddle-de-dee!" said Lavinia. "All that nonsense about spying! I know you better. Anyway, with poor Job dead and Mark not yet home, *I* give the orders here. I'll tell Renzo you're going with me and that's all there is to it. As for Gumry, let Renzo put him in his place. The very idea! Nessa! Where is that girl? Nes-sa! Find Mr. Holdridge and tell him that Miss Arabella and I are pleased to accept his kind invitation." She fluttered and panted. "Oh dear, the excitement is too much for me. Where are my pills?"

Next morning, when we three had breakfast together, I told Holdridge that like most Newport women I knew how to sail a small boat. He said he was delighted to hear it. Because of Miss Lavinia's being in mourning, he knew she would not want to meet other people, and it would be good for her to get out with me on the water.

Aragon Wells was situated on a little cay that was separated from Eleuthera only by a narrow channel. Excitedly I realized that when Holdridge gave me his boat to sail, he'd be playing into my—and Thomas Jefferson's—hands.

The *Argo*'s cabins were airy and pleasant. Holdridge gave us the use of his balcony, where Lavinia and I sat beneath an awning and watched the barge's wake unroll across the sparkling water. The wine, kept cool below, was excellent, and the food was very good.

When Eleuthera showed as a long, gray line in the far distance, the wind turned fitful, then died. A long, oily swell set in. The sky contained mist, rather than cloud, and it seemed to hang just above our mast, full of rain that, when it fell, would be heavy. The rowers were put at the oars. So breathless had the air become that the little blackamoor was set to work, throwing buckets of seawater onto the sweating oarsmen. I noticed how he shrank away from those men, who rolled their eyes at him and made mocking motions, as though to bite him, while the long sweeps pushed us like some great, spraddle-legged insect through the water.

Holdridge's land was all a luscious green. The stretches of forest that remained among the prosperous-looking fields bore enormous trees and huge ferns that like to keep their feet in moisture. When the *Argo* was spotted, a man went running from the landing on a lawn so green it might have been in England. His faintly heard shouts made black faces appear at windows of the extraordinary house that stood not quite at the top of a hill, but partly down the slope so that the hill's shadow could cool it.

My father had once said I had a nose for houses. I recognized this one as Jacobean, in the style favored in the early seventeenth century by James I, that stormy man whose mother had been the stormy Mary, Queen of Scots. I saw a trace of old Gothic, but mostly the decoration was small columns and pilasters, round-arched arcades and rows of dormer windows. It was all so English that one half expected to see ivy hiding the brick garden wall, rather than bougainvillea.

"How lovely!" I said to Holdridge.

"I call my plantation Mistletoe, after the plantation I once had on the Cooper River in Carolina. There is no mistletoe in the Bahamas, but . . . I suppose I have a streak of sentiment somewhere. All those thousands of yellow bricks that make the house were transported down the Cooper and across the sea. I have my Carolina home just as my ancestors built it."

A procession now left the house. It was led by a huge, bull-like black man whose periwig and entire costume was full of antique splendor. He was surely the majordomo, and his exaggerated dignity and white staff of office quite delighted me. The group of house slaves who trooped after him wore smaller, powdered wigs with horizontal curls above the ears, and a red-and-green livery that showed none of the shabbiness that was customary with liveries on San Isidro.

At the landing, the majordomo—his name was Percy—bowed deeply, creasing his great paunch. The servants of lesser rank then bowed. They were youngish, I thought, and most of them were Ashantis with sharp, straight features and a graceful way of walking. The majordomo banged his white staff once on the planks. Four liveried men scurried aboard to collect our chests and wicker hampers. Two others stationed themselves to help us debark.

When Holdrige noticed how badly Lavinia puffed for breath as she climbed the hill, he had slaves carry her up in an armchair. I noticed that despite his half-dead appearance, Holdridge himself acted in no way disabled.

Inside the house, standing on broad, polished boards of Carolina oak, I saw that it must have been refurnished during the mid-eighteenth century, when Carolina plantations had been at their most prosperous. But the entire choice of furniture, rugs, and hangings had been on an extravagant scale, like the European courts of that period.

I asked for a trip through that fascinating house. Lavinia, rallying, said she would accompany me. Upstairs, Holdridge showed us an immense, curtained bed in a truly enormous boudoir. At first I thought he maintained the boudoir in memory of his wife, who, I had heard, died after having had some dreadful hysterical upset. Certainly it was a delightful eighteenth-century chamber. Fanciful scrolled cutouts set off niches in the walls where statuary stood. Light, graceful furniture, much of it handsomely inlaid, stood about in little islands, always with thin-legged tables handy, as though various groups could sit together for a chat or for tea or for fancy sewing, with the lady of the house flitting from one group to the other. I had heard of such boudoirs. They had once been favored by titled ladies, who would hold a kind of court every morning before their beveled triple mirrors—such as the late Mrs. Holdridge had had—while a hairdresser spent an hour arranging the day's coiffure.

Yet a pair of boots, a tankard, a shaving stand told that Holdridge slept here amid the Aubusson rugs, the Bergère chair, and the fresco of idealized shepherdesses. Perhaps the streak of sentiment ran deep.

As I looked around, exclaiming my appreciation, Lavinia went to examine a little pink marble statue. I saw her turn away from it, scarlet-faced, and go hastily to look from a window. Holdridge seemed faintly amused. As I drifted about, I told myself I had poise enough to inspect any nude statue—for what but nudity could have so shocked Lavinia? Still, when I really looked at the statue, I felt the heat of my own flush rise to my face.

"One of my English ancestors brought it from Pompeii, where I suppose he stole it," said Holdridge, flashing his jeweled rings as he patted his hair. "He sent it to one of my ancestors in America. Certain tastes always have run in our family."

Overbred? It required rather too much sophistication to display that little statue, so beautiful in its lines, so startling in its details. Its organs were not exaggerated like those of the African statuettes in Mad Anne Burney's cabin on the *Bridgewater*. But the nature of those organs made me turn away. I did not like to see the male private parts and the female private parts put together in one body.

Meanwhile the wind that had failed us on the water had been returning in fits and starts. Soon it began to howl, and told us its destructive power when broken fronds of palms were blown across the windows. When the rain came it was flung by the wind in nearly horizontal streams. I hardly slept during my first night at Mistletoe. The wind raged, trees came crashing down, and great waves thundered madly on the shore. In the bright sunny morning we found amazing amounts of seaweed and dying sea creatures on the beach, and even a wrecked fishing boat. There was no trace of its men. Heavy damage had been done throughout the plantation, although, as we learned later, we had escaped the worst of the storm. The strongest blows of the *huiravacan*—to give it the ancient Arawak name that Holdridge used—had fallen upon outlying islands to the north and east.

I caught myself worrying about Mark. He might very well have been at sea. My worry was tinged with a certain sting of conscience, for really it should not have been left to Renzo to tell Mark of his father's death. But why was I concerned with a man I'd never see again? The fate of the United States counted far more than a mere expression of sympathy that Mark no doubt would have brushed aside.

Holdridge had to spend days on his horse, traveling around his plantation with the little blackamoor jouncing miserably after him on a Shetland pony. He told us he had to assess the damage done by wind and rain, confer with his foremen about rebuilding the windmill and other ruined buildings, and get replanting started. Certainly he was no outdoorsman. When he came to us in a state of reeling fatigue, asking us to excuse his wearing rough clothing instead of his usual finery, I begged him to leave us to our own devices. At the same time I wondered why he did not delegate more of the estate's supervision to his foremen. At last I became sure he didn't have as much money—nor as many foremen—as he wanted others to believe. Then Mary Crow reported that the cotton crop would average less than 900 pounds per acre, rather than the 1,500 pounds Holdridge had been bringing in. She told us that our host was driving his slaves mercilessly to salvage cane and other crops that had been half buried in mud, and I became sure he was short of ready money.

Still, each morning, Lavinia and I each received a basket of fresh flowers recovered from the ruin of the beautiful gardens, and each basket was accompanied by a note of apology in Holdridge's hand. By next week he'd surely be at our service. We'd always reply on the scented notepaper we found in our rooms. Lavinia assured him she felt better—as indeed she did—and that she never had forgotten his little talks on human courage and God's will. I wrote that I understood an estate owner's responsibilities and only wished I could help in some way. In fact, Holdridge had my sympathy. Seeing him so occupied with mere survival made him far more human.

Meanwhile, although the emergency had put the household staff into a scurry of making repairs, we lacked nothing. Every morning Percy came to stand in the pretty sitting room Lavinia and I shared, solemn and attentive in his vast wig, his white staff held to one side at an unvarying angle. I never gave him orders. I only requested: "Might we have a guide to show us the trail that leads through the forest?" It also led toward Aragon Wells. Or, "Might we have the landaulet?" It was a darling little wagon, painted with flowers, that probably had belonged to Holdridge's wife. Behind a happy little donkey, we drove it along the beach—and I watched the water for signs of significant shipping. Or, "Might we have the sloop today?" We could not go out without a slave to handle the anchor and lines—but the quickest and easiest way to visit Aragon Wells was by water.

At every request, Percy's fat-pouched eyes seemed to look inward in weighty consideration. He was so large, so solemn, so tremendously self-important! Having considered with the gravity of a prime minister, Percy always struck the floor with his staff, once. A footman always arrived within ten seconds. He listened, silent, to a rumble of orders. When the staff banged twice, he disappeared. Percy then bowed, retreated backward three steps, bowed again across that enormous belly. When Lavinia and I went downstairs through the house that once had stood on South Carolina's Cooper River—the house that had been moved across hundreds of miles of ocean, yet never had been moved into the nineteenth century—we always found the day's outing made perfectly ready for us. If a man was to accompany us, his black face shone with scrubbing. At least two handsome young footmen would also be there, anxious to know if we wanted anything more. The slave quarters had quite a population of naked toddlers, some evidently half-white. I wondered if Holdridge was their father. If any came to stare, their thumbs in their mouths, they were led out of our way and made to bow, along with everyone else, as we went off.

Lavinia seemed especially soothed and pleased by the outings in the little sloop. The slave baited the light hooks with which we fished, and we brought in finny rainbows. I kept sailing us closer and closer toward Aragon Wells, always interested—I said—in what rocky bluff or pretty beach lay around the next point. Will, our slave, a well-formed Mandingo with skin like velvet, agreed I handled the sloop well. On our third sailing trip I landed us at Aragon Wells and we went to see the sights of that storm-battered village.

We found a few shops on a sandy street. In one, we were able to buy from a skimpy stock of ribbons. I asked Will to choose a present for himself. He giggled and protested, then chose a high tortoise shell comb that he stuck rakishly into his tightly curled hair.

We found a little jail with its door left open, and goats wandering in and out. A flight of steps outdoors, going up one wall, led to nothing. But you could see the foundation of the gallows that had stood there in the days of the pirates, when whoever walked up those stairs did not walk down again. *Days of the pirates!* But never mind that now. Lavinia was tired. I left her sitting on the steps, in shade, with Will squatting nearby, and I said I'd walk about.

Idly I strolled to a couple of sketchy piers that straggled out into the water. The day before, I had seen a schooner heading in and had known by her style that she'd been launched in New England. I found her. My heart sang when I read the sea-faded name across her counter: *Tiger*, and her home port, *Salem, USA*. Just up the coast from Newport!

I turned to Mary Crow, who, properly, had walked one step behind even though I had refused the parasol. Mary had been attending me with her usual fierce, silent faithfulness; but I knew she was disgruntled. She hadn't wanted to leave Gumry, and indeed, the night before we'd left for Eleuthera she'd been out till dawn, no doubt sleeping in his arms.

We were out of Lavinia's sight, but still I decided to stay a good distance from the *Tiger*. I sent Mary down the length of the pier with instructions to find her captain and tell him that Miss Arabella Downing of Newport wished to speak to him.

She returned with a fair-haired, harassed-looking young man who first of all had recognized Mary as a Narrangansett, then, pointing to the *Tiger*'s starboard hook, informed me that it had once been repaired at my father's shop. This was a good beginning. But Robert Pease was no more than the schooner's second mate, acting as captain. Indicating the newly repaired damage to the *Tiger*'s spars, he told me sadly that the captain and first officer had been lost in the recent hurricane along with two seamen. "And there'll be more widders in Salem, as you've your share in Newport too, walkin' and waitin' for men who'll never come home," he said.

I knew the "widow's walks" on the roofs, from which a woman could watch the sea.

In a while we were chatting about conditions in New England. Business was fair. Mr. Jefferson had suspended the Non-Importation Act, which would have prohibited the importation of a long list of articles from England. But at the same time, there'd been trouble about English captains impressing American seamen on the pretense that they had deserted from the English Navy.

I said—as I'd heard my father say—that this could give rise to a dangerous situation, even war.

Yes, said Pease, there was already talk of war. And *that* would help Boney. He meant Napoleon Bonaparte, of course.

I kept up the talk about such affairs, hoping to lead into my own pressing business. But I had to sound Pease out. He was not much older than I, and had little of the swagger of command that went with ruling from a quarter-deck. He might very well be among those who thought New England should secede—for many restless young men favored the plan, which was opposed by most, though not all, of the older people.

"You're visiting down here, Miss Downing? Hot, ain't it?"

"Yes it is," I said, glad of the opening. "And I'm so grateful for news from back home. Tell me, what's been happening with those men up in that county in Massachusetts . . . oh, Essex County. The Essex Junto—is that what they call themselves?"

Pease frowned. "Essex Junto, aye. They're always shouting for protective tariffs that the South and West don't want, and now they're saying louder than ever that New England and New York should leave the Union. I don't go for that, Miss Downing. And from what I've heard of your father, he was a strong Union man. Why . . ." he leaned close for a confidential whisper, "I even heard that some o' the Tories we kicked out, that came down here—they're connivin' with the Essex crew! Watch out for 'em, Miss Downing."

To have Pease completely on my side was almost too good to be true. I smiled up at him. "Captain Pease . . ."

"Aw now, Miss Downing, I'm not really the—"

205

"But you *are* the master of the ship, and I speak to you as to a person of authority." He accepted that even though he rubbed his neck in embarrassment. "May I tell you something in strict confidence?"

"Why, yes, sartin," he said in the New England way.

"But you'll keep it absolutely secret?"

"Depend on it all the way through," he said, now eager to hear.

"Well, it's very important that I get to Washington, D.C., or any Northern port from which I can travel quickly to Washington. But I'll have to come aboard your ship secretly, with my maid. And you must make sure your men say nothing about me. I've little cash, but I own Downing Ironworks so I can guarantee payment for the passage."

"You want to go on the *Tiger?* Well, Miss . . ." He glanced around uneasily at the gently swaying schooner. "Well, miss, you see . . . it's not the money . . . the Downing family, why . . . no question at all. . . . And as for a cabin . . . you'd have Mr. Caulfield's . . . he was the first mate . . . I didn't take his cabin nor the cap'n's, out o' respect . . . but"—his voice took on a quick desperation— "the Commodore—Commodore Arkwright—he'll have no women aboard his ships. Now, I mean, if you was marooned on a desert island and I took you off, that's savin' a life. But you're not. The Commodore . . . owns fourteen ships, he does . . . but not a man ever holds his command of an Arkwright bottom if he takes a woman aboard! Not even the captain's wife!"

An eccentric New England shipowner. There were too many of them looking for ways to show their tyranny. And Mr. Pease might be made a real captain, now—but certainly not if he allowed a petticoat to rustle along his deck!

Time was passing. "Very well," I said swiftly. "Then will you take a confidential letter I'll prepare? You'll get it tomorrow. But it has to be secret . . . secret, please! It's . . . it's about a private commercial venture that my father was interested in and if the Tories here ever found out I've been prying into their commercial affairs . . ."

"Oh, I'd like to put a twist in their noses," said Pease.

"Then you'll take the letter to Patience Bentley on

Spring Street, in Newport? I'll enclose a draft on Downing Ironworks to pay double your expenses from Salem. . . ."

"Why, ma'am, I've an old granny in Newport and she'd be glad if I visited her. My pleasure, Miss Downing, to be of aid to as fine a family as yours."

I thought: If Robert Pease is ever to make a good ship's captain, he'll have to become less deferential.

But I said, "I can't tell you how grateful I am." Hurriedly, then, for I didn't want to be seen near a ship, or talking to a seaman: "If I can't bring the letter my maid will bring it."

"But how soon, Miss Downing? All my heavy-weather damage is repaired, and I'm off for Salem on the morning tide, short after sunrise."

"Oh . . ." Could I meet such a schedule? "Couldn't you wait a day or two? You see—"

"Couldn't, I'm sorry. The *Merchant*, out of Salem, was here when I arrived and is on her way back now, with news of the deaths and word that I'll bring the *Tiger* home as soon as she's seaworthy. If the Commodore ever found out that I had loitered . . ."

"I see. Then Mary Crow"—who could make her way through dark woods—"will be here with my letter before sunrise."

"Good. Let her wait on the opposite shore, there, and I'll have a boat go to her at first light."

"Someday we'll meet again in Salem or in Newport, Captain Pease, and I'll be able to tell you what you've done for me . . . and your country. Now I must run."

I smiled at his puzzled face, walked away quickly and just in time. Within two minutes I met Will, who was searching for me. Lavinia had begun to fret about my being away so long; and anyway, it was time to return to Mistletoe.

To my surprise, we found Holdridge sitting in a little gazebo near the water, a glass at his side and a book in his hand. He was again handsomely dressed, and he looked rested. He mentioned he had just risen from a nap. "A well-earned nap," he added, "for the plantation is in order again."

"Poor, dear Mr. Holdridge! You've had so much trouble!" Lavinia exclaimed.

"It's merely the price of prosperity," said Holdridge. Seeming to include both of us in his remarks, but really watching me, he went on: "I'm glad you ladies are back from your outing. You'll have time to rest, then dress. We'll have our welcome dinner this evening, at last, and start your visit all over again, this time with the ceremony it deserves."

I was pleased neither with the plan nor with the glint in his hooded eyes. I needed time in which to write that critical letter. But I saw no way of avoiding the dinner, and I had no wish to spoil the evening for Lavinia, just when she was becoming capable of feeling joy again.

That lovely dining room! There was a long, graceful table with rounded ends, flanked by rush-seated chairs in the same glowing mahogany, with backs carved of one piece that seemed many interlaced components. The darkly elegant sideboard was inlaid with circles and ovals of tulip wood, and graced, on top, with gilt leather knife racks and the handsomest of silver coffee urns. The tall windows and the six-paneled door were crowned with wreath designs worked into the plaster. All the paint was a soft, cool, light green. It blended with an Oriental rug that was so old its colors had become muted, like those of long-dried flowers. The epergne in the middle of the table was worth a fortune, and the silver and the napery would have put even eighteenth century Downings—when we had been rich—to shame.

A slave bowed us in, a slave slid our chairs beneath us.

I had explained to Lavinia that I felt obliged to wear my daring gown, little though I might wish to. She had said, "Oh, if Mr. Holdridge admires it so, why, of course! As long as there's nobody to be scandalized." Then, with a coquettish wink that showed how far she had recovered: "You do look so lovely in it—and our Mr. Holdridge would be quite a catch, you know!"

At least he had not placed me at the foot of the table. It would have been improper to accept the place and yet most difficult to refuse. I sat at his left, and Lavinia was at his right, a place of honor, as she well knew.

I still remember the turtle shell filled with buttered turtle and crabmeat, the *daube glacé*, the *coq au vin*, with a *filet de boeuf* ready if anyone still had appetite for it. I think the names of the dishes linger because Holdridge used them as examples in a discourse on New Orleans food—for they were all favorite dishes of the Crescent City. He said he liked to salute New Orleans, that oasis of gracious living, that bit of European civilization that was so badly needed in a—he begged my pardon—still savage land.

I remarked, "It seems to be a favorite haunt of Colonel Burr's."

Holdridge said suavely, "The Colonel is known for his good taste. Percy! Your men are slow with the wine." Five kinds of wine.

The cadaverous Holdridge, whose fine lawn neckcloth sported a considerable diamond, said he was glad he could once again find time to go over his European investments. It had become a delicate matter of switching funds from one country to another, ahead of Napoleon's marching armies. He had had to give the Rothschilds more leeway than he'd wished in handling his funds. But what else could one do when one lived an ocean away and decisions had to be made quickly.

"Oh, money, money, money!" said Lavinia. "In Carolina we never thought of money."

"Ah!" said Holdridge. "You mean the ladies never did."

"Now, Mr. Holdridge, it simply isn't proper for ladies to even mention money."

"Yes, Miss Lavinia, in an ideal world they shouldn't have to. And if I ruled the world, so it would be."

It was on the tip of my tongue to pooh-pooh that gallant notion, but I let it pass. Holdridge went on: When would he see Rome again? And Florence! Venice! An esthete's soul demanded to be nourished at fountains of beauty. He'd never give up Mistletoe—he had to admit it was the source of his income—but still it made for a lonely life. Did either of us remember our Plato? Surely even women received a little Plato in their early years? I didn't like the way he said "even women," and it occurred to me, at that moment, that there was hardly a woman at work in the entire big house. Well, Holdridge was saying, he referred to Plato's notion about men of iron and copper, men of silver, and men of gold. The men of iron and copper were the peasants. The men of silver included the better class of merchants, the administrators and such. The men of gold were those who had been born to rule.

"And so we are, all of us, born to our destiny. . . ."

Thus he went on, urbane, learned, entertaining if one were not too annoyed at his completely aristocratic view. And gradually, as the meal approached its end with *torte* and *crème glacé,* the half-hidden glint of his gaze turned almost entirely to me. Gloated on me. Undressed me. Devoured me. Shifted significantly, sometimes, to indicate the vacant armchair at the foot of the table, I looked straight ahead, sat motionless, wishing I could stop breathing and so stop the rise and fall of my bosom, more than half-exposed to his view and touched with mellow candlelight that shifted upon my skin.

With all this, Holdridge said not a word that was offensive. But he seemed to anticipate something, plan something, and I felt a chill of fear. Was it possible that his concern for Lavinia had been only a ruse to get us into his house? He once had been frank about wanting my body—and now I had put myself into his hands. So had Lavinia, but I realized she could be only a pawn in the passionate game.

What to do? What might a later hour bring? Should I try to slip out of the house, make my way to Aragon Wells, beg Pease to take me aboard the *Tiger?* No, he wouldn't. But if I offered myself to him? Even offered to be his bedmate for the entire voyage? No! Not Pease! Moreover, if I tried to reach him and was caught, I would jeopardize the arrangement I had made for him to carry the secret letter. All I could do was to get that letter written and send Mary slipping off with it, in the hope she could reach Aragon Wells before the sun rose and the tide turned and the *Tiger* left for Salem.

After the meal, Bartley Holdridge took us to his music room, next to a library lined with the works of the great poets and philosophers. He had a fine harpsichord and he played well. Haydn. Mozart. Nothing more recent. At last, with a significant glance at Lavinia's nodding head, he murmured that Miss Lavinia must not tire herself. I knew he wanted me to remain with him, but I too pleaded fatigue. He rang for a servant to light us upstairs. As he bowed his goodnight I saw that same gloating, and there was a kind of knowing ease about him, as though he knew he could afford to wait.

Chapter Thirteen

"Mary! Listen carefully."

Mary Crow had been waiting to undress me, but I had no thought of sleep. Softly I explained I had to depend upon her and told her what she must do. First, wait for me to write the letter that must be carried away secretly on the *Tiger*. Then, around two in the morning, when everyone would be asleep, take that letter and slip away. Follow five miles of rough dark trail. At the first glimpse of dawn, show herself opposite where the *Tiger* lay. Give the letter to Pease or some trusted man he would send. Return.

Mary said only: "Yes'm."

For now she must guard me against interruption or discovery, just as she had in Wentworth Hall. But this time we dealt with no temperamental Highlander, and we *would* get a letter aboard a ship.

I began to write the letter in my bedroom, with the door ajar and Mary sitting by it watchfully. A window was open at the end of the corridor and my own window was open too, but still there was hardly enough draft to stir my candle. Mary hissed a warning. Will had come upstairs. Apologizing for disturbing me, he said he must close the corridor window because there was a threat of rain. "Of course," I said, standing to hide my letter and smiling to him, glad he had been recently promoted from deckhand to house slave. I only asked him to tiptoe because Lavinia and Nessa—thank goodness!—were long asleep.

After he left I sat down again to my letter. So important was my message that I addressed the letter directly to the President of the United States, the author of the Declaration of Independence, and gulped at my temerity. But as I wrote to Thomas Jefferson he became less the president and more the Virginia planter, a man who knew what it was to worry about crops and taxes. To such a man, whom my father had called a great patriot, I poured out every detail I knew of the plot to dismember the United States, every possible name and locale . . . about the Spanish captain . . . the maps seen through the skylight . . . the cannon being assembled and fitted with wheels . . . the Bahamas Corps of Horse . . . and at last, when my eyes were going bleary, I wrote about the hidden cannon that must hold some great treasure, because it was immensely valuable to the Loyalist cause and badly needed by Aaron Burr.

"But," I wrote, "when Mr. Wentworth was sending the directions to Colonel Burr by way of the ship *Bridgewater,* that ship was sunk at sea. Meanwhile Mr. Wentworth had died, so Colonel Burr does not know how to find the cannon." Then I sat and thought. Should I tell Thomas Jefferson of my copy of the clues, secretly scrawled and hidden in a bottle? No. Instinct told me not to put that key secret into writing.

I sealed the letter, addressed it to Aunt Patience along with a short personal note. I glanced out at the stars, asked Mary if she did not agree it was about an hour past midnight.

She nodded, and said she ought to go outside and make sure of the way to the trail, where we had been only once.

"But what if anyone sees you?"

She said she'd claim she'd had a quarrel with me and that I had sent her out to cool her head.

When she had gone I felt alone and vulnerable, and even a bit foolish. With all my spying I had not yet been effective, had brought myself only to humiliation and failure. Was it to happen again? Too hurried to undress, I covered my ball gown with a dressing gown that had a large, low pocket. Tucking the letter into the pocket, I sewed a few stitches invisibly, on the inside, so the letter could not possibly fall out.

It was a big letter, and it thumped awkwardly against my leg as I paced the corridor, trying to relax my nerves. At last I paused at the window that Will had closed, looked out again at the stars. Not a cloud was in the sky. What had made anyone think it might rain that night?

For a long time I had been hearing only the scratch of my quill. Now, standing in tense silence, I became attuned to other sounds . . . the faint scratching of a mouse in the wall . . . a night bird outside . . . and then, very faintly from the back stairs, I thought I heard someone laughing.

In very dim light that came from my open bedroom door, I peered down the stairs. Yes, voices. Then more faint laughter. Servants, and no doubt slaves, might make their own little routs below stairs. But who would risk disturbing his master at one in the morning?

I crept down the stairs till I came to a little storeroom. At its back wall there was a gap in the boards, and light came through. I heard men's voices, kept low. Then a strange cry. A child's voice. The woman in me reacted to that plaintive cry, and I peered through the crack into a between-stairs room such as is often used for storing old furniture. Sure enough, I did see chairs, hassocks, and sofas standing about in the light of lamps.

But also there were several men in that room. I saw young, graceful, black, smooth-skinned men, and every one of them was naked. Several showed clearly that they were sexually excited. But they were not being excited by women. They were excited by the look and touch and caresses and admiration of each other. Others lay about on the sofas, languidly drinking from bottles. But as I watched, two of them—no! my mind refused the knowledge—two of them became engaged in applying their mouths to each other's parts.

I wanted to run and I could not move. I wanted to shut my eyes tightly but kept staring. I saw Percy. That mountain of flesh was standing naked, save that his private parts were concealed by his huge belly. At last I saw Bartley Holdridge himself hidden behind Percy and pressed tightly against him and moving . . . moving . . . gasping and moving in the act of sodomy. I saw it and I smelt its sweat, but still, although my hands clawed at my face, my eyes remained open. I saw Bartley Holdridge fling back his head in ecstasy, then fall upon a couch, gasping, flaccid. Instantly my friend Will and another velvet-skinned young man moved to caress him.

The child's cry of pain sounded again. It was the little blackamoor. They had him in midair, one man penetrating him, while a second man came at the boy from the front. . . .

What they did to that dull-witted child I cannot bring my pen to write. But I remembered Holdridge coming from the woods behind Wentworth Hall with the blackamoor

215

toddling after him in a state of shock, and the master's face sunken and ravaged by debauchery.

Now Percy, grinning, lifted his great abdomen out of the way and Holdridge prepared to play the female part. He had another voice. Not the deep, buried tones I had often heard but a weird falsetto.

While he gave himself to his majordomo, Bartley Holdridge motioned Will to come to him. He had decided to keep his hands vilely busy.

I found I had bruised my lips by forcing my knuckles against my mouth to keep myself from screaming.

I made myself return very slowly and silently to the stairs, and as I climbed them I gritted my teeth in still-unbelieving horror. The orgy continued behind me, and then I heard Holdridge say in his normal voice: "Ah, you're good lads, all of you. Come, let's dance."

In my room, I tried to make myself stop shaking. A voice within me seemed to scream, "Get out of here, get out, get out, get out, get out!" Even so, soul-shaken and nauseated as I was, I knew I had to stay and wait for Mary to return. Let her only go to Aragon Wells, return, and tell me my letter was safely aboard the *Tiger*. Then I'd have it out with Bartley Holdridge!

Half an hour later I was seated at my table with my head in my hands when someone entered the room behind me. "Mary?" I asked, turning. But I found myself looking into Will's black face.

He was liveried and correct. "Marstah wish to see you in his study downstairs, Miss Downing."

At that hour? "I'm about to go to sleep," I said.

"Marstah say you come see him in his study."

Holdridge could have noticed the light from my candle. At any rate, Will's manner told me he had orders to bring me downstairs. I had no one to help me. Still in my dressing gown, I went, carrying my candle, and he followed me along the corridor and down the beautiful flying staircase that curved unsupported to the floor below.

Bartley Holdridge, neatly clothed, sat behind his desk in a study lined with books and statuary. When he did not ask me to be seated, I took a chair and stared at him. His own candle cast weird shadows on his pale face and the reflected flickering that ran along the polished top of the deck made him seem like a figure from another world.

He said, "You spent a long time writing a letter. Don't try to deny it. Will saw your papers and quill and ink."

"What of it? Surely I'm entitled to write a letter to my aunt in Newport."

"That depends on what the letter says. But first of all— I know you've been trying to get back to New England."

"How did you—?" I bit my lip.

"How did I know?" Holdridge laughed gently and dangerously. "You went off by yourself in Aragon Wells. Later Will found you. But before that he had been watching you talk to Robert Pease, acting master of the schooner *Tiger*, Salem, Massachusetts. In addition, I know much of your history at Wentworth Hall. And I know a good deal more. I had an informer."

My shock came through in my voice. "But who—?"

"Tibbal."

Yes, Job Wentworth had been afraid that someone had suborned one of his slaves.

"All of which leads me to suppose, Arabella, that when the *Tiger* sails at dawn you had hoped to be aboard. But something changed your plans. Otherwise, you'd have waited till you were safely at sea before you put your thoughts into a letter. Instead, you scribbled away a long time tonight, when you should have been in bed."

Both in outrage and to get him off the subject, I cried, "Yes, I was up late. Late enough to hear voices from the back stairs, and go down and see you at your—your—"

"Orgy?" Holdridge allowed himself only faint surprise. "How clever of you to find a peephole somewhere. Did you enjoy the view?"

"It was the most disgusting, the most horrible—"

"I thought you were more of a woman of the world. For all the thousands of years of human history, there has been a segment of society that takes its pleasure in its own sex."

How could I voice my disgust? "You shop for the right kind of house slaves, I suppose!"

"Why, yes. It assures them good treatment and it assures me good company."

"But you've forced a young boy to—"

"Quite. And I understand that the first sight of man-to-man mating could be upsetting to a young lady. Hadn't you better have a cordial? Really," he went on as he poured his own liqueur, for I could accept nothing from his hand:

"I'm bisexual. I enjoy the best of both worlds. I could take you or I could take a delightful young man with equal aplomb. The touch of the whitewash brush you've noticed in the slave quarters is all by courtesy of myself. The wenches are proud to bear the master's progeny. As for my young men . . . some of them wish pitifully that they were women. Or like the statue in my boudoir . . . that would be best of all."

"That frightful statue!"

"That beautiful statue," said the cavernous voice in reproof. "It represents a hermaphrodite. Hermes, messenger of the gods and conductor of souls to Hades, combined with Aphrodite, goddess of love and beauty and fertility. In short, the man with breasts . . . and rather more, if you look closely. The view at the fork of the legs was unusual, was it not? Such creatures were reverenced in ancient days. Cripples went to them to be healed by their touch. Some of the more dissolute Roman emperors, like Caligula, used them in special ceremonies of sex. Ah!" Holdridge whispered beyond me into the shadows that hung about the room. "That is the ultimate pleasure . . . when the sexes flow and merge into each other . . . unbelievable ecstasy . . . unbearable . . . yet borne . . ." He gave me a sudden widening of his usually half-closed eyes; it was a new and terrible expression. "If only I had a hermaphrodite here in the flesh," he muttered.

My skin crawled. When my hands went to my mouth in an instinctive gesture of loathing, Holdridge laughed at me. "So New Englandish! But still you are beautiful, and your body is wonderfully shapely, and how kind of you to have brought along that spectacular gown. I must see you better." He touched another candle to the shivering flame of mine, that I still held as though ready to run, and gloated over the desk at me. "By the way," he said, "don't think you can escape. Every door is guarded. Also I have a special guard. Percy!"

A huge bulk shuffled in from the dark hall outside, like a moving shadow. Percy, still naked—strangely, terribly, invisibly naked—bowed to me."

"Thank you, Percy. You may wait outside. I merely wanted you to know, Arabella, that Percy shares my own taste. My—ah—shall we say double standard in sex? I have promised him that if you try to escape I will hand you over to him. You recoil? But it would be for one night only." He flayed me with his affected, falsetto laughter.

I saw a little clock that stood on his desk, held up by two gilt statuettes—a naked little girl and a naked little boy. It was a quarter till two of the morning. Helplessly I realized that Mary might already have returned, might be waiting for me to give her the letter. And time was running out.

As though he had read my mind, Bartley Holdridge murmured, "Concerning that letter you were writing. I'll have it if you please."

"I have no letter with me."

"Foolish girl! The heavy letter that I saw making a lump in your pocket and bumping your leg when you entered this room."

"But it's a personal letter to my aunt!"

"I wonder." Holdridge held out a slim, aristocratic hand.

"No!"

"I also promised Percy that if you acted too stubborn . . ."

He could not have frightened me more. Hastily I ripped the stitches I had taken, pulled the letter from my pocket, handed it over. I, the spy! I the fumbling fool!

"Forgive me," said Holdridge in a travesty of politeness. He ripped open the seal and read aloud: " 'To Thomas Jefferson, Esquire, the White House, Washington, D.C.' " Sparing me a pitying look, he read on silently, muttering to himself now and then: "Yes . . . you found out a great deal . . . yes . . . just what Jefferson would want to know."

He paused at the last page, read it again, slowly turned his sunken, ravaged face toward me. "Just as you say here, the transcription of the clues to the cannon was lost when the *Bridgewater* went down. Yes, I know that Job Wentworth dictated it all to you. I even know that Tibbal burned your shorthand notes."

Yet he could have had no chance to see the freed slave before Tibbal had sailed for New Orleans. How much had Holdridge seen from the *Argo*? I remembered the strange flash of light. It must have been the sun flashing on the polished tube of a telescope . . . yes, the very telescope with which Lavinia and I had amused ourselves while sailing to Mistletoe! He even could have sighted Tibbal and me along the ridges, here and there, as we had traced our way toward the underground road to the cannon. *Had he also seen me scribble the clues in shorthand when Tibbal wasn't looking?* No! I had ducked down every time.

Holdridge had leaned back. He crossed his legs, waited, then said with slow emphasis, "Arabella, I want that cannon. The clues to its hiding place no longer exist in writing. But they do exist in your head."

"I couldn't possibly remember them all! Mr. Wentworth purposely made them complex so they'd be difficult to remember. And they have to be exactly in order, too!"

But the sepulchral voice said only: "Those clues are in your memory. You heard them spoken by Wentworth. You wrote them in shorthand. Then you wrote them again in plain words. Then you rehearsed them as you went around with Tibbal, I'm sure. *I* know those clues are in your mind. And I will have them, Arabella!" He leaned toward me, his hands fisting on his desk. I will have those clues because *I will have that cannon!*" Now there was something reptilian in the avid glint of the hooded eyes. "Do you know why I have given so much money to the Loyalist cause? To make them trust me. To be one of them and know their secrets. But that accursed Job kept *his* secret." He slapped my letter onto his desk. "Now I'm closer to finding the cannon than anyone else alive, save you. And you are going to find it for me. Do you understand? *You are going to find that cannon for me whether you like it or not!*"

I sat and waited, wondering what would next befall me. It would be evil—that I knew.

Holdridge muttered, "If Burr ever finds it, he'll waste its value on the cause. *I* know it's a lost cause. Not that I favor anything so ridiculous as a democracy. No," he went on, his voice haunted and almost lost. *"My* world ended when Louis XVI's head rolled into the basket below the guillotine! Now—though I dutifully pretend to hate Napoleon—I want that great conqueror to become ruler of Europe and restore aristocracy to its rightful place. But my finances are in disorder. If I had that cannon . . ." A long moment passed in the nearly dark, hot, silent house, broken only by the clock's ticking. "If I had that cannon, I'd soon regain my family's estate in England. I'd be the foremost squire of the county. And Rome . . . Venice . . . Madrid . . . they'd know me again. Arabella, *you are going to lead me to that cannon.* And I tell you this. Listen well.

When that cannon is mine, and the Loyalists have no chance to fight for a Burriana . . . when they realize that however mistaken and foolish the United States may be, it is stronger than they . . . then, Arabella, then—no, even before then—you'll be sharing the benefits of that cannon with me."

What did he mean? My bewildered, fearful face asked the question.

"You will marry me," he said.

Shock kept me speechless and motionless. My only thought was: *Never!*

"But first the cannon."

I swallowed, said, "It's impossible for me to give you the directions. No one in the world could remember—"

"The mind is strange," said the man who, without touching me, kept me captive in that cursed house. "When Burr was in the islands years ago, we held excellent discussions on the powers of the mind. You must know that matters we forget for many years can return suddenly to the memory. It is as though the mind had been jarred, and old stored-up facts came down from some dusty shelf. But what jars the lost memory? Sometimes it's hearing or seeing a reminder of the past. But also, when people whose memories fail them are put under torture . . ."

Torture!

Holdridge said, "I should regret having to force the secret of the cannon from your screaming throat. You might not see me as the ideal husband, then. *But I will have that cannon.*" He rose, went to a cabinet, took out heavy objects, showed me one. There was a threaded shaft, a handle with which to turn it. The other end of the shaft went into a small iron case.

"I have amused myself by having my smith make replicas of devices found on old wrecks around here. This is a thumbscrew. The thumb goes into the hole, here. Pressure is brought to bear upon it. The pain is excruciating. The thumb is often cracked and crippled. Still, a woman with a maimed hand could bear an heir for me . . . and that is what I want of you. A son."

"No!" I screamed, and leaped up, shrinking against the wall.

"Here's another clever device. It's called the boot." It was, indeed, a sort of iron boot, quite heavy. "Your dainty foot would go in there, do you see? Wooden wedges would be added to fill up the space. Then would come the final wedge, slowly driven down with a mallet to the tune of your screaming . . . till your foot bone—there are a good many little bones in the foot—ground upon each other and crumpled within your skin. It might be advantageous to have a crippled wife. Other men wouldn't go after her. Come, Arabella. What was Job Wentworth's first direction?"

My shivering, gibbering words came tumbling through a dread that had reduced me to helplessness. "The wall . . . on the point . . . where we sat . . . walk thirty paces from its eastern end. Find a mound of shells hidden in a clump of poisonwood. Under the shells is a block of coral with an arrow chiseled into it. . . ."

"Wait," said Holdridge swiftly, taking paper from the cabinet. He made me repeat the directions. "you are being very sensible, Arabella. Give me the second direction."

It poured from fearful mind to shuddering mouth. "Go the way the arrow points. Climb a rock wall ten feet high. At the top, stand in line with the poisonwood bush and the northwest corner of Wentworth Hall." I waited, staring at the boot. I sat suddenly, drawing my feet beneath the chair. "Turn directly around . . . go in a straight line . . . find the skull of a cow. Go the way the left eye socket points."

" 'Left eye-socket points.' Very, very good. Now, the third, if you please."

But I gasped helplessly, "I can't remember!"

"Take a moment," said Holdridge almost genially. "We have all night. Meanwhile . . ." He frowned at the letter I had written so carefully. He rolled the pages into a shape he could hold conveniently, touched the pages to his candle. They began to burn slowly, as rolled-up paper will. He tossed them into the handsome little fireplace that had come with the rest of the house from Carolina, where they continued burning.

"Well?"

"I can't remember! It—it—there was a hollow gouged in a rock. It looked natural . . . or was that the fourth . . . or the fifth . . . I can't remember, I can't remember!"

Holdridge picked up the iron boot, held it close to me. "Look. Isn't it ingenious? Your dainty foot goes in here. Then the wedges are driven in. . . ."

The paper, half burning, half smoldering, cast a waver-

222

ing light. The fate of the United States might be burning there. The light wavered on my feet as I stared down at them in horror . . . made highlights on the high-heeled green shoes I still wore. I remembered something, then. I remembered kicking Aubrey Brinton, the lecherous domino. Leaning back as though avoiding the boot, I whipped up both feet violently and kicked my heels into Holdridge's arm, saw his face contort with pain as he dropped the boot onto his own foot. In his moment of helplessness I rushed to the fireplace, seized the roll of paper at its unburned end, thrust fire at his face. When he reared backward he fell over the chair. I rushed out just in time to thrust my torch at the advancing Percy, who cried out when the flame touched his cheek. I got past him before he could recover, dropped the burning papers onto the end of a drape where it touched the floor.

Instantly flames began to skitter up the fabric while I raced upstairs, screaming, "Fire! Fire!"

I counted on turmoil, men running to put out the blaze. I had it. Mary dashed down the stairs toward my voice, ran into me in a cloud of smoke.

I grabbed her, speaking rapidly. "Run to Aragon Wells. Shout and scream till someone on the *Tiger* comes for you —don't wait! Tell Pease that for the sake of the United States I beg him to come and rescue another lady and me from Mistletoe. To come with men armed with knives or belaying pins—guns if he has them. But come instantly. For a day's delay in his sailing I offer him five hundred dollars! Run, Mary!" Then I slapped my hands together and said loudly, "Get out of my sight, you Indian bitch! I have more to worry about than your apologies."

Holding a hand to her cheek, Mary gave me an understanding "Yes'm," as she went down the stairs and woefully toward the back door. Already, house slaves had pulled down the drape and were stamping out the fire. I rushed farther up the stairs, saw Lavinia in her nightgown, all confused, and shouted, "Go back, dear, it's nothing! Go back to sleep!"

Fortunately she had already turned away when I was captured. I had known I'd have no chance to escape.

Now all hope rested with Mary.

Chapter Fourteen

In a cold rage, Holdridge had two of his handsome slaves whipped for allowing Mary Crow to get out of the house. Poor young men! I heard their shrieks when the lashes were laid on, and their sobbing attempts to explain—it was only that the girl had had a quarrel with her mistress, tried to make it up, couldn't, had gone out sulking. Besides, shouldn't people be allowed to leave the house when there was a fire? They knew their backs would be scarred and they'd end up as field hands. Sitting miserably in my room with guards at the door, I wondered what would happen to such as they when they outgrew their fresh young handsomeness.

But my own troubles outweighed theirs. It was now broad daylight. The *Tiger* had been seen heading out to sea in a spanking breeze. I knew Holdridge was worried about Mary's having gone off in the schooner to spread word in the United States of what she knew. I knew she would not have gone even if Pease had been willing to take her. But where was she?

And where was the group of seamen I'd expected to come storming up the trail with Mary in the lead? I stopped expecting to be rescued, lost hope, sat with my head in my hands.

Holdridge came in, limping, savagely out of sorts. I had thought him incapable of showing temper. Percy was with him, dressed for the outdoors. Percy grabbed me while Holdridge fettered my wrists with iron bracelets so heavy they dragged my arms down. Ruefully I recalled three hundredweight of fetters delivered to the slave ship *Bridgewater*. Now I knew how fetters felt.

Grabbing the chain that linked the bracelets, Percy dragged me, still in my ball gown, down the stairs, across the lawn, down to the beach. When I stumbled and fell, Holdridge kicked me till I stood again. I called him a coward, said it was no sign of manhood to mistreat a woman. I didn't seem to penetrate the fury of his face.

Down at the beach, in a little cove to one side of the landing, we came upon a strange object. A long pole rested horizontally on a high stump, on which it could be swung around or up and down like a seesaw. From its far end, out over the water, hung a crude armchair made of planks. It was weighted with rocks.

"Tell me what it is," Holdridge demanded.

"A ducking stool."

"Yes, and I had it made especially for you." In New England it brought punishment to the scold, sometimes to the prostitute. The woman was strapped into the chair, then ducked into a pond while the villagers laughed at her. But in the days of witch-hunting the ducking stool was used in a sterner way. To make a woman confess she is a witch, simply hold her under water a minute at a time. It is very frightening to almost drown . . . and almost drown again.

I stared at the device. "You wouldn't!"

"I would. I was only scaring you with the thumbscrew and the boot. Would I, a lover of beauty, marry a maimed woman? The ducking stool breaks no bones, leaves no scars. But when you are under water, unable to breathe, your lungs bursting, I hope your mind will respond to the emergency. *I want to know the way to the cannon.* And quickly. I had time for patience before, but now I'm sure your maid is on the *Tiger* and will soon be telling Jefferson all she knows. I want to take that cannon and get to Europe with it. So here we are, you and I and Percy, with no one to bother us. Well?"

Standing chained to a tree, I noticed that the inland end of the beam was tucked under a rock. When it was pulled free, the chair would fall and sink along with the person secured in it. When Percy put his weight on the end of the beam, the chair would be drawn up out of the water and could be swung around to shore.

Carrying a drowned woman?

Stiff with fright, I told Holdridge, "I—I think—yes—there was a big arrow made of stones piled together."

Holdridge had a board with paper tacked to it. He wrote my words. "You're being very sensible," he told me. "Go on."

"There was a lot of sand on the arrow. And . . . and . . ."

"You went the way the arrow pointed?"

"No! You faced that way but you walked toward the right."

"Excellent. How many paces?"

"Right into a gully."

"Ah! But what was the number of that clue? As you yourself said, they must be followed in order."

"I . . . oh, I can't remember. Perhaps it was number twenty . . . perhaps . . . I don't know, I don't know!"

Holdridge came to me, grabbed the chain between my wrists and twisted it till I shrieked with pain. "Does that help your memory?"

"There . . . there was an old musket stuck into the ground. Vines had been trained to grow around it. You had to know where to look. A number was scratched on the barrel. You took that number of paces. . . ."

"When? After you walked away from the cow's skull?"

"No . . . oh, oh, don't, please, please!" He had twisted the chain again. "Later . . . but how can I remember when? There were so many directions, so many!"

Holdridge said to Percy, "Put her into the chair."

They tied me in and swung me out over the water.

"Well?" said Holdridge from the shore.

"The number scratched on the gun . . . I do remember . . . it was forty! But . . ."

"I have no time!" shouted Holdridge. "Percy, duck her."

The chair fell down into the warm, clear water. In the instant before it touched, I saw starfish on the bottom, and sea urchins, and tiny fish. Then came the splash and the water closing over my head.

I sat there with bursting lungs, my eyes wide open in the water that would have seemed beautiful, all struck with sunlight—at another time. Bubbles rushed up past my face. Suddenly the chair rose and I was swung, gasping and sputtering, to the shore.

"Well?"

"I can't, I can't, please believe me! Oh . . . wait . . ."

"Ah-ha!"

"At one place you'd find an iron collar—the kind they put on slaves to punish them." I had to stop and gasp. Water ran from my hair into my mouth, and I gagged, but went on babbling, hardly knowing where I was or what was happening to me. "The collar stands under a

227

Spanish bayonet plant where it's hard to see. He'd had it painted and greased to keep from rusting through."

"Well, well?" demanded Holdridge. "You look through the circle, I suppose, and—?"

"No. It was on a hill, half buried. You had to notice which way it would roll. But I . . . I . . ."

"You can't remember where it stood in the order of directions? Swing her out again, Percy! She goes under twice as long this time!"

I gulped in air, and as the water closed around me I tried to pray. Very soon my lungs were bursting again. Craning my head back I saw the surface of the water not a foot above me, but it might just as well have been a mile away. The sunlight was fading. Explosions seemed to go off inside my head, leaving black and red streaks behind my staring eyes . . . which strangely saw less and less . . . and still they did not haul me up . . . but I didn't seem to care . . . a strange peace came over me and a quiet darkness. . . .

I was lying on the sand, retching.

"Close call," said Holdridge. "But now you know how it feels to drown. Shall we try again?"

"N-no! Please . . . have . . . mercy. . . ."

"Mercy won't get that cannon for me. Percy, put her back in the chair. Your face is blue, Arabella. It's not very becoming."

The huge black man didn't expect my sudden striking with the fetters. I bruised him where his cheek was blistered, causing a roar of pain. He almost hit me—I think he could have taken my head off with a blow—but Holdridge stopped him. They got the ropes around my shrieking, squirming form. My wet hair was down over my eyes. I thought I saw something white out on the water. My sight blurred, then cleared as my hair shifted.

It was an island sloop coming along swiftly, close to shore, appearing suddenly almost at the landing. It turned and men leaped from it as it smashed against the pier and Percy, wheeling, shouted, "Marstah, look out!"

I saw a flash, heard a shot, and Percy wheeled around, blood spurting from his throat in a red arc. He grabbed at the place and fell backward. There were shouts and men running and suddenly I was looking into a copper-and-black face I knew. Gumry!

I saw Mark—Mark!—bending over a prostrate figure,

rifling its pockets, finding something, rushing toward me. The figure that lay face down, groaning, was Holdridge, and the object in Mark's hand was the key to my fetters. When he had taken them off and flung them into the sea he rubbed my hands and I saw the red marks on the knuckles of Mark's right hand. Holdridge rolled over, and moaned, holding his face.

Then Mary found me.

Running in the darkness, she had mistaken one channel for another, had lost a precious hour. Only after sunup had she found the *Tiger,* but already it was a leaning tower of canvas growing smaller, out at sea. A San Isidro sloop was coasting by and she waved and screamed. Its crew recognized her. I did not find out till later why Mark and Gumry were in that sloop, along with six of the men whom Renzo had armed to defend Wentworth Hall, nor why they had sailed to Eleuthera as quickly as they could make the sloop move through the water.

Slaves came running from the house, found Percy dead and their master half-conscious, milled about in bewilderment. Mary was pulling my water-soaked gown back onto my shoulders. Mark was asking anxiously about Lavinia, Gumry was securing the sloop. The armed slaves had gathered around to see if Miss Arabella was all right.

It was during this confusion that Holdridge got to his feet, and surrounded by his slaves slipped into the fringe of sea grapes and away up that very green lawn toward the house.

As he approached the door, Lavinia came out and held up her hands in fluttering horror as she saw Holdridge's condition. He pushed her aside so roughly that she fell. He waved his slaves to stay outside, and stumbled into the house.

Gumry was up there a moment later with the Wentworth Hall slaves. He knew Holdridge was trapped. Wise enough not to risk lives—for Holdridge might have a gun —he deployed his men around the house, making them keep under cover.

With Mark holding me on one side and Mary on the other, I came slowly up the lawn. Mark shouted, "Holdridge! Come out! You can't get away!"

We all heard the wild deep laughter, like a corpse laughing from the depths of a tomb.

Upstairs, a dormer window was flung open. We glimpsed

a small figure in a turban. It opened another window and another, down the line.

Up there, it was easy to guess, spare lamps and kegs of whale oil had been stored, and old drapes and sheets that could be soaked in oil. Flames burst suddenly from a window. Holdridge had wanted draft for his fire.

The brisk wind that had carried the *Tiger* away . . . the brisk wind that had brought the sloop so quickly along the shore . . . that same brisk wind made the upper floor of Mistletoe a mass of roaring flame that ate all the old wooden beams and all the furniture with a hideous crackling. Slaves who came running from the house told us that Holdridge had poured burning oil down the staircase. Already the lower floor, too, smoked and flamed.

By the time men drawn by the smoke came riding from other plantations, only the walls and the chimneys of the house still stood, blackened. Within those walls the remains of timbers and furniture and flooring still flickered in a fierce heat. Little could remain of the two bodies that lay somewhere in that hell.

The sloop was no more than forty feet long, and the builder had wanted more space for cargo than for cabin. Four women and eight men had to travel two hundred miles in that boat. We expected to be two nights out, at least, with little privacy and less comfort.

Still we were safe, and the boat held a large supply of food—enough for a month. Mark was puzzled at the sacks and barrels of food that Gumry had taken along, plus two huge casks of drinking water.

Before we embarked we had left depositions to be taken to the governor in Nassau, and had arranged for another planter to care for Holdridge's slaves and crops till his estate was settled. Then Mark had given Gumry the order: "Our course is nor'-by-west for Wentworth Hall." As Eleuthera dropped behind I noticed that Gumry took full charge of the sloop, and his slave crew deferred to him. Not that Mark was unwilling to command. But he had been sleepless on the *Royal Arms'* quarterdeck when she had come through the fringes of the hurricane on her way from Charleston. Then, threading the tongue of deep water amid the tricky shoals that lay off San Isidro, Mark had realized that the great tides and currents of the hurricane had shifted some of the bars to which he was long accustomed. Careful as he was, he ran the schooner hard aground within sight of his home. She had not been badly damaged, he told me, but was leaking.

Coming home, Mark learned of the death of his father and read the note saying that Lavinia and I had gone to Holdridge's house.

In Charleston, he had met people who knew Holdridge in the old days. And he had heard certain stories that only now were coming out. Stories of little boys—both black and white—who had disappeared while hunting in the woods near the original Mistletoe plantation. Tales muttered by a dying slave, shot when he tried to run away, of males and females writhing together in frantic orgies that turned into horrors of sadism when Holdridge brought out whips. And there was the beautiful but unsteady wife who had had to be "put away" in insane hysteria, and died soon after babbling of unimaginable horrors. Still, no reliable witness had appeared, nothing could be proved, and Holdridge had taken care even back then to make himself a pillar of Loyalist support.

"So you can understand," Mark told me as we sat close by where the silent Gumry stood at the tiller, "when I heard that Holdridge had lured you to his house, I dared not take time to sleep."

That was all he said. But I knew his concern for my safety had overridden fatigue, grief, everything else. I was still shaky, and suddenly conscious of a great need to rest upon Mark's shoulder. That thought opened the way for other, deeper desires—for there was much more that my body wanted. But I kept myself from even touching him. No matter that we had shared times of ecstasy and tenderness . . . Mark remained my enemy because he was still the enemy of the United States.

Now, stifling a yawn, he told me that when the sloop had come in at Wentworth Hall, trading, he had chartered it instantly. Gumry scurried about for men, arms and provisions. Leaving the bewildered Renzo again in charge of the plantation, they had set sail. After picking up the frantic Mary, he had found me in the ducking stool.

"What was it all about?" Mark asked, and I told him from first to last—about the orgy, about Holdridge's wanting the cannon, everything. He gazed at me speculatively. "Then you really know all the clues?"

"I *don't* know. It would require a superhuman memory."

"But you know more than anyone else, don't you?" Then, hastily, because I had recoiled from him: "Good heavens, Arabella, I'm going to keep you on San Isidro and you damn-sure are not going to get away again, but I'm not going to torture you!"

Yet he was right; I knew more than anyone else. And even the shreds of directions I might be able to remember could be of value to anyone searching for the cannon. Put enough men out there on the point . . . let them work their way from the few known clues while they searched for others . . . let them find only the big stone arrow that pointed the wrong way and they'd know they'd come to the right gully. Working by trial and error, then, they might find the stone that opened to an underground road.

I must say nothing. Whatever happened—absolutely nothing!

Lavinia was not in good condition. When Holdridge had made her fall, she hit her head against a stone. Now she continued to have spells of dizziness. And her realization of Holdridge's actual nature seemed to have put her into a condition of shock. She was a person who had never endured the least hardship; conditions on the sloop made her weep, and the coarse diet gave her pains in her stomach. She no longer fluttered or acted girlish, even pushed away Nessa when that dedicated girl, who had risked her life to save a few of Lavinia's things from the fire, wanted to renew the dye in her hair. She stifled in her mourning dress, fainted, wept, sometimes doubled up in real or imagined pain.

By comparison, my own trouble was minor. Having grown used to wearing the ruined gown that, when new, would have pleased the Emperor Napoleon, I forgot to shield a tender area of skin from the sun. Miserably sunburned, I suffered beneath a cape of prickly gunnysacks that Mary made for me and snapped at Mark when he made solemn-faced remarks about the well-cooked condition of his bosom friend.

Not that we were intimate in any way. But I think neither of us could have borne to quarrel in those cramped quarters. And we did share hours of beauty and peace, when, as we entered our second night out, the boat eased along gently below the far-flung banners of a marvelous sunset and then darkness that seemed to fill the water with wobbling stars. I was to remember those timeless, space-

232

less hours, when the cares left behind us and the cares waiting for us meant nothing compared to the cool softness of the air and the beauty of the sea and the sky. That precious, brief surcease! We didn't know how short it was going to be.

When I awoke the next morning I found myself uncomfortably squashed against the cabin bulkhead. I shared a three-foot-wide berth with Lavinia, who, as I have said, was a large woman. Mary and Nessa were only a little less uncomfortable in the opposite berth.

Wentworth Hall might be in sight, I thought in the first daze of half-waking when I heard motions and sounds from the deck. Then Mark's voice, sharp and concerned: "Where the devil are you steering, Gumry? The course is nor'-by-west. You're going northeastward, by the sun."

"Been goin' nor'east by the stars all night while you sleep, Mistah Mark."

"What?"

Gumry's voice was triumphant. "That's right, Mistah Mark. Didn't go where you said go. Went where I said go."

I pulled on my tatters and rushed out on deck. The low sun showed me Mark in his canvas trousers, shirtless as he had slept, dew shining on his torso. He faced Gumry, at the helm, and shook his fist. The six other slaves were standing nearby and they had muskets. Their faces were half-eager, half-frightened.

"Gumry," Mark grated, "I've told you twice. I tell you for the third and last time—the course is for Wentworth Hall."

Gumry laughed in his face.

I saw Mark's fist swing in a destroying arc, but it never hit Gumry. One of the slaves thrust his musket between the two and Mark punched the gun's wooden stock. Holding his hurt hand, he glared around, realizing he faced mutiny.

"Miss Arabella," Gumry said courteously to me, "do you mos' kindly wake up Miss Lavinia and Mary and Nessa. Mary knows."

Mary was already awake, in fact, and watching Gumry worshipfully from the cabin door. She came to him and he slid his arm around her, and somehow I knew, before I heard the rest, that my maid was lost to me.

Then, as Gumry spoke, I was glad the Wentworths had

233

always treated their slaves kindly. Otherwise he might have fed us to the sharks.

He told us that down in Guiana, in South America, runaway slaves had formed a shadow nation in the jungle. He and his men were going to sail down there and live free.

Mark said tautly, "Yes, the *marrons*. They're living with the Indians who know the jungle ways. But look here, Gumry—"

"Indians my people too," Gumry said proudly, pressing Mary to him while his high, copper-tinged cheekbones glinted in the sun.

"But Gumry—" Mark protested.

"We goin', suh."

Mark glanced around again at the men, the guns, and pounded his palm with his fist. He did not take kindly to being defeated. "Be reasonable, Gumry. Possibly you could stay alive in the Guiana jungle. But you don't have a hundred-to-one chance of reaching South America in this boat, no matter how much food you have. Give it up. Steer for Wentworth Hall. We'll forget everything that's happened."

"No, Mistah Mark. Too long we chop your cane, we pick your cotton. Now we go live fo' ourselves, in jungle almost like back in Africa. I headin' now for Flamingo Island. Go' put you, Miss Arabella, Miss Lavinia ashore on west side, mebbe nobody see us. We go away quick. You walk across island, a mile. White folks live there, Willard by name, they take care o' you, you get back in few days."

A shuddering moan from the cabin doorway told us that Lavinia had heard and could hardly comprehend.

"Mary," I said painfully.

"Yes'm?"

"You know you're free already. Stay with me, and—"

She said, "No'm, this a different kind of free." She took off her starched maid's cap and tossed it into the water. Sad but resigned, I knew she would bear Gumry's babies in the jungle. I wondered what kind of race would live in those jungles, in a hundred years.

So it can be, I thought, when a woman has found her man. I knew I'd miss Mary badly, but I never said another word to try to make her change her mind. I only went and kissed her cheek, and when she kissed mine and choked up, she told me enough. I was able to wish her well.

Not so with Lavinia, who wept dreadfully when Nessa

234

decided to go to Guiana with the others. "What will become of me? How will I manage?" Gently I led the distraught woman below.

Flamingo Island, three miles long and a mile wide, lay low in the water save for small bluffs at one end. Mark told me the Willards had lived there for several generations, evaporating salt from seawater and selling scores of thousands of bushels a year. He had heard they lived quite well, and they'd certainly take care of us. We saw no one, and no boats, when Gumry put us ashore on a wreckage-strewn beach. When the sloop sailed away, its sails dwindling into specks on the sea, I saw a figure standing at her stern, watching, and I saw Mary's arm rise, then fall, bidding me farewell. Sadly I waved my own farewell.

We made Lavinia as comfortable as we could on the side of a grassy dune. I stayed with her while Mark went to find the Willard house that was somewhere at the high end of the island. He was sure he'd return long before sunset.

Trying to please Lavinia, I waded into the water and found sea eggs. They're a ball of spikes you must handle carefully, but when you break one open you have a bit of tasty orange meat. Lavinia nibbled, despaired, fell asleep. I walked up and down on the littered sand. Obviously Flamingo Island had been hard hit by the hurricane. Palm trees lay flattened and coconuts had been scattered all over. There were great gaps where the sand had been washed away and the island's rock foundation lay exposed. It was terribly lonely, for no other island could be seen. Once I saw a long-legged flamingo, but there seemed little that was alive beyond the ever-present land crabs, golden-eyed lizards, and locusts that hopped everywhere.

I'd begun to worry when at last Mark appeared at the top of a dune. He beckoned silently to me, and I climbed up to meet him.

"Look," was all he said.

The main part of the island was shaped like a great, shallow dish. This had enabled the Willards to run seawater into the hollow and form ponds. The sun then evaporated the water from those still ponds, leaving salt behind.

So it had been, and you could see remnants of the dikes that had formed the ponds. But hurricane waves had smashed them. The sea must have swept clear across the

235

island. It was almost two islands now with a muddy, soaked area between. You could see bits of odd little horizontal windmills—like a series of toy sailboats turning in a circle—that had worked paddles to move the brine from one pond to another. But bits were all you saw. Fluttering cloth and broken wood.

Shielding my eyes, I tried to identify strange gray shapes that lay in the mud. Naked-headed turkey vultures wheeled low above them.

"Donkeys that used to draw the salt carts," Mark told me. "But I did see a live goat."

"You mean you didn't see a single person?"

"To the best of my knowledge, Lavinia and you and I are the only human beings on this island. The house is damaged and abandoned. The loading pier is wrecked. The little harbor is full of sand. I suppose some ship called for salt, found there won't be any more, and took the Willards and their slaves away. Probably they had injured folk among them."

"But won't they come back?"

"I don't know. You can see there's mighty little to come back to. It would take years to get the saltworks going again."

"But Mark," I asked, still unwilling to believe we were marooned, "won't other ships come calling for salt?"

"I hope so. But I don't know when. We had best take shelter in the house and see if they left any food behind. The Willards' own boats are all smashed, and I'm afraid Lavinia has a long walk ahead of her."

We helped the poor woman as best we could. At long last we reached the house and made our way through a sand-drifted garden. We could see how salt had gotten into everything—even before the hurricane—and had killed most of the vegetation. We saw how someone had set up woven screens—now blown flat—to shelter a few flowers. They'd grown garden vegetables in barrels of earth, but all these had been blasted with salt spray. The house had been built of strong coral blocks, so the walls and heavy roof had survived. A few windows remained unbroken. The veranda had been lifted by the awful wind and stood up vertically against the dwelling.

We clambered over wreckage to the front door. Mark, with his grim humor, banged the brass knocker. It took heavy pushing to force the door open, and I almost wished we hadn't, such was the desolation within.

Lavinia lasted not quite a week. Poor lost woman, the foundation was gone from her life, and of her many illnesses, at least one—a lump that had been growing in her abdomen—was grimly real. Nor could she face life in fear of future shocks. She seemed unable to exist save as a lady. Nor did she have anyone left to live for, and that, perhaps, was worst of all.

I nursed her as well as I could and watched her life ebb away. She lay in a big, airy bedroom where the walls were still streaked from the hard-blown spray that had gone through every crevice. The Willards had had to abandon a huge chest full of fresh linen, and every time I changed the bed I sprinkled orris root on the sheets, which pleased Lavinia, for she always had used orris root in Charleston.

She knew she was going, and worried about being buried in the wrong side of the cemetery. We must make sure to dig her grave in the white persons' side. We promised.

She fell into a coma, wakened again. At the very last, when we had to bend close to hear her voice, she whispered, "I always . . . have been . . . virtuous. I die . . . a maiden. But I confess . . . I wanted . . . Job . . . terribly . . . but he . . . after Prudence . . . left . . . never touched . . . another woman . . . and he told me . . . he told me . . . that the only blessing . . . of his . . . blindness . . . was that he could see her . . . better . . . in his memory."

Her eyes closed. They opened again, but no life was left.

Mark shaved with Harvey Willard's razors. But Willard had not been a big man, so Mark wore clothing left behind by slaves. Clarissa Willard's gowns were big for me, but I worked at them at her sewing table—with an abandoned portrait of her mother, I think, watching me disapprovingly—and made them fit.

We never starved on Flamingo Island, but we did grow thin. When long and weary bailing got the water out of the cellar, we found a great deal of food; but it was mostly spoiled. We rounded up a few hens that had been blown from their roosts. In the pantry I found eggs neatly marked with the dates they had been gathered. Some were still good. Mark put together a raft and we fished from it. Or we gathered conchs, a mainstay of the Bahamas diet—although I had never liked them. At first we made a pet of the goat. But she gave no milk, and in the end, Wilhelmina had to face the fact that man has dominion over beasts. Mark made a clumsy butcher and goat meat is very tough.

And the wind whistled, and the birds called, and a pair of herons took up housekeeping in a brackish pond. Walking on the beach, I found a lovely rose murex and a jingle shell. But there was never a more salt-blasted, windburned, sun-scalded, drearier place than the ruin of Flamingo Island.

But it was the only home we had, and we had to share it. Lavinia's passing made it all the more pointed that Mark and I had been left alone together. But we did *not* sleep together. Never, I think, had a man and a woman said such awkward goodnights, I going upstairs to the master bedroom, Mark going to a downstairs room that seemed handy if he wanted to get out very early in the morning. He often did, even if all I saw him accomplish was standing on the beach and glaring at the sea.

After a couple of weeks, Mark announced he would build a sail boat. It was a painful job for him, but it did keep him busy for hours every day. When he told me gruffly there was no way I could help, I kept myself busy making the house livable again. This was a vast project. At least I had plenty of fresh water, for rainwater was fed into a big cistern that had survived. Laboriously I washed the salt off the walls and floors and tacked old sheets across the broken windows.

Of course we'd soon see the sail of some fisherman or trader, and we'd set fire to a great heap of broken timbers from the old wharf, and men in the vessel would see the smoke. Of course some boat would come by, we told each other. But it didn't happen. The sea lay empty. Nothing broke the horizon's curve.

And the days passed and the waves swished and the birds called. And my body quivered, and memories marched in my mind and haunted my sleep. Memories of Mark at sixteen, when I had been too young to know anything of passion, but certainly had known he was an heroic male. Memories of Mark walking back into my life as a man, a captain, a customer, an enemy. Mark changing my life, my thoughts, by body, my feelings, everything—forever—on Mad Anne Burney's berth. Mark coming too late to save me from the horror in Thatch's wagon, but killing two men to save me from more. But I'd felt I'd hated him. Memories of the time in the sail locker when I discovered that the Tory wretch could woo me into helpless surrender. Where had been my hatred then—or when I had saved him from having Macgillivray smash his head?

Or when we had lain naked on the grass near the Pirate's House?

Hatred was gone, but caution was not forgotten. I could not help being a woman alone on an island with a virile man, but I dared not give in to him—or to myself. Because I *did* remember a few of the many clues to finding the cannon; and I *could* be of aid to any party of searchers. In short, it was still highly possible for me to do great harm to my beloved country—and I must not become familiar with a man who wanted me to do that harm and might find a way to trap me.

One day Mark came into the kitchen, where I was frying fish-and-conch. In all my life I had done little cooking, and that mostly for fun—but now I was learning. Silently he handed me a couple of precious papayas that had clung to a sheltered tree. I handed him a plate of very handsome china, a silver knife and fork.

Nodding his thanks, he looked at me with so deep a meaning that I flushed and looked away. It seemed to me he had questioned me silently, and the question was not, *will you?* It was, *when?*

Hastily seeking a neutral subject, I said, "We needn't go on eating in the kitchen. But the dining table is so warped. . . ."

"I'll see what I can do with it."

"Is there any sign of *anyone* out there?"

He laughed shortly, shook his unkempt head. "Not a sign. I'll have plenty of time to work on the table. I've figured it out—the word has gotten around that this island has become a wasteland. There's no reason for anyone to come here. And it's leagues away from the usual trading routes."

"I see." I fell silent.

He said, "I found some Guinea corn that I think will sprout. Anyway, I'll try. We might set a crop because there isn't so much salt blowing around anymore."

I nodded helplessly. Yes, we had better settle down for a long stay.

"And I'm having a lot of trouble with that sailboat. Well, anyway, I found a set of chess. Do you play?"

"A little. My father taught me."

"We might sit in the drawing room—what's left of it—and try a game. Just have to remember there's no use in ringing for a servant and asking for coffee."

Tension hung over the board. A man and a woman, utterly lost and alone. A virile man and a woman who moment by moment felt a stronger tug of yearning. I played badly. When Mark said, "You're taking too long to move," I snapped at him, "What's the hurry?" When he said, "Checkmate in three moves no matter what you do," I was ready to throw the board at him. It was an unreasoning annoyance that reflected my panic. Yes, *when* was the only question, and how well Mark knew it! I wanted to run. Where could I run?

Later, when it was very late, and I had almost fallen asleep, I heard the creak of boards in the corridor outside my bedroom. There was no lock on the door. Why hadn't I blocked it?

Why didn't I scream at Mark to leave me alone? What would I do when he came to lie beside me? When he slid his hand beneath the hem of my nightdress, what would I do?

After a while I heard him go away.

The next day we both were on edge. We couldn't find a pleasant word for each other. At last, because it was our day to go fishing, and two people can help each other, I followed him onto the four-by-ten raft.

Mark had found oars with which to push the raft along, but it was heavy and awkward, and there was no way of keeping dry when water squirted up between the logs. When I cooled a hand in the sea I heard a sharp, "Take your hand out of the water." I should have known better, for the water was deep enough, right there, to harbor big, voracious creatures. But I resented the warning nonetheless.

"Give me the anchor," said the sunburned man whose ever-longer hair had reached his shoulders.

"You might speak to me in a less *commanding* voice."

He glared, rose, lifted the anchor—a broken gear wheel from the wreck of the salt-grinding machinery—and tossed it over, making its rope run down after it.

He took up one of the conchs we carried, chopped into the knobby, spiral-curved shell with a hatchet, pushed his knife through the slit and cut the tissue at a certain place. The slippery white conch came out of its shell and he cut it up and baited hooks, all the while neither looking at me nor speaking.

Almost instantly he caught a foot-long fish called a coney that he tossed into a bucket of seawater. I found a very large hook and knotted it to a roll of heavy line, because I was childishly determined to catch a bigger fish than Mark had caught. In fact, I would *bait* with the coney.

He snatched the wriggling fish away from me. "We don't want anything big enough to take that as bait."

"*I* do!"

"You're sure you do?"

"Yes, I'm sure!"

Raging, he said, "Then let me show you how to make it stay on the hook. And *you're* responsible for the consequences."

He ripped open the coney's belly, and with a flip of his knife he tossed its insides away, narrowly missing my face. He folded the fish inside out and wove the hook through it.

I hated him when he looked at me and asked, "What's the matter? You seem pale."

I grabbed the fish and hook away from him and let it down into the water on the line, which was weighted with bits of sheet lead.

Nothing happened save that the sun broiled us. The only cool-looking thing in sight was the coral reef that lay just beyond, protecting us from the huge ground swell. Those mighty swells met the reef slantwise and smashed themselves into a series of heavy, spouting geysers, half water and half foam, that fell back raging upon the rock. We fished in protected water, but it seemed as though the open sea would reach and grab us if it could.

Mark, reclining in his ragged shirt and baggy trousers, said, "That reef looks spongy, but it's hard as iron. It's ripped the bottom of many a ship. It's the wreckers' friend. Which reminds me. On the way to Eleuthera we saw Macgillivray in the *Grappler*. He didn't seem anxious to communicate."

"What makes you think I'm interested?"

Mark's submerged grin told me he knew I *was* interested, and that made me angrier than ever. "Thought you might like to know he had a woman aboard."

"How pleasant for him."

"How pleasant for *her*," Mark said pointedly.

"Well," I said, "at least he's not hauling up any more cannon for you to take to Louisiana. As though you'd ever get there."

"We *will* get there. And by the way, as to that certain cannon, the one my father hid—you and I will take up the matter again when we return to Wentworth Hall."

"How shall we return? Swim?" Then, the old topic breaking through: "Oh, Mark, you Tories with your cannon that shoot and your mysterious cannon that can't shoot, and your wild young men ready to slice off heads with their sabres! And Aaron Burr leading you on and on! I know you can't proceed till you find that hidden cannon, but even if you could, Burriana wouldn't last six months." Should I tell him what Holdridge had said? I told it in my own words: "You're all so angry at the United States that you don't see the real situation. Once we gathered our forces, you'd be wiped out, and much worse off than you are now."

"We have allies."

"Spanish forces, such as they are, would help you establish Burriana. But would Spain risk war with the United States?"

For a moment Mark look flustered. But he said, "We have had assurance of Spanish aid under any circumstances."

I demanded, "Don't you see how much better it would be for everyone to let the quarrel die? I know the older folk can't forgive, but the younger ones should know better. If you don't want to be friendly with the United States, go on living here . . . getting poorer and poorer on the plantations England gave you. But you can't turn history backward. Look how the United States is growing! Look how—"

Just then my fishing line ran through my hand with a speed that burned my skin. I would have lost it if it had not looped around a thole pin. Shaking my hands, I stared down into the sea. "Something got away," I said.

Marked used the Willards' water glass to peer beneath the surface. He raised a sweating face and said, "It's still hooked. Cut your line."

"No. I want to see how big it is."

"Too big. I said, cut your line."

"I caught it and I want it."

"All right then, pull it up," he shouted, reaching for the hatchet.

Whatever it was, it was sluggish. But Mark, if I could judge by the slow, anticipatory way he nodded, had known it would follow the tug of the hook in its mouth. A heavy green tangle showed near the surface of the wind-rippled water. When I saw the thing's head I jerked back, frightened. My motion pulled that awful head out of the water above its slithering, green-and-black coils. It went for me. Its jaws snapped shut, would have taken off my hand if I had not snatched it away. The creature tried again. At the sight of its teeth I shrieked and fell backward as Mark swung the hatchet. When the thing was dead he dragged the red-dripping coils onto the raft.

"No! Throw it back!"

"But you caught it and you want it, don't you?" Mark laughed mirthlessly, kicked overboard the thick, flexible body that still twitched. "Well? Did you enjoy meeting a moray eel?"

Despite the heat I was in a cold sweat and sicker than I wanted Mark to know. I sat in stupefied silence while he roared at me. He told me I belonged among the damned fools who go fishing and never come back because they deserve not to come back. I learned I was one of those women who can't believe that a man may have found out something she doesn't know, and that it was useless to try to protect an idiot who was not worth protecting. He told me that if in the future I ever disobeyed his orders when we were at sea I could take the consequences and he'd not mourn my passing.

After that he scourged me with his hard glare while I was helpless to do anything but shiver. At last he said gruffly, "You've got a scare-chill; you'll be all right in a few minutes," and turned away and fished.

When I felt better I tidied up the raft and even threaded a carrying line through the gills of the several small fish that Mark had caught. Anything to show him I was more than a useless woman. And then . . . time passed, and Mark looked over his shoulder at me, and although I didn't want to smile, I did smile because he had smiled. And then . . . we said nothing. But those great ground swells outside the reef seemed to become part of something within us. We felt the eternal ground swell of emotion that moves every man and every woman, all around the world.

When we had enough fish Mark grounded the raft on the beach. I stood up, but he stooped, stretched an arm behind my knees, another around my shoulders, and carried me ashore. He looked steadily at me and I gazed back as steadily and as warmly out of a deep excitement.

When he lowered me to my feet, we did not move apart.

"I've missed you," he murmured. He was wonderfully transfigured with open, eager desire. His kiss sent all my long-starved instincts clamoring for his embrace.

We flung away our clothing and sank together on the warm sand, caressing, kissing, exploring, rediscovering all the secrets of each other's bodies. It had been so long! Then there was nothing in all the world save the need to hold that strong man tightly upon me and join my body to his, giving myself in frantic hunger that soared into glorious fulfillment.

Chapter Fifteen

The weeks and the months flowed blissfully together.

We did not mention Burr or Burriana or Thomas Jefferson or the United States, or France or England or Spain or the hidden cannon.

We became primitives who spent a good part of every day in hunting for our food. But at night we returned to the Willards' comfortable furniture and the soft light of their lamps. We found their wine. It would be too much to say that we dressed for dinner, but at least we cleaned up.

The season of shorter days and longer nights came in. The Pleiades, heralding winter, peered over the eastern horizon, and a blessed coolness came with them. Naked and happy, we stayed longer in bed, wrapped in each other's arms.

It was all as real as sore muscles and a fish hook in one's finger, or dodging huge spiders while taking coconuts from a fallen palm. But our sensual life ran through it all, delightful as a dream.

I remember how we walked along the beach, one warm afternoon, noting with satisfaction how the island's plants and scrubby trees were coming back. I remember how I bragged about the cabbages I had coaxed to life, and, just as important, the rose bushes I had made to bear again. Mark swung his big arm lazily and sent flat stones skipping out over the water.

There must have been a great storm in the east. Swells thundered right over the coral reef and sent water sliding up where the beach was rarely wetted. Those swells had such impact that one could feel a vibration with the soles of one's tough bare feet.

Where the sand had a small, natural rise, we poked about for interesting wreckage. But after a while we were merely looking at each other. Mark drew me to him, and our mouths sought each other's with a hunger that was never appeased. When he couldn't easily slip my dress down from my shoulders I helped him, wriggling in what I once would have called a shameless manner to make my dress—all I wore—drop around my feet.

He told me to walk away from him because he wanted to see my hips sway, and I did, wondering at men. He told me to walk toward him quickly because he wanted to see my breasts joggle, and I did, smiling at him with anticipation and excitement. He told me to let down my hair and draw it across my breasts.

"Lady Godiva!" he said. He thrust aside my hair to kiss me and nibble me and make my heart race.

"Now it's my turn to command you," I told him. I made him stand still while I stripped him. I kissed the ridged muscles of his stomach and chest while my fingers wandered.

He gasped, "You don't know what you're doing to me."

"I'm not blind," I said.

He answered with a hearty push that sent me on my back, laughing. He gave me tiny love bites up and down my body, front and back. He could be quite ungentle, but even his slapping the sand from my skin increased the eager warmth I felt in my groin.

"You forgot it's my turn to be bossy, mister! I'm going on top this time so *I'll* conquer *you*."

He scoffed, "A likely story!"

But he pleased me by lying back, and it was strange but good to go that way, and go and go and go. One vast swell sent water rushing up the sand, and Mark had to splutter water off his face, but it never stopped us in our wild delight, and the sudden coolness only increased our ecstasy. We shared the exquisite moment and then lay panting and content.

He felt my sides. "Your ribs are too near the surface." he pinched my buttocks. "But you're all right down there."

"Don't move," I sighed, blissfully resting.

After a while he said, "Now it's your turn to lie on the wet sand."

It was uncomfortable at first but I soon warmed that sand . . . oh yes, I warmed it well and left a hollow imprinted by our moving weight.

"You're nothing but a stallion and a boar and a ram,

and you had better leave yourself strength to chop wood or there'll be no fire for dinner."

"You're nothing but a Lilith and a Sheba. But my source of strength is within you, don't you see? That's why I have to seek it again and again."

Sometimes we sought the safe, shallow water, and the way it buoyed up my body helped us find new delights. I had had experience with very few men, and some of that experience had been by no means pleasant. But I began to know with a safe, quiet certainty that nowhere in the world could I find another man who could complete my passion the way Mark did. And I knew the ever-renewed delight he found in me, and that it never palled and never failed.

Over and over, our search for food turned into a bout of passion on the sand, on the grass, anywhere; even on the improved raft, which now had flooring and cushions. At night, if the day's exercise and air and sun sent us quickly to sleep, we'd waken all the more eager in the morning and by sunlight we'd renew our delight in each other's flesh. Rainy days had their own special joy. Why bother to get out of bed?

Still now and then, Mark's new smile disappeared in his old dourness. He'd go off alone to stare across the sea while his fists pounded his thighs in frustration. But in time he'd get over his despair, and when he found me again it seemed all-new and especially wonderful. Moreover, I could lead that bull-voiced captain into scenes of near fantasy. I remember how we danced a minuet on a stretch of hard sand. Our bodies were touched with silver moonlight, for we were nude, we were Adam and Eve.

But sometimes, especially when Mark worked on that hard-to-build boat and I sat alone, I had to realize that probably, someday, we would return to Wentworth Hall—and then Mark would be my enemy again, and the memory of our idyll would fade as though it never had been. So it was as well we had not fallen in love. For this *wasn't* love, I told myself. Call it nature, call it fun, call it giving in to the mating instinct, call it a woman enjoying a man and a man enjoying a woman. But—almost desperately I must repeat—it could not be love because it *must not* be love. Why, not in all of our scores of times of so-called lovemaking had we mentioned the word love!

247

So the weeks ran by. We lost track of the date, but knew it was winter when a "norther" made it too cold for swimming and the great constellation Orion slid up into the sparkling darkness. In those nearly-cold nights we slept pressed together. And sometimes, in the late dawn, as we lay between waking and sleeping with Mark's head upon my breast, my heart seemed to whisper to his ear, "I love you." Then I'd be wide awake and full of panic and denial, with Mark looking at me with one sleepy eye and wanting to know what was the matter.

"Oh . . . nothing," is easy to say. But it became harder and harder to say as the days slowly lengthened and I knew I'd have to tell him something that is more easily said if two people have declared their love and much more easily said if they are married.

We were standing outside the front door, watching shooting stars. His arms had gone around me. I wanted it and I didn't want it.

"Mark . . . I waited till I was sure before telling you. I'm pregnant," I said.

His arm went taut. "Well," he said after a moment, "I guess it's not surprising." We watched the to-do in the sky. It was almost like a Fourth of July celebration. "You know," he said, "I once offered to marry you. Then I withdrew the offer."

"Oh, yes! The gentleman's code!"

The bitterness in my voice made him look at me sharply. "As you wish. What I meant to say was, we should certainly be married."

"If I wanted to marry you, who'd marry us?"

"Well . . . we should certainly be married when we can."

It came out then, harsh and hard. "Mark, how could you and I be married? With all our disagreements and our quarrels! With all our being poles apart in our loyalties! With you knowing I'd ruin the entire Loyalist cause if I could! With my knowing you're an enemy of my nation! Marry? No, Mark. I'm your enemy, you're my enemy. We can't be husband and wife."

He wasn't holding me anymore. "But the baby?" he asked.

"I can bear my baby whether or not I wear a wedding ring."

"Out here you'd have no choice. But remember, it's *our* baby. And we won't be here that long."

248

"Maybe we'll never get away from this island."

"You forget the boat will be ready soon."

He had slaved over that boat, sometimes stopping to swear and tell me he'd gladly trade his captain's papers for a boatbuilder's skill if he could. But he had only a few planks of the right length; the rest had to be pieced together. He could not manage the subtle, precise tapering of the planks that is needed at bow and stern, and only hoped the boat would swell watertight after a few days in the water. The sail he intended to use was an old jib taken from a craft that had been wrecked and its pieces scattered, and the more he patched that sail and renewed its bolt ropes, the less I trusted it.

The boat was only fifteen feet long. He had explained that a small boat can rise and fall with waves that may break a great ship. He had told me we wouldn't have to sail more than twenty-four hours, or perhaps thirty, before we found one of the larger, inhabited islands.

I'd always been doubtful. Still, we could watch the weather and set sail when the indications were good. But now, pregnant, I was suddenly frightened and protective. The very mention of the boat made me cross my arms below my ribs, where the baby was growing.

"We could come to some agreement," Mark said. "I wouldn't want you to go unmarried."

"Oh, no! Once we were married you'd have legal control over me!"

He scowled in the darkness, drawing those heavy brows together. "Let's see when the time comes. Meanwhile, you do the fishing and I'll work full-time on the boat. Wait," he amended. "You shouldn't try to row that raft. I'll repair the pier enough so you can fish from it."

From where I fished I could watch him working on the boat. He had built it upside down so as to be able to plank the bottom. He had made its ribs out of curved tree limbs, but he hadn't been able to get precise curves and you could see that one side of that boat was not the same as the other.

We slept together. We cohabited. But an invisible wall had formed between us. I felt now that I was merely satisfying Mark's male need. And he was becoming more and more a stranger as he worked over that boat, hardly took an hour of daylight away from that boat.

He rigged tackles and turned it right side up onto a

249

cradle he had made that ran on salt-car wheels. He pushed it on plank tracks till it rolled into the water. The boat, named *Rescue,* floated with a list.

"Just a matter of ballast," he muttered. "We'll carry a few sandbags."

He stretched tarpaulins on frames over two-thirds of the boat to keep waves from swamping her. He rigged a mast made from a palm-tree trunk and stayed it strongly with ropes. When the boat had rested in the water for three days, the planks did swell and it leaked very little. Mark knew he had done an amateurish job, and I saw by his face that he detested his creation. Still, when he took her all around Flamingo Island, *Rescue* sailed crookedly and slowly but she sailed.

I had sun-dried numerous fish, and had packed several pounds of corn and beans. Mark carried aboard bottles of drinking water. We had a box of sand that held a charcoal pot for cooking.

"We could sail all the way to Florida if we had to," Mark said.

The wind blew fair and cool. Mark brought aboard a mattress that he placed on planks to keep it out of the bilgewater. We made tarpaulin coverings with holes for our heads to keep us dry in the spray.

When all was ready I looked down into the boat from the pier and said, "No, I'm not going. I'm afraid."

Mark demanded, "What the devil, Arabella! You saw me sail for at least three hours."

"Yes, with my heart in my mouth. Mark . . . my baby! I'm really afraid. You go alone and get someone to come here and get me with a bigger boat."

"No," he said flatly.

"I'm not going."

With that muscular flow I knew so well, he put a hand on the pier and vaulted upward, grimly faced me. "I can't leave you here alone."

"I'll—"

"You'll come with me, Arabella, if I have to tie you up and carry you into the boat."

In the end, I joined him. But when we passed the slanting reef where the swells spouted I couldn't look at the rearing masses of spray and water.

An hour. Two hours. Three hours. I saw how hard Mark had to work at the tiller to hold a course. But at least

Flamingo Island, behind us, seemed slowly to sink into the sea.

I crouched over the charcoal pot, almost cooking my face over the gruel of corn and beans and conch. I went below and still huddled. I bailed the bilge dry with a coconut shell and watched water form in it again. I went out and sat close to Mark, but felt far away. The boat gurgled and creaked through the small waves and a lazy wind filled our sail.

But in the afternoon the wind increased, whitecaps appeared, spray flew over the boat. She took on a plunging motion and when I checked the bilge I found three inches of water. While I bailed, Mark told me that the boat's motion was making her *work*. She was made of so many small parts that water was bound to find its way in as the parts rubbed upon each other.

I said nothing, bailed till I was tired, rested, now all wet and chilly, and bailed. And bailed. But still the wind increased and the boat plunged and rocked and weaved, and you could see planks moving and water spurting in. Sunset gave Mark a pink, grim, tired face.

"We'll heave to," he said. "We'll just drift till morning and I can bail."

But as he brought the boat around to face the wind, a sudden wind shift made our boom gybe over, narrowly missing our heads, and a rope pulled out of a fastening. The mast leaned and the end of the boom was in the water, the sail flapping wildly, the boat out of control. The wind whooped, the sail pulled the boom across again and this time the great leverage and pressure brought the mast down across our gunwale, smashing planks, so that gallons of water poured aboard before Mark desperately found a balance.

"Are you all right?" he shouted.

"Yes, but Mark—look—the boat is coming to pieces!"

He flung the sandbags overboard. We had a wooden keel, and we'd float. He tried to row with the oars we carried, but the mast, still held to the boat, pulled it this way and that. He cut the rope and at last got *Rescue*'s head into the wind. But the boat was hardly a boat anymore. She was planks and tarpaulins held sketchily together, and we were waist deep in water, planks hurting us as the waves moved them.

In the darkening dusk Mark put ropes around timbers

251

and bound me to them. When night came we floated together, little above water but our heads. It was cold, very deep ocean water. I cannot tell you how cold it felt as the hours of the night went past and Orion hunted across the sky, and the waves slapped us and jostled us. Sometimes I threw back my head and gazed wildly at the stars, but if God was watching He didn't help us.

"Hang on," Mark begged, his own teeth chattering. He tried to warm me by keeping an arm around me.

I said, "You took chances because you want that cannon."

"Please, Arabella, don't talk. Save your strength. See . . . is that a little gray of dawn?"

"You took me to sea in an unseaworthy boat because your cause is precious to you, not my baby."

The soggy sail twisted around my limbs and dragged me down. Mark pulled me to the surface. He chafed my hands and retied the ropes. But the cold gnawed at my vitals. It was in my womb. It ate at my baby.

"Arabella, it's really gray in the east, now. Hang on! Arabella, the sun is coming up. The sun will warm us." How could it? He slapped my face till I came to. "Stay awake," he pleaded. "If you go unconscious you'll . . ." And then he reared out of the water, fell back, reared again. "A ship!" he shouted.

My bleary eyes at last made out the sails. In that instant, the pain began. I doubled up, and for a moment looked down into the depths before Mark desperately pulled me up by my hair. But the pain . . . the pain! I saw his face wavering in the water that ran from my hair across my face and I heard myself scream through my agony, "You've killed my baby."

After that it was all half-consciousness and lances of pain, and glimpses of a ship coming closer, and flashes of Mark's desperate face, and the sight of blood swirling around us in the water. And then . . . something else that had come from my body floated briefly and I screamed and screamed and screamed till my screams ended in bubbling. Mark pulled my head up again.

I thought he told me: "There, girl, there, hold onto me. I won't let you go. I'll drown before I let you go. Oh my darling, hold onto me . . . I'll take care of you, my love. . . ." I was never sure. But I screamed again when I saw the triangular fin cutting the water—a shark attracted by the blood. The ship had come around with a thundering of sails and a small boat was being rowed swiftly toward us.

One man in that boat—I was vaguely aware that his hair was cut in bangs across his forehead, and of the strange cap he wore—slapped his oar into the water to drive the shark away. I saw the side of the boat and felt hands grasp my arms, and the men lifted me, sodden, my dress falling away from my body. The man with the odd hair and cap was bending over me with concern. Mark was saying, "Give me shirts, anything dry." I was aware that he shouted at a savage-looking, loose-lipped ruffian who was staring at my exposed body: "Take off your shirt, God damn you, before I break your neck."

Dimly I knew they had hooked the boat onto the dangling tackle that had let it down and were heaving it upward. Mark climbed out onto the ship's deck and had me handed to him.

"Brandy for her! Quickly!" he was saying as he held me sagging backward in his arms, my wet hair trailing on the deck.

It was in this position, as my head dangled limply, that I saw legs that seemed upside down. Those legs were shapely rather than muscular, and clad in sheer white silk. They led up to thighs clothed in blue velvet breeches. My gaze found a ruffled shirt worn loose above a broad belt that had a pistol stuck into it. I saw the man's face upside down. So smooth a face, such red lips. Such abundant bright-blond-hair, its color much like my own. . . .

I realized I was looking at a blue-eyed woman in man's clothing.

It was thus, on the deck of the *Queen of the Caribbean,* that Mad Anne Burney and I met again.

Chapter Sixteen

I slept the clock around twice, wakened and lay drowsily watching how the low morning sun made shifting, barred patterns on a bulkhead. A brass lamp, swinging on gimbals that kept it level, also told me that the *Queen of the Caribbean* was still at sea.

I wore an elaborate nightdress which I later learned had been put on me by Mad Anne's quadroon maid. My hair had been neatly brushed and was held in two swags by ribbons. I lay on fresh sheets in a comfortable berth with gleaming white paint and shining, varnished woodwork all around me in a small, neat cabin. Dull pain brought back that nightmare in the sea, and I wept for my baby.

In time I dried my eyes, told myself to be glad I was alive and able to hope—since Mad Anne had treated me so kindly—that my future might be more sparing of terror than my past had been.

It took some time before I realized that the barred patterns the sunlight made were caused by stout iron bars that crossed the cabin's window. But I had no sooner begun to think myself a prisoner than the door opened—it had not been locked—and a beautiful face, marred only by the madness of its eyes, looked in and smiled to me.

"Then you're awake, Lady Arabella. I've a draught for you."

She acted as though we had parted only yesterday. Was I to upbraid her for having left me drugged and helpless on the *Bridgewater*, a year and a half ago? I had better judgment. "How gracious of Your Majesty to bring me medicine," I said.

To her man's costume she had added a diadem of gold set with pearls; part of her pirate loot, I supposed. She felt my pulse and my forehead, seemed satisfied. She gave me three spoonsful of some black and bitter liquid, smiling quite tenderly when I made a face.

"It will do you good. Now have some water."

She could as easily have poisoned me. But the draught did perk me up, and I recalled the late Captain Chance's saying that Mad Anne was a good chemist.

"You mustn't mind the bars at the windows," she told me. "This little cabin is handy for keeping people of rank whom I might hold for ransom."

"Then your ship is very well equipped, Your Majesty?"

"Oh, yes. And now I daresay you're hungry?"

"Indeed I am, thank you for your concern, Your Majesty."

"You shall have a tray in a moment. Soon you'll be able to sit at a table."

"How kind of Your Majesty."

She kept me another day and night in bed, coming often to visit me with all the solicitude of a good nurse. Then she came with her well-mannered maid, who bore a selection of ladies' robes, taken, said Anne, from the clothing chests of ladies who no longer had use for them. I went on deck in a robe of very fine embroidered silk, silk slippers on my feet, my hair held in a fall down my back by a magnificent jeweled clasp.

The man whose hair was cut so straight above his eyes and around his head—like a dark-blonde bowl set on his cranium—was adjusting a canopy that shielded a cushioned chair at the foot of the mainmast. He helped me into it, and in a thick accent told me, *Bitte,* Fräulein—good—the air."

He was Werner—pronounced Verner—the ship's carpenter. He kept hovering about, adjusting my pillows, watching anxiously lest a change in the ship's course bring the sun into my face. The crew inspected me as they went about their duties, but Werner was the only one—and I include the mates—who had any hint of gentleness. The rest looked and talked as I might have expected—like men found sodden on the floor of gin shops, men running from the law, with nothing to lose if they added a few more murders. A placard tacked to the mast gave a table of compensation: so much would be paid a man if he lost an arm; so much if he lost an eye, and so forth. Also each man received a percentage of captured treasure. It reminded me that these sweepings and dregs knew more of their captain than her kind side. The vessel's guns had left deep scars on the deck where they had recoiled after firing. The deck, although scrubbed with holystone—so called because seamen have to be on their knees to scrape the soft stone across the planks—still showed places where great red stains had been scrubbed nearly away.

Mark strolled toward me. He wore excellent white linen taken from the chest of some man who wouldn't need it because he was turning into a skeleton on the ocean's floor. He doffed a broad-curled straw hat to me.

He also winked, not letting Mad Anne see it as he said, "May I offer my congratulations on your recovery, Lady Arabella? I have tried to express to Her Majesty my great gratitude for having saved our lives."

"But Lady Arabella is my chief lady-in-waiting," said Anne. "I never could hold court without her."

"I see," said Mark, "I see."

"And have you recovered from your wetting, Mark?" I asked him.

"Oh, you must say Sir Mark!" Mad Anne protested. "I knighted Sir Mark this morning."

"Pray forgive me. Have you recovered from your wetting, Sir Mark?"

"Thank you, Lady Arabella, I have indeed."

"Lady Arabella, it's as well that you miscarried," Anne Burney said. "Much as I regret your pain and distress, still, my ladies-in-waiting must be of the utmost respectability. Questions would have been raised about that child."

The words came hard, but: "I understand, Your Majesty."

"As for the pregnancy itself, and its implication as to your virtue—we'll put the matter aside," said she who had been whore to slavers. "After all, when a woman is marooned on an island for so many months, alone with so vigorous a man as Sir Mark . . ."

The black steward came with a table, and refreshment was brought for the Queen and her guests. I found it difficult to make conversation. So vigorous a man as Sir Mark . . . and Anne's gaze sweeping him up and down as she had said it! That white linen suit was tight on him. You could see the swell of his muscles and how the span of his shoulders thrust his coat open across his broad chest.

The *Queen of the Caribbean* cruised up and down through the Bahamas, always moving as fast as the wind

257

would allow, men always in her tops to watch for the government cutter. Once we coasted San Isidro and I saw Wentworth Hall in the far distance, then the rocky point. Anne was on the quarterdeck with a telescope, examining the shore. I didn't know whether I wanted to return to land or go on cruising. At least, while Anne searched for prey and found none amid the well-warned shipping, the problem of the hidden cannon could wait. But if Mark and I were set ashore, my troubles would begin again.

I saw Mark speak urgently to Anne, no doubt asking to be put ashore, but she shook her head. We took a turn out to sea, then, two days later, came back among the islands from a different route to confuse the cutter.

I made friends with Werner. I had grown to know lust when I saw it in men's eyes, but I saw only worship in his. He told me in his halting English that he came from a section of Pennsylvania where many Germans had settled in the time of William Penn, and where the children still grew up speaking German, so that English was a foreign language. Poor Werner! Heeding the call of the sea, he had shouldered his tool kit and gone to Philadelphia. Soon enough he was the carpenter of a coasting vessel. But Anne Burney caught and looted and sank that ship. Werner spoke in horror of the wanton bloodshed he had witnessed, and of Mad Anne shouting as she swung her sword: "Watch me, Anne Bonney! Am I not worthy to carry your soul on earth again!" And of foolish men who forebore to shoot or slash a woman, and found out they had thrown away their own lives.

Fortunately for Werner, Anne's carpenter was killed in that battle, and he'd been brusquely informed he was to take the dead man's place. He whispered to me that he was afraid to try to escape. The penalty for leaving a pirate crew without the captain's permission was a thousand lashes—death, in short.

Also, during that time, I found out where Mark was spending his vigor. I told myself I didn't care, it meant nothing to me, let him have Mad Anne like the stud he was, for I certainly did not intend to let him touch me again.

It hurt nevertheless.

Mad Anne dined alone in her "great cabin" that over-hung the ship's stern. Mark and I had been dining in the officers' mess. But unless I timed my meal to coincide with his, I found the officers' mess most unpleasant. The officers (and gentlemen?) at first couldn't keep their eyes off me and then they couldn't keep their hands off me. That, and a wish to be alone, caused me to take trays in my cabin. I tried not to brood over Mark and Anne in bed together.

When Mark rapped at my door I told him to go away. He said, "No, I'm coming in," entered, and slid the door closed behind him. "I want to speak to you privately," he said.

I shrugged. A bottle of wine stood more than half full, and fine wine it was, the pick of dozens of cases of port that Anne had taken from a plundered ship. But I offered him nothing.

Yet I couldn't help looking up at him. I found him as compelling and vital as ever, with that male *presence* about him that I had first felt so long ago. His long lashes were very striking on a face that was cordovan-colored from the Flamingo Island sun.

I started when he told me: "Anne knows about the hidden cannon."

"She told you in some intimate moment?"

He scowled. "Never mind that. I came to give you important information."

"How did she find out?"

"She mentioned no names. But I think she has spies among the *blancs* in the San Isidro area."

While Mark's father had been dictating to me, the day he had died, other craft beside *Argo* had sailed past the rocky point. I had thought them the usual fishing boats. They could have been more.

"Well?" I asked. Somehow the cannon seemed unimportant compared to the bitterness in my heart.

"Anne also has been told about my father's having dictated something to you. Something that everyone knows had to be the secret of the cannon's hiding place."

"Hell and damnation!" cried William Downing's ladylike daughter. "I can't remember more than a few of those blasted clues!" I shoved aside my food, for which I had no further taste. "Damn the cannon! Let me take this opportunity to offer my belated congratulations. You're sharing a berth with the queen."

Mark flushed. "Arabella, let me explain something to you."

"You owe me no explanations, Sir Mark. I'm sure she

259

knighted you because she wouldn't sleep with a commoner. Now go away." To my annoyance, my voice trembled.

Mark's face darkened, and he was silent for a long moment, glaring, till he said, "I'll tell you only this. During the months we were on Flamingo Island, no action was taken in regard to Burriana. No action *can* be taken till the cannon is found. I still have my cause, Arabella, and what I can do to further it, that I will do. But there are times when I almost wish I hadn't saved you from being drowned in that ducking stool."

"You didn't save me. Gumry did. Holdridge wouldn't have drowned me anyway. But speaking of drowning, kindly don't forget that you very nearly got me drowned because that cannon is more important to you than your baby would have been."

Mark turned so savagely that he banged into the bulkhead. He kicked it and walked out.

I couldn't sleep after that. Going topside, I leaned on the 'midships bulwark and watched the mild night. The ship whispered along, nodding its bowsprit toward the water as though occupied with quiet thoughts. One could forget that Mark and I sailed on a ship of blood. But I couldn't forget the agony on Mark's face when I said, *your baby.*

It was one of those nights when the mate of the watch yawns on the quarterdeck, and the seamen play at dice in the light of a lantern, with nothing else to do. I saw them grin at me. One spoke behind his hand while he motioned sternward toward the great cabin, nodding and winking.

I didn't care!

Gradually I took notice of a storage box—or so I thought—that I had vaguely seen before. It was a stoutly built box, almost five feet high, about the same length and two feet broad, and it stood upright against the break of the poop. I noticed a small opening near its top, covered with a stout wire mesh. Perhaps they stored ready-powder there when they went into battle. Perhaps the powder needed ventilation.

The dice players shifted their lantern, and in the dim movement of light I thought I saw a face in the box, behind the mesh.

Of course nobody could be in that box. But I strolled over to it.

There *was* a face pressed against the wire mesh. There *was* a man inside that box, and when I heard a faint jingle I knew he was chained. He'd been locked up for punishment, no doubt. And punishment it was, for there wasn't room in that box for a man to lie at full length or stand upright.

I wondered if I could slip him a bit of meat or a sip of wine. But if someone saw me . . .

The thought turned into stunned surprise when the confined man whispered uncertainly, "Aren't you Miss Downing?"

Gradually, as I stared through the crisscrossed wire, the face took on features. I made out a short, two-pointed black beard and a mustache waxed into long points. The man's hair had been twisted into a number of grotesque little pigtails. His eyes stared like the eyes of the dead blackamoor . . . as though he were constantly in a state of shock.

He said his name: "Hiram Chance."

"Captain Chance! You didn't drown!"

"She killed everyone else on the *Bridgewater* before she burned my ship. But she wanted me alive."

"But why are you kept in this box?" I asked in horror.

"I live in it."

"But—"

"She lets me out sometimes. She whips me to make me caper. I'm her court jester."

It took a moment for the awfulness to sink in. Soon I was to hear worse.

Meanwhile, I asked, "Where's the door?" I found it, a low trapdoor just big enough to crawl through. It was padlocked. "Wait," I whispered, "I see a loose screw on the hasp. If I can turn it with my fingers . . ."

"Don't," he said. "It's no use." He moved, trying to ease his position in that cramped, tiny place. "No use," he said again. "There's no hope for me."

I thought of the slaves this man had brought from Africa by the hundreds. They lay chained in long rows, between decks that were eighteen inches apart. They lay touching each other, back to face. On a good ship they might be taken topside, a few at a time, to eat and stretch twice a day. In bad weather they might lie chained for a week. But they were well fed. If they refused to eat, they were whipped until they did. They were expected to look sleek at the slave market; those whose bodies were not tossed over to feed the waiting sharks.

I thought of that, and I told myself to have no pity for Hiram Chance. And yet I saw him suffering, and I could not escape my pity.

I realized that the seamen were watching me now. And the mate had come to the rail of the poop and was looking down at me. They did not interfere, but seemed expectant, as though waiting for me to find something out.

I whispered, "But while there's life there's hope. She's made me her chief lady-in-waiting and she's . . . friendly . . . with Mark Wentworth . . . so perhaps I can persuade her to give you better quarters, if nothing else."

"No."

"But back on the *Bridgewater*—back in Newport—she showed me a knife and said she'd kill you, she hated you so, and since she hasn't—"

"No," said the dull voice from the darkness of the box. "I'm alive, but I've nothing to live for."

I remembered that Anne Burney had not said she'd kill Chance. She had said she would cut him.

"She still hates me," I heard. "She had four men hold me down on her cabin table." He swayed as the ship swayed. "She cut me," he said in a voice without life, without hope.

I understood, but I didn't want to understand. I had only a single word to say—a whimper: "No."

"She cut me, just as she always had said she would. I'm not a man anymore."

To answer "I'm sorry," would have been worse than useless.

"I've plenty to eat and drink." Like the slaves, I thought. "She likes me frisky. I caper. I dance. The more she whips me, the more I turn funny somersaults."

I heard the mate chuckling above my head. I returned to my cabin and for a long time sat motionless, saying to myself, "Oh God . . . oh God!"

Once again the *Queen of the Caribbean* skirted Little Bahama Bank and approached the shore of San Isidro. Anne Burney came to my cabin. I knew by now that the only way in or out was through a narrow, angled passage, and recently she had posted a man with a gun to guard the exit.

She settled herself pleasantly and said, "Dear Lady Arabella, I've been neglecting you."

"I am grateful for any moment of your attention, Your Majesty."

"I'll soon have what I need to enable me to found my court. I must have a real crown and sceptre made by the Havana goldsmiths."

"They do good work in Havana, Your Majesty."

"I'll need an orb too," she said, thinking.

"Oh yes, Your Majesty. A crown on your head. A sceptre in one hand. An orb in the other, and your purple robes, edged with ermine, draped around you . . . oh, how regal you will be!"

Pleased, Anne gave me a warm smile and adjusted her diadem.

I ventured, "I haven't seen Sir Mark in two days. Is he ill?"

"That great strong man? Nothing could make him ill. He's allowed the deck, but I've put him under guard. We'll be sailing in waters near his home, and I don't want him trying to escape. Nor you, for that matter. If either of you tried, you'd be punished as a deserter. However, Lady Arabella, you and I are going ashore, well attended." Offhandedly, she changed the subject. "Did I ever tell you I have an uncle who is a member of the Royal Society?"

I hoped to hear his name, but she was clever enough to hide her past as she went on: "He was a friend of Dr. Samuel Johnson. Once he took Dr. Johnson and Johnson's friend, Mr. Boswell, to visit my father on our family estate. I heard them speaking about people who lost their memory. They forget their own names, they forget where they live, they wander around and have no place. Dr. Johnson insisted it was a form of insanity. My uncle said it couldn't be, because sometimes, when such a person happened onto a familiar place where he'd been before, his memory began to work again. Aren't we fortunate that we live in the Age of Reason, Lady Arabella?"

"Yes, Your Majesty," I said while my heart began to thud and the chill of danger came upon me.

Speaking like the well-bred English lady she once had been, Mad Anne told me she had discussed the hidden cannon with Sir Mark and had inquired especially about the time when Mark's late father had dictated certain directions to me. Sir Mark—the wild eyes went tender when she said his name—had assured her that I could not recall even one-half of those many clues.

So Mark had tried to protect me.

Then, while my nails dug into my palms, I wondered if he hadn't really tried to protect the cannon until he himself could force me to help him find it.

"But," said the madwoman, turning her dreadful gaze directly on me, "you were seen taking Job Wentworth's dictation. You certainly transcribed the shorthand into plain words that were sent to Aaron Burr . . . and went down with the *Bridgewater*," she muttered glumly. "If only I had known! Too late now . . . and you also went over the route to the cannon with that slave who was drowned; Job Wentworth's valet."

Be calm, I told myself. "His name was Tibbal. Yes, it was exactly as you say, Your Majesty."

"Now, Lady Arabella, tonight we'll go ashore, you and I, on that rocky point, and you'll take me to the very place where Sir Mark's father dictated the directions to you. We'll sit there comfortably, and I'll give you a quill and paper so everything will feel quite familiar. Of course, you haven't really lost your memory, like those people whom Dr. Johnson called insane. Your recollections are merely hidden in your mind. So, as soon as the familiar surroundings stir up your power to recall, you'll write out all the clues for me." She rose regally. I too rose and curtseyed. "Take a nap this afternoon, my dear. Be rested. Calm your mind. Your sovereign depends on you. I need the treasure that is in that cannon."

"I shall always serve you faithfully, Queen Anne."

Somehow I was able to nap, perhaps because my emotions had become worn-out.

I awakened to the sound of chain rumbling through the hawze-hole as the *Queen of the Caribbean* dropped her anchor. It was growing dark, with a three-quarter moon silvering the southeastern sky. A man came to escort me out onto the deck. I saw Mark standing silently at the taffrail between his guards. He paid me no attention.

Anne and I were rowed ashore in the gig. Another boat carried men, well armed. We landed on a beach on the north side of the rocky point near Wentworth Hall, where the mass of the point hid the ship from the house and there were no other dwellings for some distance. It was utterly lonely amid the cry of the night birds and the waves' eternal rushing on the sand.

Supplied with lanterns and helped by moonlight we all climbed up onto the rough, gully-cut part of the point. It was difficult for me to find the trail that led to the wall of coral blocks, but Anne was patient. She even told me to be careful on rough places. But what would the madwoman do to me when she found I could not remember all those clues?

Out of breath and weary, we found the trail and then the wall of coral blocks. The ship was just visible at her anchorage. The sea stretched away, peaceful and lovely. As I settled myself at the stone table I glanced casually toward the cleft where a bottle lay hidden; a bottle of which Mad Anne must never know.

The men posted themselves on rocks all around us, out of hearing but well within sight.

"Now, Lady Arabella?"

I sat in the familiar stone seat. Mad Anne told me to place writing tablet, inkpot, and even my arm just as I had while taking Job's dictation. She sat where he had sat. I had a lantern at my elbow.

Anne rose and called to one of the guards. "Carsten! Come here and sit where I've been sitting!" She whispered to me. "You should be looking at a man."

It was all unearthly, wild, dreamlike. Where Anne stood to one side, her eyes glinted like specks of hard silver. Disturbed lizards skittered at our feet. The waves in the caverns seemed like the voices of ghosts muttering to each other.

My hand began to move the quill across the paper.

Anne came to look over my shoulder. When she saw I was writing in shorthand, she told me eagerly it was good, yes, but I must immediately write my transcription on the same page. I did so. Anne looked eastward from the end of the wall and saw the poisonwood bush.

"Good, good! Go on!"

Increasingly tense, I took the clues along until, in imagination, I had Mad Anne standing on the top of a little cliff, lining up the bush with the corner of Wentworth

Hall. That straight line having been established, one turned directly around and walked . . .

And found the cow's skull.

"Yes, yes, you're doing wonderfully, Lady Arabella."

I really tried to force my memory, for I was deathly afraid of failing. But I knew all the time I could never repeat all the clues. Soon enough I was holding my head and Anne was glaring at me. Ah, the gun. The slave collar. But again I had no sequence, and the very essence of the long list of clues was that one led to another to another to another. Break the chain and you were lost.

The moon had passed the meridian and was going down, and Anne was growing distraught. I was bone-weary and cold and frightened when I finally remembered one more clue. It was true that one's memory *can* be stirred. But how much?

I said aloud as my shaky hand wrote: "An Arawak carving . . . a turtle . . . on a slanted rock . . . go forty paces the way its tail points. Be careful . . . the tail is slightly curved . . . go the way the *tip* of the tail points. . . ."

I did not add how hard it had been for Tibbal to find that carving. Vines had grown over it.

Nor could my recollection do much good. Again I didn't know the sequence. Anne and I both shivered and huddled in the January air although it was a warm winter's night by Newport standards. She took wine. She had taken quite a bit of wine. I wondered when the idea of torture would occur to her. Her eyes had become saucers of madness, and cruel lines had appeared upon her face.

I had an inspiration, and blurted: "But Your Majesty, I always took dictation by daylight, and now it's dark!"

She uttered an oath I had never heard from a woman's lips. "Yes, of course. Daylight will make the scene familiar to you. We'll get some sleep, and come back here again. Then you'll remember. *You had better.*"

As she called in her men, we heard two shots fired in rapid succession. They weren't the boom of cannon, but the sharp crack of small arms, and they came from the direction of the ship.

"Run!" Anne shouted. But she still remembered to call back two men to guard me. Then she too ran, falling sometimes, then running on.

When I got to the beach she was berating her first mate,

a one-armed brute named Hoskins, who had been left in command. He had come ashore with most of the remaining men, and they were hunting up and down the faintly moonlit beach and looking hopelessly into the woods, where it was hard to see at all.

The sweating Hoskins was frantic with rage and frustration. "I've got 'em triced up for flogging! I'll flog 'em myself!" he roared.

He meant Mark's guards.

After the gig had reached shore and Anne and I and the men had had time to settle down on the ridge, Mark had said casually that he'd take a bath on deck and turn in. A sailor brought up a tub of seawater. Mark began to strip—Hoskins said—and was in his drawers when, without warning, he smashed the full bucket onto one guard's head, and almost in the same motion he punched another man so hard that he went rolling into the legs of the third. Oh, I could visualize that punch!

Before the third guard could draw his pistols, Mark had leaped over the rail. He'd known the current would carry him a hundred feet underwater before he came up, gulped in air, went under again as two bullets missed him in the dim light. He swam powerfully to the beach and was running into the woods before Hoskins could get another boat swung down to the water.

"Gone!" said Anne harshly. "If I ever catch him . . ." She went into a terrible tantrum, raging, screaming, kicking sand, wildly cursing while the men stood around helplessly. Suddenly she calmed, turned to me hardly knowing that her mad gesture had caused her hair to fall over her eyes. "Lady Arabella, where would he go?"

"To Wentworth Hall, Your Majesty."

"He'd spread the alarm?"

"Yes, Your Majesty. Slaves would be dispatched to bring men from every direction. By dawn they'd—"

"And besides," muttered Anne, "the sound of those shots carried far. We've no chance of finding the cannon. May Wentworth rot in hell! He's no more knight! I withdraw his knighthood! Everybody aboard! Hoskins, make around the end of Lucaya Island and out to sea."

I had gained a respite. And Mark now would have the point guarded day and night, the beaches watched.

And still the cannon would lie in its unknown hiding

267

place, and nothing could be done about founding Burriana.

Next morning we could see nothing but the rolling, open sea. Werner was showing me how to whip a rope with marline when Anne came along and sent him about his business. She didn't seem to have slept, for she still wore male clothing that was dirty from her run through the woods, and she was gaunt with fatigue.

I curtseyed. "Your Majesty."

She said, "Torture is often used to extract the truth."

I closed my eyes, stood straight and waiting.

"But, in your case, I don't think a hot iron applied to the breasts would do the trick. It's not merely stubbornness that's in our way. It's the limitations of the memory, that you can't help. So we're going to New Orleans."

"New Orleans, Your Majesty?"

"Yes. You've heard of New Orleans *obeah*—or voodoo?"

I remembered the *ouanga* bag I had seen hanging in that cluttered cabin on the slave ship. "I've heard vaguely about it," I replied, playing safe. But really I had heard a good deal in the Wentworth slave quarters, where every door was painted blue to ward off evil spirits. I knew that obeah was strong in New Orleans, and had heard that a person who believed in it would die if you made a wax doll containing some of his hair, and stuck that doll through with a needle.

At first I had laughed at such matters. Nor would I believe that a stuffed rat could make you invisible if you blew on its fur the wrong way, pointing its snout at the one who must not see you. But gradually I had come to see that beneath such trappings lay a religion with its roots deep in mystery—and perhaps in truths that would remain forever unknown to white men.

"Some of the best Haitian witch doctors came over after the revolution there," Anne Burney was saying. "Those *papalois* . . . they know so much about drugs made with rare herbs and snake venom. There's one who's very old. M'bala. I tried to get him to tell me the secret of a certain drug, but he wouldn't tell me."

"What kind of drug is it, Your Majesty?"

She didn't answer, but looked blankly out across the sunstruck sea. "They bring him young wives who won't tell the names of their secret lovers. He'll find out anything!"

"But Your Majesty, the name of a lover? Wouldn't that be in the recent memory—and anyway, hard to forget? And only one name, after all!"

"But they babble . . . they go back to their childhood and back and forth . . . all kinds of forgotten memories are set free . . ." She stopped and cursed Mark for leaving her bed. Then, as though there had been no interruption: "M'bala will drug you into a deep trance, almost like death. He'll waken you suddenly and ask you questions—the first clue, the second clue, and so forth. You'll babble, but eventually you'll give him the answer. There's only one thing that worries me. . . ."

"May I know, Your Majesty?"

"You'll have to answer so many questions that he'll keep you drugged a long time. And it's a powerful drug."

She brooded while fear crawled along my skin.

"And I've heard that the drug can be destructive to the mind. People who have had too much may lie like dead for days, then waken, but not entirely. They go around like the living dead. There's a word the Haitians use. . . . Oh yes: they become zombies."

Searching desperately for a way to prevent that fate, I said, "But Your Majesty, if I become a zombie I won't be a suitable lady-in-waiting."

In the most calm and reasonable voice, Anne said, "That's true. But there's only one cannon in the world like the one I need. On the other hand, I can always find another lady-in-waiting. Hoskins!" she shouted. "Set a course for New Orleans."

PART FOUR

THE TRAITOR

Chapter Seventeen

We followed the long, low coast of Florida southward, turned westward around its end, and followed a long line of small islands, the Florida Cays. They were mostly wilderness overhung by vast clouds of birds, but here and there I saw a large house with a cultivated area around it. This was Spanish territory, but a few retired New England mariners had come down, made their peace with the Dons, and were soaking up the sun. It was also said that they engaged in wrecking, for, like the Bahamas, beautiful and dangerous shallows strewed those waters, and we saw the skeletons of lost ships. At the end of the cays we set off across the rough, windy Gulf of Mexico toward New Orleans.

During that voyage we saw other sails, but Mad Anne never wavered from her course. Sometimes she brooded in her cabin. Sometimes she came on deck to give her officers the sharp edge of a tongue that was blunted neither by rum nor drugs—although she took plenty of both. I wondered if she was intimate with any of the men. But I thought not, because Anne Bonney, a century ago, had been notoriously hard to bed. Only such as the handsome pirate captain Stede Bonnet were said to have won the body of that terrible female. Yes, of course: captain sleeps with captain. It had been quite within protocol for Anne to have slept with Mark.

When she called me to watch her court jester entertain us, I couldn't refuse. They took the mutilated man out of his box, put him into a suit of motley and gave him a little wand with bells. Ringed by pirates, he capered about and sang bawdy songs. The men roared. Anne Burney smiled tightly, running her whip through her hand. When Chance tired—he had little strength—she whipped him. She kept him jumping up and down, jingling his bells, to avoid the whip she aimed at his ankles. And all the while, his face, in its ridiculous frame of whiskers and pigtails, stared with awful hopelessness.

When I could, I fled.

For most of the ten-day voyage to New Orleans I stayed in my cabin, preyed upon by dark memories, asking myself question after question, each more futile than the one before.

Why had I sat in a window seat where the sun would strike through my dress and make Aubrey Brinton feel he had to have me?

And *why* had I, a Newport lady, not been more of a lady and *not* gone to do business aboard a slaver?

And *why* had I taken tiffin with a slaver's whore, merely because it was raining?

Why had I gone to the Bahamas? *Why* hadn't I known that wherever Mark Wentworth went, I should go the other way? He was my nemesis, my destroyer. *Why* had I ever so much as touched the hand of a Tory? And *why* and *why*, till I'd end weeping for the baby that I'd never had a chance to mourn. Even then, I wished strangely that its father had been some masked, unknown man. Anyone but that damned Tory!

I began to find forgetfulness in wine. The lower the level dropped in the bottle, the dimmer my memories became, till at last they blanked out.

One person worried over me. Werner often poked his round face and cap of thick hair in at my door. Mad Anne had forbidden her men to become familiar with me, but nobody worried about Werner, who still seemed to have come straight from a field of fresh hay and cornflowers.

He worshipped me and worried over me, and for him, somehow, I found a wan smile. He told me he had been busy carving a new name board for the ship, to hide her well-known pirate name. She was now the *Maid of Baltimore* and flew the seventeen-starred flag. He told me about square dancing in Pennsylvania, and about the black-garbed Amish who had settled there, and about the pies his mother baked. I don't think he knew how good it was for me to listen to such innocent talk. But when he left me I'd fall back into my depression and my drinking.

The low, swampy coast of the Territory of Orleans—the southern part of the huge Louisiana Purchase lands—appeared on the horizon. The Gulf's blue waters became muddy. At last we threaded our way up the vast Mississippi, with the swamps and bayous of the Delta all around us, along with the unaccustomed smell of swamp. But it was winter, so there'd be no fever.

Once six boats sortied from a bayou and threatened us with the cannon they carried in their bows. Mad Anne must have made some signal they recognized, for, instead of surrounding us and invading our deck, the river pirates waved us on. I vaguely remembered having heard that the nearly impenetrable Delta was a last stronghold of the brotherhood of buccaneers. Werner told me that the passageway outside my door was now being watched constantly lest I try to get ashore. It didn't seem to matter. Sometimes, when I had had too much wine, I seemed to see a *papaloi,* a voodoo priest, bending over me in his hideous mask. Behind him a slaughtered goat hung from a rafter. The priest crumbled a drug into a bowl of blood. He made me drink. He demanded to know all the clues to the cannon. One by one I found them in my mind. Then I had no mind, for I had become one of the walking dead. . . .

Eventually the ship began to pass the long, busy levees at New Orleans. I came-to enough to be surprised at the largeness of the city, the amount of shipping in the river, and the many long lines of slaves that loaded and unloaded ships and barges while they mournfully sang their songs of work. I did sit up when I saw a flatboat that must have come down from the far reaches of the river. Its crew were lanky men in fringed leather jackets, and they wore the coonskin caps that were the mark of the American frontier. These certainly were the so-called Kaintocks. They were great drinkers, great fighters, great shots, and mainstays of the bordellos on New Orleans' Basin Street. I'd heard it said on San Isidro that the Crescent City trembled when the Kaintocks came to town. But they were welcome to spend the money they got for their furs and the angular flatboats that were broken up for lumber.

Yes, we had come to the famous city of many church spires and rampant sin, where convents and bawdy houses existed side by side. The city where no rich or even well-to-do white man had any status unless he kept a quadroon, or, best of all, a beautiful *cafe-au-lait* octoroon mistress in a little house on the Ramparts, with her own maid, and never worried about his wife finding out, because all the wives knew anyway. This was the city that could not help being wealthy, sitting where it funneled-in the Mississippi-Missouri-Ohio River trade, shipping enormous bonanzas of cotton and receiving an endless procession of ships from all over the world. This was an American city—but only in name, for it had been French, then Spanish, then French again, and was still French in language and style. Here lived the Creoles, proud of their whiteness, touchy as to a hint of the tarbrush or kinky hair, jealous of their women's honor, tolerant of the well-known ways of men. New Orleans was a transplanted European city. New Orleans was like no other city in the world.

If there had been no slave revolt in Haiti, Napoleon would still hold the island of Hispaniola that he had intended to be the pivot of his West Indian empire. But after Haiti was lost, the Emperor of France lost interest in continuing to hold the rich middle of the American continent—for he knew he might not hold it very long. Otherwise, Thomas Jefferson would not have been able to buy that enormous territory and add it to the United States. More important for me, the Haitian revolution had brought a certain *papaloi* to the Creole city.

My head swam. Fate . . . fate . . . fate . . . deciding the destinies of millions of people and me . . . me . . . me. . . .

The *Queen of the Caribbean,* avoiding embarrassment to the authorities because she had a new name, tied up just above the main shipping area. New Orleans, like Newport, welcomed anyone who came to trade. If the *"Maid of Baltimore"* did not stay too long, her false registry would not be questioned. Soon she was unloading well-wrapped goods that were taken away in small batches. Brisk men came to sit with Mad Anne and, I am sure, leave money. Meanwhile, watch by watch, the sailors had leave ashore. They'd return roaring drunk, accompanied by bedraggled levee doxies. The men sometimes flung them down on the levee for a farewell mating; and if the sun was already coming up, who cared?

Not I. Nothing seemed to matter. I saw Anne being driven away in a gilded carriage. She had put aside her man's clothing and was most elegantly dressed and plumed. Was she off to make arrangements with M'bala? I reached for my wine and didn't care.

Werner had taken to going back and forth in the passage. The reason, told by heavy bangings from the stern, was that the rudder needed repair. He told me there was a trapdoor at the stern end of the passage through which he could reach the steering quadrant. Also he had a little boat out in the river, tied to the rudder, and thus could work from the outside. I heard what he told me, saw his worry about my condition, but I don't know what I said.

With the ship unloaded, even the deck watch considered it their duty to get drunk. It was in an atmosphere of shouting and roistering, and reeling hornpipes danced with whores on the decks, that Werner once again came to my door. This time he shoved his shoulder against that sliding door and pushed it off its track.

"*Donnerwetter!* I will quick fix, Fräulein."

While he worked at the job he had made for himself, he whispered to me over his shoulder. Fräulein, you will not tell? But I wish to make run away. Escape, *nein?*"

Dulled though I was, I felt some interest. "I won't say a word."

"Ach! But *ein* thousand lashes! I am afraid."

"You'll be whipped only if you're caught, don't forget. But do you have a plan?"

He checked to see if anyone was around, then whispered his plan. I saw nothing wrong with it. All he'd need was good luck.

For a long time I had not thought of escape. Now, becoming animated, I got off the berth, came close to him. "Take me with you, Werner."

He stared at the hand that touched his arm, and I saw his respect for me—it had always been clear—and I saw his horror. "Ach Himmel! *Ein* thousand lashes on your little back!"

"She'd never have me flogged. I'm too valuable to her. Anyhow I'll take the risk. It's very important that I get away."

But that simple soul saw me as a kind of ethereal being, and he could not think of subjecting me to discomforts and undoubted dangers. In my turn I grew more alive and eager, seeing escape within my grasp. But how to persuade the lad? Tell him my entire story? It would take a long time, and I didn't think it would work. To him I was someone who should be wrapped in lamb's wool and cherished. I had to make him meet me on some common plane.

Drunken laughter came from the deck, and rattling.

Anne had returned and I gathered she was leading Chance around the deck like a dog. She made him bark, too. No doubt the guard still stood at the end of the corridor, but he could not see around the angle in the passage. Also, he'd be watching the fun.

I stopped thinking and acted. First I told Werner to fix the door quickly, knowing he'd only been using up time. While he had his back turned to me I sat on the berth and reached around and unbuttoned the top of my bodice. It was a modest bodice; I'd have been mad to show skin to the pirate crew. But when I had myself somewhat unbuttoned, it wasn't modest any longer.

"Close the door," I said to Werner softly. "And stay inside. I need you with me . . . just a little while."

He turned, found me smiling and patting the berth beside me. Aghast, he flushed hotly. I crooked my finger and he inched toward me as I murmured, "Come closer, Werner, come, don't be afraid." Slowly his hand rose toward my bosom, although I saw how hard he tried to hold it back. "Touch me, Werner. Here." The bodice fell away. I guided his trembling fingers across curved, warm flesh. "Here, and here . . . oh, Werner, you don't know how much I want you! Take me quickly. Then we'll escape together. And later, when we're safe, we'll have plenty of time and you'll take me again . . . and again. . . ."

Now both his hands were stroking, cupping, even while he reared back and seemed hardly able to breathe. Rising, I let my opened dress slide farther down my body, taking my chemise with it. "I'm only a woman, and I'd never be able to escape if I couldn't depend on your strength and bravery. I'm so glad and proud to give myself to a man I admire. . . ."

His hand traced down along my belly, sought inside the dress that still clung to my hips. He spoke in broken gasps —all in German—and when he found my womanhood his hand closed upon it, kneading, making me shudder with molten want.

But he was a peasant descended from Old World peasants, and he groaned, "How can I touch—the woman—of Captain Wentworth?"

"Bah, Captain Wentworth! Did I choose to be his woman? He had me alone on an island and what could I do? Later when he saw a chance to go home and tend to his money-making he ran away and left me at Mad Anne's mercy. Surely you're not like him? You wouldn't deprive me of the only friend I have. Take me, Werner. Help me forget that coward, Mark Wentworth. Help me know you, you brave, resourceful man. . . ."

I raised my lips to his and the seconds passed in a mad kiss. I forced his lips apart. I pushed my tongue into his mouth and felt his hand madly seek all over me—groin, breasts, hips, till I felt that if I didn't have him, I would die.

But he pushed away and backed to the door, flattened his hands against it. "I can't," he moaned. "My Gustl, my Gustl!" When I moved toward him he almost pressed himself backward through the wood. "No, no, Fräulein, *bitte,* do not do. I to Gustl promise made—to come back from the sea. We twenty acres from her father will have . . . we marry . . . I promise made to my Gustl, never I would to be like other sailors. . . ."

He was gone, half-running down the passage. I huddled myself back into my dress, passion gone, terribly ashamed. Hopelessly I stared out at the lights of the city of romance and wealth and festivity and wickedness . . . and dark mysterious voodoo running in a deadly current beneath.

I reached for the wine. Soon a black, red-slashed mask seemed to bend over my prostrate form, coming and going in the mist that a snake-venom drug put before my eyes. A voodoo drum, close to my ear, thrummed a soft, insistent rhythm. Boom-tatta-boom-boom . . . boom-tatta-boom-boom . . . boom-tatta . . . the turtle, yes, follow the tip of the tail, and then the boom-boom and then and then and the boom-boom then and then . . . ?

It was so real I almost screamed. But I was still in my barred cabin. I swallowed more wine.

I was lying in a near-stupor when I heard the door open quietly in its well-tallowed grooves. My lamp was still lit. I knew that the hand that reached into my room was Werner's. The hand held a roll of clothing that it pushed toward my berth. The door slid closed.

Hoping again, I staggered to my washstand, splashed my face with water. At last I was able to open the bundle. I found a seaman's canvas trousers that had been hastily sewn double at the bottom to make them short enough for me. I found a sou'wester, much too big for me; but no, Werner had intended it to hold my hair pinned up and out of sight. There was also a knitted jersey that might have belonged to some cabin boy in times past; and there was a short blue shore-leave jacket that I realized could be worn open to shield the outline of a female body.

A bit of hope, like a single star seen in the midst of storm clouds, came to me then. I dressed like a man. I dared not encumber us with luggage, but hid a few items on my person and blew out the lamp as though I had gone to sleep. The entire vessel was quiet, save for the measured tread of the watch on deck. But a quiet ship is never entirely silent. She creaks in her moorings with every slight motion of the water that holds her. That little noise would help.

All I whispered, when Werner came silently, was "Bless you."

We slipped sternward along the passage. Werner had taken care to know his way in the dark. We found the trapdoor that led down into the hidden tackles that moved the rudder post, where Werner had been tightening and renewing and adjusting. We felt our way and found a little door that opened astern, alongside the rudder, very near the water. It would be dogged tight when at sea, but now it was held only with a loop of rope. Werner lowered me into the little rowboat. He followed. We heard the lookout humming to himself. Then, as we lay flat in the bottom of the boat, Werner pulled a slipknot he had prepared and the boat came loose from the ship and drifted downsteam in the Mississippi current and away . . . a hundred feet . . . two hundred feet . . . into a patch of mist. When we came out of that providential mist, Werner was rowing and I was sitting up, yawning like a tired, belated riverman although I was so excited, I thought I'd never sleep.

Once out of sight of the *Queen of the Caribbean*, Werner slid the boat below a staging that had been built along a levee. Waiting till a watchman had passed, we scurried across the levee and found ourselves amid warehouses and dram shops on a riverside street where the odor of sugarcane hung thickly in the still air. I knew that odor well.

We paused beneath a sign that said *Tabac*. Werner faced me with something of a manly swagger. I was glad the escape had reinforced the inner strength he'd need before he won his way to Gustl; and I'm sure he was also proud of himself because he had been able to resist me.

I said, smiling up at him beneath my heavy sou'wester:

"Werner, I'm happy for you and I'm happy for Gustl and the children you'll have on your farm. . . . But Werner, when you tell her how you escaped from the pirate ship, don't say a word about me."

He protested, "But Fräulein . . . when to you I talked I grew in the heart strong. . . ."

"I know. I'm glad of that most of all. But I tell you as a woman—don't say anything about me to Gustl, ever. Now you must get out of New Orleans quickly."

"*Ja.* To north I go, to the long trail, the—"

"The Natchez Trace?" It was hundreds of miles of trail used by flatboatmen who had brought their goods downriver but wanted to avoid the long, hard trip back against the current. They sold their boats in New Orleans and walked home.

Werner nodded. "To Tennessee I walk. I find the river Ohio. Up the Ohio go and Pennsylvania it is, and over the mountains and I am with Gustl home. But you, Fräulein? How can I leave you not safe?"

"I'll keep out of sight until daylight. Then I'll find the Customs Office or the Post Office—anywhere I can talk to a United States official." I said no more to Werner's puzzled face, but searched in my bosom while he looked away, embarrassed. The emerald ring that had been my mother's was warm when I pressed it into his hand. "Give this to Gustl. You can tell her truthfully that it came from England long ago and you got it in New Orleans."

He still wanted to protest I wouldn't be safe, but I knew I must not delay him. At last he took both my hands, kissed them, and turned away into the mist that was wreathing along the street.

I spotted a handcart in the corner of an alley, and beginning to shiver with the cold, I crawled behind it. I hoped that if anyone saw me he'd ignore me, thinking me just one more drunken sailor sleeping it off. In truth I dared not sleep. Or so I told myself as I curled uncomfortably on damp grass . . . but I had had much wine, and I drifted off, never knowing I had slept until my eyes opened in wide terror as I realized I was being inspected by a roughly dressed man.

I'm sure he did think I was just another drunken sailor and that when he saw my small stature he told himself he'd have an easy time robbing me, especially since no one else was stirring in the alley or the street.

He reached inside my jacket, where a man might keep his money stashed. I froze, wildly hoping he'd find nothing and go away. But he found instant evidence that I was a woman and he flung away the sou'wester, stared at my face and my hair.

I knew him. He was one of Mad Anne's bloodthirsty crew. But he was so riven with astonishment, and so full of rum, that he stood looking at the jacket when I slipped out of it and ran. When he ran after me, he tripped over the handcart and gave me a chance to get out into the street.

I ran frantically on the cobbles, but the big trousers hampered me, and in a moment the pirate had me by the shoulder. "How now, missy! Back to the ship with you and we'll see what Cap'n has to say about this! Or mebbe"—he looked around, saw nobody—"we'll first go down the alley and I'll give you a bounce. Weeks, now, I've been lickin' my lips over you. . . ."

A door opened farther down the mist-touched street and a man silently hurried out, turned the other way. He had a cloak drawn around him. Struggling, I tried to scream, but the ruffian pressed my face against his duffel coat, held me helpless. "Come now, Miss Downing. I'm entitled to a little sample o' what Cap'n Wentworth had so much of." He forced me into a loathsome, reeking kiss.

I realized he had not seen the man in the cloak. But that man had not seen us either, and he was going away from us. I gave up. My knees sagged. To be raped, then dragged back to Mad Anne, to the witch doctor—that was my fate and I could no longer struggle.

But the man in the cloak had the gift of moving silently. His keen ears had heard two names—he was upon us—and as the pirate, still gripping me against him, turned snarling, I saw how the cloaked man's hand reached lightning-swift and jammed three fingers into the other's neck, just below his ear.

The pirate's arm fell away from me. I rolled on the cobbles as he fell too. He was getting up when the cloaked figure leaped like a flying bat and hit again in the same spot, but harder, with the edge of his hand. The pirate lay quietly, flat on his face.

I was hauled to my feet and found myself running as

282

the cloaked man dragged me along. He said over his shoulder, "I've a hansom waiting around the corner. Quick!" The hansom's driver, dozing on his box, snapped into alertness, asked no questions, but clucked to his horse instantly when the door closed behind us, and we rattled down the street.

The cloaked man kept his hat pulled down over his eyes. His face was almost hidden in his cloak's big lapels and high collar. In a quick voice that was not Southern, he said, "It's unlikely that there are two young women named Downing who are of your age and appearance. But tell me your late father's name."

Dazed, I answered, "William."

"Where is your home? In what section of the city?"

"Newport. On The Hill. But who—"

"Did a man ever come to see your father several times, in the spring of 1805, about secret matters, and if so, what was that man's name?"

"Why it was . . . it was a Mr. Hedrick . . . but please . . . I'm so mixed up. . . ."

Mr. Hedrick pushed back his hat, opened his cloak, and regarded me across his beak of a nose with a bird's alertness and intensity. He said, "Have you any idea of the job I do?"

"I . . . I believe you're an agent for Thomas Jefferson. I hope you know I'll always be a patriot like my father. . . ."

The lean face, framed in lank black hair, gave me a smile that came and went so quickly, it seemed this man had no time even for smiling. "Good. Say no more. Let me put you in a safe place. I'll also find you adequate clothing."

The safe place was a quiet rooming house on Bourbon Street, in the old French Quarter. Madame Brissaud, who conducted me—a strange ragamuffin—to an upstairs room, was an iron-haired, iron-faced woman whom one would not trifle with. She also knew Hedrick and asked no questions. He said only: "Bath. Bed. Something that's pretty much her size that she can wear while she goes to a dressmaker."

God, the bath was good and the bed was welcome!

"Well, Miss Downing," said Hedrick when, toward evening, he returned and sat to talk with me, "that man on whom I used an ancient Chinese technique is back aboard his ship with a sore neck. I know something of that ship's

283

captain, too. You escaped from the Queen, didn't you? But why were you aboard?"

My father had trusted Hedrick. I must trust him. In order to tell him why I had been aboard Mad Anne Burney's ship, I had to tell him about Mark Wentworth and Flamingo Island. This led me back to Holdridge, and a story that made the silent, intent Hedrick wrinkle his nose in disgust. I returned to the reason I had left Newport, and the added reason—spying—and so to the doings of the Loyalists and the dictated history of the Bahamas, and all I knew of Aaron Burr, whose name made Hedrick watch my face very sharply. Also I told him of the cannon that everybody wanted, that had been so bafflingly hidden, that seemed so important to Burr and the Loyalist cause.

It was no easy matter for me to tell of my—in some ways—immoral wickedness. But when you spoke to Hedrick you spoke to a human information cabinet that merely took your information and filed it accurately away. I finished, "And so I was going to look for any United States official to whom I could tell my story. Oh, Mr. Hedrick you were sent by heaven!"

He said drily, "I'm in New Orleans on a mission that has to do with Aaron Burr. It's good you've spoken to me rather than certain officials. New Orleans is a hotbed of bribing and plotting. You might have found yourself sunk in the river. Miss Downing, your action in writing those shorthand notes with the bullet was worthy of the greatest praise. You trust me. I am going to trust you. I know we both would do anything for the integrity of the nation."

"Yes! But Mr. Hedrick, you *will* get word to Washington about the preparations being made in the Bahamas? And about the cannon?"

"I will. But the fact is that as long as the Loyalist cause is suspended, the cannon can wait. Also, Anne Burney is making preparations to leave New Orleans, no doubt because she knows you can't harm her if she's at sea. Let me tell you what has occurred in the past few weeks."

As he shifted in his chair I saw the gleam of a small pistol beneath his jacket, in his belt. He said, "Burr once again came down the Mississippi. Along the Ohio he collected fifteen boatloads of men and he was heard to say: 'If a separate government were set up at New Orleans controlling the mouths of the Mississippi, all the states and territories in the West would within a few years take up

284

with it.' In Kentucky he was brought to trial on a charge of conspiring to cause the separation of the Western states from the United States. But a very clever young lawyer named Henry Clay helped him defeat the warrant. He lost some of his men and boats but he continued down the river. All that while, he didn't know that General James Wilkinson had betrayed him."

"Wilkinson betrayed him!"

"Betrayed him to the degree that last November Wilkinson was calling patriotic mass meetings to rouse the populace against Burr. This means he betrayed the Spanish too, who certainly have been bribing him, and all to save his own neck, of course. Well, another warrant came from Washington and Burr was briefly captured but he got away! He's now at large, somewhere in West Florida or southern Alabama or Mississippi. I have been instructed by Mr. Jefferson to capture him, using any means at my disposal. Until Burr is captured, tried, and sentenced, the Burriana menace remains. Thanks to you, we know the extent of the Loyalist preparations and the Spaniards' willingness to fight in the same cause. Alexander Hamilton warned years ago that Aaron Burr is a dangerous man. He is very dangerous."

Hedrick sipped the marvelous coffee that Madame Brissaud had brought us, and nibbled at a tiny almond cake. He said suddenly, "Miss Downing, I want you to help me capture Aaron Burr."

I watched my hands twisting upon each other. "Mr. Hedrick, I've been through a great deal."

"So much so that I marvel at your bravery. And I ask you to find more. I'll do all in my power to protect you. But I cannot guarantee your safety; that you must understand."

How terribly I wanted to write out my report and go home . . . go home! "Mr. Hedrick, Aaron Burr knows it was someone named Arabella Downing who took dictation for that so-called history, and he knows it was the same person who heard Job Wentworth tell the secret of finding the cannon. Mr. Hedrick, suppose Burr captured me and decided to get the secret out of my mind. It's something I can't face again." My voice rose shrilly. "I can't, I can't!"

Hedrick said, "You're right; Burr would like to capture you."

"Then for God's sake, Mr. Hedrick, put me on a ship that's going to Newport or—or anywhere away from here!"

"I won't do that, Miss Downing, but neither will I stop you from going away if you wish. I can only tell you that your nation needs you here, now, because you are completely indispensable."

"I can't believe I am."

"Believe me, you are. Because New Orleans is full of Creoles who work with the Loyalists and are secretly in touch with Burr. Everyone who is anyone in New Orleans has heard the name Arabella Downing. You didn't know that, did you? You fascinate them. You're a Yankee, but you gave blind Job Wentworth such admirable aid in getting his coded messages through to the one great leader of all the groups, Aaron Burr. Now, I want to introduce you into New Orleans society. You'll be the center of attention, and they'll surely let Burr know you're here. Then, in a little while, I'll take you on a trip into West Florida and Burr will try to capture you. That's when he's going to fall into my trap."

"You mean . . . you'd make me the bait in your trap?"

Had I thought the man's quick eyes were like a bird's? Now I could name the bird. He had the eyes of a hunting hawk.

"You have it exactly right, Miss Downing," he said. "I want you to be the bait in my trap."

Chapter Eighteen

Gerard Dulain was short, slender, swarthy, and very much the dandy. The black curls he wore above his forehead had not been put there by nature but by the curl papers he wore at night. His snuff box was of delicate porcelain in a pattern of violets, and he carried a gold-rimmed quizzing glass on a ribbon around his neck. He was always scented with his excellent Havana cigars and the lilac toilet water that he touched to his handkerchief's lace edge. He was monied, he was mannered, he was Creole to his fingertips. But upon his elegant neckcloth rested a grim chin surmounted by a straight mouth that was patterned to his level eyes and his air of watchfulness. He looked *quick.* He looked as though more than one man he had met in a duel now lay beneath a marble slab that was inscribed: *Victime de son honneur.*

We had decided Gerard was my distant cousin. And—so ran the story—he had been expecting me to arrive in New Orleans and had come down from his plantation near Natchez with his wife, Claudine, to chaperone and entertain me. The Dulains were spies, working under Warren Hedrick. So was I, for how could I have refused to help the United States? The rooms I shared with the Dulains at the Hotel Marengo, on Rue Chartres, had been newly decorated with elegant French sofas and little gilt chairs, as favored by Napoleon. I became used to having hot chocolate and a brioche in bed every morning, and I thought it a most pleasant custom. I would rather not have been served by my black maid, but she helped me play the part I had to play.

New Orleans society was accustomed to visits by the elegant Dulains. Presumably it was as clear to them, as it was to others, that the Crescent City had so much more *ton* than Natchez, which was practically an outpost of England. In fact, Natchez had been taken over by Loyalists who had streamed southward and westward even before the American Revolution. Now, since France and England had long been at war in Europe, one would think that the Loyalists and the fiercely French Creoles would hardly be on speaking terms. But the common goal of separating from the hated United States had drawn them together.

"And so," I heard Gerard say to a planter in the next box at the French Opera House, "one welcomes these transplanted people who are lost between England and England's ex-colonies. Their cause is our cause. Independence!"

"But they will not take away our business, eh, my good Dulain?"

"No, we Creoles will always hold the reins of commerce and banking."

When the haughty planter put his own quizzing glass to his eye and inspected me, Gerard lowered his voice and went on speaking conspiratorially. I knew he was assuring the planter, as he would assure others, that the beautiful Yankee, Arabella Downing, could be trusted. After all, such a person as Job Wentworth would not have chosen her to handle his "history" without reason. And of course Colonel Burr was well acquainted with her name.

I exchanged a glance with Claudine, then coolly looked around the opera house, all aglow in the light of gorgeous chandeliers. A number of people in the other boxes had been watching me. Ladies whispered behind those remarkable New Orleans fans that are made of stretched chicken skin, painted so you'd never recognize it. I wanted them to whisper about me. I was to be seen and known. I noticed the flutter of a curtain that ran across a discreetly veiled loge. Some gentleman was in there with his favorite woman of the *demi-monde* who must not offend the ladies by showing her face; but they too were interested in me.

Even my gown was part of the scheme to make me remembered. Next to my perfumed skin I wore a sleeveless shift of the most delicate pale-yellow silk. Over this I wore a green gauze tunic, open in front to reveal the shimmering yellow. My hair was all in come-hither ringlets. Since unmarried ladies of New Orleans did, on occasion, wear elaborate jewelry, I wore a fringe of emerald-bordered combs in an arc above my face. The bodice of my gown was cleverly boned to swell the breast, upward. Right there, a bit of seemingly artless lace was pinned with a ruby that

Holdridge would have liked. The lace covered my entire bosom. But it was very airy lace.

Knowing this, I leaned from the box to gaze down into the *parterre*. Only male faces looked up because females were not allowed to sit in that section. It was the great gathering place for bachelors, and of course *roués*. I fluttered my fan indifferently and looked toward the musicians who were filing in. Even after the curtain rose on *Così Fan Tutte*, quizzing glasses, directed my way from the pit below, continued to glint in the reflection of the footlights.

Later we took sedan chairs to a gaming house. The sedan chair persisted in New Orleans, it appeared, so that ladies could keep their evening slippers out of the mud of the very muddy streets.

The grandeur of that gaming house reflected the money that flowed through the city. There were green silk sofas, deep-piled gold carpets, gold velvet draperies everywhere. The gaming rooms themselves were discreet and small, each devoted to a single game—faro or *vingt-et-un* or roulette. As though to distract attention from the deadliness of those rooms—entire plantations had been lost on the turn of a single card—they were banked high with fresh roses, larkspur, violets, lilacs, and all the other blooms that clever gardeners forced, in or out of season, to cheer the Creoles and to battle the undoubted smells of New Orleans.

A few women gambled along with the men. The intricate and seemingly contradictory rules of that proud society permitted not only wives and unmarried women—if, like myself, they had grown beyond the *jeune fille* stage—but also mistresses to enter gaming rooms. And so, at the roulette wheel, I at last came face to face with two of those *placées*—"placed" women—who seemed to require a black grandmother or great-grandmother to bring out their sultry beauty. How proudly they held themselves in their jeweled turbans! One of the last Spanish governors had yielded to the wives of New Orleans, who complained that the *femmes de couleur* were outshining them in elegant dress, and had decreed that such women must wear a white *tignon*—really a bandanna—on their heads. Gradually those *tignons* had become beautifully draped headdresses of precious cloth, bedecked with topaz and other jewels that went well with brown eyes.

A potbellied man who was three-quarters gone in liquor came with his *placée* on his arm to talk to me. He would not have approached me alone save with Gerard's permission. At first I hardly heard him because of the thoughts that ran through my head when the woman's unflinching gaze met mine. Imagine her bringing-up! Lessons from her own mother on how to please a man in bed! And how to arouse a man who was growing old, or who was worn from his attentions to other women, so that his passion stirred again and he was grateful, and the next time he visited you in your little house on the Ramparts he'd bring more jewels to grace your lovely throat or your little ears or your graceful fingers. I'd even heard that some rich men sent their *placées* to be tutored by a Hindu woman who had settled in New Orleans to teach the secret love rites of the East.

The potbellied little man, resplendent in a waistcoat woven of gold and silver silk, twisted his moustache and said, "Permit the liberty. I am André Pluton. Indigo," he added boozily, thus specifying the crop that had made his fortune. "A great honor to address Miss Arabella Downing, the most admired woman in New Orleans." Bowing, he almost fell.

Of couse he did not introduce his statuesque mistress, who unobstrusively pulled him back by one arm.

"M'sieu," said I.

Swaying gently, and gesticulating in the Creole fashion, he told me: "I have friendsh—friends—in the Bahamas. The Carolina families . . . much indigo grown in Carolina . . ."

"So I have heard, M'sieu Pluton." I thought I should nod to the *placée,* but she only looked back haughtily. In the North she could have passed for white.

"And you are from a fine family in Newpor', in Rhode Island, *non,* m'amselle? Is it that in Newpor' all young ladies of good birth learn the shortpen . . . the shorthand, I mean?"

The *placée* gave him a sidelong glance and a little tug on his arm to indicate he might be growing offensive.

I smiled.

"And it is said you were at Holdridge's house when the poor fellow died." Pluton belched. "Burned up in that big house of his. Poor fellow. I had the honor of his acquaintsh—acquaintance when he visited New Orleans. Burned up! Never could understand."

I was prepared, and said, allowing myself to show lady-like embarrassment: "Mr. Holdridge seemed to have been engaged in some . . . ah . . . oh dear . . . rite or custom of which he was fond . . . that required a young attendant. . . ."

"Ah-ha!" Pluton waggled a finger. "When he was in New Orleans he attended a certain establishment on Tchoupitalous Street where young men are supplied who . . ." A tug at his arm reminded him of the proprieties. *"Pardon.* But the fire? How?"

"Perhaps a candle was turned over."

"But a candle by daylight?"

"One can only guess. There was a high wind, and once the fire started . . ."

Pluton had a trader's shrewdness. "But we heard that Mark Wentworth had arrived with armed men."

"Oh, yes. To give his second cousin and me a safe trip home. There was a pirate in those waters."

Hedrick and I had agreed I was to squelch any possible clue to scandal or violence in my background.

Now it occurred to Pluton that Mark Wentworth and I had disappeared for several months. When I had told Warren Hedrick I'd be at a loss as to how to explain it, he had said that all I'd have to do was to wait till someone offered an explanation. Now that explanation came from Pluton. After some leering and insinuating, to which I only smiled, he opined that most likely Mark and I had gone off to Europe on a secret mission for —one must whisper— —"The Colonel." Ah, Pluton was a man of the world. He could put two and two together. And the poor Miss Dermott of whom he had heard . . . desolated . . . returned to her relations in England?

I smiled.

The *placée,* in her lovely swath of pink linen, adjusted the rosette of diamonds she wore on a ribbon around her bare, tawny arm. She pulled her man gently toward the door.

Now Gerard and Claudine took me off to meet Prosper and Thérèse Charpentier, with whom we had a midnight supper. Delicious onion soup, jambalaya, lobster gumbo, pecan pralines, iced gâteaux. I whispered to Claudine that I could not find room for it all.

"But it's the men who eat!" she told me softly. "New Orleans ladies only taste here and there. It is the secret of the New Orleans figure."

The Charpentiers were elderly, and Prosper treated me in a fatherly way. *"En fin,* little one, it is said about town that you disappeared from the Bahamas for some time. And in that time so did Mark Wentworth disappear, and he is not handsome, eh? But the Mam'selle Dermott who was so useful to Job Wentworth, whose passing we lament . . . she was of years of discretion, *non?* And so . . ." The old man motioned us all to lean close around the table and put our heads together. "And so," he whispered gleefully, "she kept propriety while you all went to the mainland and so . . . somewhere . . . no-no, don't tell me where lest I talk in my sleep! . . . somewhere you made the confer*ence* with a man known well in Washington city, but we mention not his name, eh? And you, *ma petite,* were chosen to meet this man and tell him what Job Wentworth would not put in writing. I am honored to sit with you." He was impelled to pause and kiss my hand. "And then you all part? The young Wentworth goes to the Bahamas, where he has important duties. Mamselle Dermott home to her native Charleston, no doubt? And our Mamselle Arabella to appear suddenly in our midst—pouf!—from nowhere! And everyone whispers! Who sent her? Where is she going? What message does now she bear for . . . don't say his name! Bah! Is she not lovely? Let us enjoy her for her own sake."

I smiled.

We did have one bad moment. As the wine flowed, Madame Charpentier recalled that she had heard of a certain cannon. Yes, Job Wentworth had had trouble with —those dreadful degenerate *blancs,* was it?—who had tried to steal that cannon. Since I had stayed so long at Wentworth Hall, surely I must know about that cannon. Where had it come from? What made it worth stealing, in comparison with other cannons?

My smile came uneasily, and my mind was blank when Gerard cleared his throat and said, "Now Thérèse, since we know that my cousin is trusted by The Colonel, it is also possible she may hesitate to discuss certain matters."

"Of course!" cried old Prosper. "Not everything is subject to female gossip."

"You'll forgive me for not answering?" My smile, directed to Madame Charpentier, was as kindly as I could make it.

"But of course, when it involves . . . a certain matter. Ah," she sighed, "in my day women were not entrusted with political secrets." She brightened. "But if any woman is to serve as an agent for The Colonel I am glad it is you, sweet, for I see how careful you are."

I smiled and fluttered my fan.

It was now February, and Mardi Gras was approaching. Mardi Gras means Fat Tuesday. It comes just before Ash Wednesday, and so marks the last night before the subdued period of Lent. I could not have chosen a better time in which to savor the delights of the fabulous city. New Orleans approached its Mardi Gras with a roaring season of parties, dinners, dances, spectacles, soirées, operas, ballets. Every family was entertaining visitors. Every hotel was full. The famous brothels ran full blast at double prices. Certain famous courtesans were carried through the streets in sedan chairs borne on the shoulders of their admirers. It couldn't happen in Newport.

For a ball on Dauphine Street, Claudine found me a gown of transparent taffeta, gave me a gossamer oriental shawl to pin to my hair. It floated as I danced and lay coyly across one bare shoulder when I was conversing. Soon enough I found myself encircled by several bachelors who had received Gerard's permission to talk to me. "Don't think a spy is a lonely person," Gerard had told me. "Some of the most successful spies are very popular and well known." Good enough! When one young man invited me to demonstrate my shorthand on his back, I made circles and slants with my finger. When I said I wouldn't dare translate them, there were whoops from his friends who claimed they could read everything on the cloth from, "I love you," to "Your father does not have enough money."

When I danced with those gallants, I found it does not take long for rumor to become gospel of a sort. In a conspiratorial whisper, I was asked how you-know-who's health had appeared to me when I had met him in the forest. The young man meant Aaron Burr. Of course I was the Colonel's confidante! Two scions of good family even offered to guard me. It was certain that United States spies were in the city, and they might do me harm.

"United States spies? But how dreadful!"

I smiled, danced with abandon, said that the romance was not frozen out of Newport men during our cold winters, but still, Southern men were undeniably more gallant. Bachelors pressed me to tell them what I would wear at the Mardi Gras, that combination of outdoor *bal masque*, parade, riot, and continual feast. Since I didn't know what costume Claudine would find for me, it was easy to be mysterious. One *bon vivant* asked me to watch for him in his pirate costume. Another said I'd receive a wink from a Chinese mandarin. Another said to watch for the flower tossed by a troubador. But whom were they to look for? A ballerina? A Persian princess? It was fun to tease them, and if I enjoyed the attentions of young men— well, why should I not? My heart was free. My last possible tie to Mark Wentworth had vanished in the ocean. It was true that somewhere in my soul I was growing nervous . . . but I must not admit it, must go on being entranced with seductive, enchanting New Orleans.

Two nights before Mardi Gras I was seated at my dressing table, in my peignoir, with my black girl preparing me for bed. Heavens—the papaya cream, the cucumber lotion, the bitter-orange oil! It seemed to me that if New Orleans women took all that trouble every night, they'd hardly have time for sleep. Underneath, the nervousness had taken over. All very well to have played the butterfly, but I knew I'd soon have to deal with more grim affairs. And that thought I'd had of Mark kept returning. The last I had heard of him, he had been fleeing for his life through the San Isidro forest. Had he really reached home? Where was he now?

The devil take him! I didn't care!

When Gerard in his brocaded robe and Claudine in her own fluffy peignoir came to speak to me, I was sure it was about the Mardi Gras. Claudine carried a roll of cloth that was undoubtedly my costume. I dismissed the maid and invited my guardians to have seats for a cozy boudoir chat.

"Well, Arabella," said Gerard, "you've done wonderfully. Everyone's seen you, everyone's talking about you, and by now there isn't the slightest doubt that Burr knows you're in New Orleans."

"Bravo for you!" Claudine clapped her hands. "It was a wonderful act."

"Now tell me," said Gerard "what am I to do with a young man named Robert Piquery who has asked my permission to visit here and court you? And wait. How shall I prevent his dueling with another young man—what was his name, my dear?—Etienne Vaudreil, who also wishes to court you? They're both from wealthy families." He winked.

"Good gracious!" said I as lightly as I could. "Tell them I have a fiancé waiting in Newport."

Gerard chuckled. "Perfect." But his smile faded. "Arabella," he said gently, "do you know the story of Cinderella? The clock is about to strike twelve."

Still lightly: "The coach turns into a pumpkin? The white horses turn into white mice and scurry across the floor?"

But now the couple watched me seriously, and my own smile faded. Claudine said, "Dear, you're so lovely in gowns . . . it's a pity . . . but in a few hours we're leaving. I've brought you the dress you'll have to put on as soon as we're away from the hotel. It's the only dress you'll wear for the next two or three weeks, I'm afraid."

She unrolled a cheap dress of faded linsey-woolsey, a plain bonnet. She gave me a pair of thick, ugly, black stockings and a pair of scuffed, clumsy, flat-heeled, high leather shoes.

Stunned, I asked, "Then we're not going to the Mardi Gras?"

They didn't have to answer.

I sighed, "Well, it was all fun while it lasted." Fingering the shabby dress, I tried not to cringe as I remembered that I was to become the bait in a trap.

Chapter Nineteen

When we formed up—men, women, mules and one baby in its mother's arms—we were already in Spanish territory. Or so the Spanish would have claimed. But the United States claimed that the boundary of the Louisiana Purchase reached farther eastward to the Pearl River. A few settlers from Alabama and Mississippi had already drifted in. They found fertile areas that were high enough to have drainage, and even on the dangerous other side of the Pearl they built cabins and hoped the Spanish would not wipe them out.

Thus it was natural enough to have another party set out into that wilderness. I found it would not be the first party that Hedrick had led. But there was this difference: a shapeless woman who walked among the other shapeless women was myself, with my bonnet pushed back to reveal my golden hair. Hedrick wanted to be sure that Burr's agents would relay word to the fugitive that I had left New Orleans and was in the forest.

There was also another difference. Each of the men in the party, in return for a deputy's fee, had sworn to help Hedrick if he found a chance to capture Aaron Burr. It was all one to those lanky, solemn ex-farmers, who thought they'd make out better if they pioneered as their fathers had done. Some of them had never heard of Aaron Burr.

February was extraordinarily cold along the Gulf in that year of 1807. Not far north, across the shadowy Mississippi line, there had been five inches of snow. At night the men built fires against rocks that would reflect the heat. We slept in little lean-tos that I can tell you grew damp and cold, and I'll never forget how it felt, each morning, to have to put my feet into cold, soggy shoes. Sometimes a Chickasaw drifted out of the forest, wanting to trade, and I was thankful they were friendly. Sometimes lone hunters came to our camp to ask for salt or 'backy. Any of them could have been scouting for Burr.

But one of our men had a banjo. Tired as we were, most of us joined in singing "Turkey in the Straw" or "Old Dan Tucker," and a few would shuffle about in a reel on the grass. I remembered the balls in New Orleans as I danced wearily beneath the hanging moss that draped great live oaks and sometimes heard the roar of a bull alligator, angry at our fire and angry at the cold.

Sleep, waken, see that the mules' loads of household goods were properly secured with a diamond hitch, trek eastward through swamp and forest, cypress and tupelo. A panther's scream. A wildcat's squall. The strange face of an opossum peering from a tree. At first I could think of nothing but the state of my legs, that had grown used to walking in high-heeled shoes. But I toughened. I guess I was still tough from life on Flamingo Island. I begged to carry the baby, and I cooed to it as I walked. Only when it cried for food did I reluctantly return it to its mother, envying her because she had milk in her breasts.

One afternoon we made an early camp. By petition of the women, Hedrick had agreed it was time to do laundry, although I think he would not have stopped if we hadn't had to mend harness as well. At last having energy to spare, I wandered amid the tethered donkeys, patting noses, offering bunches of grass. Alone with my thoughts I went a little farther. The weather had warmed a bit, and I made a pleasant game of finding open spots among the huge trees where I could take the sun. I saw a squirrel. Perhaps he didn't follow the habits of Northern squirrels, who sleep through most of the winter, or perhaps the sun had wakened him. At any rate, he was curious. I discovered last year's black walnuts in the forest mold and tried to tempt that perky little beast to eat from my hand. This seemed to be too much for his bravery. But he led me on and on.

Too far from the camp, I thought. Hedrick had warned me against straying. But I'd loll a while where the sun had warmed a rock ledge. To think that luxury could mean toasting one's back against rough, mossy rocks in the Louisiana-Mississippi-Florida jungle!

I saw the hunter when he waved to me in a friendly fashion. He wore buckskins that had been blackened by smoking to make them tough and greased to make them

298

waterproof. A two-week growth of black, wiry beard and mustache seemed almost to grow down from his coonskin cap. He walked bent-kneed, as all the hunters did, and carried his long rifle as though it were part of him. He approached me with the sun behind him, and I squinted but could not make out much of his face.

When he reached me he dropped his pack to the ground, slanted his rifle against it. As he did this he turned away from me. Still wearing his powder horn, bullet pouch, and other accoutrements, he squatted down and faced me squarely.

"Howdy, mum," he said in an obviously exaggerated drawl. "Been right cool, hain't it?"

The familiar lineaments of a dark-browed face seemed to pull together inside that villainous scrubby beard. It came to me in gasping shock that this was Mark Wentworth. But I fought back any word of glad welcome, made myself seem hardly surprised. "So it's you, Mark? Permit me to tell you that you don't smell very good."

"Why, mum, yer oughter sniff these yere buckies when they're wet. Drive a skonk pure envious, they would."

"Never mind the sassafras dialect." Why was I *glad* to see him? I moved away a foot. He was Burr's scout, of course. He had come to help Burr, of course. Later I learned I was right in my guesses. "I suppose you've been spying on us," I said.

"I have. And what are you doing out here?"

"I hope to become the schoolmarm in some settlement."

"That's a very flimsy story."

It was. I shrugged, began to get up. A hand whose strength I knew caught my shoulder and pressed me back against the rock.

Mark said, "I daresay you enjoyed being the toast of New Orleans."

"I daresay I did." Why must I thrill to the hand that stayed warm and hard upon my shoulder? "Of course I first had to get away from Mad Anne, after you abandoned me in the cowardly way you did."

"I didn't abandon you. I came back with Renzo and all the men and guns I could find. But the ship was gone."

"You expected them to wait? Oh, it was the act of a poltroon to run away and leave me in the hands of that crew, completely at Anne's mercy!"

299

"It would have been the act of a fool to try to snatch you away from that group of armed men when I had no arms but sticks and stones."

"I had a terrible time! She was going to turn me over to a witch doctor! She—"

"But you obviously escaped and I see you're in good health, although I have seen you better dressed. And goddamm it, there are other matters in the world to be considered beside the doubtful use I could have been to you on a ship full of pirates."

"Of use to me? Your use was all to Mad Anne. Stud use."

How well I knew his glare, and the way his thick brows drew together in annoyance. "I told you I would do anything for my cause, and you know I will. My . . . intimacy with Mad Anne was part of my effort to get her to aid Colonel Burr with her well-gunned vessel."

I turned my head slowly to look at the sinewy hand I could not escape. Did I want to escape Mark? His face was so close to mine. . . .

"Oh, Mark, Mark," I said, my voice breaking, "Burr will be hunted down. He'll hang for treason. If you stay with him, you'll hang too."

"Would you be sorry?" he asked in a strange, too-quiet way.

Rather than answer that disturbing question, I said, "Mark, your ancestors helped settle our country—yes, *our* country—and mine did too. Why do you go on scheming over a lost cause when you could be part of our nation again? They say there'll be war with England. If there is, you're a skilled shipmaster and you'll be needed. If there isn't, you and the *Royal Arms* can help build United States trade. Mark!" I cried as I reopened the ever-festering wound of the old quarrel. "Come home. Be an American again."

I expected a tirade. Instead, Mark clamped his mouth and looked away. He picked up a twig and drew aimless lines upon the earth. At last he muttered, "we can speak of that another time."

Standing in front of me so I could not move without brushing past him, he secured his rifle to his pack, swung up the heavy load. Now he had both arms free. I found out why. As though I weighed nothing he jerked me up from the ground, twisting me so I faced away from him.

My cry of dismay was smothered when his hand muffled my mouth.

"Walk," he whispered, whipping his other arm around my waist. He jammed his knee painfully into my thigh to turn me the way he wanted me to go.

When I tried to bite his hand he withdrew it long enough to slap me. Lights flashed in my head. Gagged again, I stumbled on, wetting his hand with my helpless tears. Thus we clumsily made our way along a trail. When Mark had me a quarter-mile from Hedrick's camp he released my mouth, warned me to make no noise on pain of severe punishment. He tied my hands behind me with a strip of buckskin. When I tried, even in a soft voice, to beg for mercy, he told me to shut up. When I stumbled, he pushed me along.

Once he said, "I know this forest better than Hedrick does. I explored it years ago—at the time we Loyalists began making plans."

At last, when it was growing dark and I was staggering, he took me off the trail and over a ridge into a little hidden glade, where we made camp. It was a cold camp. I knew he didn't want to show a fire.

He told me sharply as I sat exhausted on a log: "Of course Hedrick brought you into the forest to tempt Burr. But as you see, the trap has worked the other way."

I turned my head in chagrin. Perhaps I could escape during the night. But could I find my way back through all the twistings and turnings we had taken?

The setting sun had drawn all the warmth with it. When Mark saw me shiver, he roughly thrust a bottle into my hand. I recognized the label of the fine French brandy his father had preferred. I was raising the bottle to my lips when Mark said, "Since you're a lady—" and handed me a wooden noggin. Pouring brandy, I wondered if I should throw it in his face. But I drank it slowly. It restored me.

Because Mark was not really occupied with hunting, he had a pack full of food. We did well on cheese, nuts, and bread he had baked the night before by winding dough on a stick and slanting the stick over a fire. Meanwhile a slow rain had begun. Using his heavy hunting knife, Mark made a lean-to that he waterproofed—more or less—with strips of bark. He had a deerskin that he spread on the lean-to's floor over springy boughs.

He told me: "That's for both of us. Get in."

"No."

"Yes." His hand reached toward me, hovered as though ready to rip away my bodice. The hand dropped. "We'll keep our clothes on. It's warmer that way. You take the inside; I'll take the outside."

Helplessly I lay in the lean-to and turned my back. My face touched the scratchy ceiling on top, the deerskin below. The boughs beneath it were short of being comfortable.

Sometime during the night the rain stopped and left the forest dank and dripping. I knew because I had awakened. I had awakened with my face against Mark's pulsing throat and his arms around me. This was the warmest way to pass the night, and in our sleep we had found it. Carefully I disengaged myself. Mark went on sleeping, his breath slow and deep.

Pulling up my skirt, I carefully maneuvered my way across that large, quiet form. When I was standing outside the lean-to I could not remember the way to the trail. I dimly made out the loom of the ridge. Good. I'd find the trail, turn southward. Men would be searching for me. As an afterthought I reached for the rifle where it glittered faintly, loaded and primed, greased leather covering its action.

Just as my hand closed around cold steel, Mark's hand closed around my ankle. In one motion he was on his feet and wresting the rifle from me.

"So, Arabella? Without even saying good-bye?" He flung me back onto the deerskin. I think his strength was three times mine. He leaned over me and growled, "You're coming along with me, like it or not. If you act up, I'll spank you."

"Where are you taking me?"

"You'll see when we get there." Dropping to the deerskin beside me, he let the message of my helplessness sink in, then said in a less threatening manner: "If we make good time I can promise you better quarters tomorrow night. Dry, anyway, but not what you had in New Orleans." I thought he had fallen asleep when I heard his voice again: "I was glad to hear you were in the city."

"So you could kidnap me and abuse me?"

"Goddamm it," he said savagely, "I was glad to hear you

302

were in New Orleans because I hadn't known whether you were alive or dead."

"Oh, you care so much for me! As though everything bad that has happened to me hasn't been your fault! Everything!"

"Well," he said with exaggerated patience, "I get more understanding from your aunt than I do from you. All a man wants is a little understanding."

I was so outraged that I lifted myself almost through the roof of the lean-to as I faced him, glaring. "I was a decent woman till you got hold of me. Do you understand *that?*"

Mark had been goading me, but he was serious when he said, "Arabella, you're a decent woman and you'll always be one. People have strange ideas about what 'decent' means." He caught my hand. "I have had you many times, and I never have had you when you didn't enjoy it— even the first time. But I suppose your womanish viewpoint requires you to call that indecent."

Not knowing how to reply, I shouted in raging sarcasm: "How fortunate I was to have you as my tutor, that first time!"

"You taught me a thing or two, later out there on Flamingo Island."

"Let me sleep!"

"Hush. You'll waken the bears."

"Have me captive and mock me. Have me captive and beat me. You're such a brave man,"

"I haven't really beaten you yet. But if you'd consider it a sign of affection, as some women do, I'd be glad to oblige."

He was grinning, the wretch. My rage broke through and I hammered upon his chest, tried to rip out his beard, all to the tune of "I'll kill you . . . I'll kill you." He only protected his eyes with one arm and let me go on hammering and ripping and kicking futilely with my bare feet till exhaustion came and I dropped across him.

"It's just as well you stopped when you did," Mark growled. He held a fist to my face. But he didn't punch me, only let me lie till my sobs quieted.

I didn't seem able to move. The woods made a slow, restful drip-drip and Mark's great chest rose and fell beneath me, and I was strangely comfortable and calm now that the storm of rage had passed. The minutes passed.

Then I cried, "No!" But I didn't strike away Mark's hand. After all, he was only running his fingers through my hair, finding bits of leaves and twigs, tossing them outside.

I don't know when that same hand began smoothing my long hair down my back with a caressing motion. "No, please!" I begged, yet made no move to stop him or get away. It felt too good to lie upon the warm, solid body and be soothed and relaxed. Slowly, inevitably, the soothing began to send tremors through my body. "No!" I said to the warm, well-remembered stirrings. "No! I hate you!" But those were only words. I didn't move even though I knew Mark felt my quivering and even though I knew by the thrust up against me that he was in the manly way.

Now he moved me, putting me on my back beside him. His hand trailed along my cheeks, my eyelids, my lips. Gradually my own fingers rose to that springy beard, and although I thought I wanted to pull it again, my hand moved tenderly, my sigh was tender. He kissed my throat, pulled my dress down to let his lips find more burning skin. I remembered an old tingle as it came again to make hard points on my treacherous breasts.

"No!"

But it seemed we had returned to Flamingo Island, when our days and nights had flowed together in one endless sigh and cry of mating. He was kissing my mouth. My lips did not know how to close against his. Why should they? This and only this was glorious life.

Slowly Mark felt along my body, rediscovering the swell of the bosom, the fullness of the hips, first through my dress but very soon upon my yearning nudity, bringing delighted gasps as he rubbed his palm across my eager, thrusting nipples. He kissed and nibbled and tugged there till I hardly could bear the pleasure, and yet it increased as his fingers sought and found the warm womanhood below.

Even as he entered me I was surging, and he had hardly filled me before I lost myself in shaking, throbbing rapture. We rose and fell together, and out of my long starvation for his body I must have gone wild with sexual climax twice before he found his own. But he found another. He withdrew then and we lay side by side, tightly embraced. Till his hand began to seek between us, and mine followed and found his manhood and brought it up strong and made it welcome within me again.

Afterward he lay on his back and I lay across his chest as he slowly caressed my buttocks and I whispered in my purring contentment: "Oh Mark . . . oh Mark," till I fell asleep.

I awakened shivering in the first dim light that filtered through the trees. When I would have covered myself with clothing and gone blissfully to sleep again, Mark shook me, not gently.

"Up with you, woman. We leave in half an hour."

"No . . . let me be. . . ."

He yanked me outside and onto my feet. "Wake up, damn it. We've a long day coming. Also, at least one of those men in your party is bound to be a good tracker, and the ground is wet so our tracks won't be hard to find. We've got to get 'way ahead." As naked as I, he eyed me hungrily. "Not that I wouldn't like to take you again. . . ." For a moment he buried his face between my breasts, and his sex stirred. But he forced himself away.

"Let me sleep . . . jus' sleep. . . ." I fell against him.

"You've got to wake up!" He flung me across his shoulder. Dangling as I was, I was still more than half asleep when cold water closed over me. In awful panic I thought I was drowning in the sea again, in the wreckage of the sailboat. But I was sitting on smooth pebbles waist-deep in an icy brook.

Then I was trying to smash Mark's head with a rock I found in the stream and he was warding me off, startled, unable to understand my hysteria.

Bitterly I regretted my weakness of the night before. I told myself over and over that Mark Wentworth had not changed. He still was out to dismember the United States, and how could I ever have forgotten he was anything but an enemy and the enemy of all I held dear? Thus I stumbled on and on. I grew so tired that I walked into trees, but still he forced me along, up into rising country where snow still lay in shadowed places.

It had been raining on and off, which both helped to wash away our tracks and made more mud in which we could not help leaving traces of our passage—I deliberately stamped my shoes into the damp earth. But Mark had also hauled me along in the beds of streams, not caring how cold the water was as long as we traveled a way and left no traces. At last we rested against rocks in the meager

305

sun. I found myself looking straight ahead, my jaw sagging. I didn't have the strength to hold my mouth closed.

Mark, seated a few feet away, tossed something into my lap. It was parched corn. I fell asleep, sitting, with the corn unchewed, and he let me sleep an hour, I think, for the sun had moved in the sky when I dazedly opened my eyes again.

"I won't take any favors from you!" I cried, ready to scream with futility.

"I thought you had more stamina but you're pretty weak, even for a woman. Let's get along," was all he said.

A dozen times I might have run away, but every time I stopped myself. My plight was very like that of most of the freed slaves in the Bahamas; I had nowhere to go. As night fell and the rain began again, I found strength in hatred. I coldly decided I would really kill Mark. Of course we'd find no such thing as comfortable quarters, and that night we'd have another lean-to somewhere among the trees and hills. I'd conceal a heavy, hand-sized rock beneath my mattress of boughs. And after Mark fell asleep, I'd take out the rock and smash his head. He couldn't waken in time to save himself.

I would hold my hatred. I would make it stay. I would smash Mark dead. But then could I find my way back to Hedrick? I didn't want to be bothered with such thoughts. I would smash Mark dead. Be rid of him and his cruelty toward me and his shameful, unwanted power over my body.

I wonder if I would have done it.

It was quite dark, and we were slipping along in mud, and I was hugging my hatred and nourishing myself on it when Mark stopped and peered around. Vague shapes of rocky outcroppings thrust up through the forest. Mark made a soft, low, shivery sound. If I had not been standing next to him I would have thought I had heard a screech owl.

He listened, made the signal again. This time it came back to us from somewhere. Then a voice said from the rocks, although the speaker was invisible: "Lean yer gun agin a tree and stand away from it."

Mark did that. A man appeared. He was long-bearded, and also in wet, fringed, smelly buckskin. He leveled a pistol at us. He took his time about examining Mark's face, then said, "Yeh-up." He then scanned me from several angles and said, "Yeh-up, goldy-haired is what he said." And to Mark: "Take yer gun and foller me."

He led us among the rocks and told us to wait. It didn't matter. I couldn't have been colder or wetter. He went somewhere and returned in a few minutes. "Yeh-up. He says to come."

The frontiersman brought us to a hidden cave that was curtained with deerskin. We made our way in. The cave was not large. It was lit by a candle and a tiny fire that drifted its smoke up into cracks in the rocks. There was warmth in that cave, held in by the deerskins. My knees sagged, and I sat heavily on a box near some bales of furs.

A man who sat on another box watched me. "Wentworth," he said, greeting Mark, then: "And this must be Miss Downing." He picked up a stone jug. "You both need a few swallows of Monongahela."

I don't know how that Pennsylvania whiskey came to be in a Mississippi cave, but like the fine brandy that we had finished along the trail, it did me good.

While I drank, the man—he was short, not young, but vigorous in his actions—put a coffeepot on stones in the fire. He worked with one hand. The other hand held some object that I supposed he had been examining when we'd come in. Now, in a resigned way, he placed the small object into a pack that stood open amid other dunnage. He was clothed in a fine-looking riding suit that showed wear, but even its torn places did not take away from the little man's air of elegance. Out there in the forest he had kept himself clean-shaven, and wore his hair neatly clubbed. The flickering firelight revealed a sad face of great intelligence and large, lambent eyes.

He put a few more sticks on the fire and said, "Let me have your shoes, Miss Downing." When I silently handed them to him he placed them on their sides, open toward the fire. Even his hands were elegant, and his speech was the speech of a gentleman, but definitely not that of a Southern gentleman. Near him I noticed a neatly arranged pile of papers and a rolled case that might have been a map case.

"Any trouble?" he asked Mark.

Mark said wearily, "Once Miss Downing knew she could not escape, she became fairly cooperative. But Colonel, we won't have much time. Hedrick is certainly track-

307

ing us, and I'd expect him to reach this area within twenty-four hours."

One word rang in my mind. *Colonel.*

This little man, who nodded thoughtfully, had been tied with Thomas Jefferson in a presidential election that the House of Representatives had had to decide. After thirty-six ballots, Alexander Hamilton's influence had swung one deciding vote to Jefferson and Aaron Burr had become Vice President. He had still been Vice President when he had killed Hamilton in that famous duel.

This was the man who, earlier, my father had admired at the siege of Quebec. This was the man who, like General Washington, had honored my home in Newport before my father had broken with him because of his treachery. This was the clever lawyer, statesman, and schemer who still might have a chance to carve a renegade nation out of the United States.

And this was a fugitive with a price on his head. He reached into a sack, found half a ham, cut two thick slices. One he gave to Mark. The other he gave to me—but first he folded a clean sheet of writing paper around it so I would not get my fingers greasy.

He said, "You should eat something. Meanwhile ,forgive Captain Wentworth and myself if we confer in whispers. We'll turn our backs, however, and it will be quite safe for you to undress and set your clothing to dry at the fire. Wrap yourself in that blanket." He nodded at it. "It's clean." He took out a handsome watch. "In half an hour, Miss Downing, I'd like to have a talk with you."

Chapter Twenty

Wrapped in that scratchy blanket, with my wet hair falling around me, I could not have been very prepossessing. Mark, sitting at the fire with steam rising from his shirt, glowered at me; but Burr was very gentle, very quiet.

"First of all, Miss Downing," he said, "remember that you will come to no harm here. Captain Wentworth has told me some of your recent misadventures. I regret that such horrors should come upon a lady of fine family . . . I knew your father well. But I am no Holdridge. Be at ease."

He listened to a rising wind that keened in the trees outside. "Let us hope the rain will blow away. Well, Miss Downing, I wish first of all to thank you for the neatness and precision with which you wrote Job Wentworth's history. I wished at the time that I could meet the lady who wrote so delicate and clear a hand. But as I think on it, I realized I did meet you long ago. I looked into your cradle and remarked you were a beautiful baby. That was in your father's house."

I could not help but return his smile. He could be very pleasant. But that little man glowed with power. Napoleon, too, was a man of small body and intense mind.

Not wishing to seem cowed, I said, "I heard you also visited Mr. and Mrs. Wentworth in Newport at that time, sir."

He said "Yes," rather quickly, and with a kind of withdrawal. Instantly pleasant again: "And I held Captain Wentworth on my knee. Is it possible?" Chuckling, he assayed me. "My dear Miss Downing, I know how sleepy and tired you must be, and we'll only talk a little while."

"As you wish," I said, on guard.

Still watching me, he began to tap his fingertips lightly together. I went uneasy in the aura of his intelligence and the lambency of those wide eyes. They seemed to draw forth information. I understood why Burr had been a successful lawyer and how, when he had turned traitor, he had won so many powerful men to his side.

"Have you heard," he asked, "that history is often made by the merest trifles?"

"Yes. My father told me that Quebec would have fallen if there had not been so much smallpox in his—your—attacking army."

"Precisely. And if Quebec had fallen, Canada would have fallen. And then—who knows? I am minded, too, of Washington's defeat at the Battle of Long Island. He saved his army by taking them back to New York City, across the East River, in small boats. English warships were in New York Harbor. They could have sailed up the East River and blown those boats out of the water. The Revolution would have ended. The United States would have died a-borning. But the English warships could not sail that very short distance in the narrow river. The wind was wrong." He nodded slowly. It was hard to take my gaze from his face. "So goes history, Miss Downing. 'For want of a nail, the shoe was lost. For want of a shoe the horse was lost. For want of a horse the rider was lost. For want of a rider the message was lost. For want of a message the battle was lost. And all for the want of a horseshoe nail.'"

"I remember that. I read it in *Poor Richard's Almanac.*"

"It was first said by George Herbert, an English writer, long ago. Ben Franklin was a great borrower."

"I am grateful to Mr. Franklin for having helped to found my country," I said, bridling.

"Ah well," said Burr. "He was a great borrower and a worthy man. Another dram of Monongahela, Miss Downing? No? Well . . ."

A subtle change came over Aaron Burr. A kind of concentration of his forces—a focusing of his wits. He said, "It is no secret to you that I am ready to found a nation somewhat to the west of where we sit. Let me tell you that even without the support of that weakling Wilkinson I still can do it with the aid of the Loyalists in the Bahamas—"

"And the Spanish," I said.

Firelight flickered, but it seemed as though an inner fire had flickered in Burr's eye. "And the Spanish. You have learned a good deal. And so I have men waiting,

310

and a secret invasion fleet. The time is ripe and more than ripe. But for want of a cannon, a nation is lost."

I glanced at Mark, who was watching me steadily. But my eyes returned to Burr's as though a magnet drew them.

"Job Wentworth told you the way to that cannon, Miss Downing. I understand that you recall a few of the clues. Will you be kind enough to tell me as much as you remember?"

Since I had already told Mark, it could do no harm. I revealed the direction in which to take thirty paces from the end of the coral-block wall; I told about the clue to be found in the poisonwood bush; about the little cliff, and the lineup to be made with the bush and the corner of Wentworth Hall . . . the cow skull, the rifle barrel, the turtle the Arawaks had carved, the slave collar. I made it clear that for some of the clues I had no sequence, and how important it was to follow from one to the other.

"So you see, Colonel Burr, I can't remember enough."

He had been watching my face. He said, "I know you're telling the truth. Well, Miss Downing, perhaps I have made a mistake in having you brought to me. But since you are here, and not of your own free will, at least I can make you comfortable." He rose, pulled pelts from a bale of furs. "It pains me to see you leaning back against bare rock. Allow me to place this fur behind your back. Isn't that more comfortable? And I'll roll this other fur so you can rest your head upon it."

He did make me much more comfortable. But I was tense and watchful nonetheless.

Returning to his own box, the fugitive leaned on his hands, steepling his fingers beneath his chin. His voice went very soft and pleasant. "No harm will come to you here, Miss Downing. You need not be tense. Do relax. Can't you relax? Of course you can. Loosen up in the limbs and the shoulders . . . ah, that's the way. And now take the tightness out of the forehead. And now the chin. It's very hard for some people to relax their lower jaws. But you can, can't you? There . . . oh, you're doing very well." In truth, I simply had decided I might as well trust Burr . . . not much choice . . . and really, his soft, pleasant voice did relax one . . . he was a great persuader . . . and all one had to do was to allow the tiredness to seep along the arms and legs and spine and make them rest . . . and let the face smooth itself, which is a way to ward off

311

wrinkles, anyway. . . . And all the time, Burr helped me relax by tapping his fingers together in a gentle, regular rhythm, watching me fondly with those great eyes that made me feel as though I were looking into pools of warm light.

"Your hands are lying so loosely in your lap," he murmured. "Loosely . . . loosely . . . you're all loose and resting and content . . . and your head is so nicely pillowed on the soft fur, and you're warm and safe, safe and warm, warm and safe, safe and warm, ready to rest, rest, rest, rest, rest, rest, rest, watch my eyes and rest, rest, rest, rest, watch my eyes and rest, rest, rest, rest, rest, rest . . . a little drowsy rest, rest, your eyelids are drooping now, the eyelids drooping, eyelids drooping, feels so good, good, good, good, good to rest, rest, rest, rest, rest, rest, rest, rest, rest with your eyes closed, closed closed, not sleeping, resting, resting, resting, safe and warm, safe and warm, warm and resting, resting resting till I clap my hands you will rest, rest, rest but you will hear me and you can speak while you safely, softly close your eyes and rest, rest, rest, rest. . . . remember and rest, rest, rest, and your memory knows, your memory knows, the clues to the cannon, cannon, cannon, cannon, cannon, cannon, deep in your mind, deep, deep, you're remembering, remembering, rest, rest, rest, rest, soft, soft, quiet, quiet, remember, remember, the cannon remember, the way to the cannon, the clues, the clues, the clues, the clues, Job Wentworth is telling you, telling you, telling you and your pen writes, writes, writes and you know, know, know, the clues, clues, clues. . . ."

I knew I was not asleep, but beyond that only felt the bliss of that peaceful resting with consciousness held just at the edge of my mind in a dreamlike state. It seemed a voice murmured and it seemed I spoke . . . or did I? Nothing was sure, nothing was solid, but what did it matter when I was safe and warm and so wonderfully at rest? . . .

A sharp noise sounded far away. Again, this time very close. I opened my eyes just as Aaron Burr once again clapped his hands before my face.

"Oh! I must have fallen asleep!"

"No, you were only resting."

"But it was . . . hours!"

Burr glanced at his watch. He wore it across his waistcoat on a chain. "It was only seven minutes, Miss Downing."

Confusedly I looked around the cave. Something had changed. Yes, Mark had picked up the writing materials and had them on his lap, on a board.

Burr said, "Thank you for answering my further questions, Miss Downing."

"But you didn't ask me any more questions."

"I did. You were in a trance, and I asked questions and you answered. I suggested to you that you were sitting again with Job Wentworth and he was dictating, and that now, at last, you remembered all the clues perfectly, one after another. We made progress."

"But you *didn't* ask me any more questions and I *didn't* answer!"

Burr smiled regretfully. "Wentworth, will you read the answer Miss Downing gave when I asked her where one goes after he finds the cow's skull?"

Mark read from the paper before him: "Go the way the left eye-socket points, twenty-three paces, and you'll find an old stone bowl lying upside down. A piece is cracked out of one edge. Go that way. You can't go in a straight line because of clumps of cactus. Walk around the cactus, but count the paces you take in doing this. Go thirty-eight paces and—"

"Yes!" I cried, remembering, and clapped my hand to my mouth.

"Be kind enough to complete that one," Burr told Mark. "It would be number four in the series."

Mark read, and I nodded, defeated. Mark glanced at me narrowly, read on, and when I realized he also had the fifth clue exactly right—just as my stirred-up memory told me—and also the sixth, I pulled the blanket tightly around me in a futile gesture of self-defense. I could be naked in Burr's presence and trust him to keep his back turned. Yet he had reached my inmost mind and plucked forth my hidden memories.

"That's all," Burr said. "You began to falter, and I thought it as well to awaken you. We'll try again tomorrow morning. You are quite susceptible, and the second trance should come easily. Wentworth, will you make Miss Downing a bed on the furs? And give her another blanket so she'll feel assured she's well covered. Miss Downing, Captain Wentworth and I shall sleep at the opposite side of the cave, and when the lookouts change a man will come in and sleep on that side too. Pray have no fear.

You will not be harmed or insulted here, ever. In the morning you'll have a chance to dress yourself in privacy, and you'll join us in a breakfast of our poor best. You may also have the use of my pocket comb if you wish."

The sky was clear in the morning and the air was warmer. Burr took me on a little walk amid the rocks and woods. Having slept long and eaten my fill, I had to admit the walk was pleasant. Burr told me that the trance state gained attention when it had been used by a Dr. Mesmer in Vienna, who called it animal magnetism and claimed to have used it in curing nervous afflictions. Another experimenter had said that people in a trance might recall long-forgotten, hurtful events that had occurred in their early childhood.

"I conclude it's akin to the religious trance that has been observed among fakirs in India," the freshly shaven Burr told me as we strolled along. "That kind of trance, however, is self-induced. But it appears that an occasional person has the power to induce a trance in others—or in certain others. I find myself blessed with that power."

He went on to speak of memory. What he told me reflected a keen, inquiring mind; but it was little different from what I had heard before. "No one knows what makes us remember or what makes us lose a memory. But it does appear that no memory is ever really lost; it merely fades, but a trace remains. When a man or a woman becomes profoundly relaxed, as when in a trance, it appears that the person who helped induce the trance has access to long-lost memories. He is able to get the entranced person to relive old experiences. In trying to induce trance I have failed more often then I have succeeded . . . but sometimes it works."

But he had never asked me if I was willing to be entranced and answer questions, especially questions about the hidden cannon. Well, he was not going to entrance me again! Meanwhile, Hedrick and his men must be drawing closer to the cave. They'd have lost the trail in some places, but with many keen eyes at work they would find it again. Burr did not seem worried, but I noticed he posted four bearded, buckskinned men in hidden places high among the rocks. Also I knew Mark had slipped off down the trail that morning.

When Mark returned he said he had seen no sign of

pursuers. He had enlisted the aid of a Chickasaw who would watch for men coming up through the forest.

"We've another day and night of safety," Burr told Mark. "Then we'll leave and have weeks of safety at the other cave."

Mark frowned, said he thought they should leave right then. Burr did not agree.

In a while he took me back into the cave. "Do make yourself comfortable," he said, offering me a box with all the ceremony that might have gone with the offer of a well-upholstered chair. "Would you like another fur behind your head?"

If he thought he'd get me relaxed so he could lure me into a trance, I'd fool him! But he seemed only to want to chat. He mentioned he had been in the Bahamas, and we talked about the islands. When I remarked on the clarity of the water, this well-informed man told me that because there are no streams in the Bahamas, no sediment is carried down into the sea. He had been as enchanted as I by the colors in the water.

"Lovely," I agreed. Then, seeking for the right words with which to express myself, I said, "And it's so beautiful to see a ship come in just after sunup, across that water, with the morning on its sails."

Burr, who had been winding his watch, said with a smile: "Why, that's poetry! Morning on its sails. Let me see. The ship came in with morning on its sails. Yes, it scans the way poetry should. The accent is very regular. The *ship* came *in* with *morn*ing *on* its *sails*. The *ship* came *in* with *morn*ing *on* its *sails*." Idly he swung his watch in the same rhythm, back and forth, making it glint, holding it just below his big, deep eyes. "The ship . . . came in . . . with morn . . . ing on . . . its sails . . . swing . . . swing . . . regular swing . . . swing . . . swing . . . watch it swing . . . swing . . . swing . . . see it swing . . . swing . . . swing . . . swing . . . gleam . . . gleam . . . gleam . . . gleam . . . in . . . your eyes . . . gleam . . . gleam makes your eyes . . . want to close . . . gleam . . . gleam . . . close . . . close . . . rest . . . rest . . . eyes close. . . ."

The restful rhythm carried me along, for I was still tired, and my eyes closed to the words, "safe . . . warm . . . safe . . . warm . . . rest . . . rest . . . safe . . . warm . . . don't open your eyes . . . until I . . . clap my hands . . . gently

315

rest . . . gently rest . . . my voice fades . . . fades away . . . fading . . . fading. . . ."

Then, in the wonderful quiet, perhaps he spoke.

A sharp sound broke my rest and I opened my eyes to his hands' brisk clapping.

"You didn't put me into a trance?"

"I did."

"But you didn't ask for my consent," I cried.

'I didn't ask because I knew what your answer would be." Burr held up a sheet of paper on which he had been writing. "We've reached number fourteen. The turtle was number ten, and the gun was number eight."

"But I forbid you to put me into trances!"

The former Vice President's face showed all the discomfort of a gentleman who is forced to disagree with a lady. "I'm truly sorry, but it's something I really must do."

"Then I refuse to look into your eyes. I will not pay attention to any trancelike rhythm."

Burr shook his head. "Some people can resist being put into a trance, but you are *very* susceptible, Miss Downing. I can only promise you there will be no ill effect."

But after all my months of desperate, dangerous effort he would force me to fail in my duty toward the United States.

He gathered up the writing materials and other papers and took them out of the cave, leaving me alone. For some time I sat with my indignation. At last I rose, kicked the box I had been sitting on, and flung the furs back among the rest. My eye caught the open knapsack. I remembered that when Mark and I had arrived, Burr had been inspecting some small object that he'd then put away. Now it seemed there had been something familiar about that barely-seen object. Its shape? Its size?

If Aaron Burr was going to pry into my mind without my consent, I'd pry into his knapsack. I rummaged through it and found a flat, hard oval, small enough to fit into a man's pocket. One side was blank. I turned it over.

How beautiful Mark's mother had been at thirty, with an ageless beauty that turns into handsomeness but never goes away! And oh so sultry, posed just as I had seen her on the miniature her husband had carried, with the same huge opal on the hand that rested at the base of her throat.

I wondered how many duplicates of that miniature she had had painted to give to her men. It was clear, now, why Job Wentworth had shown hatred of Aaron Burr. But he had forced himself to work in the same cause with his wife's lover.

That woman Prudence! I was musing over the seductive and infinitely charming face when I heard shouts and the sound of running outside, and I hastily put the painted oval back where I had found it.

Mark and Burr dashed in through the deerskin curtain. Mark told me the Indian had arrived with reports of men coming close from the south. Burr, who had waited too long, was in desperate chagrin. "Get the maps. My books. All the food. The blankets. The pistols. We'll have to abandon the furs."

Mark told him, "The time has passed when anyone would believe we're a party of trappers."

The four sentries came scrambling down from the rocks. Everyone loaded himself with goods and guns. Burr told Mark and another man, Scoresby, to walk close alongside me, and they forced me to hurry along with them.

Burr said, "Whatever happens, don't let her get away."

We walked on rock ledges as far as we could. Then we split into two groups so Hedrick's men would not know which track to follow. "Meet me at the other cave," Burr panted. "It is of the utmost importance that I finish my business with Miss Downing." For a moment he fixed me with his magnetic gaze. It was very difficult for me to turn my eyes away from his. He left me feeling dizzy.

He disappeared northwestward with the other two men. Scoresby and Mark and I were to go in the opposite direction, then around in a long circle. They raced me along till my breath burned in my lungs and I staggered, begging to stop, but they kept me going. At one point we waded an unnamed river—the Pearl, perhaps. When we climbed its bank and were in the forest again, I fell and whimpered, "I can't go on."

"We'll have to let her rest," Mark said.

Disgustedly, Scoresby slid his burden of sacks and other gear to the ground. "Stay here with her while I go back and make a false trail. Damn the woman!"

Mark sat and watched me. I wasn't as tired as I had pretended to be. I *wanted* to be captured! I lay moaning, but was aware that Mark went away from me and looked after Scoresby. I didn't realize he was making sure that Scoresby would really go some distance.

When Mark returned, he yanked me to my feet. "You're coming with me. Right now."

"W-what?"

His face was savage. "I said you're coming with me right now whether you walk or whether I drag you by your hair." He lifted a sack of food and thrust it at me. "Carry this. And if you make an unnecessary sound, I'll—" He threatened me with a fist that would have smashed me.

He chivvied me to the river. Farther downstream it grew narrower and deeper. He found dead trees along its bank, lashed them together with vines to make a small raft. That raft was not to carry us. It carried only Mark's rifle and our sacks and blankets. We were to hold onto it with one hand and paddle with the other, trying to keep the raft in the middle of the stream. That water ran deep and I refused in terror. I screamed that Mark had tried to drown me before and now was trying again. Two minutes later, with my head ringing from a heavy slap, I found myself in the water, holding onto the raft for dear life.

It was cold mountain water, but Mark kept me in it for half an hour and gave me no time to dry out when we went trekking through the woods again, southward. I knew that now it would be almost impossible for anyone to track us, but in my daze of fatigue I knew little else. For three days we walked from earliest sunup till darkness closed in. I was fortunate when Mark allowed me to stop long enough to eat a little parched corn and a mixture of dried meat and suet he called pemmican, for again he built no fires. Often we ate as we walked. At night he tied my hands to posts he drove into the ground. I had to sleep on my back, but nothing could have stopped me from sleeping. There was no tenderness. Mark touched me only to pull me along, growling at my weakness. Once I heard him ask himself in numb despair: "Is this the twenty-third of the month or the twenty-fourth?" I had lost track long ago. Obviously he was in a desperate hurry to arrive somewhere in time for—what? I had no way of knowing and I was beyond caring. It had grown warm enough to make us sweat. The blossoms of spring were bursting all around us in the woods, and the mating birds sang beautifully, but I hardly had a glance to spare them.

The forest gave way to swamp, where our feet sucked in mud and we dodged copperheads. I knew we had reached the Gulf Coast. The land rose in a fringe of little

318

hills that had once been sand dunes pushed up by wind and water. We threaded through them and came out of the shade into a bright noon sun that hurt our eyes with its glitter on a long, empty beach and the endless blue Gulf of Mexico.

Peering beneath his hand, Mark inspected a sandy point, bearing a few trees, that stuck out into the water. "I've found the right place," he muttered. "But if we've missed her . . ."

Who? The question found small lodgment in my mind as, without caring that sand would get into my hair, I dropped my burdens, fell on my back, pulled my ragged bonnet over my face and simply lay still.

The sun was markedly lower before I wakened. I rose on one elbow and watched the man with the short beard try to build a driftwood fire. He had a weary time of it with his flint and steel, but at last flames licked around dry, strawlike weeds, then larger pieces. The wood was full of salt, and it crackled, and the minerals in the salt made strange darts of color.

I glanced both ways along the beach. Mobile lay many miles eastward, New Orleans many miles westward and inland. It was utterly lonely. We might have been the only two people left on the earth.

"You're awake? Want a drink?" Mark had brought water from a stream behind the dunes. It tasted of rotting vegetation, but it eased thirst.

The rasp was gone from his voice. I didn't know where we were or if we'd arrived in time to meet *her,* whoever she was, but I felt better. Surprised, I watched Mark slice pemmican into a pot, add the last of our potatoes and a bit of onion. While that meager stew simmered he baked a pan of bannock bread, and in the last remaining utensil —a saucepan—he boiled water for coffee. I hadn't known we had coffee.

Again to my surprise, he brought the finished stew to me. We sat close together on the sand and ate with wooden spoons, used the hot new bread to wipe up the last bits. My gaunt ribs told me I'd lost weight during that mad dash to the sea; but I'd had little appetite. Now, the more I ate of the hot food, the hungrier I grew.

We still said almost nothing. But a strain had left us. Not that I didn't bitterly resent having been driven like a mule! But the ordeal was over and we had entered a different, peaceful world full of breeze and great spaces; and we were being treated to the sight of little red clouds scattered like roses in the darkening western sky.

Because we had no cup, we took turns drinking coffee from the saucepan. As I've said, in New Orleans they know how to make coffee and they make it in all kinds of wonderful ways. I had become especially attached to a frothy brew topped off with lime meringue, always served in an exquisite *tasse*. But I never had tasted anything so good as Mark's rank, black, unfiltered, unsugared coffee with ashes floating in it.

His hand was gentle as he handed me the saucepan so that I might drain the last drop. He scoured the utensils with sand, rinsed them in seawater, then in fresh water. The fire was flickering down. Mark banked the coals with sand so we could blow them alight in the morning.

Again he sat beside me and we watched the sky fill with stars.

"Arabella?"

"Yes?"

Out of a long pause came: "Will you forgive me for kicking you around?"

Mark Wentworth was asking for forgiveness.

A tirade rose within me—a tree of bitterness with its roots in a berth aboard the *Bridgewater* and its branches spreading to all the roughness and all the quarrels, and the loss of my baby. I choked when I remembered all I had suffered because of that man.

Then why was I saying, "I forgive you, Mark." It simply came out of the other memories I held in my heart, of his bravery and the tenderness we had known together, and was said.

More stars came out before he spoke again. "The cause has been badly hurt."

"Do you think Burr will be captured?"

"Yes. If not this week, then next week. Wilkinson will come searching with whole companies of men."

Something impelled me to give comfort. "There was no way you could have saved Burr."

"I know. And even if the cause is staggering, it still needs a leader. I hated to run away, but—" He turned to me in the gathering darkness. "I'm the leader now."

320

I sat silent.

"If only we could find that cannon! It will finance us—keep us on our feet—and the Spanish are still ready to help us. We might not have a Burriana, but we could still hold enough territory to give us a small nation, the nation of Orleans. With the city itself in our hands, the Cajuns holding the swamps, the Creoles pouring in their own money as they've promised, Spanish soldiers and arms backing us . . . why, we'd strangle Mississippi trade long enough to force the United States to recognize us. But. That cannon."

More time passed with nothing said. Mark stretched, sighed, said, "I still feel like a coward having run away from Burr."

"You couldn't save him from being imprisoned or hung. But I don't understand why you insisted on taking me along. I only impeded you."

"I had to take you with me. I don't know if I can tell you why . . . I don't know if I *should* tell you."

"Why not?"

"Maybe you're better off if you don't know."

"I want to know."

"Oh, God!" said Mark, and he was not swearing. He was appealing.

He rose and walked to the edge of the Gulf. I saw him dimly where he cut off stars. At last he returned, sat next to me again. He was trembling.

"Arabella, we've had our good times and our bad times."

I echoed, "All kinds of times." He took my hand and kissed it. A strange, soft warmth crept through my body. I tried to make it go away, but that was as futile as telling the stars not to shine. Trying to be brisk, I said, "But you haven't told me why you made me go along when you left Burr."

"I had to do it."

"What do you mean?"

It was a suddenly panicky Mark Wentworth who said, "It was absolutely imperative. I *had* to take you along."

"But you knew that when Burr was captured, *I* wouldn't go to prison."

"But if I had left you behind, I'd have lost you," Mark said. "And I love you, Arabella, I love you, don't you see?"

He caught me by the shoulders. "How can I tell you how long I've loved you?"

How could I tell him how long I had loved him and fought my love? I think he knew, in the wondering way I touched his face, that my heart had become a great drum thudding a great truth.

Mark whispered, "Every time we were together I wanted to tell you, but we had our quarrel, and I made myself believe that a man and wife dare not have a basic disagreement. But I love you, I love you! Dearest, I can't let go of the cause, not while I have life in my body. I must return to San Isidro and keep the men drilling, keep in touch with sources of help, try to raise funds, do what I can to keep everyone together. And I know you won't help me. But still I want you to be my wife. I say, let's marry and share our lives, and what will happen will happen. Will you marry me? I promise you faithfulness. I promise you devotion. I promise you that whatever I may own will be yours as much as mine. I promise you that as long as I can lift an arm it will be to cherish you and guard you. Arabella, I beg you to marry me."

"Mark, Mark, I've just realized how long I've waited to be your wife!"

He was a long time in making our bed. He gathered great bunches of that strawlike seaweed, shook out the sand. He arranged it carefully in a space about seven feet by four, stretched a blanket across, pegged down the corners to make it tight. When it was ready we undressed each other and went hand in hand to the sea, bathed, and stood and watched the stars while the breeze dried us.

We went to bed and tasted each other's salty skin. One might have thought this would be just one more time of Mark's caressing me and my returning his caresses while the yearning grew and grew until our two bodies merged into one. But oh, the difference! At last we knew that we possessed more of each other than our throbbing bodies. We mated with our hearts, too, and our very souls. We had often known ecstasy, but never before as we felt it that night when each really possessed the other.

When the rising sun brought a new day, I lay quiet and blissful in my man's arms. As Mark opened his eyes, a thought came from nowhere and I said, "But my dearest, wasn't some woman supposed to meet us here?"

He grinned gloriously. "Not anyone to be jealous of. In

fact, not a woman but something else that is always called 'she.' There she is."

It was the *Royal Arms,* standing in to keep a rendezvous made weeks ago for the twenty-sixth of February. On she came with morning in her sails.

Chapter Twenty-one

We paused a day in Nassau, where the astonished governor married us. Before we left I wrote the news to Aunt Patience, and also wrote a good deal else, in case Hedrick's message to Washington had gone astray. I told Aunty I would like nothing more than to return to Newport, but my duty was with my husband . . . and we would see.

Three days later we were greeted by faithful old Renzo, who was submerged in tears of relief and joy. "I don' muches bein' marstah here, and I don' muches to worry over Mistah Mark and Miss Arabella, specially Miss Arabella, 'cause to me she still ten years old."

Renzo asked us to wait outside while he filled the house with flowers. Mark carried me across the threshold. Thus did Wentworth's Yankee become the mistress of Wentworth Hall.

The house had deteriorated along with the staff's willingness to work. I rounded up the reluctant maids and bustled about with them. I sent out word that Captain and Mrs. Mark Wentworth were "at home." Neighbors, then planters and their families from other islands, rode up or sailed up. They offered congratulations to the groom and good fortune to the bride. And how awkward they were, and how askance they looked at us! It was only after weeks of argument and doubt that the planters condoned Mark's marriage to me and acepted him as their leader. News of Burr's capture came as no balm to their distress.

But however feeble the cause had become, Mark kept it alive. Men came to confer with him secretly. Sealed dispatches came and went—and you may be sure that none of them were dictated to me. Mark went off for a day to see trials of wheeled cannon that had been prepared to roll through the Louisiana swamps. He returned muddy and grim, said nothing to me, and I kept my silence, difficult as it was for a loving wife to ignore her husband's gloomy discouragement. Only I knew of Mark's hours of despair, when he sat with his head in his hands at a table littered with maps and papers. It was terribly difficult to stop myself from comforting him . . . except that I did comfort him, wildly and silently, late at night.

Mark cheered up somewhat when the Bahamas Corps of Horse galloped up to do him honor. They performed in squadron column and half-column, wheeled into line with pennons flying, saluted Mark with a magnificent flash of swords. Then off they galloped—thoughtless young men who ruined our lawn—and I waved to them because I couldn't help it. It really is heartbreaking for a man and wife to have a basic quarrel. I kept my silence and hoped for the last bugle call to fade and the last hope of conquest to be forgotten. Meanwhile, in every way I could, I let Mark know I loved him and that if he suffered, so did I.

At least I was able to show real enthusiasm for the new squad of musket-bearing slaves that Renzo had formed to replace the old plantation guard, now gone to Guiana. The ten men had no uniforms, but they were all sharpshooters and that was what counted. Wisely, Mark sent to Nassau for sets of white cross straps, pipeclay to keep them white, and handsome brass-trimmed powder horns, plus a single epaulet that Renzo wore proudly on a blue jacket. The men were delighted. They knew their importance, for the cutter came by to warn us that pirates were increasing in the area and we should be ready to defend ourselves.

Thus we settled in, Mark and I. He retained nominal command of the *Royal Arms*, but Mr. Lynd, the first mate, took her on her trading voyages. Mark missed her. But he knew he had to give his full time to the plantation. He bought me a gentle mare and I often rode around with him, inspecting the cotton fields, the baler, the windmill, the smelly vats that produced our best cash crop, molasses. We could be out half a day and hardly say a word. Our marriage was still a great wonder, and all we needed was to be near each other, now and then touching hand to hand.

Spring came once more with a rush of growth. But I knew enough about the plantation to know that things weren't right, and Mark's increasing gloom told me of trouble. The Wentworth soil was the best on San Isidro, but even before Job had gone blind he had known it was too thin and would one day become exhausted. Also, cattle and sheep never had done well in the islands, so the supply of manure was scanty. We saw bad harvests coming. Meanwhile, the increasing fury of the Napoleonic Wars had almost stopped direct trade with Europe. Even ports on the American mainland were badly affected. It all added up to poor trade on top of poor crops, and growing discouragement throughout the Bahamas.

I thought of siphoning off some of the profits of Downing Ironworks, knowing that Mark would be too proud to ask. On the other hand, as Aunt Patience wrote, the slowness in shipping meant fewer orders for anchors, chain, and the like. I'd wait and watch. My fortunes were Mark's; his were mine. It had been months since our unsolved quarrel had been mentioned.

Rosemary Trumbull married a dull Jamaican planter who had four children, a forty-room house, three ships, and four hundred slaves. Captain and Mrs. Wentworth were invited to the wedding. The bride greeted us with a straight back and a flashing eye. In a way I was sorry for her, but I knew she never had loved Mark; she had loved the wonderful social position she had hoped might be hers. First lady of Burriana! A position that now had one chance in a million of falling to *me!* But I hardly could take the thought seriously, and decided to cross that bridge in the unlikely event that I ever came to it.

Returned home, Mark and I sat out on our airy wicker settee and watched the rolling water and the spouting reefs. I rested my hand on my husband's knee, felt a familiar thrill as his hand came to cover mine. "Rosemary made a lovely bride," I said. Then, with a laugh: "I can afford to be generous."

"All the more so because she went virgin to her husband. To the best of my knowledge," he added.

"Indeed, sir!"

"Indeed."

"Men!" I said, but was pleased when Mark kissed my ear and glad, too, that he had come out of his brooding.

"I wrote to your aunt, he said. "I sounded her out on looking around among the Narragansett girls and finding you another maid."

"Oh, Mark!" I said in bittersweet delight, for I still

longed for Mary. "But I can do without a maid, and we shouldn't undertake the extra expense."

"I'd like you to have one."

"Let's see what Aunt Patience says. I must say she wrote most kindly of you."

"Why not?"

"Why not indeed, indeed!" I considered the little cays that always seemed to be swimming, out there in the beautiful water. "Mark, I've had a letter from Washington, D.C."

"Jefferson?"

"No, from the Secretary of State, Mr. Madison."

"Thanking you?"

"Yes."

Mark looked bleak. "Did he say anything about the cannon?"

"Yes, although he never used the word. He said that since the United States had no claim upon the object in question, and because there was no reason for warlike action that would be necessary to obtain it, and still doubt as to whether it could be found, and since at any rate it was of unknown value, the Department of State would prefer to table the matter for the time being." I went on: "Mr. Madison also felicitated me upon my marriage and asked me to convey his congratulations to you."

Mark cried. "A mocking salute to a defeated enemy!"

I sighed. "Dearest, I didn't know if I should tell you."

He scowled at the sea, but after a moment he put his arm around me. "The devil! In his place I would do the same. Yet I have to live with the knowledge that Burr will soon be brought to trial and there's no way I can help him. It embitters me . . . but I must be fair to you. I'll say no more than . . . what will happen will happen, and whatever may happen, it can't hurt our love. I love you, Arabella, till death do us part . . . no, I love you to eternity."

"Mark, always remember I love you, I love you, I love you!"

He caught me in a kiss that, as our lips moved upon each other's, grew more and more exciting. He rose, lifted me from the couch straight up into his arms, holding me as easily as though I were a child.

"We have business upstairs," he said.

As though I were a young girl again, I felt heat rise in my bosom, my throat, my face. "Mark! I'm a matron!"

"At twenty-one? No, you are Lilith and Salome and Cleopatra. You're the complete temptress." He had me inside the house and was carrying me up the stairs.

"Mark! The house slaves!"

"They took one look and scattered."

"But they'll giggle about us! We're not in the woods!"

"A pity. That's where I do my best work. But a bed has its advantages."

Thank goodness the slaves had "remembered" they had duties that took them out of sight. We weren't halfway up the stairs before Mark bared my bosom, pressed kisses deeply into my hot flesh. At least he closed the bedroom door before he fully stripped me and possessed me with eager hands and hungry lips, reducing me to wild need of him.

I lay in bright sunlight that bathed our bed. He tasted here and tasted there, and nipped me where he said my body had the petals of a flower. In mad abandon I went for him with both hands, stroking and squeezing till he cried, "No, woman stop! I almost . . ." I laughed tenderly to think of the power I had over him, with all his ruggedness. I surged upward to meet the organ I needed to assuage me, and my body held it wonderfully deep. I had my man, and we ran away from the world into our private place of ecstasy . . . rested, murmured, stroked, kissed . . . panted for paradise . . . ran away to paradise again.

The next day a welcome gun signaled the arrival of a ship. Peering from a top-floor window, where I was overseeing a long-overdue inventory of linens, I thought that ship looked familiar. Familiar or no, I sent a messenger to fetch Mark from the fields. Meeting me at the front door, he said in a foreboding way, "Yes, she looks familiar. I know the Spanish way of making ships . . . she's the *Nuestra Señora de los Dolores*."

Her captain was the same big-mustachioed mountebank in a great cocked hat and cascades of gold braid. Bowing over my hand, he was enchanted. He was overwhelmed. He praised the saints for having vouchsafed another glimpse of the glorious *señorita* he remembered, But now, *señora*? Ah, had he but known, he would have ransacked the seven seas to bring a wedding gift even half-suitable for one of my beauty.

He was a trial at dinner, where his table manners

329

lagged behind his ability to compliment. At least, after dinner, he begged leave to withdraw himself from my ravishing presence . . . but it was of the essential most that he and his *compadre* Captain Wentworth exchange a few trifling words, after which he begged to be allowed to bask again in my delicious presence.

Those few words went on for over an hour, and they were private and low-voiced. I noticed that as the Spanish captain consumed rum and cigars—always dipping his cigar into his rum—Mark argued with him and my husband's face gloomed darker and darker. Also the Spanish captain, an ear-to-ear smiler, seemed to have forgotten how to smile.

He slept aboard his ship and left very early in the morning. Mark was up as early, after a disturbed night that made me worried. He went off about plantation business, leaving word that he didn't know when he'd get home. He seemed bothered and evasive, and he took a lantern from the stable, which was odd.

All morning I felt uneasy, and in the afternoon I sent a house slave to find Mark and ask him if he'd be home for dinner. The slave returned and said that Mister Mark had been very briefly in the fields and then had gone away; no one knew where. I puttered in the garden, stopping often to look around and see if Mark was coming. The sun sent low shafts of light through clear air. Over on the point, in the rocky, broken area, something moved and the sun caught it—a tiny white speck. Mark had not worn anything over his old white shirt.

The point and its rocks and bluffs meant only one thing. The cannon.

I put down my garden shears and began walking, following the path I had so often followed in Job Wentworth's sedan chair. I begrudged the pause when I met Renzo, and told him I was off to the point to gather cactus apples. Wouldn't I need a basket? No, I'd carry them in my straw hat. And I'd be careful of the spines. That dear black man! But my thoughts returned to Mark, who had slept so poorly and had been so disturbed and glum. I climbed steep areas and slippery areas, and at length, in the midst of ridges and gullies, I paused, panting, hot and not knowing where to go.

"Arabella! Up here." His voice was strong but it reflected discouragement. Oh, I knew him well!

330

I found Mark at the coral-block wall, cooling himself in the sea breeze. I could see he had been climbing around, for his clothing and his face were streaked with dirt.

"What made you come here?" he demanded, giving me the black V of his scowling brows.

"Love," I said truly. And, just as truly: "Worry. What's the matter?"

"I'm all right." But he wasn't all right. There was a desperate, sunken-eyed look about him.

"Still, I wondered why . . ."

The unasked question hung in the air while Mark glowered, and it seemed to me that he debated whether to confide in me or send me away. Suddenly he showed me a rectangle of rumpled paper. "Burr gave me this list before I left him."

"The clues I was able to remember? But there are so many missing."

"I know. But I thought . . ." He glared at the list hopelessly. He had thought that after he had found the last clear clue he might fumble his way to the others. He hadn't. He had taken along a lantern in case he had to enter a cave. The cave remained unfound.

There he stood, defeated and undeniably desperate, his hands clenching and unclenching and his mouth tight. But why, after all the months that had passed, had he suddenly tried to find the cannon?

"Mark! The Spanish captain?"

"Yes. He came to serve notice on me. Time is running out. The Spanish position in Florida, with Burr captured and the United States looming to the north and west, is badly compromised. They've given me two months in which to find the cannon and set the invasion plan in motion. Otherwise, the Spanish offer of aid must be considered withdrawn."

The word *withdrawn* fell like lead. The Loyalist cause was at its last gasp. I felt no happiness, only a relieved weariness, as though a long illness were over.

Mark leaned back against the wall of coral blocks. He was not a yard away from the crack that held, beneath a scatter of earth, a bottle that contained all the directions for finding the cannon and the treasure in the cannon. With a word I could give my husband all he wanted. But I must not. Ridden with guilt, I tried not to look at that crack in the wall.

331

"Let's go home," I said gently. I must be very soft with Mark while he suffered with his defeat.

But he remained leaning against the wall, his arms folded and a darkness had come across his face—a terrible darkness. He was not going home, I knew. And he had something to tell me. Instinct made me wish not to hear it, but I heard.

"Arabella, I hoped I could leave you out of this. But now I must ask your help."

"My help?" It was a useless, frightened question, because I knew exactly what he meant.

"Your help in finding the cannon."

"No! I mean—how can I help you? You know there are many clues I can't remember. And really"—I searched for reasons— "really one's memory is bound to grow worse as time goes on."

"And unlike Burr I know nothing of entrancement. But if you and I followed the first clue, then the second and so forth, right through to the fourteenth as I have them on this paper, and then we kept on looking around in areas where you've been before, where you'd recognize landmarks, your memory might be stirred up enough to let you remember the rest."

It well might! Mark's plan was akin to the idea that Mad Anne's learned uncle had had—he who was a member of the Royal Society. Go back to the scene. Recreate the old conditions as nearly as possible—just as Mad Anne had tried to do. But going through the entire route of the treasure clues would be an even better way to recapture the clues that lurked in my mind, only waiting to be formed into words again.

But it must not happen! "Mark, do you realize you're asking me to be disloyal to the United States?"

"Yes," he said harshly.

"My dearest, you mustn't ask it of me."

"But I do ask it of you."

"No!"

He pushed himself away from the wall, came very close. "I demand it, Arabella."

It is hard to describe my fright. The wind, the sun, the rocks, even the breeze seemed laden with terror.

The man I loved breathed heavily and raggedly, and his shoulders bent beneath an invisible weight of resolve. There was no mercy in the voice that said, "I tell you that you are going to help me. I am your husband. You are my wife."

Trying for courage: "Mark, that's not fair! And it's futile! Can't you see that history is on the side of the United States? Why must you—all of you—now lose all you have? Involve yourselves in war and blood and misery in order to create a shaky little nation that won't last, can't last, may drag Europe into the conflict. Dearest, dearest, come back with me to Newport. Be an American again. Or stay here and I'll gladly stay with you, or I'll live anywhere in the world with you, happily, as long as you give up the idea of Burriana."

He shouted, "Never mind all that! You're my wife and I require that you help me find the cannon."

"I can't."

"You can and you will."

"I won't!" I stamped my foot.

"I tell you I demand it of you," he snarled as he reached and dug into my arms with all the steely strength of his fingers. But when I screamed in agony he let go, stared at his hands, thrust them wildly to his head. "No . . . no . . . I didn't mean to . . ."

Holding my arms and moaning with pain, I sobbed, "Go away from me."

"Arabella, I was beside myself. I would never try to force you to—"

"Stay away from me! Don't follow me! May the cannon rot and your cause rot and you rot with it! Don't ever come near me! If that's what I mean to you . . . after you swore you'd never lift an arm save to cherish and guard me . . ." Still writhing with the pain of crushed flesh, I stumbled toward the trail.

He came after me with great strides. "Wait. I love you. I can't tell you how it hurts to know I've hurt you. It's just that . . . so many people depend on me. The entire cause is *me*, now, and the cannon. I'm so torn inside . . . I too have loyalty . . ." He was holding me desperately. "If you'll help me of your own free will, then I beg of you to help me. But if you won't, I can't force you." He fell to his knees and held me around the legs, shaking, his face on my thigh, looking up with a wild soul-agony that hurt my heart. "You mean more to me than anything else in the world. Let the rest go—Burr, the new nation, my friends, my oath, anything. I will not force you. I will not

333

hurt you. I love you too much." He hid his face against me.

It was terrible to see Mark humbled. I wanted him brave and rough and never retreating. I lived through a moment in which I almost gave in because I *was* his wife. But I didn't give in, only pulled him upward till he was taller than I again and I rested where I belonged, on his chest, in his arms. It was only then, when the strong man had been reduced to his inmost self, that the truth came out, told haltingly, and at length with his tears wetting my cheek.

"My dearest," he gasped, "what you've told me . . . about history being on the side of the United States . . . is what I began to know . . . back on Flamingo Island . . . back in the Florida jungle . . . then that night on the beach . . . then back here on San Isidro, with the cause coming to pieces around me. Couldn't admit it. But now I have to admit it . . . because it's true that the United States could overwhelm any country we set up . . . and so our cause was lost long ago."

And my cause had won. But all I wanted just then was to find a way to comfort my husband. "Mark, you Loyalists were *loyal*, after all. Being loyal is no sin."

He wiped his hand across his face. "Loyal, yes, and human enough to have chosen the losing side in the Revolution. Later, human enough to resent the way we were treated. Do you know that many of us would have been glad to get rid of George III and his ministers? But we thought the colonies still needed Great Britain's strength. Now I see that with the French Revolution only a memory and Europe going back to its old monarchy and tyranny, the United States must not be weakened. We are the hope of the world." I noticed that Mark had said *we*. "And you were right; the quarrel shouldn't be passed along to another generation. It's time to heal the wound."

"Yes!"

He kissed me, tried to smile. "Let me say the words. I who was born in the United States want to return to it and be a part of it. Oh, my darling, it isn't easy to abandon all my father lived for and that he reared me to live for. Tell me that you love me. I need your help to see me through."

"I love you, I love you!"

We clung and murmured in our gathering joy. We had

334

made an end to old sorrow and conflict. We had found a wonderful new beginning. The waves swished below our feet, in the secret caverns where, for all we cared, that cannon could lie for a thousand years.

"Shall we go home?" I whispered.

He nodded, still embraced me. I'll always remember how completely happy we were . . . for just a little while.

Mark had picked up the lantern and we were ready to leave when he paused—holding my hand—and gazed back at the sea. He said thoughtfully, "A couple of hours ago I saw a ship. She was pretty far out, but she seemed familiar. Nothing out there now."

"Could it have been the *Nuestra Señora* returning?"

"No. Two-masted. I thought she was heading this way, but she may have changed her course. Well . . ." He laughed a little. "Come on, old lady, I need my dinner."

I laughed too, still gloriously happy.

As we began walking, something down the slope to the right—the direction away from Wentworth Hall—caught Mark's attention. He stared down the tumbled slope, leaped up onto the wall to see better. "There's a brig anchored close inshore at the base of the point, where she's hard to see against the woods." He leaped down. "Arabella, that's the vessel I saw. Look at her, but keep yourself hidden."

I peered around a corner of the wall, then back at Mark, worried.

He said, "It's the *Queen of the Caribbean*. This seems to be the week to be visited by familiar ships." He grimaced.

I peered again. "Mark, she has her small boats on the beach. That means men are ashore."

"Damn! And I exposed myself to clear view."

"Someone on the ship is signaling with flags."

"That's it! Telling the men ashore that I'm up here."

"Mark! Remember, Anne Burney wants that cannon— but for herself, the way Holdridge did. Do you suppose she's after it now? But she still has no clues. . . ."

Mark slumped into a stone chair, banged the table despairingly. "The Spanish captain told me that two of Burr's men were able to slip away with letters the Colonel wrote before he himself was captured. One letter was to Anne Burney, who was hiding with other pirates in the Mississippi Delta. It contained a copy of those fourteen

335

clues. It told Anne that if she could work out the rest of the clues and find the cannon, and if she then delivered the cannon, unopened—"

A cannon unopened? What could he mean?

"—to the Spanish officials at a certain spot in Florida, he, Burr, promised to make Anne the Empress of Mexico."

"She'd wanted the cannon so she could found her court!"

"Yes, and think of the grand court that Burr used to tempt the loony. Empress of Mexico."

"But the other letter?"

"It was a short note to those nameless Spanish officials with whom Burr worked. It enclosed a copy of the letter to Mad Anne and explained that Burr wasn't really giving away Mexico, which of course belongs to Spain. But if Anne delivered that cannon, intact, the war for Burriana could begin. He also pointed out what a great name those Spaniards would make for themselves in Madrid if they stopped the United States' westward expansion."

Bewildered, I asked, "But Mark, if the Spanish were still to keep Mexico, how could Anne become Empress?"

"Burr also suggested that it would be a good thing for the world if Mad Anne lost her life on her way back to her ship."

I shuddered. "So Mad Anne is here to find the cannon and insure her death. But I don't think she'll find it."

"I don't think so either. And it seems strange to hear myself say it—but I hope not!" We exchanged a brief, understanding smile as he added quickly, "At any rate, we certainly don't want her to find *us*. She warned me that if I ever tried to escape from her, I'd die the death of a thousand lashes. As for you—"

"I escaped too!" I cringed, almost able to feel those lashes ripping skin and flesh from my back.

"Worse yet," Mark growled, "Anne knows how Burr secured all those extra clues, right down to the fourteenth and all in order. *From you,* my dearest, which means that Anne would stop at nothing to plumb your mind for the rest. Yes, you may well look frightened. Come on!"

But we had hardly taken ten steps toward the trail when Mark stopped, pulled me down. Wordlessly he pointed. Men with swords and muskets had appeared between us and the house, between us and the forest, between us and the bay where the *Queen of the Caribbean* rode at anchor, a man watching from her masthead, a man ready with signal flags on her deck.

We looked back at the edge of the bluff and the sea beyond. If we leaped into the ocean we'd have a terribly long swim in deep shark-infested water. Men would be after us in small boats while others fired from the cliffs. It would be suicide.

Anne had us trapped.

Mark said grimly, "As they close the circle they'll look into every corner, every gully. Worse yet, they know I'm up here at the wall. I don't have a gun, a sword, anything more than a pocket knife." He stamped back and forth, trying to think; turned to me. "But they don't know *you're* here. Hide, quickly! There—beneath the stone table. I know it's scant shelter, but I'll make sure they follow me, and no one has any reason to search for you. After the ship leaves you can get away."

"No," I said.

He took me to him. "My beloved, if you're captured with me we'll both die. At least let me have the comfort of knowing you'll stay alive."

How to explain I could not leave him? How to show him that after all we had suffered before we had found each other, I would rather join him in death than give him up?

But there was a place where we both could hide and never be found! And yet I dared not take him there. And yet, if I didn't take him to that place, he would die.

I had to make a choice and my heart twisted with indecision. But I really had no choice. With heart and soul and mind I knew I must save Mark, and I knew nothing else.

I ran to the wall and thrust my hand down into a wide crack. I pulled out the wine bottle, smashed it, found the tight roll of paper that had stayed safe and dry.

Mark stared uncomprehendingly at the fuzzy shorthand I had scribbled with a bullet. When I told him that I held all the clues to finding the cave, he hardly could speak above his shock.

And I, in growing terror, whispered hoarsely, "We'll find the cave and hide in it. And wait till Anne has given up and gone away." After that, not another word could pass my dry lips. I waited for Mark to cry out in triumph that he and his cause would possess the cannon at last. And

337

even so, and even if it meant turning my back on the United States, I would still save his life. I must.

I could not hear his first few words, I was so stunned with dread. But others came through as he bent to kiss me: ". . . and then let the cannon lie there for a thousand years, where it can do no harm. You'll know where it is and I'll know, but no one else will know, ever."

I think I smiled and whispered my love and my trust. Then we were running, crouched, breathing hard. We slid and scrambled through the first fourteen clues at a frantic pace, I sometimes wild with frustration because a line of shorthand had smudged. But I managed to decipher everything. We risked broken limbs as we cut across rough rocks. Once Mark swung me down a steep shelf with my notes in my teeth. The wind brought the voices of Anne's desperadoes shouting to each other. Suddenly we heard her own voice: "Find that bastard Wentworth! I want to watch him die!"

Fortunately for us, the pirates had to pause to investigate every angle and declivity while Mark and I kept going at reckless speed. Often we lost precious moments because one man's thirty paces may be another's twenty-five. We heard Anne cry shrilly, "Come along, you!" to someone unseen. We ran and climbed wildly on.

At last we found the large, sand-hidden arrow where I had had to wait while Tibbal entered the gully. I gasped to Mark that this was the right gully, and we rushed into the stiflingly hot air that was held between its high rock walls. Hastily I read the final instructions. But nothing seemed to be the way Job had described it. No wonder! Another landslide had covered many of the flat stones and had tumbled great masses of vine that had been nourished in one of those soil pockets.

Even so we were able to puzzle out the first two clues on the rough floor of the gully. But when we faced those tons of rock that had slid down, and tried to count nine stones, we couldn't tell where to begin.

I looked up, screamed. A man had appeared at the edge of the gully and his musket pointed down at us. But Mad Anne wanted Mark alive, so the pirate fired a shot that skipped and buzzed off the rocks.

"This way!" he roared gleefully as he disappeared to guide the others. "And 'e's got the woman with 'im—the one what ran away with the German in New Orleans."

338

Anne's scream rang echoes. "Don't let her escape!"

I thought I heard the distant rattle of a chain, but I was too busy with frantic searching to know anything but our need to find the cave's entrance. Of course it was well hidden. We pushed and pulled in despair at dozens of flat stones . . . scores of flat stones.

Mark said, "At least I can fight with this," and went to pick up a long, heavy stone sliver. But it pivoted at one end, where it had been drilled and fitted to a stone pin. Beneath it we saw a finger-wide crack.

Mark got his fingers into the crack and pulled. Now came the groaning sound of rock grinding upon rock. Slowly the crack widened and other cracks appeared, showing a square, hewn stone that also swiveled at one corner and displayed a black hole beneath.

While Mark moved the stone I had luck with his flint and quickly lit the lantern. It showed us a ledge four feet below. When I was down there with the lantern, Mark followed, stood on the ledge, tried to swing the stone back over the opening. But some loose pebble had wedged into the pivot. He couldn't move the stone, couldn't take time to clear it as shouts drew closer. He grabbed at hanging vines, covered the hole and the stone as well as he could. The lantern showed us steps cut in the whitish rock. We followed them down into a region of cool darkness. Would Anne find the opening and follow us with her armed men? If so, we were lost and the cannon would be hers. Yet we could have done nothing else but flee and hope.

It appeared the sea had made that underground passage long ago. The rock had been worn smooth, and we walked on sand—where we could see others had walked before— and saw bits of shell, seaweed that had dried into dust, a rotted crab claw. Mark led me, holding up a hand to warn us of projections from the rock roof. Ancient blackness kept moving away from the lantern light and closing in behind. We began to smell the sea.

Sometimes we had to squeeze through narrow places. Sometimes the cleft widened till its sides grew dim. The tunnel went upward. The sand disappeared. The sound of our heavy breathing grew different, and we realized we had entered one side of an extensive cave.

"Careful," Mark whispered. "We're following a narrow ledge. We're yards above the floor of the cave."

It was black down there. It became a trifle lighter, but

still very dim, when Mark held the lantern outward. He thought he had seen something. He had. Something lay on the white sand floor.

Gripping into a crack for support, Mark held out the lantern farther. We saw that the dim object was itself a dull white, and knobby at one end. It was the size of a man. We still could not quite make it out. But I saw odd, faint shadows that fell on the tumbled sand. They were curved shadows, close together.

Gradually the vague shape became something the eye recognized. We were looking at a skeleton. The strange shadows were made by its fleshless ribs.

"Whew!" said Mark, pulling himself back to safety. He peered ahead. "The ledge slants downward."

We followed it, and it led us to the cave's floor. We turned back along the sand. Gradually the bones swam into view. We realized there were two skeletons, and we knew why the two had looked like one.

Mark uttered a cry and almost dropped the lantern. I took it from him. Frightening as it was for me, the sight was truly terrible for my husband.

He had found his mother's last remains.

Chapter Twenty-two

They lay upon the sand they had disturbed with their love-making, long ago when their bones had been clothed with passionate flesh. Their bones were still entwined in the attitude of love. The skeleton on the bottom still had long black hair. Her skull grinned up at us. The larger skeleton lay face downward. Their cheeks had been pressed together when they died.

The arrow of waxed hardwood remained fixed in both rib cages. It had come from above, from the ledge where Job Wentworth had stood very quietly in the darkness. But he had been able to see the lovers. Near by, a bit of tallow still remained of their candle. The arrow had been shot with great force by a man still strong and keen-eyed. Directed downward, it had gathered extra speed, and the steel arrowhead my father had made—only flakes of rust now—had spurted into the man's back and through him into the woman's breast, stopping both hearts.

Thus had Prudence Wentworth and Brendan Stratton died in their ecstasy. If there could have been any doubt that the smaller skeleton had once been Mark's mother, it was dispelled by her left arm. The right arm still clasped the long-lost English statesman, but the left arm and hand lay stretched outward. One finger pointed. A great opal glittered on a gold ring that loosely circled bone.

Mark sank to his knees and held his face.

I touched him but he remained motionless. I tried to whisper comfort but he didn't hear. Sadly I moved about, found where the lovers had left their clothing. There still remained a few coins and buttons lying on moldering shreds of leather and cloth. Nearby lay wine bottles and dishes to show they must have come often to their secret rendezvous. Till they disappeared. Not gone to Florida. Not killed by Indians.

I remembered Job's saying, "I know where they went."

Mark had not moved. I listened, heard nothing, so did not disturb his mourning. My thoughts turned to Job Wentworth and Aaron Burr; two clever men. Why had Job waited so long, and very nearly too long, to send the clues to the archplotter?

One reason was clear enough. If Job had told the way to the bodies he'd have revealed himself as a murderer. The crime of passion is often condoned, but Brendan Stratton had been an important man and had been much missed by Lord Grenville's government in London. There would have been questions, perhaps a trial, much trouble, and a long-dead scandal would have walked again. Then, too, the way to the secret cave would have become known to many.

Another reason was rooted in the miniature that Aaron Burr carried and still sighed over. Job had reached from the grave to recoup his name as a man. That was why it had had to be Burr and only Burr who was to have discovered the bones. To know that moment would occur, Job had waited till his death was upon him before dictating the clues, and thus had risked the entire Loyalist cause and the hope of a Burriana. *See?* he had wanted to say from the grave. *This I did to the wife who cuckolded me, and the man's bones might have been your bones.*

That too was the reason he had not buried the bodies to hide all evidence of murder. I thought of Job going all those years, working and plotting with Aaron Burr while his heart was gnawed with all the bitterness that a helpless cuckold knows. Meanwhile, Prudence, seeing that Burr had too much business away from the islands, found another man she could take to the cave she knew. But even Job had reached his breaking point. And had followed them quietly. And at last had stood in the darkness on the ledge and had notched the string of his heavy hunting bow to a razor-sharp arrow.

But with all that, was it really possible that the entire Loyalist cause had been left hanging on Job's last heartbeat? Had been so gravely risked because a husband had killed his faithless wife and had wanted to prove his manhood to her lover?

Yes, it was possible; yes, it was quite true. Back in my father's house I might not have thought so, but since then I had learned much about men and women.

I waited, standing close to Mark. At length he rose

heavily. "Mother's lain there so long unburied," he whispered in a way that almost broke my heart.

In the next moment our thoughts were wrenched away from the sad and dreadful sight. We heard faint sounds echoing from far back in the passage we had followed. We were being pursued. Anne and her men had found the moving stone.

Hopelessly we looked at each other. Wherever we went, Mad Anne could follow us. If we found the cannon, she could find it. With her overwhelming, armed force she certainly could leave us dead and bring the cannon to the Spanish governor. And so Burr would make his desperate move. Cannon would roll through Louisiana swamps. Trained troops from Florida would follow the wild charges of the Bahamas Corps of Horse. And . . .

"There's no denying that the war might be won," Mark whispered as he looked all around as though for a weapon —but of course there was none. "Because . . . who knows . . . ?

Who knew what forces might come from France or England or Spain? Or what might happen in Washington?

All this because we had not been able to close that moving stone behind us. And Anne had found it.

But Anne would not have been led to the stone if I had not been so determined to save my husband's life. And so in the end I had gravely hurt the United States after all. I could not cope with the knowledge—could not speak, could not move, had no tears.

Mark said chokingly, "Let's keep going . . . while there's life there's . . ." He never said *hope*. Again he stared around. "My father never said how Burr should proceed from here."

Forcing myself into motion, I pointed downward. "But he left a signpost."

Job had arranged his wife's dead hand so that Burr would be guided by the pointing bone that bore the well-known opal ring.

Stonily Mark took the lantern, turned his back on the finger and the opal, and walked across the cave. All we saw was a slanting crease in the rock. But when you looked carefully into the shadows you found a crevice hardly more than a foot wide.

I held Mark back. "We don't want Anne to see that signpost!"

He started toward the skeletons, hesitated. "Arabella . . . can you?"

"Give me the lantern."

I walked to the remains. Steeling myself, I picked up the bones of Prudence Wentworth's left fingers. They were very dry. As I moved them, they came all apart and I bit my tongue to keep from screaming. But the pointer did not exist any longer. When I hurried back with the lantern, Mark had squeezed himself through the crevice and was waiting to guide me with a quivering hand.

We heard the shouts of surprise when the pirates burst into the cave and found the skeletons. Going as quietly as we could, hoping it would take Anne a long time to find the cleft, we followed another sand-strewn passage. The smell of salt water grew stronger. We began to feel the tremor of the waves through the rock. Here the stone was not so old, and you could make out the structure of the ancient coral that had been formed out of sea lime by trillions of tiny creatures. Fresher shells and seaweed lay about, as though the great storm of last year had rolled water far in.

We came to a spot where the cleft divided, branching to the right and the left. Which way to go? I saw something small on a ledge in the left-hand passage. Mark rubbed it on his sleeve and we caught a gleam of silver, saw the rose pattern.

"One of my father's buttons. He must have put it there to guide Burr. Now we'll let it show Anne Burney the wrong way."

He placed the button in the right-hand passage where anyone would see it. For a desperate moment he debated hiding with me down the left-hand passage, waiting till Anne and her men had followed the false clue, then slipping back the way we had come and so out of the cave. But Anne was not a pirate captain for nothing. She'd know enough to post a man with a gun at the doubtful turning, and she certainly had left an armed man outside to guard the swiveling stone.

So we went on, leftward through the winding tunnel till its walls began to grow damp. We heard the swash of waves. A crab scuttled ahead of us. The sound of the sea grew stronger, and again we entered a large cave.

We stood breathless on its slanting, smooth floor. At the bottom of the slant, that rock floor went underwater. The

344

cave had a broad entrance from the murmuring sea, but the opening was covered by a curtain of heavy greenery that came down from the bluff outside. It would have been very difficult for a man in a boat to find the cave. But someone had found it. He had hammered two large spikes into the coral at the water's edge, so that a boat or small barge could be moored inside the curtain of creepers. It was an ideal place to land a secret cargo.

At first our attention was held by the lapping water and the mooring pins. Inevitably we turned to look up the slope . . . and up . . . in the vague light. At the back of the cave, where the roof was low, loose rocks had been piled into a low wall. Looming behind that wall lay something monstrous.

Was it the cannon?

It was a cylinder, a kind of broad black metal pipe. If you had put it on its end, three people could have stood in a close circle inside it and their heads would not have shown. Heavy black rings of metal had been molded around it.

Very slowly we walked up the slope. Mark did not say at first that we had found the cannon. He said the metal rings were an old kind of mounting that would hold a cannon securely on heavy timbers. He said that *that* had been cast in Lima, Peru, in the mid-sixteenth century, and was of even older, medieval pattern. He told me that such monster guns had once been used to fling stone balls that could batter down a castle.

"But *is* that the valuable cannon?"

"That's it," he said, seeming almost not to care.

Deep scratches in the rock showed where men had hauled the cannon up the slope. I realized they had piled stones against it to keep it from rolling.

"That cannon isn't black," Mark said. "It's only painted black. Its walls are four inches thick and it's made of gold. The gold was cast in the shape of a cannon and painted so that pirates or privateers who might intercept a galleon wouldn't know its value. It was discovered some years ago, crusted with sea growths, just off the coast here."

I touched the incredible gun that had never been fired. "Made of gold!"

"That's only part of the reason it's valuable. Let me show you." Mark tapped a wooden disk that closed the cannon's mouth. The disk had been tightly fitted, but with the aid of his knife he worked it loose and let it drop. "Reach inside, Arabella."

I reached, felt hard objects that clinked. I pulled one out by its thin golden chain. It was a marvelous pendant of pierced jade carved into an Incan face, with the jade mounted in heavy, chunky gold. It told of ancient times and devoted artisans. It was both primitive and sophisticated, and wonderful beyond description.

"Probably that's the portrait of an Incan prince," Mark said. He showed me where sand had abraded the gold, then put the chain over my head and let me wear the gorgeous piece. He did not say: *Wear it in the few minutes we have left to live.*

Reaching into the cannon, he found a heavy crucifix studded with jewels, a chalice that glittered with gems worth a king's ransom. He found bracelets of gold and cloisonné and diamonds, and the decorated front piece of a corselet made merely of silver; but designs had been worked upon it with a thousand pearls.

He explained that some pieces had come from various parts of Asia to the Philippines, then across the Pacific by galleon, then across the Isthmus of Panama on a donkey's back to be shipped to Spain. The crucifix might have been fashioned of melted Incan or Mayan ornaments in Havana. There was even a fantastically costly table service that bore royal arms, and might have been destined for the palace in Madrid.

"All from wrecked galleons and pirate ships," he said, heavy with thought.

My husband looked around the cave, searching the walls, which were blank stone except where the passageway entered. Coming back to the mass of fabulous treasure: "Loyalists picked this out of shoal water, mostly. Some was found washed up on Bahamas beaches. Plantations were already failing. Everybody needed money. Nevertheless the planters brought all this to my father to be hidden in the cannon. For our cause."

"To finance Burriana." Later, I knew, some of the planters had tried to get their treasure back, when they'd grown desperate.

Mark said, "And to finance the war, also the mercenaries from the West Indies, the invasion ships, great new capitol buildings that Burr planned, money for the new nation's treasury. Burriana became all the world to us."

He would never see the new nation, nor would I. But it now had a good chance of coming into existence. Even if it were reconquered by the United States, there would be bloodshed and woe. The Loyalists might never know it, but they'd have me to thank; William Downing's daughter. And Thomas Jefferson and James Madison and John Adams and the other founders of my country who were still alive would never know it, but they'd have me to curse; I, whose name was temptress and patriot and traitor.

Mark watched me. He touched my cheek. I saw his eyes glisten and his face become wet. I knew it was for me he wept; not for himself; not for his mother.

We heard a faint murmur that was not the murmur of the sea. It was the sound of voices that funneled down the dark, sea-carved passage we had followed from the skeletons to the cannon. If Anne and her men had taken the wrong turn, misled by the silver button, they could not have gone far.

Mark gazed around again. "There's no way out."

"No way out."

Whatever was going to happen to me, it would be small punishment for betraying my country. I held Mark's hand and waited.

Mark put a foot up on the wall of stones, inspected the great bulk of black-painted gold. He still held my hand, but for a time he seemed to go far away.

He seemed to return as he said, "A man lives and learns. I learned too late."

Silently I reached for him. There was nothing but our kissing and our clinging.

He whispered, "At least I'll die a better man than I have been. Because I saw my error and because I feel I am once again what I was privileged to be born—a citizen of the United States. But mostly, my dearest—mostly I am a better man because I have become a man who is worthy of your love. Let us hope we die quickly and die together."

I felt neither panic nor fear. This was the end, and I accepted it, and thanked God that I could be with my husband.

Embraced, we stood and waited. The murmur from the passageway gradually grew. It filled the cave with strange echoes. Our time was running out, grains of sand in the hourglass of the Grim Reaper.

Mark turned his face fram mine and stared at the

squatting tons of that fateful cannon. He said resignedly, "There's no way we can hide it."

"If only we could! Then, even if we're killed, Mad Anne might not find it."

I had hardly finished before our heads turned together and we looked down the slope that ended at the dimly seen water. Together we looked back again at the hulking cylinder of the cannon.

"Arabella!"

"It will roll!" I cried.

Instantly we began pulling away the stones that had been piled against the cannon to keep it from rolling after it had been dragged uphill, away from storm water. Those stones were heavy, but I found a new strength that made them slide and clatter away. Some rolled straight down into the sea. They disappeared with a hollow splash, and we knew they'd sink a thousand fathoms deep.

So must the cannon. The rocks tore one's fingers, yet my heart sang as I worked away beside my man. Sinking the cannon could not save our lives, but it would help the United States, and as we labored together it seemed that at last we were really married.

Rock followed rock, Mark flinging them as though they were pebbles. One rock remained, wedged beneath the edge of the cannon. Mark banged it away.

The mighty mass of gold and jewels stirred, hesitated, rolled very slowly. As Mad Anne Burney ran into the cave, dragging a long chain, the cannon rolled faster, thundering, rumbling, clanging, filling the cave with reverberating echoes.

"I, Anne, Empress of Mexico, command you to stop that cannon!"

We did nothing but hold each other. The five men who had dashed out of the passage tried to wedge cutlasses beneath it, even shot at it. One pushed the stock of his musket beneath the rolling juggernaut, saw it broken like a matchstick. We had not replaced the wooden disk, so the chalice and a few other items of glittering wealth spilled along the rocky floor.

"You! Throw yourself in front of it!" Anne was whipping someone with a loop of the chain. It was Hiram Chance in his motley, hauled along on the search for some reason known only to the madwoman. The pathetic captive staggered toward the cannon. I knew a man's body would be instantly smashed by the awful weight that crushed stones thrown in its way. Hiram Chance had nothing to live for. . . .

But as Mad Anne gave him slack in the chain that led to his slave collar, Chance whipped that chain into a loop and flung it around her neck, twisted it. With frantic strength he dragged her, choking and gurgling, toward the water. Just as a pirate fired, the great gun splashed ponderously into the sea. Chance stumbled and his eyes rolled upward. But he took the last step, uttered his last sound, a wordless cry of triumph.| He fell with Anne. The water closed over them as they followed the golden cannon into the eternal silence of the deep.

Someone else—he was black—leaped from the passage. Mark forced me against the wall, sheltered me with his body while bullets ricocheted and shots resounded and the cave filled with reeking smoke. I remember sliding down the rock wall till I sat on the floor. I remember an end to the shooting, cries of surrender, and vaguely I knew that eight or ten black men were rounding up the pirates. Renzo had heard the shot fired from the edge of the gully, had suspected trouble, had overcome the sentry left outside. Now he went about picking up precious items of treasure, and with great concern he brought them to Mark and me.

We allowed one disarmed pirate to go and tell the others there was no longer any treasure and their captain was dead. We sent out the rest in the pirate ship's last boat only when the *Queen of the Caribbean* had sailed more than gunshot away. Already we saw the cutter coming swiftly down the wind.

And so we returned to Wentworth Hall, Mark and I and Renzo and his men, save for one who had been killed. He was buried in the cemetery near the remains of Mark's father and mother.

But that came later. That night we sat and watched the stars. We kissed and touched. We whispered and planned. It was a new beginning.

When we returned to Newport we took only two pieces of treasure. One was the Incan pendant. I wear it with pride when we give dinners or go to balls, but I never explain. The other piece, the chalice, we sold to a rich patroon in the upper Hudson Valley. With the proceeds we bought back my father's house, where Aubrey Brinton visits no more, for he'll never been seen in Newport again.

Back on San Isidro, the black people, all freed, own the Wentworth plantation. The other four pieces of treasure that fell out of the cannon will see them through for many years. We're looking for a traveling teacher. A physician makes the rounds of all the plantations that reverted to their ex-slaves when the Loyalists went home. The black people now concentrate on food crops and fishing, but one day may go back to foreign trade. Meanwhile Job's windmill has stopped turning. The sugarcane rollers are rusting away. The doors of Wentworth Hall swing idly open. Perhaps ghosts dance in the wind that blows through the broken ballroom windows.

But in Newport, on The Hill, the Wentworth house rings with love and laughter. Mark's schooner, renamed *Arabella*, swings at Long Wharf, ready to take us trading wherever we want to go. But we'll pause a while. I am waiting. We have persuaded Aunt Patience to live with us, and she too is waiting to dandle little Mark upon her knee.

a note from the author . . .

History records that Aaron Burr was again captured, tried, and finally acquitted of the charge of
treason. He had written to the British Minister
to ask his aid in "endeavoring to effect a separation of the western part of the United States," but
no one could prove treasonous action. It was only
vaguely reported that he had connived with Bahamas Loyalists, and to this day we cannot accurately fill in his secret travelings and meetings
along the Gulf Coast. Thus *Traitor's Bride* is
based on events that *could* have been. It is mostly
a view of a turbulent time and above all a tale of
loyalty and lovers.

J.H.